"I can't go back, Jake," Caitlin whispered. "What we had . . . it's over."

Jake reached out and caught her wrist. "Cat . . . "

As he was seated, his arms encircled her hips and Jake bent forward to rest his forehead against her belly. "It's not over, Cat . . . I won't let it be over . . . "

His voice, dark and hoarse, raked deep inside her. Her heart ached for him, for her. She felt his need, his pain, felt her own—a savage yearning to regain the tenderness they'd lost, to find the magic they'd once shared.

"It's not over, Cat."

Oh, Jake.

He was right, Caitlin acknowledged with painful honesty. It wasn't over between them. That was the hell of it.

W9-CFJ-008

Praise for
THE OUTLAW

"THE OUTLAW is a fast-paced western romance filled with two great star-crossed lead protagonists. Anyone who likes their romance to steam, simmer, and sizzle must read Nicole Jordan's latest work."
Affaire de Coeur

THE OUTLAW

NICOLE JORDAN

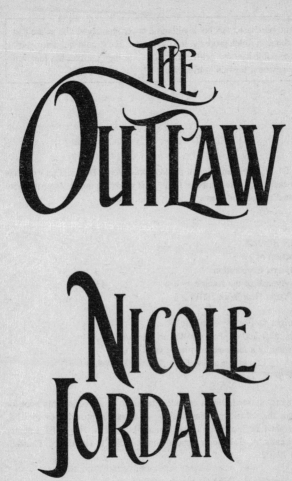

AVON BOOKS ◆ NEW YORK

THE OUTLAW is an original publication of Avon Books. This work has never before appeared in book form. This work is a novel. Any similarity to actual persons or events is purely coincidental.

AVON BOOKS
A division of
The Hearst Corporation
1350 Avenue of the Americas
New York, New York 10019

Copyright © 1996 by Anne Bushyhead
Inside cover author photo by Wayne Johnson
Published by arrangement with the author
Library of Congress Catalog Card Number: 95-94930
ISBN: 0-380-77832-7

First Avon Books Printing: March 1996

AVON TRADEMARK REG. U.S. PAT. OFF. AND IN OTHER COUNTRIES, MARCA REGISTRADA, HECHO EN U.S.A.

Printed in the U.S.A.

RA   10   9   8   7   6   5   4   3   2   1

For Gin (aka "Lyn") Ellis,
kindred spirit and supercool lady

Who can give law to lovers?
Love is a greater law to itself.

BOETHIUS

Prologue

〜◦◦◦〜

Colorado
August 1882

The golden haze of summer cast an enchantment over the glen and bronzed the naked
shoulders of the man bathing in the pool below.
Caitlin watched spellbound as he rose slowly from
the water, her breath catching at the magnificent
sight of his wet, nude body glistening in the sunlight.

He was as beautiful as the jeweled setting, the
place where she came to dream. Sheltered by towering ponderosa pines, the secluded hideaway in
the foothills of the Rockies was her refuge, a jealously guarded haven she had shared with no one
until Jake McCord. A snow-fed mountain stream
tumbled down the granite rocks above to form a
natural pool that was deep and wide enough to
bathe in if you could stand the cold. Ferns and
moss and wildflowers grew here in brilliant pro-

fusion, scenting the clear mountain air with a perfume as heady as wine.

Caitlin drew a sharp breath of that sweet air as the man she loved climbed the rocky bank of the pool to stand naked in the bright sunshine. Rivulets of water coursed down his gleaming, tanned body, leaving crystalline droplets glittering in the dark gold hair that sprinkled his chest and loins.

Finding her watching him, Jake put his hands on his narrow hips, his long, muscular legs braced in a self-assured, almost arrogant stance as he flashed her a lazy smile.

"You're staring mighty hard. Like what you see, Cat?"

She *did* like what she saw. She was captivated by the beauty of his body, fascinated by the bronzed masculine contours that were so different from her own softer curves. He was tall and whipcord lean, slim-hipped but with well-muscled shoulders and thighs and corded forearms. Every inch of him was hard and sinewed from countless hours in the saddle, driving cattle and riding the range.

"Maybe I do like what I see," she retorted saucily, "but I don't dare tell you or you'll get a swelled head."

The corners of his green eyes crinkled with that irreverent charm that always enchanted and sometimes infuriated her. "My head's not the only part of me that'll swell if you keep looking at me like that."

At his blatantly suggestive remark, her gaze dropped involuntarily, down Jake's wet, glistening form, where his chest hair narrowed over his flat belly and widened again at his groin. Helplessly her attention was drawn to the masculine flesh that could give her such wild pleasure. Caitlin felt hot color rise to her cheeks, even knowing Jake was teasing her just to see her blush. He was so casual about his nudity, so unself-conscious, a healthy male animal for whom sex and pleasure were as natural as breathing. He was determined to make it natural for her, too. To make her shed the repressive inhibitions young ladies were taught from the cradle.

She was no prim and proper miss exactly. As the daughter of a once-famous actress, she'd often been called a hellion by the ladies of the Greenbriar community. And she had a temper that was easily riled. But Jake's habitually audacious frankness was outrageous even for her.

She wasn't shy, either. She was just still so new to all this. This was only the third time she'd given herself to him. The third time they had shared a wanton afternoon of lovemaking, with Jake initiating her into the mysteries of love.

He was her lover, this man who was supposed to be her enemy. For a full generation their families had been locked in a deadly fight over the land—cattle kingdom versus sheep empire. Every time she came here, she knew she was betraying her father, yet she couldn't stay away. Despite the bloodshed and destruction, she'd fallen in love with Jake. For two summers she'd defied her father to meet in secret here in their special hideaway, until finally she'd given in to the heated passion that had built to an explosive level—an outcome Jake had confidently predicted months before.

When she'd arrived here today, he'd been waiting impatiently for her. He'd barely given her time to dismount before tugging off her shirtwaist and pulling up her camisole, baring her breasts to his hungry mouth. At his request she hadn't worn a corset, a daring move even for her.

Now a bold smile flagrantly teased his lips, challenging her with its brazen arrogance. And his eyes . . . His spectacularly green eyes reflected the vibrant color of the ferns that surrounded them, with tanned laugh lines fanning out from the corners. Just now his beautiful eyes gleamed like heated emeralds as they roamed her sun-flushed skin.

She loved the way he looked at her, as if she were beautiful when she wasn't really. As if she were infinitely special to him. At eighteen, she was still not very womanly, and probably never would be. Small breasts and smaller hips gave her a youthful figure that in trousers could be mistaken for a boy's. Jake didn't seem to mind, not if the way he seemed to worship her body when they made love was any indication. He made her feel as if she were the only woman in the world, the only one he could care for.

His heated look now filled her with a tingling self-awareness, deliciously wanton. The hot sun beat down on her bare skin, warming the beads of water that still clung from her dip in the pool, but the sun's rays were nothing compared to his smoldering gaze. Jake was studying her pale body, as if she were his prey and he was trying to decide the best way to devour her.

"Well, I don't mind admitting I sure like what *I* see," Jake mused. "You have beautiful breasts. All rosy and hard. Begging to be sucked."

"*Jake!*" Her cheeks flooding with color, Caitlin scowled at him.

He returned a shamelessly irresistible grin. "You're going to be my wife soon. I can admire you if I want."

"We're not married yet! And you shouldn't say such scandalous things."

"Your ass isn't bad, either," he said thoughtfully,

totally ignoring her protest. "Even if it's barely big enough to fill my hands. And that rosebud between your legs . . ." Slowly he licked his lips, making a great show of relish, like a cat savoring cream.

"Jacob McCord, you *stop* that!"

His teasing eyes invited her to share his game. "Sorry, Cat. It's too late."

It *was* too late, she realized. To her dismay and delight, she could see his naked arousal swelling, thickening, rising between his muscled thighs.

Caitlin shook her head, letting her raven hair fall forward to hide her flaming cheeks. He was incorrigibly shameless. And he was making her shameless, too. At the sight of that rigid erection, she felt heat rise within her again, a vibrant yearning, a hot, coiling tension he'd taught her to crave.

Helplessly she watched as Jake came toward her. He called her Cat, but he was the one who looked like a cat . . . a sleek mountain lion with his tawny mane and vibrant green eyes she could lose herself in.

Like a cougar, he moved with a graceful freedom that was spellbinding, climbing up to the sunbaked rock where she lay. There was both purpose and devilment in his eyes as he stood over her, letting her see how hard and heavy and aroused he was. To her bewilderment, he leaned over her and shook his overlong, unruly hair, scattering icy droplets of water over her heated body. The shock was both refreshing and breathtaking.

"Jake!" she gasped.

He was laughing when he dropped down beside her. "Hot damn, now I get to lick it off."

He targeted her left breast, wrapping his tongue around the budded nipple. The wrenching pleasure made Caitlin arch so wildly that he had to pin her shoulders down to keep her from escaping. When he stretched over her, the intimate contact with his chilled body was a greater shock than the shower had been.

"Jake! You're freezing!"

"I know. Warm me, Cat," he said, his voice suddenly turning husky, his lean features softening with tenderness. Giving her no time to protest, he settled his finely muscled body between her thighs, letting her feel the hardness and detail of him. Twining his fingers in hers, he raised her hands over her head and lowered his mouth to hers for a slow, burning kiss.

When she yielded helplessly, as they'd both known she would, Jake released her fingers and began stroking her body. She loved the feel of his work-roughened hands on her skin, loved the feel of his adoring lips. Before Jake she had never realized how intensely she could feel. How *desired*. How *needed*. Her body was no longer hers; he had stolen it, one caress at a time.

His lips left hers, moving downward, over the sun-kissed flesh of her throat and collarbone, to her bare, trembling breasts. She gasped when his tongue circled a rosy crest, now pebbled and urgent, and arched up to him shamelessly. She could feel her nipples swell painfully to rigid peaks of desire. Throbbing and aching, she pushed her breast against his hot, loving mouth.

"That's it, wildcat," he murmured in approval against her skin. "Let me teach you to purr."

Still feasting on a taut bud, he moved his hand downward, between their bodies, and dipped his fingers into the spirals of dusky hair at the crown of her thighs.

A whimper escaped Caitlin at his sorcery. Jake seemed to know everything there was to know about a woman's body, how to find each exquisite pleasure point, each sensual hollow and curve, how to drive her mad with wanting. Her pulse racing, she clutched at his naked, wet shoulders, her fingers pressing instinctively into his hard muscles as his lips mimicked the slow, arousing rhythm of his hand.

"That's it . . . purr for me, Cat. . . ."

Her blood igniting, she strained against him, hungry to find release for the delicious torment between her thighs.

"Jake . . ." His name was a whispered plea on her lips.

She nearly sobbed in gratitude when he finally shifted his body to cover hers . . . gratitude and frustration. She could feel his lips moving upon her flushed face, feel his fingers brushing her ebony hair back from her forehead. Yet she didn't want tenderness from him. Didn't want restraint. When he poised at the entrance of her womanhood, she arched eagerly against him . . . urging him on until he pressed smoothly inside her, penetrating her, filling her . . . unsatisfied till he slid home to the hilt, hardness against aching softness.

Caitlin sighed with contented pleasure as she took his weight, welcoming his fullness. She could feel her body begin to throb, to come alive for him again.

"Hold me tighter, Cat. . . ."

At his husky demand, she wrapped her legs around his narrow hips as Jake had taught her, relishing the tight, glorious fit of his swollen flesh in the sleek velvet of hers, loving the hard tautness of his buttocks as he began to thrust with slow, exquisite rhythm inside her.

The flames started licking insistently at her then, and she drew him deeper, seeking that incredible, unbearable delight that could send her to the stars, that soul-wrenching intimacy that could fuse them together. With renewed intensity, she arched her slender body beneath his, straining against the powerful thighs that kept her thighs parted, her hips rocking against him, matching the rhythm of his hard, thrusting body.

"Easy now, easy," she heard Jake whisper hoarsely against her damp throat, yet he was breathing hard himself, as if her writhing movements excited him beyond bearing. Then she lost track of his breathing and hers as her tenuous control shattered.

Her own frenzied senses went crazy, and she twisted and bucked beneath him while his lips drank her wild moans. Suddenly she was shaking, shuddering, leaping upward in ecstasy, plunging downward in unending, heated spirals. Exploding with heat, she cried out his name, clawing mindlessly at his bare back as waves of ecstasy quaked through her.

Jake was still plunging hard inside her, she realized dimly when she could think. Through a sensual daze, she heard his savage groan, heard the hoarse, rasped words—"Oh, God, Cat . . ." Felt his body clench in her arms, convulsing around her, within her. She reveled in the violence of his explosion, cherishing every pulsebeat of his hot, shuddering release, the sheer force of his heated seed spurting deep within her womb.

Her mouth pressed against the damp silk of his chest, Caitlin managed an exhausted smile of joy that she could elicit such wildness in this beautiful, arrogant man who wanted her. She made no protest when Jake collapsed weakly against her, his face buried in the warm flesh of her throat.

Long, lazy, delicious moments later he eased off her limp body and rolled onto his back, letting out his breath in a contented sigh.

"You okay?" he asked faintly.

"Mmmm." Replete, Caitlin curled against him, never wanting to move again. This was the meaning of bliss: the heat of the sun warming her bare body, the caress of a mountain breeze on her naked skin, the hot musk of Jake's arousal . . . the overwhelming feelings of tenderness and closeness and sharing. If only she could stay here with him always.

It startled her that he craved that tenderness, too. She still couldn't quite believe Jake had chosen her when he could have nearly any woman he wanted. The McCord brothers were keen favorites with the ladies. Jake and his older brother Sloan were a hell-raising pair, both a little wild, although Jake was the worst. He was a black sheep if there ever was one—only he hated to be called that, Caitlin reflected with a drowsy smile. No self-respecting cattleman would have anything to do with sheep.

That lawless aura made Jake downright dangerous to the female sex. With his devil's smile he could charm anything in skirts; with his wild streak, every woman wanted to be the one to tame him.

Caitlin knew he was trouble from the first moment he'd invaded her own special place. Jake had been looking for calves that had strayed off McCord land when by chance he'd discovered her secret mountain hideaway where she came to dream about becoming an actress and practice her lines.

That first time, she'd pulled a gun on him in alarm, not trusting the son of her father's bitterest enemy. Only, Jake had charmed and coaxed away her apprehension, even applauding her rendition of Shakespeare's Juliet. That afternoon, they had struck up a forbidden friendship that eventually had grown into something far more beautiful.

Forbidden because of the hatred between their families. Adam Kingsly and Ben McCord owned adjacent spreads in the foothills of the Colorado Rockies and were leaders of a range war between sheep ranchers and cattlemen, a war which over the years had resulted in death and destruction.

If only she could erase twenty years of bitter feuding between their families, Caitlin thought wistfully. She would give anything to stop the bloodshed. She wanted more out of life than a perpetual battle with neighboring ranchers. Instead she dreamed of escaping the bitterness and hatred, of running away to the East.

Jake understood her dreams—to follow in her mother's footsteps and become a famous actress like Moira Flynn had been, before Adam Kingsly had dragged her off to Colorado to start a sheep ranch during the gold rush of '59.

Jake shared her restlessness, too. He hungered to explore the wild West, itched to strike out on his own. The only thing keeping him here was his affection for his father and brother and the vast cattle ranch they worked. And now *her*. He always said they were two of a kind, and often their thoughts coincided—just as now. She knew what he was going to say even before he spoke.

"When are you going to tell your father about us?" she heard Jake ask in a low voice.

He had turned on his side, lounging like a mountain cougar comfortably sunning himself. Yet despite his relaxed pose, his green eyes were intent, entirely serious.

"Soon," she prevaricated. She was afraid to tell her father she loved a McCord. Papa would never forgive her. And she feared what he'd do to Jake when he learned the truth.

"I don't want to wait much longer, Cat. I don't

like sneaking around behind a man's back." Jake frowned, plucking absently at a damp, raven tress of her hair that clung to her breast. "I've got a good mind to ride over and tell him today, finally get it out in the open."

Wincing, Caitlin shook her head. "You can't, Jake. If Papa finds out what we've been doing, he'll kill me, and you, too. At the very least he'll refuse to let me marry you."

"So? Then we'll elope. We'll find a preacher to perform the ceremony, and you'll be out from under your father's thumb. You won't be a Kingsly any longer—you'll be a McCord. You'll come live on our ranch, with me and Pa and Sloan."

"What if they object?"

"They didn't."

Caitlin's mouth dropped in dismay. "You *told* them about us?"

He shrugged noncommittally. "I had to give them some reason for skipping out on my work so often. And I wanted to prepare them for a wedding in the family."

"How . . . how did your father take it?"

"Not too bad, considering the circumstances." Jake grinned without much humor. "I didn't give him a chance to argue. Sloan seemed happy for me—even drank a toast to us. But Pa . . . Well, I'm not worried. He'll love you when he gets to know you."

"Jake . . ."

At her uncertainty, he put a finger to her lips. "You're not thinking of backing out on me now, are you, hellcat? I thought you felt what I do."

"I do, but you're asking me to betray my *family*, Jake. It isn't that easy. What if I were to ask you to leave *your* home and come live with me and *my* father?"

Jake grimaced as if in pain. "I'd walk through fire for you, Cat, but I draw the line at moving in with your pa or bedding down with any stupid woollies."

"They aren't stupid! No more so than your blasted cows."

"Steers," he corrected automatically, although he refused to be sidetracked by their age-old argument. He looked at her intently, his green gaze holding her blue one. "You could get pregnant from what we're doing, have you thought of that? Wouldn't it bother you to be carrying my baby if we're not married?"

She *had* considered that possibility. She'd thought about it long and hard. It was probably the main reason she had finally succumbed to Jake's seductive persuasions and let him make love to her. If he were to get her with child, then her father would *have* to let her marry Jake. "I'll tell him before then."

"That's good to hear," Jake replied sarcastically. "You think maybe you could do it before next year?"

Caitlin understood his impatience; she felt it herself. They wouldn't have much more time to meet even covertly. Jake was taking advantage of the last free days until fall roundup started, but come mid-September, he would be working twenty-hour days, until the McCords got their steers to the railhead in Denver. And then there would be only a few short weeks before winter set in.

"I worry about you, Cat," Jake said in a low, urgent voice. "Your father's a bitter, dangerous man, and I damned sure don't like the idea of you being near his fists when he takes one of his drunken spells."

She didn't like the idea any better, but she had

learned to stay out of Adam Kingsly's way when
the black moods struck him and he took to the bottle. "He wouldn't hurt me."

"He damn well better not."

Caitlin sighed. Jake's protectiveness warmed her,
even if his possessiveness sometimes seemed over-
powering and his domineering manner tended to
rile her. He had never mentioned love in so many
words. He'd never even asked her to marry him;
he'd just told her she would. But she was certain
he felt something more for her than just lust, more
than desire. "Neal will be there to look after me.
Papa listens to him."

Jake snorted. "Your brother is no better than
your pa."

Stiffening, Caitlin looked away. Her brother *was*
better. Neal was a loving, caring, gentle soul—or
at least he had been as a boy, before he'd been cor-
rupted by their father's bitterness and hatred. Before he'd been taught vindictiveness and rage. Neal
would still do anything to protect her.

"I thought we agreed not to talk about the feud.
Besides, Neal isn't as bad as you think."

"Hell, he's not." Jake's face darkened. "I know
what he did to a hundred head on our southwest
range."

"You don't know anything of the kind. Neal
wasn't involved with that incident, and your father
retaliated for it, in any case."

"You're right, maybe we better not discuss it.
Not when you're blind to everything they do."

"I'm not blind! I'm just—"

"Loyal. I know."

She nodded sadly. She was torn between loyalty
to her father and brother and her love for Jake, and
it was tearing her apart inside. Neal had practically
raised her after their mother died, looking after her

and shielding her when their father retreated into one of his bitter spells. He was both brother and parent to her, her island of protection and love. But he'd been caught up in the deadly feud, just like every other man in the territory, including Jake.

Hiding her hurt, Caitlin looked up at the sky, noting the sun sinking behind a pine-covered slope. "I should go. Papa will begin to worry if I'm gone too long."

"What about us? Are you going to tell him?"

"Yes. I just have to pick the right time."

"Well, make it soon," Jake said, his voice suddenly dropping into huskiness. "I want you in my bed every night . . . every day. Come here, Cat. You're not going away mad."

Caitlin felt her pulse quicken at the raw sensuality in his voice, at the soft glow of warmth in his eyes. She knew what that heated look of his meant.

Jake pulled her into his arms and kissed her then, his lips hard and hungry, instantly melting her defensiveness.

And, of course, after such an arousing embrace, he could not possibly let her go. He made love to her one last time, tenderly, slowly, lingeringly, before he finally let her up in order to dress. And then he was more hindrance than help, since he insisted on kissing every inch of exposed skin he could find.

He wore only his pants when he led her to her horse and gave her one last, hard kiss before tossing her up in the saddle. Reluctantly Caitlin smiled good-bye, drinking in the sight of him. Jake stood barefoot with his hands on his hips, his tawny hair tousled, all beautiful, arrogant male.

Her body glowing with the warm, remembered pleasure of his tenderness, she forced herself to back and turn her horse toward home. She gave Jake one last glance over her shoulder. Then he disappeared from view as she rode around the curve of a slope and began the long trek down a narrow gulch.

Jake watched for a moment longer before turning and making his way down the rocky bank to the pool. After shucking his denims, he deliberately sank to his shoulders in the icy water and ducked his head under the meager waterfall, trying to neutralize the effect his fiery Cat had on his body, trying harder to soothe his anger at her damned father. Adam Kingsly was a drunken son of a bitch who didn't deserve half the loyalty his daughter showed him. Jake just wished he could make Caitlin see it. But blood was blood. He knew he would think less of her if she turned her back on family. And he *was* asking her to give up the only life she'd known, to desert a brother she loved. He would have to be patient . . . but it was damned difficult.

He stayed there in the water for a long time, before finally climbing out of the pool, his body numb with cold. The chill hadn't driven Caitlin from his mind, though, he realized wryly as he reached for his denim pants. Not much could these days. It seemed he thought about her waking or sleeping. Especially sleeping. Jesus, the dreams he had about her. All he had to do was picture those slender legs of hers winding around him, imagine her bucking beneath him, and he woke up hard and aching.

He hadn't counted on falling for an enemy's daughter. Before meeting Cat, he'd planned on striking out on his own, seeing a bit of the world, living it up a little. He sure as hell had never planned on settling down with one woman. But it felt *right* with her. Cat was part of him, like a missing piece to a puzzle. When she was with him, he didn't itch so much to be on the trail. Hell, for that matter, if he ever did take off, Caitlin would demand to go with him. In fact, getting her away from here might be the only way to wean her from her family. As things stood now, if she had to choose between them, Jake wasn't sure which side she would come down on.

He was tugging on his second boot, thinking erotic thoughts of Cat, when over the splash of the waterfall he heard the faint scrape of a footstep on rock. Before he could reach for the gun-belt lying in a pile with his chaps and shirt, he caught another unmistakable sound: the ominous click of a hammer being drawn back.

Jake froze. Holding his hands out passively, he slowly turned his head to find a Colt six-shooter pointed dead at his chest. Glaring over the barrel were the angry blue eyes of Caitlin's older brother, Neal.

Neither her father nor brother was home, Caitlin discovered when she reached the sprawling, split-log ranch house Adam Kingsly had built fifteen years before.

He had chosen the homesite well. The ranch nestled among the eastern foothills of the Rockies, surrounded by the good grazing and abundant water vital for a stock ranch. In the distance, behind the house and pens and outbuildings, majestic mountains stood within view, their slopes covered with handsome ponderosa pine and a sprinkling of spruce. Caitlin had always loved this land, even if she hated the terrible conflicts it spawned.

Her father's absence didn't worry her, for she knew both he and her brother would be out riding the hills, checking on the stations. Raising sheep was harder than herding cattle. Sheep had to be dipped and sheared, as well as protected from

predators and the harshest elements as other livestock, and they could get into trouble faster than
you could blink. They really *were* stupid, just as
Jake claimed, although Caitlin would have chewed
a bushel of hot peppers before she'd admit it to
him.

The Kingslys employed some dozen shepherds,
mostly Basques from the north of Spain, to tend
their three thousand head. The men lived night and
day with their flocks, sleeping in wagons or rough
shacks, with only a dog for companionship. It was
a lonely life, lonelier even than a cowhand's—but
even that was subject for dispute between sheep
ranchers and cattlemen.

Caitlin found herself sighing as she entered her
bedchamber at the rear of the house. It seemed that
her entire life had revolved around the range war.
The two sides understood each other so little, despised each other so intensely.

Perhaps her marriage to Jake was a way to make
peace, she thought wistfully. Perhaps Adam
Kingsly and Ben McCord could put the past behind
them if their children made a future together. Jake
was right on one score at least. She would have to
work up the gumption to tell her father—and soon,
Caitlin realized with a wince as she caught sight of
her reflection in the cheval mirror.

Her hair was a mess, with raven tendrils straggling around her face in wild disarray. She looked
like a young woman who had been well and thoroughly loved—her blue eyes bright, her cheeks
flushed with color, her lips bruised with passion,
the outline of her peaked nipples showing dis-
gracefully beneath her corsetless blouse. Dismayed,
she hastened to restore some sort of order to her
appearance. If her father saw her like this, there

would be no need to tell him about her lover. He would know.

She had just started supper in the kitchen when she heard shouts from the yard out back. Disturbed, Caitlin wiped her flour-coated hands on her apron and went to the window, framed by yellow chintz curtains. A few of the ranch hands lived in the nearby bunkhouse, and she could see several of them running toward the corral. From her position, she could make out three riders coming in from the hills—one with her father's bulky frame. He appeared to be carrying something across his saddle.

Caitlin felt her stomach muscles clench. *Not again.* How many times had Adam Kingsly brought home the carcass of a dead sheep, poisoned or shot by enemy cowhands? Except that his burden didn't look like a sheep. It looked like a . . . man.

A sick feeling of dread suddenly crawled through her, leaving its cold, clammy footprints in the pit of her stomach. Moving blindly toward the door, Caitlin fumbled with the doorknob, nearly stumbling in her haste to reach the back porch.

The waning summer day still held an unusual warmth, even though the sun was sinking behind the mountains to the west, so perhaps it was the heat that caused her sudden shortness of breath, the erratic thudding of her heart. Trembling with inexplicable fear, Caitlin came to a faltering stop at the edge of the wooden porch, unable to force herself to go farther.

Her father rode his stocky chestnut slowly toward her, but it seemed an eternity before he finally came to a halt barely a yard from the back steps. His tanned face was twisted with anguish, while dusty tear streaks mottled his cheeks.

Caitlin scarcely saw. Her agonized gaze was riveted on the burden in her father's arms, on the blood that soaked the back of the body's chambray shirt.

"He's dead, damn you," Adam said in a tone so hoarse and ravaged it was barely comprehensible.

Caitlin had no need to ask the identity of the dead man, even though his face was turned into her father's chest; she recognized the coal black hair so like her own, a legacy of her Irish mother.

Denial clawed at her throat, while words she couldn't speak screamed in her mind. *No, please God . . . Neal . . . no . . .*

Staggering, she gripped the porch rail with one hand, while her other fist clenched over her heart, as though she could ward off the searing pain that knotted her vitals. A dizzying sense of disbelief assaulted her, a nausea so strong she thought she might faint. She moaned raggedly, scarcely recognizing the keening sound of grief as her own. This could not be happening. Any moment she would shake herself and wake up from this nightmare. She could not be seeing her brother's bloodstained, lifeless body. *Dear God, no.*

She could feel herself crying, tears streaming like hot acid down her cheeks, choking her. Stark and unfocused, her blurred gaze found her father's face.

"What . . ." The word came out a raw croak. Struggling for breath against the crushing weight in her chest, she swallowed and tried again. "W-What happened?"

Adam lifted his head sharply to glare at her, his reddened eyes suddenly burning with rage. "Jake McCord, that's what happened! The bastard murdered your brother."

"*No.*" Her voice was a hoarse rasp. "You can't mean it."

"I mean it, Goddamn you. He shot an unarmed man in cold blood. All because of you."

Ashen-faced, she shook her head in disbelief. Her father was maddened by grief at the death of his only son. He was lashing out at anyone, anything, accusing his longtime enemies, even targeting her. "I don't believe it. Jake would never—"

"There are witnesses. Shorty and Placido were both there."

Her face a mask of pain, Caitlin turned slowly to stare at the other two riders. Shorty Davis was grinning faintly. She had never liked the wiry, weathered ranch hand under the best of circumstances, even though he was one of her father's most trusted men. Shorty always made her uneasy, while his leers downright disgusted her. Now she recoiled from the look of satisfaction on his brown, leathery face.

"That's right, Miss Kingsly. The bastard gunned him down. Neal never had a chance."

"That's impossible. You're wrong. You're lying."

Shorty's patronizing smirk sickened her. "It was murder. Ask Placido if you don't believe me."

Blindly, Caitlin turned to the other rider, her gaze imploring. A dark-haired Basque, Placido Flores was one of the skilled shepherds who tended the Kingsly flocks. She had known him since she was a girl, when he'd taught her to care for her first lamb. She trusted him to tell the truth.

"Placido, it isn't true," she whispered. "Jake McCord didn't kill my brother."

For a moment the Basque shepherd sat white-faced and silent, causing false hope to well in her breast. "*Sí, señorita*, it is so." He looked away, but not before she saw the tears in his eyes, heard the quaver in his voice. "It is as your father says."

"You *saw* it happen?"

"*Sí*, I was there."

Her knees almost gave way; only her grip on the rail kept her from falling. *No!* her heart cried. The man she loved could not have murdered her brother. Yet how could she refute the mounting evidence?

Her body racked by shuddering, she shook her head. "*Why*? Why would he do such a thing?"

Shorty answered for the shepherd, a note like gloating in his tone. "Because Neal told him to keep his filthy hands to hisself, and McCord didn't take kindly to being ordered about, so he pulled a gun and started shooting."

Adam Kingsly broke in savagely, glaring at Caitlin. "Your brother was only trying to protect you, that's all, Goddamn you."

Caitlin didn't understand what her father was saying. "Jake . . . where is he?" She had to talk to him, to somehow discover the *real* truth.

"He got away," Shorty interjected. "Headed off into the mountains."

Her father clenched his fist, his shoulders shaking with rage. "But I'll track him down, by God! I'll raise a posse, despite what that worthless marshal says. I'll see Jake McCord hang, I swear it!"

Caitlin shook her head again, scarcely comprehending. Shock and grief had set in, blessedly numbing her body, dulling her mind. She could no longer feel the agony. Vaguely she realized she should be trying to console her grief-stricken father. Forcing her feet to move, she stumbled down the steps, her hand held out to him, to Neal's still form.

Her father flinched and drew back, holding his son's body in a death grip. "Keep away, damn you! You won't touch him. Slut! You're no better than a whore!"

Caitlin stopped in her tracks, more stunned than if her father had struck her.

"I know about you, whore! Traitor! This is all *your* fault. If you hadn't taken up with that bastard, my son would still be alive."

"W-what . . . what do you mean?" she managed to rasp.

"Neal would never have gone after that murdering bastard if not for your whoring. He was only trying to protect you."

She raised a shaking hand to her temple. Protect her? Had Neal somehow found out about her affair with Jake? Had he confronted Jake and been killed for defending her honor? A terrible clarity crept over her. It sounded like the kind of chivalrous thing her brother would do. Dear God, she couldn't bear to think Neal had died because of *her*.

She watched in mute shock as Adam handed the body to one of the silent ranch hands and then dismounted. Her father looked far older than his forty-eight years. His strong hands trembled as he took his dead son again in his arms and turned to carry the precious burden into the house.

Yet when Caitlin started to follow blindly, Adam whirled on her savagely. "No, you're not welcome in my house! Go! Get the hell out of my sight. You aren't my daughter any longer, do you hear me, Goddamn you!"

His words pounded into her, blinding her beneath a fresh wave of pain. Stumbling backward, Caitlin clasped a hand over her mouth to keep a moan from spilling out. The cruel hurt was growing like some malignant thing in her chest as she watched her father disappear into the house with Neal's body. Savage, raking, unbearable.

She breathed in great, shuddering gasps, swaying. She flinched when she felt a gentle hand on her shoulder. Placido had dismounted and was staring at her sadly, his dark eyes filled with grief and concern. The other men had gone back to their chores, it seemed.

"*Señorita*, are you all right?"

A harsh whimper bubbled up from her aching throat. No, she would never be right, ever again. She felt as if her heart had been ripped from her breast. Her brother was dead and it was her fault. Neal had mistakenly thought she needed protection and had been killed trying to defend her. She should have told him about Jake, should have told him of her love for their enemy.

Rigidly Caitlin twisted away, refusing to accept the shepherd's comfort. "Please . . . just leave me alone."

She was hardly aware of his retreating footsteps as he led the horses toward the corral; she only knew that she was alone with her pain.

Jake, where are you? she cried silently from the deep, grieving hollow of her heart.

Tears of anguish blinded Caitlin as she gazed up at the hills where only a short while ago she had known such bliss. She would never believe Jake was a cold-blooded killer. Maybe there had been a fight and he'd shot her brother, but he wasn't a murderer. He would never take an innocent life. Even if Placido thought he'd witnessed a murder, there had to be some other explanation. She had to talk to Jake, to hear his side of the story. She had to hear the truth from him, before her enraged father found him—

Fresh dread clutched at Caitlin's stomach as she remembered her father's vow to raise a posse and track Jake down. Dear God. She had to find him first. She had to search the hills and warn him. . . .

"Jake, I *know* you didn't do it," she whispered

hoarsely as she moved blindly toward the corral to fetch her horse.

She couldn't believe him guilty, wouldn't let herself believe. Not when she loved him. He would never heartlessly destroy what they had together . . . would he?

Chapter 1

Colorado
June 1886

The wanted poster hanging in a rear corner of the Greenbriar General Store was crinkled and yellowed with age, but the sketch seemed a true rendering of the man she had once loved. Against her will, Caitlin reached out to touch the faded handbill with her gloved fingertips.

A tightness welled in her chest as she stared at the blurred lines of the lean, handsome face she'd once known so intimately. She'd thought four years an adequate time to get over Jake, thought the sorrow and hurt had healed, or at least scarred over. But she was wrong. His likeness brought it all rushing back to her.

Taunting images swam before her eyes as memories flooded her: Jake planting his hands on his hips in that cocky, masculine way of his. Jake teasing and tormenting her with his laughing green eyes. Jake taking her in his arms and kissing her

25

breathless. Jake destroying her family . . .

He had claimed her heart, shredded it into little pieces, then vanished without a word.

Stop remembering! Caitlin commanded herself silently, yet the cruel memories she'd forced from her mind years ago wouldn't leave her. She'd waited anxiously to hear Jake's side of the story, steadfastly determined to believe in his innocence, desperately hoping. But he had never come, never explained, leaving her to believe the worst. The horror of her brother's death, the anguish and grief and despair she'd endured, had only been magnified by Jake's crime of cold-blooded murder.

She was safe from him now, Caitlin reminded herself, her heart twisting with raw pain as she gazed at his faded image. Jake would never return to Colorado, not with a price on his head. Not and risk hanging.

He would never tease or laugh at her again. She would never feel the burning pressure of his lips, the ecstasy of his hard body moving against her, within her. Never again hear his hoarsely whispered words of desire and need as he took his pleasure and sent her to paradise in return. Never know the intense closeness she'd felt with him, the exquisite tenderness that had made her feel so cherished and loved.

She would never again see him in her life. She never *wanted* to see him.

Jake McCord was a fugitive, an outlaw, wanted by the state of Colorado. He had shot an unarmed man without provocation. And in the years that followed, he'd become a gunfighter, a lawless killer, the kind of man she despised with all her soul. Rumor had it that he'd shot upward of a dozen men, from Texas to Arizona Territory.

Yet even in his absence, Caitlin realized with

aching sorrow, even after all this time, Jake still had the power to torment her. Seeing his face on the wanted poster had reopened old wounds that had never fully healed, brought all the excruciating hurt and bitter regrets surging back. She had trusted Jake, loved him with all her heart, but he had betrayed her, deserted her, taken the innocent life of the brother she loved—

A feminine throat being cleared behind her startled Caitlin out of her painful reflections. Turning, she found the store clerk eyeing her with a strange look: wariness mingled with what might be pity.

"Sorry I took so long. You wouldn't think Thursdays would be so busy. What may I do for you, Miss Kingsly?"

Caitlin smiled faintly. "Thank you, Sarah. But I no longer go by Kingsly. The name is Hughes, now. Mrs. Hughes. I am a widow."

"Oh, yes . . . I guess I had heard that. You married after you moved to St. Louis. A brief marriage, was it?"

"Yes. My dear husband passed away only a short time after we said our vows."

"How terrible for you."

"It was." Preferring to change the subject, she added, "I would be pleased if you would call me Caitlin like you used to."

"Yes, of course . . . Caitlin. Well, I must say I'm glad to see you back. It's been a long time."

"Yes, it has."

"Sorry about your father. It's a darn shame."

Caitlin forced a smile at Sarah Baxter's insincere profession of sympathy. The young woman was only being polite, of course. Like many of the ranchers around here, she had doubtless breathed a sigh of relief when Adam Kingsly was killed this past March, another victim of the range war, by all reports. A shootout with cattlemen, Caitlin had been told.

Because she was his daughter, because it was expected of her, she was dressed in mourning for him now, a simple suit of black bombazine, but after four years she still mourned her brother's death more. Neal had been a pawn caught in the grip of a destructive feud. A gentle, loving boy warped by their father's bitterness and hatred.

Caitlin could not be sorry her father was no longer alive to carry on the war. The countryside was free from his tyranny forever, his blind rages. And so was she. She'd left behind the terrible past and made a new life for herself in St. Louis, where, alone and penniless, she'd gone to live with her Aunt Winifred a month after the tragedy.

Her father hadn't thrown her off the ranch that night as he'd threatened, but she'd been glad to escape his bitter recriminations. Even numbed by grief and despair, she wasn't immune to his outrage, or the growing scandal. Few people had known the truth about her and Jake being lovers, but after her brother's murder, there were rumors, whispers, suspicions. . . .

Blessedly, her marriage made people here now overlook the past rumors, while her widowhood lent her further respectability. She was determined to keep it that way.

"Do you plan to stay, or are you just here to settle affairs?" Sarah asked.

"To settle affairs," Caitlin replied truthfully. "I want to get a decent price for our wool. And I'd like to try and sell the ranch. I'll have time to look for a buyer, now that shearing's over. If you hear of anyone who might be interested, would you let me know?"

"Certainly. Didn't I hear you have a son?"

Caitlin smiled genuinely at the thought of her precious Ryan. "Yes. He's the light of my life, but I left him in St. Louis with my aunt. I knew shearing would keep me so busy, I wouldn't have any time to spend with him. And I thought it would be safer there. . . ."

Her girlhood friend Sarah gave a sigh and nodded. "It *is* still dangerous here."

As if of one mind, both women glanced at the poster of Jake. "My husband wouldn't let me take that down," Sarah mused. "I guess because he was jealous of Jake. All the women took his side, including me. I never believed Jake McCord was guilty, that he could murder someone like they said."

Caitlin felt herself wince. She hadn't wanted to believe, either. Even after seeing her brother's bloodstained body, despite hearing eye witness accounts of his death, an insistent corner of her heart had held on to the hope that it was all a tragic mistake, that Jake was innocent. But then, she'd been stubbornly blinded by love.

Sarah eyed the poster in bemusement. "Who would have thought Jake would turn out to be a notorious gunslinger? And an outlaw? Last we heard, he was wanted for murdering a bank clerk in a holdup in New Mexico." She shook her head in wonder. "They say he's killed over a dozen men. You don't know why he went bad, do you?"

When Sarah glanced at her speculatively, Caitlin felt the sting of bitter memories color her cheeks. "No, not really. I haven't seen or spoken to him since . . . not since before he killed my brother."

"Oh, my . . . I'm sorry, I forgot it was Neal he shot. . . . Ah . . . well, what can I get for you?" Sarah asked with sudden brisk efficiency, as if realizing her tactlessness.

Caitlin shook herself from her grim remembrances of the past and handed over her list. The
ranch house lacked most necessities after being un-
occupied for several months, and the shepherds'
stores had been depleted during the exhausting
weeks of shearing and baling wool for shipment
back East. Caitlin had driven the buckboard into
town this morning to fetch supplies, rather than
waiting until Saturday, when the streets would be
crowded with cowboys and ranchers and miners
who'd made the long trek down from the mountains.

It had been a wise move, considering the discom-
fort she felt just now. Several old-timers were sitting around the pickle barrel in the opposite corner
of the store, eyeing her with varying degrees of
sentiment: curiosity, suspicion, and outright hostility. Adam Kingsly's daughter would not be
welcomed by these cattlemen, even after an absence of four years.

She had dreaded facing just such a reception,
dreaded returning home to Colorado, to the place
of so much heartache and pain. She'd come three
weeks ago, for one reason only. To secure her son's
inheritance. To sell the Kingsly ranch for her young
son, Ryan.

"Let's see now . . ." Sarah murmured, turning
away to fill the order. "A hundred pounds of flour
. . . two sides of bacon . . . I'll get Baxter to carry this
out for you."

Trying to ignore the hard stares of the old men
in the corner, Caitlin busied herself with the rest of
her shopping. When most of the supplies had been
loaded in her buckboard, she paid Sarah in cash,
unwilling to ask for credit. Refusing to look again
at the wanted poster that bore Jake's faded image,
Caitlin picked up the last of her parcels from the

counter and turned toward the entrance.

"Here let me help you with those," Sarah offered. Taking some of the packages, she accompanied Caitlin outside to her buckboard.

They had just reached it when Caitlin stopped short. Across the dirt street, in front of the small stone building that served as the marshal's office and jail, two men stood talking. One she recognized as the county marshal. The other was Jake's brother, Sloan McCord.

Caitlin felt her heart skip an unpleasant beat. This was the first time she'd seen Sloan in four years, since his brother had killed hers.

Unbidden, a sharp memory assailed her—Jake's low voice that last enchanted afternoon in their hideaway. *Sloan seemed happy for me—even drank a toast to us.*

Sloan had been willing to accept their marriage, Caitlin remembered with a wistful pang, but then that really wasn't so surprising. The older of the two McCord brothers by a couple of years, Sloan had always been known as a maverick. Almost as wild as Jake, he had gone his own way, ridden his own path, even down to marrying a woman of the Cheyenne tribe. According to Jake, Sloan had mostly been a reluctant participant in the feud. But that was before his brother had turned outlaw.

In the past three weeks, Caitlin had learned a great deal about the progress of the range war while she'd been away. The feud had intensified after Jake's disappearance. Not only had countless sheep and cattle been killed in raids and counterraids, but more human blood had been shed. Jake's father, Ben McCord, was dead now, found shot in the back over a year ago, and Sloan's Cheyenne wife had been assaulted and murdered this past winter, leaving behind their two-month-old daughter for him to care for. It was rumored that Adam Kingsly himself had led the attack on Sleeping Doe, and that Sloan, in revenge for his wife's death, had killed Adam, although neither charge could be proven. It *was* true, however, that Sloan had picked up the reins of leadership from his late father and carried on the war that showed no signs of ending.

Caitlin had wanted to scream in horror and outrage when she'd heard the terrible stories from her friend Vernon. It was all so pointlessly destructive, so senseless. And her father had been greatly to blame for the savagery.

As if sensing her presence, the two men across the street abruptly ceased their conversation, both turning slowly to stare at her. Caitlin nearly recoiled when she met Sloan's hard gaze. Even across the way she could sense the hatred shimmering in his ice blue eyes.

She found herself wishing she'd accepted Vernon's protection when he'd offered to escort her into town this morning. As the local schoolteacher, Vernon Whitfield had tried to remain neutral in the feud, but he had no illusions about the danger.

Beside her, Sarah tensed. "It's a bit scary, the way Sloan's looking at you."

Caitlin nodded. Sloan McCord looked as if he might enjoy seeing her skinned alive, with him wielding the knife. "I don't suppose I can blame him, not if what I've heard about his wife is true. If my father truly was responsible for her death, Sloan would hate any Kingsly."

"You had nothing to do with it."

"No," Caitlin said sadly. But then any number of innocents had suffered because of this damned, everlasting war. She had vowed her son would never be among them. Nothing and no one would ever harm Ryan. She would fight tooth and nail, she would *kill*, before she allowed her young son to get sucked into the hatred and bitterness, to be destroyed the way her brother had been destroyed. Never would she let Ryan anywhere *near* this blood-drenched range and the terrible violence that had shattered so many lives.

Just then Sloan abruptly turned on his heel and strode off down the street toward the saloon, his spurs jangling angrily. Caitlin found herself letting out her breath in relief.

Anxious to be away, she climbed into the driver's seat and murmured good-bye to Sarah.

"I really am glad you're back, Caitlin."

"Thank you." Caitlin smiled distractedly. "It's nice to know I still have friends."

Releasing the brake then, she slapped the reins, sending the two bays lurching into a brisk trot. She thought she heard Marshal Netherson call out her name as her buckboard rattled off, but she didn't stop. She needed to get away from here, from the bitter reminders of the past that wouldn't stay buried.

The taunting images were worse here, Jake realized as his narrowed gaze surveyed the glen. The shimmering pool with its tumbling waterfall looked much the same as it had four years ago, the day all his dreams had been shot to smithereens. The peaceful scene mocked him.

Uneasily Jake shifted in the saddle.

What the hell was he doing here? After all his years of running, why had he come back *here*, of all places? This was where his life had almost ended, where everything had gone from heaven to hell in a blaze of gunfire. This should be the last place he wanted to come. Yet he hadn't been home a day when he'd found himself drawn here against his will.

Shading his eyes, he glanced up at the rocks above the pool. He wouldn't have been surprised to still find bloodstains there—his own and Neal's—but the granite was washed clean by time and the relentless elements. Clean, unlike his tarnished memories.

Memories of Caitlin.

He'd heard from his brother that she'd returned to Colorado only a few weeks ago. He'd wondered if he would be able to feel her presence here, if he would feel closer, or if the enchantment would be spoiled by blood and death. It *was* spoiled. The scene haunted him, just as the memory of her did.

"So what the devil are you doing here?" Jake muttered out loud.

Deep down, though, he understood. He'd come here to figure out what he still felt for Cat. What he wanted from her. What, if anything, he meant to do about it. If he wanted to try and make it right with her.

He needed to know before he went looking for her.

And the answer was? . . .

Tugging off his hat, Jake shoved a hand roughly through his hair. The answer was, he didn't know. He didn't know what he wanted from Caitlin. Didn't know if he wanted to bury the past. If he could deal with the savage anger he still felt sometimes, the bitterness, the regrets. If he could forget what her bastard father had done.

The hell of it was, he didn't even know if he *wanted* to forget.

"Are you sure you'll be all right, ma'am?" her foreman asked as he gave Caitlin a leg up on her horse shortly after her return from town.

"I'll be fine," she replied, arranging her skirts over the sidesaddle. "I mean to keep to Kingsly land, and I have a derringer as well as my rifle." Her gloved fingers touched the reticule she'd looped over the saddle horn, feeling the hardness of the double-shot pistol she kept there in case of trouble. Only a fool would travel these blood-stained hills without protection. "I don't plan to be gone long, anyway."

Drawing back on the reins with determination, Caitlin turned her horse toward the ranch road and spurred into a lope, heading for the glen.

Until now she hadn't allowed herself to deal with the past. She'd been home three weeks, yet she hadn't wanted to face the painful memories of her brother's death, to confront her feelings of grief and guilt. Really, there'd been no chance to, with shearing taking all her time and energy. But she had no excuse to put it off any longer. And seeing the wanted poster of Jake this morning had jolted her—a brutal reminder that made the pain of Neal's death more real than it had been in years.

She'd ridden only a short distance from the ranch when she was forced to curb her speed. The narrow, rocky trail, with its sharp curves and steep inclines, was dangerous under the best of conditions as it wound west through the hills— and these weren't the best conditions, with her thoughts so distracted. Normally the rugged foothills soothed her spirits, but even with the magnificent scenery to comfort her, she couldn't stop thinking of Jake.

She was wrong about being over him. She was still haunted by ghosts that wouldn't die, still plagued by remembrances of a man she'd tried desperately to forget.

Forget? Caitlin gave a mirthless laugh of self-mockery. How could she hope to forget Jake McCord? The smallest details were still branded in her mind, in her heart: the way his eyes devoured her with the devil's own gleam in their emerald depths. How his tender, relentless hands caressed her skin. His scent, earthy and musky and masculine, that drove her wild. His hard, driving body that took her to the heights of passion. The closeness and warmth afterward that had bonded them together, that made her feel an immutable part of him. How they'd talked for hours about dreams and wishes and hopes, young lovers in love—

Stop thinking of him, dammit! She'd been a fool to be taken in by him four years ago. He had never loved her; she could finally admit that to herself without flinching. Jake had seduced her, stolen her heart, and then betrayed her. She was no longer even sure he'd ever really intended to marry her. He could have been lying—a cruel way of seeking revenge for whatever ills her father had caused him and his kin.

When he'd disappeared, she'd felt as if he'd torn the heart from her breast. There were times in the barren years afterward when she wondered if she'd ever find a cure for her agonizing thoughts of Jake. He'd left her with nothing but tears and grief and excruciating loneliness. . . .

But she had to put him out of her mind for good now. She had to get on with her life. She needed to take care of business and then return to St. Louis as soon as possible, to resume the quiet, uneventful, *safe* existence she'd built for herself and Ryan.

She planned to sell the ranch, of course. She would not risk her child's life to hold on to a dream she had never shared. Adam Kingsly's vision of a sheep empire built on blood and hate was not hers.

She didn't want the vast spread she'd inherited from her father, yet she wouldn't deny her son his legacy. Ryan deserved a better future than she could give him on her meager teacher's salary. And she hoped to end their dependence on her aunt, perhaps even repay Winnie's generosity. It wasn't fair to ask her aunt to keep supporting them from her small stipend as she'd done for the past four years.

Just then Caitlin came to the swift-flowing stream that ran down from the higher elevations. The tension in her body escalated as she negotiated the gulch that led to the glen.

She didn't want to face this beautiful place, yet she felt herself drawn back here, lured by the haunting memories of her last visit . . . the love she'd once known here. That last enchanted day when everything had been perfect. Everything in her life she cared about had begun and ended that day. . . .

Caitlin held her breath as she rounded a curve where the narrow trail spilled out into a sun-splashed meadow.

So many memories. The glen was filled with them, bittersweet, haunting recollections that all too easily closed around her.

This had been her favorite place in all the world. This was her favorite season, too. Summer. A time of peace and life-giving warmth, when the hills turned vibrant green and mountain wildflowers burst into bloom. She'd met Jake in the summer. Fallen in love in the summer . . .

In the distance, beyond a stand of pines, she could glimpse the edge of the pool, could hear the splash of the waterfall as it tumbled over the rocks.

A sweet remembrance stole into her mind, of a clear, warm July day, the moment when she'd first suspected she was falling in love with Jake. He'd gone swimming buck-naked in the pool, and in his shameless fashion, was trying to lure her in with him. She'd refused, of course, and given him a piece of her mind, but later that summer . . .

Oh, Jake.

She was passing the pines when she spied a lone horseman riding slowly toward her.

Suddenly her heart froze in her chest.

With his leather vest and chaps, the approaching rider could have been any cowboy, and yet somehow Caitlin knew better. His hat shielded his tawny hair and face from view, yet on some primal level she recognized that lean frame, that hard body.

Her hands clenched involuntarily on the reins, jabbing her horse's mouth and making it stumble to a halt.

Run! a warning voice screamed in her mind. But her limbs wouldn't obey. She sat frozen, immobile, unable to do anything but stare, her heart hammering wildly in her throat as the dreaded ghost from her past came closer.

She realized the instant he recognized her, for he brought his black horse to a sudden halt. For the space of a dozen terrifying heartbeats he sat watching her. His hat was pulled down low over his eyes, but even from this distance, she could feel the hard intensity of his gaze. Then, with a nudge of his spurs, he rode slowly forward.

A disjointed, fragmented feeling of unreality, of

horror, kept Caitlin rigid, paralyzed as she waited helplessly. It was too late to run now. She couldn't hope to outrace him. Not *this* man. All too soon he reached her, coming to a halt beside her horse.

Her pulse pounding in her ears, Caitlin found herself staring into the hard, unforgettable green eyes of her outlaw lover.

Chapter 2

"**H**ello, Cat," Jake said in a soft voice devoid of emotion. "It's been a long time."

Caitlin couldn't answer. Even if she'd been able to think of a reply, she could never have pushed the words past the constriction in her throat. Nor could she look away. Her anguished gaze raked him feverishly, devouring the sight of him.

For a fleeting moment the intervening years faded. She didn't see a dangerous outlaw whose face was brandished on a wanted poster; she saw a different man, the one she'd loved as a girl. She'd slipped away to meet Jake here in their magical place, to talk and touch and simply be with him. They were young lovers again, with dreams and hopes and desires that needed sharing. She felt the excitement, the anticipation, the sweet joy of seeing him again. . . .

In the span of a ragged heartbeat, the image ebbed. Instead she saw her brother Neal as he'd looked that last day; his lifeless, bloodstained body clutched in their father's arms . . . dead by Jake's hand. Pain, blinding and sharp, shot through Caitlin as reality returned. Stricken, white-faced, she stared at Jake, her mind instinctively taking in the transformation.

He had changed in the years he'd been away. The overlong, unruly hair showing beneath his hat was still the color of dusty wheat, his eyes still a vivid, breathtaking green. But wind and hard living had stripped any trace of softness from his face, while his skin was deeply bronzed from the sun. His body was lean and tough as always, without an ounce of fat, yet his torso seemed broader, more muscular than before, his shoulders wide enough to stretch the faded blue chambray shirt taut across them.

Her gaze dropped to the well-worn pistols strapped low on his thighs. He looked hard and dangerous, like the lawless gunslinger he had become.

Caitlin wanted to weep. Her heart recognized him, while it cried out against the loss of the tender lover she'd once known. He was a stranger to her now, an outlaw, a man she feared. She feared *for* him. Jake would be hanged if he were caught.

"What's wrong? Cat got your tongue?" he taunted softly.

She felt a knife of longing twist inside her at the old joke. The memory choked her, unbearable torment.

"W-What . . . what are you doing here?" she asked hoarsely. "Don't you know there's a price on your head?"

His eyes searched her face intently. "What's this, Cat? Sounds almost like you're worried for me."

With effort, Caitlin forced herself to lift the reins in her shaking hands. She was mad to still care what happened to him after all he'd put her through. "I'm not the least bit worried. You can hang for all I care. I have nothing to say to you," she added, preparing to ride past him.

He reacted like lightning, spurring his mount sideways and leaning down to grasp the bridle of her horse. "Oh, yes, you do. You're going to talk to me. You owe me that much at least." With a harsh jerk on the rein, Jake managed to pull the strip of leather from Caitlin's nerveless fingers and wrap it around his own. Straightening, he impaled her with his heated gaze. "I would have come looking for you, in any case. We might as well have it out now."

Caitlin's breath fled, while her stomach knotted in alarm. She was out here alone, with a dangerous criminal, in an isolated area, without protection. No one would hear her cry for help. But she did have a weapon. . . . Trembling, she tore open the strings of her reticule and fumbled for her derringer. When she found the small gun, she dragged it out and aimed the barrel unsteadily at the center of Jake's chest.

If a flash of pain flickered across his lean features, it was gone so quickly she was certain she'd imagined it. His face was once again closed, emotions shuttered.

He laughed softly, a sound of derision. "Same old Cat. The first time I met you here at Devil's Pool, you pulled a gun on me, remember, Juliet?" His smile, though half mocking, held a trace of his old devastating charm. "Remember how it ended that time?"

Her heart contracting with remembrance, Caitlin drew a sharp breath at the effect that crooked male smile had on her. Whatever tenderness he'd lost, Jake McCord still possessed a frank sexuality that called to everything feminine in her. One look from those hard, bright eyes still made a woman's pulse go wild; one smile made her want to melt. She was still completely vulnerable to it—and him.

A tremor knifed through Caitlin at the cruel realization. God help her, she was still nursing her terrible ache for him.

Hating herself for her traitorous attraction, for her acute awareness of Jake and the tormenting memories that stood between them, Caitlin willed her heart to slow its frantic rhythm. She would not be taken in by his false charm or his devastating masculine appeal. She wouldn't be afraid of him. Determinedly she let her anger swell, cherishing its capacity to cover hurt and grief, and raised her derringer another inch.

The air between them trembled, raw with tension. Her hand shook deplorably. She had to do better than this. . . .

"Keep away from me, Jake," she demanded, proud that her voice quavered only slightly.

"Keep away?" His mouth curled a little more. "It's a bit late to be protecting your virtue from me, wouldn't you say?" His taunting drawl infuriated her, as did his nearly insulting glance.

"It's too late for a lot of things. Too much has happened between us for either of us to forget. I'm not the same girl you once fooled into falling for you. I'm a different person. You're a different person."

She *was* different from the girl he remembered, Jake thought with a bitterness he couldn't quell. His Cat was a woman now. Time had added fullness to her breasts, maturity and softness to her face. But she was still the same vivid temptress who'd turned him inside out four years ago.

He hadn't thought it would hurt so much to see her again, although he should have expected Caitlin's reaction to him. He had the advantage of surprise, yet his sudden appearance had obviously shocked and distressed her. Nothing could have kept him from tracking her down, though, now that he was home. The gunfight four years ago had wrecked his life, but it was his abrupt separation from Cat that had left him with a gaping hole to fill, shattered dreams to resolve.

Dreams that might never be mended.

Jake cursed softly under his breath as he surveyed her taut, anguished face. She was no longer *his* Cat, though, Jake reminded himself grimly. She had married another man; someone else had taken his place in her bed. He felt a stab of jealously deep in his gut.

"Move aside and let me pass," Caitlin warned him, still pointing that puny gun at his chest.

His heart filled with a hellish hurt. "I don't think so." Negligently he crossed his hands across the pommel of his saddle, looking prepared to wait till doomsday.

"All I have to do is tell the marshal I've seen you, and he'll hunt you down, throw you in prison. You'll wind up with a noose around your neck."

"Go right ahead. Tell him."

She stared at Jake, astonished that he could be so unconcerned about a matter of life and death. "What do you want then, damn you?" she demanded in a heated rasp.

Jake felt a small measure of satisfaction that he still had the power to make Cat lose that hot temper of hers. "I want you to hear my side of the story for once." He paused. "I guess nobody's told you the news yet."

Caitlin eyed him warily. "What news?"

Jake didn't smile exactly, though his mouth twisted. "I'm a free man."

"What?" Caitlin stared, certain she must have misheard.

"I was declared innocent last week by the Colorado governor. Given a full pardon."

"That's . . . not possible," she breathed, almost too shocked to speak. "You murdered my brother. . . . "

Her hoarse charge pierced Jake like a knife to the gut. He'd always known Caitlin would blame him for killing her brother, but that she had so little faith in him, that she really believed him guilty of murder . . . He drew a sharp breath at the savage hurt.

"Now, sweetheart," Jake replied patronizingly, hiding the bitter betrayal he felt, "it's possible because it happened. Sloan wired the news to me from Denver, and gave me the papers last night when I rode in from New Mexico Territory. I'm no longer a wanted man. At least not in Colorado, not for murder. Sloan has proof I was framed for the crime—by your pa, Caitlin."

"There must be some mistake," she managed to say faintly.

"No mistake. Ask my brother if you don't believe me. He just got back from Denver. Seems like one of your pa's witnesses changed his tune."

Caitlin pressed a hand to her forehead, finding it hard to think with her head spinning so dizzily. Her father's witnesses? But there had only been two witnesses to the shooting, and Shorty Davis was dead. Which left Placido. . . . "What do you mean? What tune?"

"Your pa's witnesses lied about what they saw that day." When she remained silent, Jake raised an eyebrow. "Don't you want to know what happened then, Cat?"

"I know what happened," she whispered. "You killed my brother."

"Maybe, but it was self-defense." His mouth curled a little. "I've got me a pardon from the governor to prove it."

Caitlin flinched and stiffened at his black humor. "That proves nothing."

Jake's sardonic expression sobered. "No, you're right, it doesn't. But I'm still innocent. I was framed for Neal's murder by your father."

"No, you're lying."

His face went cold. "It's the God's own truth, Cat. I killed your brother, but it was self-defense, to keep from being gelded, or maybe even lynched. Neal came after me, looking to get even with me for daring to touch you."

She shook her head, too hurt by what had happened in the past to listen to him, unwilling to accept any explanation that painted her brother in so harsh a light. "A guilty man doesn't run. You ran that day."

His jaw hardened, reminding her of the dangerous man he had become. "Yeah, I ran."

"And you disappeared afterward. You never came back."

"Aren't you even a bit curious to know why?"

"No." She would not let Jake sway her with some made-up story after all this time.

"I had two bullets in me. Neal shot me . . . hurt me so bad I nearly died."

"I don't believe you," Caitlin replied, infusing assurance into her voice to mask her hint of doubt.

Jake's hand went to the front of his shirt, beneath the black bandanna tied at his throat. When his fingers began unfastening the buttons, a twinge of panic shot through Caitlin. "What are you *doing*?"

"Getting undressed." He smiled at the alarm on her face. "What's wrong, hellcat? You used to like looking at me without my clothes on."

"Jake . . . don't . . ."

"Settle down. I'm not going to attack you."

Holding her gaze intently, he opened his shirt, then shrugged it and his leather vest off over his shoulders, so she could clearly see his chest. His bare torso was bronzed and roped with steely muscle, Caitlin noted, but the sharp breath she drew had little to do with his masculine beauty. Two vivid scars that might have been bullet wounds scored his flesh, one on his right shoulder, the other in the left side of his rib cage.

Caitlin shook her head defensively. "What does that prove? You could have gotten those scars anywhere."

Jake shrugged his shirt and vest back on, leaving the shirt unbuttoned. "I could have, but I didn't. Your brother put them there."

"You're a gunfighter now. Perhaps another man drew faster."

He shook his head. "There's no one faster. Not in New Mexico Territory, at any rate. Listen to me, Caitlin." His voice turned low and urgent. "That day Neal shot first and I grabbed my gun. I didn't even know I'd hit him. It was all I could do to climb on my horse and hightail it out of there. I realize now he must have gone down. He'd brought his two hired hands with him, but Davis and Flores didn't come after me like I expected. Good thing, because the shape I was in, they could have caught me easy.

"I made it a few miles into the mountains before I passed out, and the next thing I knew, I was being poked and prodded by a Cheyenne half-breed named Wolf Logan. He dug out the bullets and took me to his mining camp in the mountains. I spent the next few days delirious with fever. The wounds healed well enough, but it was weeks before I could even stand, let alone travel." Jake's mouth twisted bitterly. "It was one hell of a surprise when I came back home two months later to discover I was wanted for murder."

Her heart seemed to stop. "You came back *here*?"

"Yeah, I came back, but I didn't stay. I couldn't prove I was innocent, not with your father holding all the cards. Sloan convinced me to head down to New Mexico Territory rather than risk hanging. Said he would fight your pa for me. You had left Colorado by then, and I had a price on my head. So I figured Sloan was right, that it wasn't smart to stick around. But I was framed. Your father got his two witnesses to lie for him."

"Placido Flores told me what happened, and he wouldn't lie," Caitlin insisted loyally.

"But I would, is that it?" Jake felt a wave of fury wash through him at her stubborn blindness, yet he tried to stomp it down. He was a fool to expect Caitlin to accept his side of the story just on faith. She'd evidently spent four years believing her father's lies, and it would take time to convince her otherwise. Or maybe, Jake had to acknowledge, maybe he'd just hurt her too bad. She might never be able to forgive him for killing her brother.... But he wouldn't let her go on believing him guilty of murder. "I was framed that day, Cat," he persisted.

"Why would my father want to frame you?" she returned.

"Why the hell do you think? Because I'd killed his son and he wanted me to pay. It didn't make a hill of beans that I acted in self-defense."

Caitlin shook her head, not wanting to be swayed, even while her eyes probed his for the truth. "Why should I believe you? How do I know you're not lying now?"

"Maybe because you have a little faith in me?" Jake asked sardonically. "No? I didn't think so. Well, then, because I have the proof now. Flores recanted. Sloan got him to sign a confession."

"How do I know Sloan didn't coerce Placido into signing?"

"Ask him."

"It seems just a little too convenient," Caitlin observed skeptically. "My father is no longer alive to challenge your story, and Shorty Davis is dead, too. For all I know, Sloan could have bribed the governor to give you a pardon. I hear Sloan has become involved in state politics."

"Flores is still alive. Ask him what happened, if you don't believe me."

She intended to do just that, as soon as she could get away from Jake, but she wouldn't let him know how vital it was to her to discover the truth. She wouldn't let him know how devastated he'd left her.

"In fact," she heard him drawl, "I think maybe I should have a little talk with Flores myself. After all, he cost me four years of my life."

"No!" Caitlin stiffened with alarm. The only reason Jake would seek out the shepherd would be to exact revenge. "You keep away from him, Jake."

"Or what, Cat?" His voice softened to a dangerous purr as he nudged his horse forward. "How will you stop me?"

Her heartbeat quickening with fear, she raised her drooping pistol. "Don't come any closer."

He ignored her warning, bringing his black gelding adjacent to her chestnut.

"Jake, I mean it. I'll shoot, I swear it!"

"Will you, hellcat?" His eyes, glittering like sun-soaked leaves, held hers steadily. "Could you shoot an unarmed man in cold blood?"

"You're not unarmed!"

"I might as well be. I won't draw on you. And you know it."

Her fingers clenched on the gun handle and yet . . . Caitlin knew with aching certainty she was only bluffing. She couldn't shoot Jake. She had once made love to this man. She'd known him more intimately than anyone else on earth, once loved him with all the unbridled force of her innocent young soul. The searing pain of those memories, of his betrayal, took her breath away, but she couldn't put a bullet in him.

Something of her decision must have shown in her eyes, for Jake nodded slowly. "No, I didn't think so," he said softly. "You couldn't commit murder any easier than I could."

Caitlin looked away in dismay. She'd never been any good at hiding what she was feeling from him. She'd always been weak where Jake was concerned. She still was. Her vulnerability to him made him doubly dangerous now.

"Did you really believe me capable of murdering your brother?" he asked in a low voice.

She didn't know what to believe. She couldn't trust him now, couldn't trust herself and the gnawing torment of hope that was burgeoning in her chest. It was possible he was innocent of murder as he claimed. But . . . Did that really make any difference? Jake was still her brother's killer, the man who had betrayed her trust and broken her heart. Still a lawless gunslinger with a notorious reputation. She wanted nothing to do with him. She couldn't bear to know the kind of man he'd become, so different from the tender lover she'd once known.

"It doesn't matter," she murmured achingly, unable to look at him. "Whether or not you did it deliberately, you still killed Neal. I can't forget that."

"Would you rather I had died that day? Is that it? Should I have just lain back and let Neal slaughter me?"

Her startled blue gaze found Jake's, but she couldn't answer.

"It was three against one, Cat, counting Neal's two hired hands. Those odds have never been fair." When she stared at him mutely, Jake's mouth twisted into a bleak smile. "You once claimed you were on my side. You were even willing to marry me."

Caitlin flushed as she remembered the starry-eyed girl who had been in love with Jake McCord. Unexpectedly she felt a sudden ache in her throat. "That was a girlish infatuation, nothing more."

He tipped his hat back to blister her with the force of his vivid stare. "Now who's lying, Cat?"

"Stop . . . stop calling me that. You no longer have the right."

"No, I guess I don't. Thanks to your pa."

"My father wasn't to blame for your shooting Neal."

"The hell he wasn't. He sent Neal up to find me that day. And then he framed me for murder. I owe him."

Caitlin's anguished eyes searched Jake's lean, virile face. "Is that why you came back home? For revenge?"

Revenge. Jake felt his muscles tense with a familiar rage. The thought of Adam Kingsly still was like acid in his gut. He'd once dreamed of revenge, hungered for it. Being cheated of justice because Kingsly was dead left a bitter taste in his mouth. But he'd long ago learned there was no use cursing fate. Besides, Adam Kingsly wasn't solely to blame for what had happened. *He* shared some of the responsibility. He *had* shot Neal, even though he'd had little choice. Caitlin wasn't to blame, either, for hating him. They were both casualties of a range war that had exploded out of control.

"Maybe I do want revenge," he answered tonelessly. "Having four years of his life stolen gets a man a little riled. Too bad the old bastard isn't here to pay for what he did." Jake's gaze scrutinized her. "Maybe I should make you settle up in his place."

Her mouth suddenly trembled. "I have paid, Jake. I've never forgotten my part in what happened."

"What are you talking about? Why should you feel guilty?"

"If Neal hadn't been so determined to protect me, he would be alive now."

"He brought his death on himself."

"No," she whispered.

Jake made a scoffing sound like a snort. "Did you go running to your brother, claiming I had raped you?"

She stared at him. "No, of course not."

"Neal said you did."

"I never told him anything about us."

"I didn't think so. I didn't believe him. That's the difference between us, Cat. I took your side."

It was Caitlin's turn to smile bleakly. "Did you? For all I know, you seduced me and promised to marry me, just to get back at my father."

Jake's laugh was a short, rusty sound of surprise. "Is that what you think? I seduced you?" He was silent for a long moment. "Well, maybe it's true. I sure as hell wanted your pa to pay for all he'd done to our side. And I was so hot for you, I would have said anything to get under your skirts."

The cruel taunt made her heart constrict painfully. "I don't see any point in continuing this conversation."

"Well, maybe I do." He hooked one leg over the pommel of his saddle, lounging as if he was going nowhere in a hurry. "What about you? You never made it to the bright lights? I remember you were set on treading the boards in the big city."

"I changed my mind." She had never become an actress. After the scandal of her brother's death, she'd wanted a respectable profession, a quiet life. And later, she had her son to think of.

Jake's eyes narrowed on her, holding hers again, whether she wanted it or not. "I hear you go by the name of Hughes now. Seems you didn't waste any time finding a husband."

"No, I didn't," Caitlin retorted staunchly, glad she had something she could throw in Jake's face after all the hurt he had caused her.

"I also hear you have a son." His tone was devoid of any emotion, but his eyes were bright and intent, almost accusing.

She stiffened. Jake was probing too deeply. She didn't want him knowing about her life, prying out her confidences. "My son is really none of your business."

A surge of jealous rage washed through Jake. No, Caitlin's son wasn't his business. Nor was she any longer, really. The hell of it was, his mind and heart couldn't accept that she was out of his life for good. She didn't deserve the kind of man he'd become—a hired gun with the blood of a dozen dead men on his hands. Even so, her past actions hurt him almost as much as she claimed his hurt her. He guessed that made them even. She couldn't forgive him for killing her brother, but he couldn't forgive Caitlin for marrying another man and bearing a son.

He'd learned the news just yesterday from his brother, after riding in from New Mexico. The knowledge that she'd been married to somebody else had destroyed whatever pleasure in homecoming he might have found. In some fool corner of his heart, he'd thought she might wait for him. But he should have expected her to have a husband and children. Women wanted those things. He couldn't condemn her for it. *And you wanted her to be happy,* Jake reminded himself. Just not with another man.

He'd lain awake last night in his own bed, in the house he'd been raised in, hard and aching, while he'd pictured that son of a bitch husband of hers making love to Caitlin . . . settling between her slim white thighs . . . taking his pleasure . . . claiming her heart. His worst fears had been confirmed. No, not the worst. Her husband could still be alive. She'd been widowed within a year of her marriage.

"Was he good to you?" The question was dredged from deep within Jake, from the turmoil of jealousy that was eating at him.

"Extremely," Caitlin said, forcing conviction into her tone.

Her haughty answer infuriated him. "Too bad he's gone then," he drawled, not sounding the least bit sorry.

She wanted to slap that arrogant smirk off his handsome face, but she settled for merely glaring at him. "Why did you come back, Jake?"

"Why'd *you* come back?"

For her son, Caitlin answered silently. To fight for his future. But she wouldn't discuss her innocent child with this notorious man. "You haven't answered my question."

"Why did I come back? Because this is my home."

"You don't belong here anymore."

He didn't rise to her scorn. "Maybe I just want my old life back."

"Do you?" she asked bitterly. "Neal can't have his back."

"Dammit. . . ." He took a steadying breath. "Why won't you believe me? I just explained what happened."

"You had four *years* to tell me," she cried suddenly in an unleashing of pent-up despair. "You vanished without a word! You never even sent me a *letter*!"

He saw the stark emotions in her eyes, emotions that echoed his own—familiar feelings of anger, hurt, and betrayal that had consumed him for four bitter years. There was a wildness in her face, a harsh torment.

Jake looked away, unable to abide her pain. He could have written. He could have hunted Caitlin down years ago in St. Louis and at least tried to set the record straight. But that was all he could have done. He couldn't have asked her to marry him, to share his life. With a price on his head, he didn't have the right. And he couldn't have stood seeing her again, knowing that he'd lost her. He wouldn't have been able to force himself to leave her after that, either.

"You didn't stick around here long yourself, after the shooting," Jake reminded her stiffly.

That wasn't true, Caitlin reflected with anguish. She had stayed as long as she could, desperately waiting for an explanation. She'd searched for Jake, hoping, praying—but she would never let him know that. "I had no *choice*. My father sent me away. He blamed *me* for Neal's death."

That seemed to stop him cold.

"I would never," Jake responded at last, his voice gruff and low, "have hurt you willingly."

But you did hurt me! Caitlin wanted to cry. Yet she bit back the ragged sob that welled in her throat, and closed her eyes on the tears that burned behind her lids. She wasn't going to let Jake know how devastated she'd been, how painful her exile. She wouldn't tell him of the scandal, the loneliness, the grief of losing the only two men she'd ever loved at the same shattering moment.

When he said nothing further, Caitlin forced herself to lift her chin. "All right, I've listened. Now I'm going."

"In a minute."

"Damn you, what do you want from me?"

His face seemed to harden. His eyelids drooped lazily as his gaze raked her body, sexual speculation in the green depths.

He was deliberately trying to intimidate her, Caitlin suspected. Well, she wouldn't let him. She lifted her chin, returning his stare, measure for measure.

"What do I want from you?" Jake drawled insolently. "That's a good question. We had a good thing going once. I thought maybe we could take up where we left off."

Her blue eyes widened, while her heart skipped a thudding beat. "Well, you can just think again. The past is over between us."

"No, it isn't over, Cat. Not by a long shot."

She'd had enough of this conversation. Regrettably, though, she couldn't simply ride off. Jake was holding one of her horse's reins, and she would have to retrieve it if she wanted to go anywhere. Bending forward, Caitlin tried to reach for it, but he wouldn't let go. Worse, Jake slid from his saddle and dropped easily to the ground.

Struggling to hide her panic, Caitlin raised her gun. "I told you to stay away from me!"

Unconcerned, Jake closed the distance between them. "I thought we had settled this. You're not going to shoot me, Cat."

"Don't bet on it!"

He looked up at her, his hands resting arrogantly on his hips in that cocksure way of his that never failed to rile her. His knowing smile was a taunt. "Then go ahead. Pull the trigger."

Impotence made Caitlin grind her teeth in frustration. When Jake took a step closer, barely brushing her leg with his chest, she flinched.

"You're not afraid of me, are you, Cat?"

She *was* afraid of him. Desperately afraid. Even if he'd been pardoned for shooting her brother, he was a gunfighter, wanted for murdering a bank clerk in New Mexico Territory and God only knew what else. Far more damning, she had never been able to resist him. "Anyone would be a fool not to be afraid of a man with your reputation."

"What reputation would that be?"

"You're a gunslinger, an outlaw. Brutal and vengeful. You're not the man I once promised to marry."

She was right about that, Jake thought grimly, wincing inwardly at her accounting. He wasn't the same young fool who'd made love to her here in their mountain hideaway, who'd dreamed about making Caitlin his wife. The years had made him hard and unforgiving. The last speck of gentleness had been stripped away by his life as an outlaw, as a hunted man always looking over his shoulder for anyone who might be coming after him.

His eyes narrowed. "Vengeful, maybe. But not brutal. Not with women, at any rate. I can still show you a good time, hellcat. I'll bet I can still make you purr."

Her heart started hammering at the sensual suggestion in his tone, at the promise in his words. While she stared down at him, Jake effortlessly took the derringer from her nerveless fingers and tossed it carelessly on a patch of grass.

Alarmed to find herself powerless, Caitlin fumbled blindly for the rifle in her saddle scabbard. When Jake caught her wrist, she tried to jerk her arm away, but he tightened his grip, preventing her from drawing the weapon.

"Get your hands off me!"

Smiling grimly at the edge of desperation in her voice, he shook his head. "In a minute. I'm not through with you."

"Well, I'm through with you! I want nothing more to do with you. You're a brute, a cold-blooded savage."

Her impassioned contempt ripped at Jake's heart, making him want to wound Caitlin as she'd wounded him. His lazy facade shattered. Reaching up suddenly, he pulled her from the saddle and set her abruptly on her feet, where she had less of an advantage. "Well, maybe I still want *you*. You were one hell of a fuck four years ago."

Gasping, Caitlin jerked from his hold and backed away unsteadily, coming up against the rump of her horse, making it sidle nervously. It wasn't shock at Jake's crudity that stole her breath as much as it was fear. Of him, of herself. The Jake McCord she knew had always gotten anything he set his mind to. If he wanted her, she would be hard-pressed to keep him from having her. She could feel her heart slamming against her ribs as she stared up at him.

"Is it true what they say about widow ladies?"

Jake demanded huskily, crowding her with his body. "How hungry they get without a man to share their bed? Or maybe you already have a fella who's keeping you happy. Is somebody scratching your itch, hellcat?"

She slapped him then. In blind anger and alarm she hauled back and struck him across the cheek with her gloved palm.

The blow probably hurt her more than him, but it fed Jake's dark anger. Before she could do more than gasp, Caitlin found herself pressed back against her horse, her arms pinned at her sides.

The rough calluses of Jake's palms scraped her wrists above her cotton gloves, while his green gaze bored into hers.

Her heart pounded erratically, racing in fury and fear. He was looming over her, his height and muscularity making her feel fragile and insignificant. His shoulders seemed to have acquired a disturbing new breadth in the years he'd been away, his hands a steely strength.

Those hard hands held her immobile while his threatening gaze raked insolently down her body.

It had been foolish to strike him, Caitlin thought wildly, reminding herself how dangerous he was. But then Jake had always been able to get under her skin in a way no other mortal ever could—or ever would, she suspected with despair.

"What are you doing here, Cat?" Jake demanded ominously, the sudden question surprising her more than his harsh tone. "Why'd you come here today?"

Why *had* she come here? she wondered bitterly.

"This was our special place, remember? Our secret."

Yes, she remembered. She remembered the enchantment this beautiful glen had once held for her, before grief and pain had ravaged her life. She'd known none of the hostility and anger and doubt then that bristled between them now.

"Why'd you come back, Cat?" Jake repeated almost savagely.

She couldn't answer. She'd come here to make peace with her brother's memory, true, yet that wasn't the sole reason. She'd come because of Jake, also. *His* memory had drawn her here. She'd wanted to be closer to him, wanted, if only for a moment, to recapture her shattered dreams, to experience the sweet, joyful innocence of the love she'd once felt here.

But the young man she'd loved was gone. Her hero and friend, her first lover, the man who would have been her husband if not for her brother's death that fateful day . . . that man no longer existed.

In his place was an arrogant, domineering, ruthless stranger.

The love was gone, too. This raw emotion that trembled between them was dark, edged with soft violence.

She could feel the heat of Jake's body through her dress suit, feel his hardness as he pressed nearer, crowding her. The smell of horse and man rose from that seductive heat, enveloping her, arousing Caitlin against her will.

His eyes seared her, glittering and angry, and yet she had the wild idea he meant to kiss her.

"No . . . Jake . . . don't . . ."

He didn't answer. He simply closed his fist in her hair and held her still for his kiss. His lips, hard and vengeful, slanted over hers, forcing his domination on her mouth, branding her with his taste, his heat, while the steel band of his arm drew her closer.

Caitlin struggled for breath. His mouth was hotter, harder than she remembered, his kiss even more devastating. She almost moaned, for despite her rebellion, his touch felt so *right*.

A memory stole through her mind, one more cruel than his ruthless fingers. Another kiss of pure enchantment. His last kiss on that fateful day, one that had been tender and sweet and yearning.

Oh, Jake.

Helplessly she leaned against him. His tongue plunged deeply, repeatedly, into her, subduing her, mastering her, robbing her of breath, filling her with a taste that was deliciously familiar. His hard body pressed against her with compelling force . . . his chest restraining hers, chafing her nipples within the confines of her corset . . . his hips angling to bring the stiff bulge of his erection against her lower belly.

Caitlin whimpered. A part of her wanted him to continue, the part that had once been blinded by love, the part of her that was needy and desperately lonely. She could feel the hard blade of his arousal through her skirts, could feel her breasts tighten and swell in response. A heated rush of sensation pooled between her thighs and spread to every nerve of her body . . . yet she knew she had to resist.

He had released his tight grip, Caitlin realized dazedly. Wildly her hands came up to flatten against his chest and push him away—a grave mistake, for even through her gloves she could feel the heat of his bare skin beneath his open shirt. Jake paid little attention to her defiance, though. He was pulling at the high lace collar of her blouse, unfastening the tiny buttons.

"Have you gone all prim and proper on me,

Cat?'' he murmured, his hard, chiseled face dark with concentration.

Caitlin drew a sharp breath and tried again to elude his grasp, but he subdued her by pressing her back with his thighs. "No, Jake! Stop it . . ."

"You don't want me to stop."

"Yes, I do!"

By now he had bared her throat to his mouth. "Didn't you ever miss me, wildcat? Miss this?" he demanded in the slow, deep tones of arousal as he nuzzled her skin.

Another memory surfaced, Jake's lips caressing her breasts, his tongue worshiping her nipples.

A strangled sound of protest caught in her throat, and she desperately sought to defend herself from Jake's powerful onslaught. She twisted in his embrace, but she couldn't escape him, couldn't escape the rising tension in her body as his hand effortlessly unbuttoned her basque jacket and slid inside. In only a moment he had loosened her blouse fully and was pulling at the neckline of her chemise, drawing it down as far as her covering corset would allow.

Caitlin went rigid as his hand curled over the top edges of her undergarments, gasping as his fingers dipped beneath to graze the bare swells of her breasts, his knuckles searching. . . .

Unbidden came deep, sensual images of everything his fingers had ever done to her; wildly wicked things during the lazy, stolen afternoons they'd spent in their hideaway.

"Jake, don't . . ."

He ignored her desperate plea and found her mouth again with a kiss while his fingers relentlessly sought her flesh beneath her chemise and confining corset.

In some vague corner of his mind, his ruthless

intensity startled Jake. He didn't want to be rough with her. Didn't want to be the brute she thought him . . . the hard, bitter man he'd become. He told himself to go slow, tried to gentle his touch, but he couldn't help himself. He *needed* to touch her, to hold her, to have her. Needed to kiss her until the ache in his soul had been eased . . .

"I remember . . . you used to take this contraption off for me," he breathed huskily against her lips, "to save me the trouble of ripping it off." His knuckles found what he was seeking. Caressing, he lightly rubbed a sensitive nipple, arousing her with only a touch. Caitlin's knees nearly buckled.

"Hold still, hellcat."

Hold still? How could she possibly manage that when his brazen caresses were driving her wild? Against her will, she closed her eyes and clutched at his shoulders, feeling her nipples grow rigid and aching beneath those hard, probing fingers. Caitlin whimpered as desire, reckless and wild, knifed through her trembling body. He was using both hands now, his thumbs coaxing the hard points to throbbing peaks of fire.

Then Jake bent his head to her bosom. "I want to know if you still taste as good as you used to," he murmured as he nuzzled the soft white swells showing above her chemise.

Caitlin moaned and arched instinctively. At her response, a low, hungry noise rumbled in Jake's throat. Deliberately, hungrily, his hand moved between her thighs to cup her woman's mound beneath her skirts, staking his claim.

"God, I want you. I want to take you right here, where I used to. Remember, Cat . . . how we used to make love here? What it felt like?"

Sweet mercy, yes, she remembered. She could never forget how Jake had made love to her as a lover should, tenderly yet impossibly demanding. The memory rose up around her, sending fear and excitement coursing through her.

Oh, God, she thought dizzily. Why did her heart lurch so wildly at his touch? Why did her body turn to fire? She should be ashamed of her wanton surrender, of her weakness, her inability to resist his potent masculinity. Yet all she could think of was Jake and how he would feel with his naked warmth enveloping her, his rigid flesh thrusting deep inside her. She wanted to become part of him again, bodies joining, hearts melding.

As if he could read her wicked thoughts, he took her hand and pressed it to the straining fabric of his denim trousers, making her feel the granite ridge of his manhood. "You want me, Cat. You know you do."

Panic rippled through her. Dear God, it was happening just as she'd feared. Jake was taking control of her body, her mind, her senses, making her yearn for the tenderness, the love they'd once shared. And she was succumbing helplessly to his seduction. She had to stop herself. . . .

How she found the will to resist, Caitlin never knew. Giving a rough, tortured cry, she struggled earnestly to break free of his embrace. "No . . . I don't want you! I despise men like you . . . you . . . murderer."

He let her go abruptly, as if he'd suddenly discovered himself holding hot coals.

In the taut, choking silence, his stark gaze fixed on her face as the hurtful words she'd hurled at him echoed between them. In his eyes, Caitlin glimpsed emotions that weren't foreign to her: bleakness, bitterness, emptiness, raw betrayal.

Seeing that look, she fought to hold back a ragged sob. Her chest heaving, she backed unsteadily away, toward the pool, prepared to run if he came after her.

"I t-told you to keep away from me," she repeated, breathless with fear and pain.

Breathing hard himself, Jake stared at her, anger and hurt warring with his aroused senses. She'd called him a murderer, when all he'd wanted was to make love to her. He wanted her to look at him with trust and adoration in her eyes, the way she used to.

He wanted her so much that the pain was a raw ache in his gut—and he wouldn't be satisfied till he had her, till he rested deep and tight inside her.

"Keep away?" he repeated huskily, his face harsh with strain. "Not on your life, darlin'. I want you back in my bed, Cat. And I mean to have you."

"You w-won't..." she retorted in a shaking voice.

"I sure as hell will. We're not finished with this, with us. I've been under your skirts before, and I'll be there again. And I'll make *damned* sure you enjoy it."

"I w-won't," Caitlin insisted.

"Yes, you will, wildcat. You'll spread your legs for me because you want me—just the way I want you. You'll moan for me and beg me to take you, just the way you used to."

With that grim, outrageous prediction, Jake settled his hat more firmly on his head and turned away toward his horse. Gathering the reins, he swung up easily into the saddle and looked down at Caitlin.

When she realized he was staring brazenly, appreciatively down at her partially exposed breasts, Caitlin self-consciously jerked the lapels of her basque jacket closed, clutching the fabric desperately.

Jake's mouth twisted in a mocking male grin. "I was right. Your tits do taste as good as they used to. Now I just have to find out about the rest of you."

Chapter 3

⌒◡◠◡⌒

He needed a whiskey and he needed a woman, not necessarily in that order. As Jake spurred his horse in the direction of town, he was coldly furious at himself—for losing his temper, for letting his blood overheat, for caring.

Jake swore out loud. *Forget her, dammit! Stop letting her get to you.*

And yet there was no respite from the ghosts that rose up to torment him. His rage at Adam Kingsly still burned, but it was the daughter's betrayal that ripped at his gut. Caitlin thought him guilty of murder.

He didn't know why it mattered so damn much that she believe in his innocence, except that for four hellish years, he'd always clung to the certainty that Caitlin was on his side.

His Cat should have had more faith in him.

Jake swore again at length, fluently, knowing his hope was foolish. She'd promised to marry him, but that promise had turned to dust the minute he'd pulled the trigger to save his life.

67

Bitter memories assailed him, as sharp and vivid as if they had been made yesterday: how he'd barely managed to escape the gunfight alive. The burning pain of the bullets in his chest. The long weeks of recuperation. The longer years afterward, when he'd been a hunted man. He couldn't blame Cat for turning her back on him.

But he sure as hell should have had more control. His first glimpse of Caitlin in four years and he'd acted like a stupid, lust-starved kid. His only excuse was that he hadn't expected to meet her suddenly like that, in their own special place, and he wasn't prepared.

Not even his most disturbing dreams had prepared him for Cat in the flesh. He thought he'd remembered, but he'd forgotten so much. The husky nuance of her voice. The flash of fire in her blue eyes when she got riled. That black witch's mane of hers.

He remembered streaming his hands through the long silky folds . . . remembered the sweetness of her taste and the silky softness of her body. Even now, his lungs were filled with the rich, haunting scent of her, a taunting reminder of all he'd lost.

How could he stop remembering?

It was always her face in his dreams, not the face of any of the countless women he'd had since her. Unbidden, a vision of her naked beauty flickered before Jake's eyes. He could almost see her . . . the image of Caitlin lying beneath him, slim body naked, ebony hair spread out over the summer grass, pale thighs open to him, her blue eyes luminous and trusting, welcoming him home as he buried himself inside her.

He closed his own eyes against the pain of remembering. Damn, but he wanted her. He wanted to feel the firmness of her small breasts in his hands again, wanted to feel her wet heat surrounding him, that unique sensation on his shaft, her shivering around his hardness. It was like no other sensation in the world. *She* was like no other woman in the world. Once, four years ago, somewhere deep inside him, he'd felt as if they were linked together. That she was made for him and he for her.

Forgetting her was like trying to forget he had a hand, or eyes to see with. Losing her was worse than losing four years of his life. When he'd learned about her marriage, the news had exploded like a gunshot to the belly, pain so fierce it took his breath away.

"Stupid fool," Jake cursed himself. "She doesn't belong to you anymore."

He shouldn't have kissed her. Shouldn't have even gotten off his horse. He'd done it merely to have an excuse to touch her. And he'd learned right quick that he was still fiercely attracted by her fiery spirit. That it hurt worse than any gunshot wound to hear her voice her suspicions. It cut him like a razor to think Caitlin might actually be afraid of him.

Still, she felt something for him, he was certain. He'd felt her response to his kiss a minute ago, felt the way her mouth had softened and shaped itself to his, albeit unwillingly. The way her body had weakened even as she strained against him. Caitlin still wanted him—and she wanted nothing to do with him.

It was over between them.

"So forget her and get on with your life."

Jake shook his head viciously. He would never get her out of his mind, his gut, no matter what he did. His only hope was to drown his memories in whiskey and some other woman's body, and he doubted even that would do much good.

God knew, he'd already tried that way. For the past four years, he'd tried. He'd owed it to Caitlin to forget. That was all that had kept him from looking for her after she'd left Colorado and gone back East. What could he offer her, a wanted man on the run? He couldn't ask her to share the life of a criminal. Couldn't ask her to keep one eye peeled uneasily over her shoulder, always on the lookout for some bounty hunter or lawman on her trail. Caitlin deserved better. A hell of a lot better. Even if she thought he was a cold-blooded murderer.

Damn her bewitching eyes.

The town apparently hadn't changed much in his absence, Jake noted as he reached Greenbriar's main street. A few false-fronted buildings. A church. A blacksmith's shop and livery stable. A general store that supplied the ranchers and miners. A combination bathhouse and barber shop. A small stone jail . . . He felt his gut clench as he rode past.

Coming to a halt in front of the Stirrup & Pick Saloon, Jake dismounted and tied his horse to the hitching rail, gazing cautiously about him as he flexed his taut shoulder muscles. Three days of steady riding on the long trip from New Mexico Territory had left him stiff and aching. He'd set out an hour after receiving Sloan's telegram from Denver declaring his pardon. He owed his brother for his freedom. Sloan had worked tirelessly to prove him innocent of murder and he had finally succeeded.

Jake pushed through the swinging double doors.

The place smelled of tobacco smoke and whiskey fumes and was nearly deserted, with only a half dozen cowhands and miners at one baize-covered table, playing cards—an all-night poker game that had run long, by the looks of the bleary eyes and unshaven jaws of the participants.

He got a couple of careful glances, but no chairs scraped back in alarm at his appearance. A couple of the cowboys even nodded in recognition. By now Sloan would have spread the word about his pardon, Jake knew.

He was used to making people suspicious and frightened. They were scared of his reputation as a lightning draw and his dangerous look. He'd carefully cultivated that look. One cold, hard stare had saved him more than one showdown with a green-horn trying to prove his manhood.

Jake didn't approach the game. His temper had cooled, but he wasn't good company just now. Instead he settled at a table on the opposite side of the saloon and gestured with his head at the woman behind the bar. Dressed in a low-cut, red silk gown, she sashayed over to his table.

Della Perkins was one of the soiled doves of Greenbriar. A survivor, she was pretty in a hard-lived sort of way, like a straggling bloom that was fast fading from weathering too many storms. She had black hair like Cat's, but there the resemblance stopped.

She gave Jake a warm, feminine smile of welcome, showing a chipped front tooth where some heavy-fisted drunk had punched her in the face.

"What can I get for you, cowboy?" Della asked in a husky, seductive tone that soothed Jake's raw anger.

He returned a slow grin of his own. "A bottle of your best stuff. I'm supposed to meet my brother here in a while."

"I know. Sloan came by a few minutes ago to tell us the news. Congratulations, Jake. I always knew you were innocent."

Resentment flared in his gut, not at her words but at the memory of Caitlin's accusation. A whore had more faith in him than the girl he'd planned to marry.

When she came back to his table, she was carrying a bottle of whiskey and two glasses. "Here you go, sugar."

Purposefully she leaned down and let her bodice sag, showing him more than a glimpse of generous breasts and peaked nipples. He felt himself quickening. Her interest and affection soothed his ravaged pride, while her naked charms rekindled the throbbing ache in his loins left from his unexpected encounter with Cat.

Della's fingers trailed along his arm, purposely arousing. "You want to take a little trip up to my room? It'd be on the house."

Jake eyed her speculatively. He didn't often have to pay for sex, but he knew Della couldn't afford to be so generous. Her job was attracting customers to the saloon and showing them a good time. But he could afford her price. And while she would be a poor substitute for Cat, she could provide him the oblivion he needed.

She bent down to kiss him, and he opened his mouth automatically for her. She smelled of stale sex and cheap perfume. Just what he needed to get the scent of Caitlin from his nostrils.

"Come on, sugar," she whispered. "For old times' sake." She reached down to cup his groin, massaging the hard ridge of his manhood. "You always were so much better than those other groping slobs. You know how to show a girl a good time."

"Hell, why not?"

He caught the whisky bottle by the neck and stood. Della immediately wrapped an arm around his waist, clinging to him as she led him toward the wooden stairs.

"Hey, Randy," she called out to one of the card players. "Sloan comes looking for Jake, you tell him he's upstairs with me—and he won't be coming down till he can't walk straight."

Randy nodded as a spurt of ribald laughter rose from the group, but then went back to the game.

Della's room was plain and serviceable and more than a little tawdry, Jake noted with dispassion. The brass bed in the center was unmade, the rumpled yellow sheets testifying to her profession.

He'd seen too many rooms just like this one. Had too many women like Della, too many empty nights filled with more emptiness. But then, if he couldn't have Cat, it didn't much matter who he bedded down with. He followed Della inside and, with his boot, nudged the door shut behind him.

Della wasted no time before turning to wrap her arms around his neck. Raising her face for a kiss, she pressed her ripe body against his full length, pushing him back against the door. When she was through kissing, she gazed up at him with soulful brown eyes.

"I missed you, Jake," she said softly, as if she meant it.

He smiled with a tenderness he didn't quite feel. He would have rather heard those words from Caitlin, but that wasn't likely to happen.

Eagerly Della began unbuttoning his shirt. "Whatcha been doing all these years?"

"Drifting mostly." He'd drifted as a gunfighter, hiring out his services to whoever paid the most.

Her hands paused at the buckle to his gun belt. "Can I take these off?"

Jake understood her caution. Some men—espe-

cially men living on the wrong side of the law—
didn't like being without their guns, even while
screwing. They kept their boots on and their horses
saddled, ready to ride at a moment's notice.
"Sure," he replied. "I don't have anybody on my
back trail, as far as I know."

"Not even some woman? Ain't there anybody I
should be jealous of, sugar?"

He laughed lightly, but the humor didn't reach
his eyes. "No woman."

Unfastening the buckle, Della carefully carried
the gun belt over to a wooden chair and hung it
over the back, where his revolvers could be used if
needed. Watching her, Jake took a swig of whiskey,
relishing the feel of the numbing liquor as it burned
a path down his throat to his belly. "You're not
afraid of me, are you, Dell?"

"Afraid of *you*?" Her brown eyes widened in
surprise. "Nah."

"Maybe you should be," he said, his tone brood-
ing. "You don't know what kind of man I've become . . . what I've done."

She laughed. "Jake, honey, you always were a
hell-raiser, but you were never mean. You
wouldn't hurt me. It ain't in you." Coming back to
him, Della smiled enticingly and slipped the straps
off her gown and lowered the bodice. Her bare
breasts were full and ripe and big-nippled, not like
Cat's.

Stop thinking about her, Goddammit.

"Come here," he said huskily.

"Sure, sugar . . . You don't need this, do you?"
Reaching up, Della tugged his hat from his head
and sent it sailing halfway across the room to land
neatly on the chair seat.

With a grin, Jake saluted her aim with the bottle.

"Are you home to stay?" she asked as she pulled his shirttail from his pants.

Why did you come back, Jake? Caitlin had asked him.

"Haven't made up my mind yet."

Della flashed him a seductive smile as she pushed his shirt off his shoulders. "Well, maybe I can help you make it up."

"If anybody could, it'd be you, Dell," he replied gallantly.

"Ain't you a sweet-talker? Oh..." She had seen the scars on his shoulder and ribs. "You poor man. Does it hurt?" The question was rhetorical, for she only seemed intent on soothing the pain. Bending forward, she kissed the topmost scar, swirling her tongue over the ravaged flesh, licking lightly.

Jake felt his body tighten, a tension that only heightened when Della unbuttoned his pants and his drawers and slid her warm fingers over his swelling shaft.

Jake stifled a groan as she squeezed gently. If he closed his eyes, he could imagine a different woman holding him this way, stroking him.

"You keep doing that," he muttered huskily, "and I'll come in your hand."

"That's okay, sugar. You just stand there and enjoy it."

Relaxing his spine, he leaned back against the door panel, arching his hips a little to give Della better access. She cupped the swollen sacs beneath his shaft, massaging skillfully, making Jake sigh in appreciation. She was damned good at what she did.

He closed his eyes again, drifting back into his fantasy, letting the images engulf him. It was Cat he wanted touching him like this, caressing him, making him so hard he burned. And in his thoughts he was arousing her in turn. Heated images flickered in his mind. . . . Her body welcoming his touch, his kisses. Her hips arching toward him, her small, ripe breasts straining for his caresses. He could see her face, the reverence it held. . . . He wouldn't satisfy her at once, though. Instead he would see how hot he could make her. He would savor her, taste her everywhere, starting at the dusky triangle between her thighs. . . .

Caitlin would whimper and writhe beneath his mouth, his teasing fingers. She would twist and fight like a little hellcat, but then she'd moan for him to fill her, her naked body, pale and frenzied beneath his. Only then, when he was good and ready, would he take her . . . hard and fast, driving deep, plunging wildly inside her as far as he could go . . .

A savage groan was dredged from Jake's throat as he exploded in Della's hand, his hips jerking spasmodically. Moments later his eyelids rose fractionally as he slowly came back to his senses.

Sharp disappointment hit him in the gut as he recognized Della's pretty, painted face. Her skin was flushed and she was breathing heavily, as if she'd enjoyed bringing him to pleasure.

Jake managed a forced smile as he brushed her parted lips tenderly with his fingertips. Then he felt in his vest pocket.

When he brought out a ten-dollar gold piece and tucked it in her gaping bodice, her eyes widened. "I told you, sugar, it's on the house."

"Take it—for old times' sake." He eased the straps of her gown back up over her shoulders.

"That's all you want?"

Jake's mouth curled faintly as he began buttoning his pants with one hand, the other still holding

the whiskey bottle. "That's more than enough, darlin'. You nearly buckled my knees."

"I remember a time, Jake honey, when you could
go all night and never show signs of wearing
down."

"Maybe I'm getting old."

Della laughed and shook her head. "Maybe I'm
losing my touch." Her gaze was uncertain.

"No, it's not you, Dell. I'm just saddlesore after
riding so long."

After scrutinizing Jake a moment, her look disbelieving, she turned to the washstand, where she
wiped her passion-slick hands on a towel.
"Maybe your heart's just not in it. You *do* have a
girl somewhere, don't you? You got a sweetheart."

Jake's twisted smile was bleak and bitter. "She's
not mine any longer. She can't stand the sight of
me."

"Sure, and I'm a fancy lady."

"I mean it. She wants nothing to do with a man
with my past."

"Is she crazy?"

"Thanks, Della."

"She really don't want you?"

"Nope." He took a swig from his bottle.

"The Jake McCord I used to know wouldn't let
a little thing like that stop him."

He grinned in reply, but Della's expression remained sober. "You won't be comin' back, will
you." It wasn't a question.

"Not for a while at least." Jake gestured with his
head toward the door and said gently, "I'll see you
downstairs."

Letting himself out into the hall, he paused with
his back against the door, not eager for any other
company. Della had eased the male ache in his

groin, but she couldn't fix the deeper one in his chest.

Would he ever be free of Caitlin? Free of this savage, restless hunger that had plagued him for four long years? Would he ever stop craving the feel of her, the touch and taste and smell of her?

Did he even want to stop?

No, his mind answered savagely, even as he called himself a fool. He'd thought he'd returned to Colorado because he wanted to put his life back together, because the nothing existence he'd left behind in New Mexico held no future worth living. He'd thought he wanted revenge for the years that were stolen from him by that bastard, Adam Kingsly.

But that wasn't what he wanted at all. He wanted Cat. Any way he could get her.

It wasn't over between them after all. He couldn't rid himself of the ghosts that haunted him—ghosts with blue eyes and raven hair. He couldn't pretend there was nothing between them, couldn't simply dismiss the past and act as if they were just old enemies and not old lovers. He couldn't pretend Cat wasn't different from the countless other women he'd known.

It *wasn't* over between them.

He knew the passion was still there; when he'd kissed her in the glen, he'd felt the yearning leap up between them, wild and strong, felt her need. But as sure as he breathed, he knew that more than her body was involved. The familiarity, the connection, the *bond* was still there. Whatever existed between them was unexplainable but real.

But she hates you, remember?

Jake squeezed his eyes shut, remembering how Cat had called him a murderer. He would have to prove his innocence to her first, make her believe in him, if he hoped to have a chance in hell of convincing her to come back to him. But he was going to do his damnedest to try.

He wanted Caitlin back in his life. In his bed. And he wasn't about to accept anything less.

Chapter 4

~~~OOC~~~

Caitlin urged her horse up the rocky slope toward Placido's sheep station, picking her way cautiously over the rough ground, yet she couldn't slow her racing heart or quiet the frantic thoughts that pounded in her head with a relentless rhythm.

Her body still trembled from the shock of seeing Jake again, from hearing the alarming news about his pardon.

Jake had returned to Colorado a free man.

Caitlin squeezed her eyes shut, awash in a sea of cruel memories. His sudden appearance had tapped a wellspring of pain inside her, stripping her bare, shattering the peace she'd struggled so hard to gain.

Why had Jake come back to torment her now, just when she was learning to forget him? Could she never put the past behind her? Would he even let her?

Haunting memories, dark and sweet, swept over her. Tender memories of a man who'd been her lover and her only love. She had given herself to him, heart and soul . . . to her everlasting regret.

Her throat constricted, wedged with anger and bitterness and apprehension as Caitlin recalled her confrontation with Jake only a short while ago. She could still remember the hot smell of him, the hardness of his body when he'd kissed her and told her he wanted her. . . .

If she was shaken by his return, though, she was even more unnerved by his promise to become her lover again. She'd seen the desire in his eyes, felt it in the coiled tension of his body. Yet she'd tasted the anger inside him. He wasn't the same man she had once fallen in love with. He was harder, rougher, far more dangerous. There was a dark intensity about him, an unyielding grimness, an edge of violence he hadn't possessed four years before.

But he'd proven irrefutably that the flame between them hadn't died, and the realization left Caitlin cold with fear.

Jake McCord was a dangerous man, and not only because of his criminal past. She was profoundly grateful she'd left Ryan in St. Louis with her aunt. She didn't want her son anywhere near him, especially when Jake could still be seeking revenge against her late father—

A swift surge of panic welled up in her. Ryan! She had to protect him. She *would* protect him.

She had never been away from her son for more than a day, not once since his birth. She'd left him behind this time because she was determined to shield him from the ravages and violence of the range war. She refused to expose Ryan to such viciousness and destruction.

But now she had a worse fear. Jake. Would he try to hurt her son to get back at her father?

Caitlin shivered, despite the blazing June sun

that beat down from a cloudless sky. She hoped
Jake was innocent as he claimed, that he really had
been framed by her father, but she couldn't let it
matter to her. Pardon or no pardon, Jake McCord
was a lawless gunfighter who had betrayed her
trust, broken her heart, and was now a threat to
her son.

Even so, she needed to know the truth about
him. She had to discover from Placido what had
happened that day four years ago at Devil's Pool—
whether or not Jake really had acted in self-
defense, if her brother truly had attacked him
without honor or scruples. And if so, why it had
taken so long for the truth to come out.

Just then her horse crested a hill and a wooden
shepherd's hut came into view. There was no sign
of Placido, though, or his flock. She had to ride
another half mile before she came to a mountain
meadow where countless, newly shorn sheep
grazed peacefully.

Each summer the shepherds pastured their flocks
at higher elevations, utilizing the rich, free grass of
public lands—a prime grievance of the cattle bar-
ons. To cattlemen, sheep were villains, mainly because they tended to crop grass down to the roots
and needed more water than cattle. The settlers
had fought over this range for twenty bitter years.
Much of it had been taken over by private ownership in the past decade, by ranchers like Adam
Kingsly and Ben McCord, men who had few scruples about the methods they employed to increase
their vast spreads.

Placido's black-and-white sheepdog barked once
in warning, then raised its pointed ears and followed her intently with its gaze, alert for danger.
The sight of the dog roused a painful memory in
Caitlin, of the time her father had forced Neal to

drown a young pup who was slow to train. Any sheepdog who couldn't do its job was a danger to the flocks, she knew, yet Adam Kingsly had used the cruel lesson to teach Neal to become a man, driving home a principle untempered by mercy or compassion. She would never expose her son to that harsh upbringing.

In another moment she spied Placido Flores with his shepherd's crook on the far side of the meadow. He remained completely still, watching her approach as bleating sheep scurried out of her path.

"I knew you would come, *señora*," the Basque shepherd observed solemnly when she halted her horse before him.

"Placido, tell me what happened," she said earnestly, searching his face. "Jake says he was framed for murdering my brother."

Placido lowered his gaze, unable to meet her eyes. "*Si, señora,*" he whispered.

"You lied to me?"

"Not lied. Yet . . . I did not tell the complete truth. *Señor* Jake . . . he killed your brother as your father claimed, but . . . It has preyed on my mind for a long while."

"What happened?" Caitlin asked hoarsely.

"Your brother . . . he was very angry at *Señor* Jake for . . . for dishonoring you. *Señor* Neal said the gringo had violated you—"

"That wasn't true."

"I know that now. But then . . . I believed. Your brother ordered me to accompany him and *Señor* Davis. I did not know then what he intended, but he told us to tie *Señor* Jake's hands while he held a gun on him. *Señor* Neal wanted to render him . . . useless . . . less than a man. When *Señor* Jake sought his gun, your brother fired and hit him. There were more shots between them. I heard *Señor* Neal cry out . . . saw him fall to the ground.

"I ran to him, but . . . there was nothing I could do. *Señor* Neal was dead. When your father learned of it, he made me swear to keep quiet."

"And you did? Even when you knew you were condemning an innocent man to possible hanging?"

Placido hung his head. "I know. In my heart I knew it was wrong. Yet . . . *Señor* Kingsly was always good to me. And the McCords, they were our enemies . . . bad men who caused much death of my sheep. Your father, he was maddened by grief. And . . . and he said if I told what I knew, I could not work here any longer—nowhere in this country. My wife, Maria . . . she was big with child . . . the other young ones must be fed. . . ."

His voice trailed off, but Caitlin had no need to hear more. Her father had threatened Placido's job, not just on this ranch, but in the whole state. With no wages, his pregnant wife and young children might face starvation. It was a terrible choice for anyone to have to make, and she wasn't certain that if it had been her child threatened, she would have chosen any differently.

"I have felt this terrible guilt ever since, *señora*, here in my heart." Placido touched his chest. "When *Señor* Kingsly passed away, I went to Sloan McCord and told the truth of what happened. He requested me to sign some papers, telling what I knew."

Caitlin nodded slowly. "Sloan must have used them to persuade the governor to pardon Jake."

"I am glad."

"Still . . . he could have been hanged for murder if you hadn't come forward."

"If there was a trial, I would not have lied, *señora*, you must believe me."

Placido's despairing look left no room for doubt, yet Caitlin wanted to cry out, *You might not have let Jake hang, yet you allowed him to be branded a murderer, let my father destroy his life. . . .*

She forced herself to take a deep breath, her own feelings in turmoil at the shepherd's confession. Gratitude that Jake was not a cold-blooded killer. Remorse that he'd been terribly wronged all these years. Liberation from some of her own guilt. Her brother's death had not been entirely her fault. Neal had thought he was defending her honor, true, but it was his unscrupulous assault on Jake that had prompted the shooting—although Neal *would* doubtless still be alive if she and Jake had never been lovers. She could not exonerate herself completely.

"I am ashamed, *señora*," Placido said quietly, "for what I have done. I would understand if you no longer wished to keep me in your employ."

Aching with the injustice of it all, Caitlin shook her head. She could not fire Placido now, not when he had admitted the truth. She could only blame her father for forcing the shepherd into such a terrible situation. And Placido was right. The McCords were their enemies. Over the years their side had committed far worse crimes than failing to be forthright.

"No, I won't fire you. I don't want to lose you, Placido."

"Then . . . what will you do, *señora*?"

"I don't really know. I expect Jake holds us to blame for what my father did. You will have to take care. Jake is free because of you, but . . . I will do whatever I can to protect you, but he may be set on vengeance."

"Will you be safe from him, *señora*?" Placido asked worriedly.

Caitlin smiled bleakly. She didn't think she would ever be safe from Jake McCord. He wouldn't forgive her for doubting him, she was certain. Yet she wanted to reassure the shepherd. "I don't think he would hurt me."

"I should go to him, explain. Tell him of the regret I feel."

"I don't know. Perhaps it would be better to let things die down. We could wait and see what Jake means to do. I doubt the marshal would act against him, in any case, unless he breaks any laws. Netherson always has taken the cattlemen's side over ours."

The shepherd nodded. "*Señora*, I also regret . . . that you had to learn of your brother's deed. What he did was not honorable. . . . "

"I know," Caitlin said sadly. "It is just one more tragedy I lay at our father's door."

She had expected to be relieved finally to know the truth about Jake, but Caitlin's thoughts were in worse turmoil than before as she wound her way down from the hills to the Kingsly ranch house. Whatever should she do?

A panicked voice in her head urged her to flee. She had come to Colorado to sell the ranch for her son, but Jake's return changed things drastically. It was dangerous for her even to remain in the same state with him. She could put the ranch up for sale with the bank and then leave. Once she'd made the arrangements, she wouldn't have to stay. She could run from her past, from Jake. And yet that would be taking the coward's way out. . . .

So what? a dark voice whispered. *You can't face him again. You can't stand the pain.* She couldn't bear to feel such hurt as Jake McCord had inflicted on her when he'd killed her brother and disappeared from her life without a word.

God, why had she ever returned to Colorado? She had been safe in St. Louis. If sometimes in the dark, lonely hours of night she grieved for her lost love, by day she always managed to crush the bitter feelings, to bury them under countless, self-protective layers of numbness and guilt.

Layers that had been stripped away in only moments today, exposing her, leaving her bare and vulnerable.

Now that Jake had come home.

Pain clutched at her anew as she remembered.

One thing was certain, though. She could never bring Ryan here now, not and risk Jake harming him. She would have to send a telegram to Aunt Winnie in St. Louis at once, warning her to keep Ryan away from Colorado. Her aunt was a sweet, generous soul, yet she was sometimes forgetful. She couldn't be counted on to remember all the careful instructions Caitlin had left regarding her son's supervision. And protecting her son was the only thing in the world she cared about.

To Caitlin's dismay, she found Vernon Whitfield waiting for her in the ranch yard, along with the county marshal. She hadn't regained her composure enough to face either man, although ordinarily she would have been genuinely glad to see Vernon.

When he spied her, the schoolmaster flashed her a warm smile and removed his hat to expose curling, dark brown hair.

Caitlin forced herself to return the smile. She'd known Vernon before her move to St. Louis, and his correspondence had kept her apprised of events

here during her long absence. In fact, he was one
of the few people who'd welcomed her home three
weeks ago. Originally from the East, Vernon enjoyed discussing the world beyond the Colorado
foothills, as she did, and they shared other interests
in common, as well—such as teaching and a love
of Shakespeare.

Vernon's smile faded as she drew her horse to a
halt before him. "Caitlin, are you okay?" he asked,
worry evident in his tone. "You look pale."

"Yes . . . I'm fine." She let him help her down
from the saddle, but felt herself tensing as Marshal
Netherson stepped forward.

White-haired and leather cheeked, Luther Netherson was her late father's age, with a tall, rangy
frame and the slightly bowed legs of a cowman
who'd spent years in the saddle. Being Greenbriar's
marshal was only a part-time job for him. The rest,
he spent running cattle on his ranch—which had
always been a sore point with Adam Kingsly. The
law was supposed to be fair and open-minded, but
Netherson had always held a decided partiality for
the Kingslys' enemies.

Netherson tipped his hat to Caitlin now. "Mrs.
Hughes, I wanted to talk to you, if you have a minute. I wonder if you've heard the news? I tried to
catch you before you drove out of town, but I guess
you didn't hear me call you."

"What news is that, Marshal?" she asked politely.

"Jake McCord was pardoned by the governor for
the crime of murder."

"Yes . . . I had heard."

"So did I," Vernon interrupted grimly. "And I
don't believe for a minute that he's innocent."

"Now, Verne, that's not the point," Netherson
said. "Jake's not wanted by the law here any

longer. He didn't kill your brother, Caitlin." The marshal's tone held satisfaction.

"Well, someone sure as heck did," Vernon retorted. "Neal's dead, isn't he? If McCord didn't do it, then who *did*?"

The satisfaction faded from Netherson's tanned face. "Well, I guess Jake did *kill* him, but it wasn't murder, is what I meant."

Caitlin took a deep breath. "Was there some point in your riding all this way to tell me, Marshal?"

"Well, the thing is . . . I was hoping things would settle down around here now that your pa's gone. But with Jake back . . . I just don't want there to be any trouble."

"Now see here, Luther," Vernon exploded. "You show Mrs. Hughes some respect! She never has caused a whit of trouble, and you know it. You should be talking to the McCords, warning *them* to mind their own concerns."

"It's all right, Vernon," Caitlin forced herself to say soothingly. "Marshal Netherson, I am not my father. Trouble is the last thing I want. There won't be any from me, I assure you."

Netherson looked at her skeptically. "You think you can keep that foreman of yours in line?"

Caitlin was certain of nothing of the kind. The Kingsly foreman cherished almost as big a hatred for cattlemen as her father had. But she had no desire to argue just now with the marshal. "Our side won't start anything, if I have any say about it."

Netherson nodded slowly, while Vernon fixed him with a smoldering stare. "You just make sure your side does the same, Luther."

"I mean to. I've already had a long talk with Sloan, and I have his promise to let things simmer down. Well . . . that's all I came to say." Netherson touched his hat. "Ma'am, Verne."

He turned and mounted his horse, then rode away, leaving the two of them alone.

Vernon's eyes darkened with concern as he looked at her. "I'm sorry about McCord going free, Caitlin. This is a miscarriage of justice if I ever saw one. Heck, I wouldn't put it past Sloan to bribe the governor himself. Probably helped finance the man's election with that in mind."

Caitlin shook her head. She'd heard Sloan was dabbling in state politics, and he might very well have the governor's ear, but she no longer had any doubt that Jake was innocent of murder. "No, Vernon," she said quietly. "I think justice *has* finally been served. You see, I spoke with one of the witnesses. . . . "

Briefly she explained what Placido had told her, leaving out her relations with Jake. At the conclusion, Vernon stared at her, still obviously disbelieving. "Well . . . maybe McCord won't stick around. With his reputation, few folks will be eager to welcome him home."

Perhaps so, Caitlin thought sadly, but the decision to stay or go would be Jake's. Despite his unsavory reputation, there was little possibility he would be run off by the upstanding citizens of the county. It was an unwritten code in the West: a man's past wasn't questioned. It didn't matter what crimes he'd committed elsewhere, as long as he didn't cause trouble in the present, he would be allowed a fresh start. Besides, this was Jake's home. These were his people. He would be accepted back with open arms by the cattlemen at least, although with fear and dread by the sheep ranchers.

Caitlin shook her head, preferring to change

the subject; she had something more urgent to discuss.

"Vernon, you know I'm planning to sell the ranch, and . . . I had the impression you might help me look for a buyer. Was I wrong?"

"Caitlin—No, you weren't wrong. But you're upset right now. You shouldn't be making such decisions just yet. Besides, I had the notion that . . . I wasn't going to say anything yet, but . . ." He took her hand tenderly in his. "I don't want you to leave, Caitlin. You have friends here, supporters. I could take your troubles off your hands."

Her eyes widened as she realized Vernon was asking permission to court her. She'd known his interest in her seemed more than simple friendship. An eligible bachelor, he was on the lookout for a wife to keep house for him and help with the homestead he worked. There was still a shortage of eligible women in the West, decent ones at any rate—which made her a prime candidate. But she hadn't expected Vernon to press his suit just yet.

Summoning a faint smile, Caitlin gently withdrew her hand from his warm embrace. "Vernon, if you don't mind . . . it's too soon. You're right. I can't think straight just now. Would you understand if I said I needed to be alone?"

"Certainly, Caitlin, whatever you say. But I want you to know, I'm here if you need me. I'll protect you. If McCord gives you any trouble at all, you just come to me."

Caitlin nodded gravely at his sweet offer, but Vernon was a gentle, civilized man, a nurturer of young souls and developer of minds. Physically he would be no match for Jake. Indeed, she doubted there was anyone in the entire state of Colorado who could handle that kind of trouble if Jake McCord chose to cause it.

Chapter 5

She had some hard decisions to make, Caitlin reflected as she rode at a lope across the northern acres of Kingsly land. Decisions about her life. Her future. Her son's future.

She'd seen nothing of Jake during the past two days, yet her encounter with him played over and over in her head and heart, till she felt lightheaded. Worse, she'd spent every moment in nervous anticipation, looking over her shoulder for him, expecting him suddenly to appear. It irked her that he could still affect her so keenly. Jake was free now, but she was still trapped by her past, by her bittersweet memories of him, by her guilt. His exoneration had only made Caitlin realize how terribly she had wronged Jake.

She'd gone riding this afternoon to escape, needing to find peace and privacy to think, rationally and calmly to contemplate her course of action. She was grateful for the surge of stubbornness that had welled inside her after their first shocking meeting, though; it helped stiffen her spine.

"You won't drive me away, Jake McCord," Caitlin muttered, lifting her chin.

She was determined not to fear him or let him run her off her land. Perhaps he did intend to seek revenge for what her father had done to him. She could even understand the feelings Jake must harbor toward her family after being unjustly accused of murder—the bitterness and anger and betrayal. And from all accounts, he'd already begun to get even with his enemies. Last night Jake had reportedly picked a quarrel in the barroom of the saloon with one of the prominent sheep ranchers, and the argument had erupted into a violent brawl between cattlemen and sheep men.

Yet she refused to let Jake's return influence her plans, or make her act in foolish haste. The ranch belonged to her now, and she would do what was best for her and for her son.

She still intended to sell the ranch, of course. This was no place for a young boy—in the middle of a range war, a blood feud that had fomented for two decades.

On the other hand . . . fleeing right now would hardly be wise. Not only did she have obligations here, but there were other factors to consider. Not all the influences here were evil. Vernon Whitfield, for example.

Vernon had been her friend for years, and she couldn't simply dismiss his desire to court her. His interest flattered her a little, but being sought after was of small importance. What counted was that Vernon was a good person, gentle and kind and principled, the sort of man who would make a young boy a good father.

And there was another factor to weigh. A husband in her life would fill the hated emptiness, Caitlin thought wistfully. It would close the gaping hole Jake had created when he'd disappeared without a word. Jake had left her numb, empty inside—a hollowness that started somewhere in her body and ended in her soul.

Vernon would never kindle her blood the way Jake could, never drive her to the incredible heights of passion, but she didn't want passion. She wanted peace and safety. And Vernon was safe.

But there was Jake himself to think of. Caitlin shivered, grateful for the blazing sun that came out from behind a fleecy cloud to warm her. She'd been forcefully reminded of the threat he presented just last night, when one of the Kingsly ranch hands had been carted home by the marshal, draped unconscious over his horse.

"Dear Lord," she'd rasped, her heart in her throat as she came out on the back porch holding a lantern. "He's not . . ."

"Hogtie's okay, ma'am," Netherson said quickly. "Just got a black eye and a busted lip, maybe a bruised rib or two."

Hogtie Brown groaned when the marshal dismounted and pulled him down from his horse.

"What happened?" Caitlin asked as she led the way to the bunkhouse.

The story came out while she was patching up the wounded man. Hogtie roused himself enough to claim Jake McCord not only had thrown the first punch, he'd meant to kill the other rancher—a claim the marshal refuted.

"Aw, Jake was just raising a little hell," Netherson explained. "He drank a mite too much. . . ."

Caitlin sent Netherson a cool look. "What you mean is, he started a drunken brawl."

"Well . . . I guess you could put it that way."

A wave of disappointment crushed her. To think Jake had become so much like her father, fomenting his hostility in a whiskey bottle. . . . "I'll bet you didn't arrest him, either," she said, her throat tight.

"Well, no . . . I didn't see any need."

"Yet you were the one who said you didn't want trouble, Marshal."

"Jake'll settle down. He gave me his word."

Jake had once given *her* his word not to fight, Caitlin remembered as a fresh wave of pain rose up to engulf her. He'd gotten into a fistfight with Neal over some ridiculous dispute, and they'd both ended up bloodied and aching. She'd patched both of them up, and given each a piece of her mind. Then, unable to bear to see them hurt each other anymore, she'd made Jake *swear* he wouldn't get into any more fights. . . .

Battling her tormenting thoughts, Caitlin shook herself back to the present. Deliberately she slowed her horse to a walk and forced herself to concentrate on the issue at hand. Perhaps it *was* best to return to St. Louis at once, before there was any chance of another confrontation with Jake.

Vernon could handle the sale of the ranch for her. And Hank Spurlock, the Kingsly foreman, could keep up the operation until she found a buyer. She wouldn't get top dollar if she sold in haste, certainly, but the proceeds would be large enough to ensure her son's future.

Yet she also owed something to the people in her employ. She wanted to try and find a new owner who would let them keep their jobs, who would reward loyalty and hard work.

Caitlin's gaze lifted to the jagged horizon on her left. Whatever her decision, she had to do what was best for her son. And yet . . . this was Ryan's legacy. Was she doing the right thing by taking it away from him?

The foothills were so beautiful and rugged. Broken by small peaks and valleys, the land rose west-ward toward the main range of the Rockies, lush with fertile meadows and cool forests of pine and spruce. It held a solid strength, majestic and en-during, standing nobly above the petty affairs of man and beast.

Briefly she closed her eyes and listened to the keening of a red-tailed hawk high overhead. She'd missed this place so much. If not for the tragedies that had occurred here, she would love this land. . . .

Caitlin suddenly gave a start. Seeing a rocky promontory some two hundred yards to the north-east made her realize she was precariously close to McCord land. A soft laugh edged with bitterness escaped her. Had she ridden this way by accident or design, in some subconscious act of defiance against Jake? Or some unspoken need to be near him?

She was about to turn her horse around and head back when she heard the distant sound of gunshots. Her heart lurching, she reached for the Winchester rifle tucked in her saddle scabbard. Anxiously she spurred her mount forward. She had no idea what kind of danger she might be riding into, but she couldn't simply leave. Gunshots in this rough land often meant death, and someone might need help.

Another shot echoed off the hills and she urged her horse faster, riding up a slope and down again, slowing to thread her way past a stand of scrub oak. When she came to the edge of a ravine, she drew her horse to a sudden halt.

Some twenty feet below to the right, Jake stood with his Colt six-shooter drawn. He was staring up at her, his gaze narrowed and watchful.

"Jake . . ." Caitlin felt her mouth go dry. She had

known she must face him again sometime, but she wasn't ready. Indeed, she wasn't sure if she would ever be ready.

He looked infinitely dangerous, with that hard, sculpted face darkened by several days' growth of stubble and bruised by the fistfight he'd reportedly started. His green eyes were hooded, unreadable, nearly hidden by the thatch of wheat-colored hair that fell over his forehead beneath his hat.

Her senses jolted at the sight of him.

He stood quietly, one thumb hooked over the gun belt riding low on his hips, his face hard and still. Even at this distance, Caitlin could see evidence of the brawl he'd been in—a bruise under his left eye, a cut at the corner of his mouth, a nasty gash on his right cheek that was caked with dried blood.

He looked uncompromisingly masculine, thoroughly disreputable. He had his shirtsleeves rolled up, exposing corded, tanned forearms, and sweat glistened on his skin. Even sweat and dirt, though, couldn't detract from the aura of a powerful, intensely sexual male animal.

Forcibly she averted her eyes, sweeping the edge of the ravine, looking for a way down. Seeing none, she walked her horse along the edge, closer to the man below. That was when she saw the body of the sheep, lying dead at his feet.

"Jake . . . what have you done?" The question came out a hoarse rasp.

His face was still and expressionless as he slid his revolver into his holster and turned toward his horse with that long-legged, narrow-hipped saunter of his.

"I was taking care of these stupid critters," he said coolly.

There were two other dead animals, Caitlin saw

with horror; blood from bullet holes stained the white wool at the temples. "Those . . . are Kingsly sheep."

Jake glanced back over his shoulder, his mouth curled sardonically. "They sure as hell aren't McCord sheep." He gave a soft snort as he swung up on his black gelding. "I hate these smelly things. They ought to be outlawed."

"Dear God, you killed them. . . . "

"What if I did?" he asked tersely. "I'd be well within my rights. They're on McCord land."

Her horrified gaze found his as a memory flashed through Caitlin's mind, terrible and exquisite. It was when their love was new, when her father had ruthlessly shot three dozen head of McCord cattle that had wandered onto Kingsly land, forcing Caitlin to watch because he didn't want her "going soft." Afterward, she'd run straight to Jake in the glen.

Throwing herself into his arms, she'd tried to burrow into his body, to block out the horror, her sobs hoarse and anguished.

Cat, what is it? You can tell me.

But she couldn't answer Jake's alarmed demand, couldn't tell him about her father's cruelty and spite. Not without risking the McCords' revenge. They would discover soon enough about their slaughtered cattle, but they wouldn't know who had actually committed the obscene deed. Oh, God, she felt like a traitor to both sides.

Jake had held her, though, comforting her while she cried, her body racked with sobs. She could still remember the fierceness of his need to take away whatever was hurting her so, to make her forget the ugliness, the revulsion, the pain. She'd known she loved him then. Known she needed him.

Craving him desperately, her mouth had sought

his, her arms clutching him, pulling him closer, drawing him down. . . . She remembered the wet ground, the smell of damp earth and summer rain from a storm that had passed earlier. She remembered his hands, so gentle and tender they made her want to weep. She remembered his exquisite care as he made her a woman. His woman.

They had bound themselves to each other that magical day—forever, she'd thought. But the violence that had driven her into Jake's arms that day hadn't ended then. Instead it had only grown worse, erupting in a final tragedy with the death of her brother.

Caitlin stared at the dead sheep carcasses now, feeling as if a knife had passed through her heart. Dear God, was Jake no better than her father, making innocent creatures the victims of his vengeance?

"How could you?" she whispered. "They're just defenseless animals."

"And I'm a murderer, is that it?" His gaze pinned her. "Come on, Cat, not even you believe that. Your sheep are so stupid, they tumbled down here and half killed themselves. Two of 'em had broken legs, and the third had a sliver of rock embedded in its chest. I shot them to put them out of their misery."

She choked back a sob of relief, but her spine went rigid as she realized Jake had deliberately led her on, letting her believe he'd maliciously killed her sheep. "How . . . do I know that's what happened? How does the cattleman's creed go—the only good sheep is a dead one? Maybe you drove them over the edge out of spite, simply because they wandered onto your land."

Swift, dark fury burned in his eyes. "Lady, you have one hell of a nerve accusing me of anything.

I spent four years running from a false charge, and I'm damn tired of it. I'm sick of having to defend myself!''

The words erupted between them with soft violence.

A blunt ache wended its way through Caitlin's heart as she stared at him. Suddenly contrite, she bit her lip hard. Jake was right. He had paid a terrible price four years ago, merely for the crime of making love to her. And she'd meant to offer an apology, belated though it might be, not to accuse him again. He didn't look as if he was prepared to accept words of conciliation or remorse from her, though. His eyes, narrowed and burning, swept over her in an insulting glance that made her wince.

She wanted to flee, to fight . . . anything that didn't force her to deal with herself and her renewed feelings for him.

It seemed as if his eyes had turned into green stones as he said, "You keep your stock off my land, or I'll do it myself." The words were soft, deadly.

His eyes were hard and intent upon her face as he waited for her response.

"Jake . . . I'm sorry. I didn't mean to imply—"

"Sure you did, hellcat. I'm a murderer in your eyes. And you're too damn blind and stubborn to see otherwise."

Caitlin flushed with temper as heat and tension combined to inflame her already-ravaged nerves. Before she could answer, though, she heard the distant sound of hoofbeats behind her. Jake's head came up like a wolf scenting danger . . . or a man running from the law.

Starting, Caitlin glanced over her shoulder and realized several riders were headed their way. Her fingers clenched around her rifle, then relaxed again as the horsemen came into view. She recognized her ranch foreman, Hank Spurlock, and two of his men.

"Hank! Over here," she called, directing them her way. When she glanced down at the ravine again, she found Jake staring at her. The air crackled with the strain of things left unsaid between them.

"You okay, ma'am?" her foreman asked with concern when he reached her. "We heard gunfire."

"Yes, I'm fine. Jake . . . Mr. McCord and I were just taking care of some sheep. Three of our ewes were crippled in a fall and they had to be killed."

Spurlock stiffened visibly when he recognized the man down below, and yet his new alertness suggested careful respect.

Jake remained totally still. He sat his horse easily, but he kept his gun hand near his holster, Caitlin noted apprehensively. She thought it best to separate the two of them before trouble started.

"I regret our stock wandered onto your land, Jake," she said quickly. "We'll try to see it doesn't happen again."

"We ought to take the carcasses back with us, ma'am," Hank interjected. "Leaving 'em will only lure wolves and mountain cats, and we could butcher the meat. Okay with you, Mr. McCord?"

Jake nodded curtly and gestured with his head. "There's a way down over there."

With quiet efficiency the foreman and his men descended into the ravine. Working together, they hefted the heavy carcasses over their saddles, then climbed back up the path again.

"You coming with us, Miz Hughes?" Hank asked, as if worried about leaving her alone with a reputed outlaw.

At the question, Caitlin gave Jake one last glance, her gaze filled with reluctance and frustration. She wanted to say something to relieve the tension still between them, but the challenge she saw in his eyes deterred her. Besides, she couldn't remain here alone with him and give rise to further gossip.

"You should take care of that cut on your cheek," she murmured rather inadequately, before turning her horse and riding away with the others.

When she was gone, Jake swore, soft and low. He was furious at Caitlin for finding him guilty again without a hearing, and even angrier at himself for the way he'd handled it. Growling at Cat was no way to win her. No way to make her believe in him.

Jake filled his lungs with an uneven breath as he fought to keep his resentment at bay. It wasn't just wanting her physically that left him aching and restless. That made his heart heavy with emotion. It was knowing what he'd lost. The reminder of everything he'd missed during the past four years. And the uncertainty of wondering if he could ever get it back.

She couldn't sleep that night. Caitlin tossed and turned in her lonely bed, fighting the stifling heat that was unusual for June, and the empty, hopeless feeling that had haunted her ever since Jake's return.

Her gaze kept straying to the open window and the splash of moonlight that filtered through the pale curtains. She knew if she looked out, she could see the foothills that hid the McCord ranch from her own, just as she had when she was eighteen. She'd spent hours gazing out that window, yearning for Jake—that summer when he'd been her world. She'd spent hours more after her brother died, staring out in anguish, waiting for Jake to return and declare his innocence.

Don't. Abruptly Caitlin stopped herself, as she always did when she thought of what she'd lost. It served no purpose to remember, to let herself wallow in the pain again. Even so, she wanted to cry, for a love long dead, for scars that had never fully healed. She'd convinced herself she was over Jake, but she wasn't really—

Her eyes burning with unshed tears, Caitlin rolled over again and punched the pillow, determined to banish any traitorous thoughts of Jake McCord from her mind.

She was still frustratingly awake, however, when she heard a sharp knock on the front door echo throughout the house—near midnight, by her reckoning. Her heart skipped a beat as she threw off the covers, wondering who could be calling at this hour on a Saturday night. Any of the ranch hands would have come to the back door, and those who'd ridden into town to dance and play poker wouldn't be back for hours yet.

All seemed quiet outside. Through her open window she could see the corrals and sheep pens clearly in the moonlight. Dear Lord, perhaps something had happened to Ryan. . . . A telegram might be delivered to the front door.

Quickly Caitlin caught up her wrapper and slipped it on as she ran barefoot over the polished wood floor, down the dark hall to the front door. When she flung it open, she came to an abrupt halt.

Jake stood there, lounging in the doorway. She could see nothing but a shadowed outline, but she didn't need the light to identify him when every nerve in her body tingled with awareness.

"Jake . . . what do you want?"

"We have to talk." His voice was low, cool.

"Now?"

"Yes, now, wildcat. We're going to have it out. Somewhere where you can't run away." He cast a careful glance behind him, like a man who never forgot to watch his back, and shouldered his way in.

"Jake, you can't come in here!"

"Why not?" He kicked the door behind him, his presence immediately filling the dark hallway. She caught the hot, earthy scents of sweat, leather, and man, and nearly gasped at the primitive effect it had on her senses.

"Because . . ." she stammered. *Because I'm alone here.* "Because it's late."

"So? You're going to listen to me for once. I've had enough of being accused of crimes I didn't commit."

Blindly Caitlin's eyes narrowed as she tried unsuccessfully to search Jake's face. "Have you been drinking?"

"I wish I had," he muttered in a voice so low she could barely hear. "Maybe then I'd be able to forget. Light a lamp, Cat," he added more audibly.

"Jake . . ."

"You want to stand here in the dark with me? If so, I could think of some pleasant diversions. . . . "

Nervously Caitlin fumbled for the box of matches on the entryway table and struck one. She winced when the golden flame illuminated Jake's hard, virile face. Stubble still blurred the lines of his jaw and chin but did little to hide the cuts and bruises from the beating his face had suffered. More disquieting, Jake was watching her, branding her with the intense heat of his unfathomable gaze. It was all Caitlin could do to stiffen her spine.

"What's so important that you have to sneak over in the dead of night?"

He smiled crookedly. "Would you rather I showed up in broad daylight? I didn't think the Widow Hughes would like having her hands know a 'notorious gunslinger's' come calling." His gaze traveled the length of the hall. "Can you cook?"

She blinked at him in startlement. "What?"

Shaking his head, Jake laughed softly. "Hell, I don't even know that much about you, and I was going to marry you. . . . I'd like some coffee. Can you make us a pot? Never mind, I'll do it. Where's the kitchen? We can talk there. No one will bother us. Half your boys are in town, the other half are camped up in the hills with their smelly woollies."

As he spoke, he moved pantherlike down the hall, leaving Caitlin no choice but to follow him with the lamp. She knew arguing was pointless. Jake wasn't the kind of man who gave a damn whether he was welcome or not.

He found the kitchen without much trouble and headed for the stove. When he picked up the coffeepot, she shook her head and set the lamp on the countertop near the sink. "No, sit down. I'll make the coffee. You're right. We need to talk."

She could see that she'd been the one to startle Jake this time, and that small triumph strengthened her. He'd obviously expected a fight, but she couldn't continue to live like this. She had to get things settled with him before she went crazy, before all her nerves were shredded raw.

I can do this, she thought a bit desperately. *I can look at him and talk to him without falling apart.*

She took the blue ironware pot from him, glad to have something to do, and turned toward the sink. Jake didn't take a seat at the table, though. He simply stood there, staring at her.

"God, that beautiful hair," he said finally, almost to himself, his voice soft and reverent. "I used to dream about it wrapping around me. . . ."

Caitlin's heart stalled in its rhythmic beat as she felt him take hold of a few strands of her unbound hair and rub it between his fingertips. She tried not to remember another time, a time when Jake had made the simple gesture of running his fingers through her hair an act of worship, when he'd considered it his right to touch it and her anytime he liked. . . . But he no longer had that right.

Pulling away, she forced herself to ignore his actions and primed the pump till fresh water spilled out. Carefully she filled the coffeepot and turned to set it on the stove, then poked the coals in the firebox beneath, trying her best to disregard the man hovering so near. He was standing too close to her, though. Much too close.

"Is that what you wear to sleep in?" His voice had dropped to a soft, husky rasp. When she turned with a start, his gaze flickered over the tight buds outlined beneath her cambric nightgown.

Caitlin could feel an instant stirring in her blood, a familiar quickening between her thighs, but she jerked the lapels of her wrapper closed and tied the sash tightly about her waist. "I said, go sit *down*, Jake."

With deceptive laziness he turned toward the kitchen table of polished oak and pulled out a chair, angling it to face her. Then, tossing his hat on the table, he sprawled in the seat, long legs stretched out before him, and crossed his muscular forearms over his chest, making the fabric of his faded, blue cotton shirt stretch across his broad shoulders.

Caitlin proceeded to measure some coffee grounds into the pot, but she had never been more aware of a man in her life, of the tension in her body, drumming in her veins. Jake was watching her, and his intense gaze made her feel hot, restless, not to mention vulnerable.

"I've never had you in a real bed, you know that?"

She nearly jumped out of her skin at his quiet observation. "And you won't, either," Caitlin forced herself to respond evenly.

"I wouldn't be too sure of that."

"Dammit, Jake..." She whirled to face him, planting her hands on her hips defensively. "You're going to say what you have to say, and then you'll leave," she declared in her most repressive schoolmarm voice. "Now... what did you want to talk about?"

"You. Me. Us."

"There is no 'us' any longer."

He shook his head, his green gaze intent and smoldering. "That's where you're wrong, Cat. I'm just going to have to make you see it."

Chapter 6

Warily Caitlin stared at the rough, hard-eyed gunman lounging at her kitchen table. His relaxed pose didn't fool her for an instant. Concealed in the lazy posture, hidden in Jake's deceptively negligent attitude, was an alertness, an intense awareness that was directed solely at her. His brilliant green gaze held the power to make her tremble.

His appearance made her hurt. Jake's handsome, hard-planed face bore the ravages of the brawl he'd started, while the gash on his cheek was still caked with blood. His unruly hair fell around his injured face in a thick, gold-streaked tangle, and when Caitlin caught herself wanting to smooth back a lock of it from his forehead, she scolded herself furiously.

To her dismay her hands shook as she turned back to finish making the coffee. Leaving it to boil, she searched in the pantry for some carbolic and sticking plaster, and filled a basin with fresh water, grateful to postpone what she knew would be, for her at least, an agonizing discussion.

When she set her supplies on the table in front of Jake, he eyed her warily.

"That cut needs tending," Caitlin said tersely. "You're liable to have a scar otherwise."

Jake settled back, tilting his face up for her examination. There was, he thought as his guard relaxed, something comfortable and intimate about her fussing, even if he could see no sign of the tenderness Caitlin had once exhibited when she ministered to him.

He winced when her fingertips probed the bruise beneath his eye. "Ouch . . . dang it, Cat, do you have to enjoy poking me so much?"

"It's no more than you deserve. You ought to be ashamed of yourself, a grown man fistfighting in a saloon."

"It was only a little harmless fun."

"*Harmless*?" She made a sound of disgust as she wrung water from a cloth. "One of our hands came home half-dead last night—and I can only guess what the others looked like after your savagery. Someone could have gotten *killed*, Jake. Not to mention that you've stirred up the feud again."

His mouth twitched. "I never claimed to be a saint. You know you wouldn't really want a saint, anyway."

He wasn't teasing her exactly, but almost. "What I *don't* want," Caitlin said with quiet emphasis, unable to help the bitterness that crept into her tone, "is a hostile drunkard like my father rousing the community to war."

The tension was suddenly back in the air; the dark past vibrated between them as their eyes locked.

In the strained silence, Jake was the first to drop

his gaze. He sat quietly as she gently washed the dried blood from his cheek and patched the gash with sticking plaster, unwillingly remembering how she'd once made him promise never to fight again. He could have sworn similar thoughts were haunting Cat. He could see her pain.

He looked away from her unbearably sad eyes. He'd violated his promise to her with a vengeance, just as she'd violated hers to be his wife.

They were both relieved when her task was done. Caitlin could feel her hands trembling again as she set the basin in the sink, could sense Jake's watchfulness.

Not turning around, she forced herself to take a deep breath. She couldn't put off the moment any longer. They had some critical issues to discuss, not the least of which was the terrible treatment Jake had received at her family's hands. She owed him an ardent apology for what her father had done, for the lies that had destroyed his life.

"Jake . . ." she began in a low voice, not looking at him. "I'm sorry . . . for doubting you. I realize now that the accusations my father made were false, that you weren't to blame for . . . for killing Neal. You had no choice. I know it isn't much after all this time, but I want you to know . . . I'm sorry for the way things turned out."

"So you believe me now?" His tone was taut, skeptical. "What changed your mind?"

"I spoke to Placido. He confirmed your story. It was self-defense."

Why didn't you believe me before? Why didn't you have faith in me then? The painful challenge hung between them, unspoken.

"Did Flores say why he was willing to see me hang?" Jake asked instead.

"He . . . he did it out of loyalty to us, to our side.

And because his job was at risk. My father threatened his family."

"Sounds like something the old bastard would do."

She cast a swift glance at Jake over her shoulder. His mouth looked hard and unyielding, and he seemed only slightly mollified by her apology. "Jake . . . you have every right to want revenge, but please . . . leave Placido alone. He's sorry for what he did. And really, he's the reason you're free. Because he went to Sloan and confessed the truth."

Her quiet plea disarmed him. "I know he went to Sloan," Jake muttered, before letting out a heavy sigh. "I won't hurt your shepherd, Cat. I just want to forget this whole blasted mess and get on with my life."

She eyed him warily, wondering if she could believe him. Encouraged by his reasonable tone, she crossed to the table and took a seat at one end, at right angles to Jake, a careful distance away. He was no longer looking at her with that intent predator's gaze, though. Instead he was staring down at the tips of his boots.

She could understand what he must be feeling: betrayal, anger, bitterness . . . hatred. *I just want to get on with my life*, he'd said. That was all she wanted to do, too. To bury the pain. Until now, though, she hadn't truly considered how hurt Jake must be by all that had happened to him. She knew the emotional pain *she'd* endured, knew how alone and grieving *she'd* been, but Jake must have felt something similar, driven from his home, separated from his family, branded a criminal. . . .

Her throat ached with sorrow, for what he'd suffered, for what he'd lost, for the man he'd been.

Although she knew better, she allowed her eyes to search the face she'd once loved. Life as an outlaw must have changed him, she thought sorrowfully. Jake was a stranger to her now, yet she desperately wanted to know what sort of man he had become.

Instinctively Caitlin leaned toward him, resting her palms on the table. "You said . . . you were badly wounded in the shooting, but that you recovered. What happened afterward?"

"After I learned I was wanted for murder?" Jake looked up, his gaze shuttered. "I headed down to New Mexico. Hired on at a big spread, working for a cattle baron who needed protection from his enemies. I guess you could say I was a hired gun."

"You . . . killed for money?"

"If I had to." When she gazed at him in anguish, his mouth twisted in a bleak smile. "I had to eat, Cat. I couldn't take much cash when I left here, since most of our capital was tied up in our ranch. And it was hard for Sloan to get money to me when I was on the run. I had to earn a living somehow."

He watched the expressions cross her face: sadness, acceptance, something that looked like despair. "What I did was perfectly legal."

"But you . . . still got in trouble with the law."

Jake laughed softly, bitterly. "I suppose you could say that." He'd killed men who'd come after him looking to collect the bounty on his head. He'd killed others, too. Innocents who'd gotten in his way. The kid's face still haunted him, pale, still, so young. . . . It was a guilt he would always live with. He couldn't tell Cat about that. Couldn't bear to see the horror in her eyes when she learned what he'd done.

He offered her a humorless smile. He didn't want to make excuses for himself, and yet . . . "I lived by my gun, Cat. With a price on my head I had little choice."

"I . . . I heard you've killed over a dozen men. Is it true?"

"That number's about right."

His bald confession made Caitlin's stomach churn. She had hoped it was an exaggeration.

"You'd be surprised how many greedy bastards there are out there," he added tonelessly. "My main goal was trying to stay alive."

"It must have been . . . rough."

"Living as a hunted man? Yeah. It taught me to be hard, for damn sure. I learned not to trust anybody."

She heard the raw pain in the depths of his voice, and her heart ached for him, even while the thought of his violent existence dismayed her. She didn't want to judge him, but even so . . . "Are you still running?" The question was quiet. "The bank holdup in New Mexico where that clerk was murdered . . ." Her voice trailed off, leaving him an opening if he chose to take it.

It was pride, pure pride, that kept Jake's jaw clenched. His notorious reputation was well-earned, but although he wasn't proud of it, he was too proud to defend himself to Cat, or confess all the things he'd done simply to stay alive. Besides, some of the things he'd done were indefensible. He'd made some bad choices, choices he would regret for the rest of his life. When he'd first been framed for murder, lost everything and everyone he loved, he hadn't given two hoots in hell about anything. And the years he'd been hunted like an animal had eaten away at the fiber of his soul, hardened him, turned him unforgiving and suspicious, even a trifle savage. But what really kept him silent was a stubborn conviction he couldn't quell, regardless of how irrational it was: Cat should have believed in his innocence without explanation.

"There may be some wanted posters still out on me for that murder," he answered finally, refusing to expound further.

Caitlin bit her lip, not knowing what to say. There was a haunted emptiness in Jake's eyes that sliced at her heart. A vulnerability that spoke of wounds that needed healing. She felt a sudden need to put her arms around him . . . yet she was afraid to test her own vulnerability, to risk the slightest weakening.

Then Jake shrugged, as if dismissing the subject.

"What about you?" he asked softly. "What have you been doing with yourself all these years?"

"I made a life for myself in St. Louis."

"What kind of life?"

"It's quiet. Peaceful. I teach now. At an exclusive girls school. A conservatoire for young ladies."

"Sounds fancy."

"Not really. I instruct my pupils in reading and diction and manners—" She broke off when a hint of a smile crossed Jake's mouth. Despite her best intentions, Caitlin felt herself bristle. "Don't you dare laugh, Jake McCord. I know more about polite manners than you ever will, and I'm perfectly capable of imparting rules of etiquette to pubescent girls."

"I don't doubt it, hellcat." He grinned. "Jeeze, don't bite my head off. I was only remembering how you used to hate people who put on airs."

"There is a *world* of difference between 'airs' and common courtesy. But then you never paid the slightest attention to what the world considers decent behavior, as I recall."

"Still don't, I'm afraid."

He was deliberately provoking her, Caitlin realized, seeing the sudden sparkle of laughter dancing in his emerald eyes. She took a deep breath, willing herself to calm. She would not let him get the better of her. "My best friend owns the school," she pressed on. "Heather Ashford is headmistress, but she allows me a big say in how it's run."

"You said you had a son," Jake murmured finally when he couldn't get a rise out of her. Swiveling in his chair, he faced her fully, so that he could see her eyes. "Tell me about him."

She gazed at him warily. "What do you want to know?"

"What's his name?"

"Ryan. It's Irish, after my mother. He's a beautiful child. He has my black hair and . . . and he has his father's eyes."

Jake heard the wistfulness in her voice, and it went straight to his gut. She must love her son a great deal. Had she loved that bastard husband of hers, too?

"How old is he . . . your son?"

She hesitated for an instant, her eyes clouding. "Almost three." She could see Jake doing the mental calculations.

"You didn't waste any time replacing me, did you?" he said slowly.

"You were gone. I never heard a word from you."

"I'm back now."

"It doesn't matter."

It sure as hell does, Cat, he thought savagely, but he let the comment slide. "Your husband . . . did you love him?" The question burned his throat with its searing power.

"Yes."

Jake cursed to himself. Her eyes had turned soft, tender the way they'd once been when *he'd* made love to her. He wanted to smash something with his fists. He wanted to drive that look from her eyes, wanted to make Caitlin forget the bastard who'd shared her bed, her body, her heart. The man who had fathered her child.

He looked down at her left hand. She wore her late husband's wedding ring, a thin, plain band of gold, like the one he'd planned to buy her so long ago. It should have been *his* ring. *His* son. *His* heart she shared. His bed.

The vicious, scalding jealousy that knifed through him was sharp enough to make his stomach knot. It wasn't hard to picture her husband making love to her—or scores of other men, for that matter. Caitlin was the kind of woman who would effortlessly draw masculine notice. With her inner fire, she made a man hungry for a taste of her.

"Was he the only one?" Jake asked through gritted teeth.

"The only one, what?"

"The only man you let in your bed. Or were there others?"

Wincing at the ruthless questions that tore at her heart, Caitlin stiffened. "Not that it's any of your business, but I've had no lovers but you and my husband. Can you say the same, Jake? How many women have you had?"

He stared at her, refusing to answer. He'd long ago lost track of the number of women he'd bedded. There'd been too many meaningless tumbles in too many nowhere towns. The women had helped, but only for a while. Their attractions paled when compared to the raven-haired, hot-tempered vixen he'd left behind. Cat was in his blood, and he knew now she always would be. That was the hell of it.

"Nothing was ever as good as what we had," he said quietly.

Green eyes met blue for a ragged heartbeat as they recalled the past they'd shared. He could tell Caitlin was remembering; memory lurked in her eyes, along with a deep sadness. He wanted to take away that sadness, wanted to erase that anguish and despair from her expression.

"Do you remember, Cat?" he couldn't resist asking. "The first time we made love?"

Her lips parted, but no sound came out.

Jake watched those soft lips, remembering the first time he'd kissed her, a caress he'd felt at the very core of his man's body and soul. He remembered the first time he'd taken her, the way she'd clutched at him in desperate need, how she'd sobbed at his possession, as if overwhelmed by raw emotion and the elemental, primitive beauty of becoming part of him. It *had* been beautiful. And gutwrenching. He'd never learned what had driven her to such despair that day, though he knew it had something to do with her family.

"Don't, Jake," she whispered, the words a plea, her eyes wounded.

He couldn't help himself. He felt the ache starting deep inside, a yearning that had festered for four long years. His gaze swept over the lustrous cascade of her hair, cherishing the way the lamplight looked in it, how the ebony tresses glinted with blue-black highlights. The wild, sweet scent of it taunted him. He felt his lower body harden painfully.

His gaze moved over her lithe, curved figure, lingered on her breasts. The memory of those soft breasts tormented him. They were ripe and pert, perfectly shaped to fill a man's hands. All he had to do was think about taking those taut buds in his mouth, and he grew hard as a fencepost.

Unwillingly his gaze traveled farther down her body half hidden beneath the table, to her legs covered primly by a dark blue satin wrapper the color of her eyes. He wanted those slender legs hugging him. Jesus, he wanted it.

I want to touch you, he thought. *I want to hold you and comfort you and be comforted. I want to end the aloneness I've felt since you.*

His gaze slid back to her mouth and darkened. It wasn't over between them. His feelings, and hers, were still unresolved. Regardless of the pain between them, they still shared a bond forged by the past.

"Remember, Juliet?" he murmured, his voice soft and prodding.

Memory rose up around her, drowning her. "Don't," Caitlin repeated in a hoarse whisper. She didn't want to remember how sweet and innocent their love had been, before their lives had fallen apart.

Tearing her gaze away before she got lost in the depthless green of his eyes, she desperately sought to change the subject. "What . . . what do you plan to do now that you're home?"

With effort, Jake focused his mind on her question. "I told you. I just want to start over."

His dreams were smaller now, tamer, but they were still dreams. "I want to put my life back together. Make a fresh start."

"Do you mean to live at your brother's ranch?"

Jake shrugged. He had little in common with any of the people here any longer. "For a while, yeah. The Bar M is half mine, but Sloan's doing well enough without my help. Trouble is, the cattle business isn't so profitable these days, what with prices slipping. I have a few other ideas I'm considering, but . . ."

He would settle for having his old life back, Jake reflected, as long as Caitlin was in it. For four years she'd been on his mind, but he hadn't understood what had driven him home. Not until seeing Caitlin two days ago. Until he'd kissed her and held her and realized all he had lost. But now he knew. He'd come back to claim her. Only she could fill the hollow ache in his soul. Without her he faced a future filled with emptiness.

He'd thought his heart was dead, but it had only been lying dormant, waiting for her. He wanted to care for her, to protect her, wanted to fight and argue and make love.

Caitlin would fight him, he knew. But he was prepared for it, ready for it, eager even.

Jake muttered another silent curse. The heat was rising in him now. He felt the hardening of his loins like a savage fire.

"What about you?" he made himself ask. "I hear you mean to sell this place."

She lowered her gaze. "Yes. As soon as I can find a buyer."

"You don't have to sell out, Cat."

"I do. I can't live here. I won't. There's been too much bloodshed and heartache."

"You're going to just walk away?"

"I walked away years ago. I've made a new life for myself and my son."

Without thinking, Jake reached across the table for her, but when Caitlin flinched and drew back her hands abruptly, he stopped short, a shaft of pain ripping through him at the panic he saw in her eyes. It hurt like hell to see her pull away from him in fear.

Achingly aware of what she'd done, Caitlin stared back at Jake silently, her heart crying, her eyes pleading with him to understand. She couldn't have let him touch her; such intimate contact was more than she could bear. She could scarcely hold on to her composure as it was. She felt an infinite, suffocating sadness at all they'd lost. Yet it was irrevocable. Jake had to understand that he had no place here, in either her life or her heart. She couldn't let him.

Rigidly, Jake caught his hat in his fingers, fingering the rim. There had to be a way to get through to her, he thought with grim determination.

He nodded slowly. "You're right about the feud. It's gone on too damn long." He paused. "You could end it, you know."

"What do you mean?" He had her attention at least; she sounded wary but curious.

"You could put an end to the range war. Your pa's gone, and he was the main reason it lasted so long."

"I have no influence over anyone here."

"You could, if you tried."

Caitlin shook her head. "I don't belong here anymore, Jake. And I'd rather just stay out of it. I just want peace."

He wanted peace, too. He wanted to be rid of the hollow ache that had tormented him for so long.

"You think you can find a buyer who's willing to settle here in the middle of a range war? You might be able to sell at rock-bottom prices, but that's all."

Jake was right, Caitlin thought reluctantly. No one in his right mind would become involved in the death and destruction that had lasted for twenty years. If someone could somehow bring about a peace, or at least a truce, it would help her chances of selling for a decent price.

"I'll talk to Sloan," Jake offered. "I think I can get him to listen to reason."

"You would do that? Why?"

"Because it's time for the feud to be over. I'm sick of the fighting, just like you are."

It shocked her a little that Jake was interested in burying the hatchet when she'd thought him bent on revenge. But then, he meant to live here, and she didn't.

"Think about it, Cat," he said coaxingly. "You'll never have a better chance. Working together we could make something happen."

Her nerves went on full alert at his beguiling tone. Possibly they *could* change the progress of the war if they worked together, Caitlin thought worriedly. The trouble was she didn't *want* to work with Jake. She didn't dare have anything to do with him.

Still . . . that didn't mean she couldn't act on her own. If she approached Sloan, he might be willing to listen, to work with her. She would have to give it careful consideration.

She heard Jake's voice drop to a quiet murmur. "I don't want you to leave, Cat."

Her mouth twisted briefly at hearing the same sentiments voiced by two very different men. "Funny. Vernon Whitfield had said much the same thing just the other day."

"The schoolteacher?"

At his sharp tone, Caitlin shook herself. She needed to make Jake see there was no chance for them. She felt her own bitterness at what had been taken from them, but they couldn't go back. Too many dreams had been shattered. It was time to move on.

She leaned forward, holding his gaze earnestly. "Jake, the past is over. You have to accept that."

"I don't," he said flatly.

"You have to. Four years ago was a long time. We were young and foolish—"

"You were young. I was the damn fool. I should have taken you away from here when we first decided to get married. I should have made you elope with me."

Caitlin felt an ache well up in her throat. "What we had . . . that life . . . is gone forever."

"Our relationship isn't over. I still want you. And I think you still want me. When I kissed you the other day . . . your body responded, just like it used to. I didn't imagine that."

She shut her eyes for a moment, silently damning Jake for his perception, for making her remember things she shouldn't be remembering. Gathering her resources, she made herself face him, knowing she had to do anything in her power to resist him. She had to think of her son. Jake had blood on his hands. A man with his hard soul was no model for a young boy.

"What are you suggesting? That we become lovers again?"

He smiled faintly. "That would be a start."

She shook her head, trying to keep her voice steady and reasonable. "I couldn't. Not without destroying my reputation. Not without branding Ryan the child of a wanton."

"I can be discreet."

Caitlin drew a sharp breath, believing his teasing had crossed the line. "Perhaps so, but I won't have my son touched by scandal. It was hard enough four years ago to be called a whore by my own father—" She broke off, a fresh ache in her throat.

Jake's face softened. "Was it bad? Your father didn't hurt you did he?"

"He . . . he threatened to, but no, he didn't. He wanted to kick me out of the house, but . . . he gave me time to make arrangements to live with my aunt. To 'leave the place of my shame.' " Her laugh was sharp with bitterness.

"Is that what you thought it was? That what we'd done was shameful?"

Caitlin shook her head, not trusting herself to speak. She wasn't ashamed of what they'd done, she *wasn't*. She couldn't call their loving a sin, even now.

Jake regarded her silently, wishing he could have spared her. He was largely to blame for her father turning against her. It had hurt her badly, losing her family. He didn't want to hurt her any more.

Maybe Cat was right. Maybe he should keep away from her. It would be the honorable thing to do, to go back to his nothing life and never be with her again. As futures went, it would be hell. But then he'd been in hell for four years.

Still, he wasn't willing to give up so soon.

"We could get married."

She inhaled sharply, staring at him. "Is this some sort of cruel game you're playing, Jake?"

"It's no game, Cat."

"You said you wanted to make me pay for what my father did to you."

"I was riled when I said that."

"And what about four years ago?" She needed to know. "Did . . . did you seduce me because I was an easy conquest? Was it just sex to you? Or were you pursuing me for revenge like you said?"

Roughly Jake ran a hand through his hair, tousling it even more. "It wasn't just sex, dammit. And it sure as hell wasn't revenge. I wanted to marry you, for crissakes. I never said that to any other girl. What more could I have done?"

You could have said you loved me. Yet seductive hope flared through her. Had Jake really wanted her for herself? "Would you really have married me?"

His green eyes narrowed. "You never used to be a dimwit."

For some reason, his terse, almost-savage reply reassured Caitlin far more than sweet blandishments would have. She slowly shook her head. "It really doesn't matter. I can't marry you now, Jake."

"Why not? Because you'd feel guilty taking up with your brother's killer?"

"That's not . . . the only reason." She would feel guilty for betraying Neal's memory, no doubt, but her son mattered more than any personal feelings. "I . . . the truth is . . . I don't want such a violent man for my son's father."

For an instant his jaw clenched. "That's the bottom line, isn't it? Your son."

"Yes." Her voice was a hoarse rasp. "He's all I care about."

"You cared for me once."

"Perhaps I did. But I don't feel the same way about you as I did then." Her heart constricted with pain and regret. "I don't even know you now, Jake."

"Am I so different than I was?" The question was quiet.

"Yes . . . yes, you are."

Her eyes blurred with sudden tears. The Jake she remembered was honorable and kind, strong yet compassionate. That man had been capable of infinite gentleness, of great tenderness. This hard stranger . . . she *didn't* know him anymore.

To her surprise—and vast relief—he drew back,

draping one arm negligently over the back of his chair, while he studied her silently.

"All right, then," he said slowly. "We don't have to get married. I'm willing to be friends, if that's all you want."

Caitlin tensed. She could handle Jake's bitterness, his anger, even his scorn; fighting those emotions kept her strong. But his offer of friendship terrified her. She didn't want to be drawn into *any* kind of relationship with him. She couldn't trust him to keep his distance.

"How long has it been for you, wildcat?" he asked when she remained silent.

"How long since what?"

"Since a man made love to you."

"I don't believe that's really any of your business," she retorted stiffly.

"What if I said I plan to make it my business?"

His impossible arrogance triggered a reckless response in her; her mouth set mutinously. "If your memory were better, you'd know better than to push me."

Jake held up his hands innocently. "I'm not going to push you, Cat." And he wouldn't. He badly wanted to touch her. Wanted to feel Caitlin go warm and soft in his hands. Wanted her wet and hungry and quivering with need for him. But he wanted more to make her realize what they'd lost, what they could still have.

His gaze slid briefly to the door that led to the hall. "I'd like nothing more than to carry you into your bedroom right now and make love to you till neither of us could walk, but I mean to give you time."

"Time for what?"

"To realize we belong together."

"It will never happen."

He eyed her casually, giving her the full effect of his lazy smile. "Want to bet?"

Her breath seemed to stop.

"I know you, Caitlin. I know your body, how to make you purr."

His voice was languid and dark, while a slow smile teased his lips. A smile that frightened her. There was an intense, smoldering sexuality beneath that relaxed expression that put all her senses on edge, set all her nerve endings shouting in alarm.

Defensively Caitlin curled her fingers into fists. His tone held an arrogant confidence that she would be supremely satisfied in his arms, and she knew to her regret it was no boast. Jake's lovemaking was intense, elemental, like getting caught up in a storm. If she let him touch her now, she would melt. Their coupling would be raw and hot and purely sexual—yet she wanted more than that from a man, from Jake. She needed so much more.

"Even if I wanted to take up with you again," she said shakily, "—and I assure you, I don't—I have a son to think of. He's the only thing in my life that matters to me."

Jake nodded sympathetically. "We'll deal with that when we come to it."

"Jake, stop it! You're not going to run roughshod over me!" Caitlin exclaimed, her voice too high and breathless. She swallowed and tried again. "Jake . . . you'd better go. I don't want you here."

"Want me where, Cat?"

In my memories, in my dreams, in my heart, she cried silently. "In my house," she forced herself to reply. "On my ranch."

"You don't really want me to go, be honest."

Bravely she lifted her chin. "You vastly overestimate your appeal."

"Do I?" His smile was slow and warm and incredibly sensual. "All right. I'll leave. If you'll do something for me first."

"W-What?"

"Give me a kiss."

"Are you out of your mind?"

To her infinite dismay, he rose from the table with his lithe cougar's grace and moved toward her, giving her a clear view of the desire that was so compellingly clear in the bulging contours of his denims.

Caitlin froze, her heart going wild with excitement. "Jake . . . you said you only wanted to talk. . . . "

"Just a kiss, Cat. For old times' sake. I'm not going to do anything you don't want me to do, I swear."

Favoring her with a smile of breathtaking charm, he reached down and caught her hand.

"Jake, I . . ." Caitlin licked her suddenly dry lips. He meant to seduce her, and she would be powerless to stop him, she knew it.

"Caitlin, look at me."

She couldn't look at him. If she let her eyes meet his, he would see her confusion, her *need*.

"One last time, that's all." Raising her fingers to his mouth in a soft caress, he pressed a delicate kiss on her knuckles, but it was Jake's pleading look that was her undoing.

I shouldn't, she thought frantically as he slowly but inexorably drew her to her feet. She pushed her hands weakly against his chest, even as he pulled her resisting body into his arms. Bracing herself, she waited, deathly still.

The night trembled around them. Caitlin tried to look away and couldn't. Her soft, ragged intake of breath sounded loud in the silence as, with one long finger, Jake tilted her chin up. He was going to kiss her, and God help her, she couldn't resist the temptation of that hard mouth. She hungered for his kiss, for one more taste of him.

His lean, sinewy hands were gentle on her shoulders as he bent his head. And then his lips met hers.

The caress was no more than a touch, a fleeting, questioning brush of flesh, yet it evoked a turmoil of churning emotions. Feelings that were mirrored in Jake's eyes as he lifted his head to stare down at her.

She drew a shattered breath, remaining frozen as he bent once more. Slowly he tasted her again. His touch was burningly tender, his mouth impossibly soft and loving . . . warm . . . not shadow-cold like her dreams and memories.

Oh, God, this feels so right, Caitlin thought. So familiar. So much like heaven. *Oh, Jake, what happened to us?*

She tried to hold herself rigid so she wouldn't sob out loud as his mouth savored hers, slowly, like a thirsty man drinking a rare wine. His mouth was warm and sweet as it moved over hers, coaxing, gentle. She felt as if she were being worshiped. . . . Yet it was over too soon. When Jake raised his head, she wanted to cry out at the sudden, empty longing that flooded her.

His eyes were filled with desire and a masculine satisfaction as he asked softly, "Haven't you missed that at all, sweetheart?"

"Jake . . ." she began helplessly, but he only drew her closer, making her feel the incredible, lean, toughness of his body, his heat and hardness. Caitlin felt herself start to melt, felt a hard, rebellious ache flare between her shivering thighs.

"Haven't you, Cat?"

"Yes," she whispered. She'd missed him so

much. No matter what else she'd felt in the past, Jake made her feel whole, complete, even as he was drawing the very soul from her body.

In answer, he slipped his hands to her face, his callused palms rough yet impossibly delicate against her cheeks. Bending, he kissed her again, but this time the kiss went on forever, warm, hungry, fever building to a demanding urgency.

With a silent moan of desperation Caitlin moved her hands up his chest, to his shoulders, clinging. She was trembling and she couldn't stop. She parted her lips, accepting the probe of his tongue as if she too were starved with need for him. What had been tender and poignant flared into something brighter between them, something sensual and wild, intense and burning, a blaze that threatened all defensive barriers.

Suddenly the tension within Caithlin seemed to give way, a rending she felt at the depths of her soul. To her dismay a harsh sob burst from her. The dam shattered, releasing a flood of feelings she'd tried for so long to keep locked inside.

She was crying, Caitlin realized vaguely. She could feel the tears streaming from her eyes, sliding down her face as she clutched at Jake desperately, trying to draw him tighter.

"Hey . . ." His quiet murmur held concern but not surprise. "It's okay."

Pulling back from her stranglehold a little, Jake brought both hands up to cup her face. The pads of his thumbs brushed at the swollen tears as startling tenderness assailed him.

He knew what Caitlin felt; he felt the same deep anguish at all they had lost, could feel the ache in his own throat, the stinging behind his eyelids as she tried to choke back her ragged little sobs.

Leaning closer, he bent to kiss the tears from her

cheek. "No crying," Jake whispered thickly.

When Caitlin gave a convulsive shudder, he tenderly wrapped his arms around her and buried his face in her hair, not letting her go.

For a long moment he just held her that way, enveloping her in the heat and smell of his body, letting her grow accustomed to his touch, the feel of being in his arms again, determined to wait till her shudders subsided.

He wanted to do more. He wanted to touch her. To strip every stitch of her clothing from her, then stretch her out naked on the table and plunge deep and fast into her. He wanted to take until the hunger in his heart had been satisfied. The heat of sexual arousal was building in his loins like a fever, but he forced himself to go slow, resting his lips with feather-light pressure against her temple. His shaft was iron-hard with lust, straining against the front of his jeans, but he simply stood there, drinking in the sweet, warm fragrance of her skin, her hair.

He could feel her tremble as he pressed lightly into her, rubbing the hard ridge of his manhood against her soft mound, letting her know wordlessly of his need.

How many times had he dreamed of this during the past four years? Jake wondered. Had Cat dreamed of it, too?

Needing to see her eyes, he drew back a little. Teardrops, like diamonds, sparkled amid her lush lashes, stained her cheeks.

"Jake, please...." Caitlin whispered, yet she didn't know what she was pleading for. She knew better than to remain here with him, yet danger beckoned and taunted. Her body had turned traitor. She could feel the treacherous heat of desire spreading through her limbs, making her weak, weaker. . . .

Despairingly, Caitlin closed her eyes. How frightening it was to feel such need. How sweet. It had been so long since any man had held her, since Jake had held her. She'd thought she would never again know his kiss, the comfort of his arms. She'd thought he lacked tenderness, that he'd been hardened beyond redemption, but just now she didn't care if he'd committed a dozen crimes.

"I want you, Caitlin." His voice was husky, deep, yet she could not have responded if her life was at stake. "Say you want me, too."

She did want him. She wanted to feel his lips on hers, the way she had too few exquisite times in the past. She wanted to stay here in his arms and be sheltered from the world. . . . "I . . . I don't . . . know what I want."

"Then let go and I'll show you."

When her arms fell away, Jake took a step back. His eyes were hot and held dark promises, Caitlin saw; the emerald depths were deep enough to drown in.

They held hers as he gently tugged the sash of her wrapper and loosened the tie. Her breath caught in her throat, but she didn't stop him.

It was the simple work of a moment to slip the garment over her shoulders and let it fall to the floor. Caitlin stood in only her cambric nightdress.

Jake smiled, that soft, sweet, coaxing smile that devastated all her senses.

"You don't need this, darlin'," he murmured, his voice maddeningly sensuous as he began to unfasten the three buttons of her bodice.

She remained immobile, paralyzed by desire, as he silently completed his task. She saw the quick tightening of his expression as her bare, trembling breasts spilled out. His hard, chiseled face held an awed, tender look.

Jake caught a harsh breath as his eyes ruthlessly devoured her. Her breasts were larger than he remembered, high and round and impudent. The dusky crimson peaks were darker, the nipples small and already tightly budded. God, she was even more beautiful than he remembered.

He reached out reverently to touch an aching peak, brushing the proud, taunting crest with excruciating slowness.

Hunger flared within Caitlin, fanning to instant life at his touch. She squeezed her eyes shut, cursing herself for her weakness.

"So beautiful. . . ." His husky voice stroked her senses as he aroused her, running his thumbs lightly over the nipples. She wanted to protest, but reason fled as he cupped her breasts in his callused palms, staking his claim.

She whimpered at the stunning warmth of his gentle hands. And that was before he bent his head. His hard, hot lips closed wetly over a pouting crest, tugging and stroking . . . arousing. Stunned, she gave a sob and arched upward against his mouth, straining against the searing wet heat.

"Look at me, Cat."

It was a struggle to raise her heavy lids. His eyes were hard and bright and hungry, narrowed in a look of sexual intent as old as time.

"I want to make love to you."

A stab of panic trembled through her. She couldn't do this. Surrendering to Jake would destroy the careful, sedate life she'd made for herself and her son. It would leave her reputation in tatters. . . .

"Jake . . . I *can't*. . . ."

Blindly Caitlin turned away, needing to escape,

but she only came up against the rim of the table. When Jake slipped an arm around her waist, she was trapped.

"Don't run from me, sweetheart. Cat, don't. . . . " His plea raked at her heart, while his touch burned.

Sweetly, with exquisite skill, he brushed aside the wild tangle of her glorious hair and pressed his lips against her neck.

"I know your body, hellcat. I know what to do to you to make you wild. Don't you remember how good I can make you feel?"

"No . . . I don't want this. . . . "

"Liar. . . ." His breath was a warm shiver against her neck. She could feel the searing heat of him at her back. "You can't forget what we used to have. Neither can I. . . . "

A reckless urge prodded her to surrender. She wanted to give in to sweet, mindless abandon, to blind passion. An insidious voice called to her. They were alone, with no one to see them. Only Jake and she were here. What would be the harm? If it created a scandal later, she just didn't care. For just this moment, she wanted to pretend that they were young lovers again, that they had discovered each other again. . . .

"You know I'll please you, honey."

"No," she pleaded, but the word was uttered in such a thick, helpless, wanting tone that Jake smiled.

Searching, his hands slid slowly up her body to cup and squeeze her bare breasts. Caitlin's breath caught in her lungs. She could feel her nipples throb against his palms, could feel them ache as he rubbed the peaks to hard little points of fire. Jake's touch was hot and rough and oh so tender. . . . Her skin was aflame as he pulled and caressed her flesh. Only the shredded remnants of her pride kept her from moaning in wild pleasure.

God, how she'd missed him, missed this. All she could think of at this moment was how desperately she still wanted him.

"Remember, Cat? How you start getting wet as soon as I touch you. . . . "

She felt a cool draft against the back of her legs as he raised her nightdress, felt the hard outline of his manhood as he pressed against her. "Jake. . . ."

"I know. I know what you want. I know how tight and hot you are. . . . "

Her limbs weak, she braced her hands against the tabletop. Behind her, Jake's hard thighs grazed her soft, bare bottom, letting her feel his blatant need.

"God, you're so soft and sexy." His voice was thick like dark honey, his hands incredibly arousing as he drew back and began to caress the bare curves of her buttocks.

Shameful pleasure flared wherever he touched her. Palms flat, fingers spread, he grasped the cushioned roundness of her bottom in strong fingers, squeezing and kneading the twin cheeks, stroking the dark crevice between, giving her no opportunity to evade him or the coiling tension that was building inside her to an explosive level. It was a sensual assault in which her own body assailed and betrayed her, and Caitlin could no more have broken free than she could have taken wing, even if she'd wanted to.

"Just think, Cat," Jake whispered to her, his voice going even softer, deeper, stroking her senses like dark velvet. "How you're going to moan for me when you take all of me inside you."

She whimpered again, the sound Jake had been waiting for. He levered his knee between hers and spread her legs, pressing his hips against her buttocks, wanting her to feel his rigid erection. Anticipation and arousal were riding him hard, just the way he wanted to ride her. He wanted to drive into her hard and fast, thrusting into her hot womanhood from behind. He wanted to feel her release deep inside, shivering around his hardness. . . .

When Caitlin arched back against him, his throbbing shaft cramped beneath his pants. It was a pure, primitive male instinct, the reaction of a male to a ready female. He almost came right there; his hunger was that raw, that explosive. Yet he clenched his teeth and forced himself to go slow.

He wrapped his arm around her, his hand spread flat and burning hot against the quivering softness of her belly, while his hoarse murmur resonated in her ear. "I'm going to get inside you, deep inside you, and listen to you moan." Even as the words caressed her, his fingers delved down into the hot, wet darkness between her legs to brush the soft, silky female cleft. "And then I'll start moving harder and faster . . . going deeper and deeper till you cry out for me. Let me hear you, Cat, honey. Let me hear you purr for me, baby."

Caitlin shuddered, unable to halt the flow of erotic images his dark voice aroused in her mind, or keep herself from surrendering to the pleasure he promised. He was slowly circling his rough fingertip around the small nub at the tip of her sex, pressing against the moist cleft, slipping inside.

When she gave a gasping cry, his embrace tightened. "That's it. . . . Easy, honey, I'll take care of you."

Her body was arching shamelessly for him, just the way Jake wanted her. She was aroused but not enough, he thought with satisfaction. He set about exciting her with all the sexual skill he possessed, stroking her slick flesh, exploring, plundering.

"That's right, give in to it, baby," he whispered hoarsely. Her hips moved jerkily against his fingers, straining for the release only he could give her.

When his exquisite ministrations tore a wild moan from her, desire, savage and blinding, shot through his groin. His own breath was ragged as he kept up his deliberate, sensual assault. In only moments her body went rigid, her thighs clenching around his hand. Then a raw sound ripped from her throat as the spiraling climax began.

She shook with spasms of ecstasy, but Jake held her tightly, reveling in her helpless response, supporting her when she half collapsed weakly, panting, against the table.

But he gave her no chance to recover her equilibrium. He turned her limp body gently in his arms, drawing her close against him. His eyes were intensely green, burning and tender, as he gazed down at her.

The desire she read there was compelling, fierce . . . expectant. He expected her to make love to him, Caitlin realized. To finish what he'd started.

Oh, no. In the quiet of the kitchen, she could hear her own uneven breaths, smell the aroma of boiling coffee as reality came rushing back to engulf her. God, what had she done?

Shame flooded Caitlin. Shame and guilt at her lack of control. Jake had demonstrated very aptly with his brazen caresses how weak she could be, but she was to blame for not stopping him. She couldn't let it go any further, though.

"Don't," she whispered when he bent to kiss her again.

"Don't, what, sweetheart?"

"Don't touch me."

She felt Jake's sudden stillness, yet he didn't

seem to understand she was serious. He wouldn't release her when she tried to escape his embrace. "Jake . . . let me go."

He smiled down at her in tender challenge, clearly doubting her resolve. "You want me, you know you do."

"I d-don't."

His look was both confident and satisfied. "That isn't what you were saying a minute ago."

No, it wasn't. She was disgusted at herself, at him. Her protests had been no more than half-hearted, and by not refusing adamantly, she'd given her consent. She'd been foolish to let things go so far, foolish to get Jake so aroused and then tell him no. But she had to end it here.

"I *don't* want you," she insisted, infusing her voice with conviction. "I want nothing to do with you."

His eyes grew cool, while his expression suddenly shuttered. The pain that stretched Jake's facial muscles could have been from physical denial, or hurt from her rejection. "Then . . . would you care to explain your little display just now?"

Caitlin winced. "My body may desire you—I can't help that—but my mind knows better."

"What does your heart say, Cat?"

The rough-edged question stopped her. She drew a sharp breath, unable to respond.

"Damn you, Jake," she whispered finally, unable to look away from his relentless stare. "Get out of my house and leave me alone."

The earlier tension was back between them with a vengeance; she could see it smolder in Jake's eyes, feel it vibrating in the hard lines of his body.

"No, hellcat." The reply was soft. "Leaving you alone is the last thing I mean to do. I'm going to have you, Caitlin. If not now, then soon. After all, we have four years to make up for."

Her own eyes dark with frustration, she pushed helplessly against his chest. "We have nothing to make up."

"Sure, we do. And you're going to enjoy it." His lips finding her temple, Jake murmured huskily, outrageously, against her skin, "You'll be begging me to take you."

"Oh, you . . . you! . . ." She had only one defense against him: anger. Caitlin released a moan of fury and twisted impotently in his grasp. "Get out! Get out of my house, before I call the marshal. Or I fetch my gun."

Jake just smiled that wicked smile of his, one that never quite reached his eyes. He freed her, though. Simply let his arms fall away. Off-balance, Caitlin caught the edge of the table to brace herself.

Turning, Jake picked up his hat from the table. "I'll show myself out; I know the way. But I'll be back. That's a promise."

"If you come back," she called shakily after his arrogant, retreating figure, "I really will shoot you, I swear it!"

His harsh chuckle infuriated her, but not enough for her to risk going after him. Trembling, she listened to the echo of his bootheels as he strode down the hall.

When she heard the front door close behind him, Caitlin exhaled a quivering sigh of relief. She had escaped Jake's devastating assault with her pride in shambles, but she might not be so lucky next time—Dear lord, she had to make sure there was no next time.

Turning on weak limbs, she collapsed in the chair and buried her face in her shaking hands, the scent of hot coffee mocking her.

Chapter 7

❦

"I'm not sure I like this," Vernon Whitfield observed as he handed Caitlin into his buggy two afternoons later. "You could be putting yourself in danger, calling on Sloan McCord. He may be up to some trick."

Caitlin gathered her black skirts closer to allow Vernon room on the seat beside her. "I don't think he's planning anything. I asked for this meeting, and Sloan agreed. It's possible he wants to end the feud as badly as we do."

Vernon looked as if he wanted to argue but was too polite. Snapping the reins, he sent the chestnut into a brisk trot, heading away from the Kingsly ranch, toward the road north.

"There's a greater risk in simply doing nothing," Caitlin said consolingly. "It's certain more blood will be shed if we don't act."

"You really think you can stop twenty years of fighting?"

"Perhaps not, but we might be able to arrange a

truce of some sort. Even that would be a step forward."

"Still, I'd feel better if you stayed out of it, Caitlin. I don't want to see you hurt."

Vernon's concern warmed her. The schoolteacher was troubled by the danger she might face in trying to end the feud—unlike Jake, who had urged her to take the situation in hand. The two men couldn't be more different, Caitlin reflected. Jake not only wouldn't fear the risk of acting, he would think less of her if she turned her back when she could do some good.

Vernon, on the other hand, was kind and gentle and sweet and highly protective of the female sex. She couldn't imagine him barging into her house and practically assaulting her the way Jake had two nights ago. He didn't seem capable of the kind of dark passion that smoldered in Jake's every pore. She didn't dare even mention Jake's offer of help, either, for fear his late-night visit would become common knowledge. Vernon would doubtless consider her behavior scandalous, which it was.

Caitlin hoped fervently Jake wouldn't be at the private meeting she'd requested with his brother. She had no desire to face him after nearly surrendering to him the other night. Her cheeks flushed whenever she remembered the intimate way he'd touched her, the devastating pleasure of his kisses and caresses. Her body still tingled, while her heart still ached. The bittersweet memories Jake had aroused in her had left her wounded and vulnerable. For a few mad moments she'd even fancied the tender warmth in his eyes was due to something more than carnal desire.

Devil take the man, but it wasn't fair, him using their past against her. Her reaction to him was just what she'd feared would happen. She'd turned into a helpless wanton in his arms. And Jake, damn him, had planned her downfall, she was certain. His hands and mouth might have reduced her to liquid heat, but that didn't make his actions any less outrageous. In future, though, she would have to put up a better fight. He'd proved how meager her defenses were against him, but she couldn't allow Jake to endanger the tenuous security of her new life. She'd been earnest about wanting to put the past behind her and get on with living. She wanted, needed, to make a fresh start—

Beside her, Vernon cleared his throat, making Caitlin give a start. "Have you thought any more about what I said the other day?"

"I'm sorry, I was woolgathering. Said about what?"

He sent her a covert, almost shy glance. "I'd like you to stay in Colorado, Caitlin."

"Oh."

"I know I've surprised you. And I know it's rather sudden. But I think we would make a good team. And I would make you a dependable husband. I'd like to try."

"Is this . . . a proposal, Vernon?"

"Yes." His voice softened, while his tender gaze found hers. "I'd like you to be my wife, Caitlin."

"I . . . I don't know what to say."

"You don't have to say anything just yet. Just think about it for a while. My home is here, but if Colorado holds difficult memories for you, if you don't want to stay, I could doubtless find another teaching position back East. We could live in St. Louis, if that's what you wanted."

"Vernon, I have a son to consider. Ryan comes first with me, you have to realize that."

"I do. And I would try to be a good father, Caitlin. I'm good with children, you know that."

"Yes." Vernon was wonderful with children of all ages. Teaching was his passion as well as his vocation. He would make an excellent father. As for a husband . . .

Caitlin fell silent. Could she contemplate marrying a man when her heart wasn't engaged? Could she afford *not* to? She could think of no one who would be a better father than Vernon Whitfield. He would take her son as his own, she had little doubt.

Just as reassuring, he was her friend. She enjoyed his company. Life with Vernon would be calm and peaceful, which was precisely what she wanted. She needed someone safe and stable to curb the restless streak in her. She wanted a companion to share her thoughts with, the minor sorrows and joys of everyday existence. Perhaps she didn't love Vernon, but did that really matter? She didn't *want* to lose her heart again. Never would she allow herself to be hurt so deeply again as Jake had hurt her.

Still, it was a leap to think of taking Vernon Whitfield as her lover. After Jake, any man would seem tame. Vernon would never inflame her senses or make every nerve ending feel intensely alive— yet was that so bad?

She'd had passion, and look where it had led her—nearly destroying her. She had control of her life now, and she wanted to keep it that way. She longed for peace. Jake couldn't supply that. He had the power to comfort or arouse her, to console or anger, to break her heart or take her to paradise. But he couldn't give her what she needed most.

Vernon would be safe and reliable. Dependable and trustworthy. He wasn't dangerous. He wasn't a notorious gunman or suspected criminal. She couldn't imagine Vernon killing men for a living.

There was much to be said for choosing safety

over passion, Caitlin knew. Her own mother had married her father during the first flush of infatuation and spent the rest of her days regretting it, longing to escape. Moira had died unhappy.

Her father had begun drinking heavily then, Caitlin remembered sorrowfully. Only then had his feud with the cattlemen become an obsessive hatred, tearing their lives apart.

There was another consideration, as well. Having a husband would perhaps protect her from Jake. If she were safely married, Jake would have to accept the finality of their separation. And a husband would prevent him from ever getting too near her son—and that was perhaps the most important consideration of all.

She'd ridden into town this morning, as soon as the telegraph office opened, to wire Aunt Winnie, reminding her to keep Ryan safely in St. Louis, but her own escape was still some time away—until she found a buyer for the ranch.

"Will you at least consider it?" Vernon asked quietly.

"Yes," Caitlin replied. "Of course I will. But . . . I'll need time, Vernon. I couldn't make so important a decision without careful thought."

He grinned. "As long as you don't say no just yet."

No, she wouldn't say no. She would do what was best for Ryan, for his future. And that included settling her affairs so she could return to him as soon as possible.

It would be a relief, though, to turn her attention to something productive, like trying to end the range war. Ever since Jake's startling return, her stomach had been tied in knots, and focusing on the future was the best possible remedy for what ailed her. Besides, Jake was right. Ending the feud would be vitally important to the successful sale of the Kingsly ranch. And Sloan McCord was the key.

She rode in companionable silence with Vernon for another quarter of an hour, sharing small talk now and then as the buggy wound through the foothills of McCord territory. The Bar M Ranch was a sprawling, prosperous spread with thousands of acres of good grazing land, both privately and publicly owned. They passed vast herds of cattle lazily dozing in the summer heat, guarded by armed cowpunchers who eyed them warily.

The McCord ranch house was not so different than her own family's, except that the handsome, split-log structure boasted two stories. A Mexican housekeeper answered the front door and showed the visitors into a study decorated in a masculine style, with few of the knickknacks or lace doilies or daguerreotypes that adorned the Kingsly parlors at home. A gleaming oaken desk strewn with open books occupied the far corner of the room, while shelves lined with leather-bound volumes adorned the adjacent wall. Caitlin settled herself in a black leather settee at right angles before the empty fireplace, while Vernon inspected the titles of the books.

"Looks like someone's been studying law," he commented curiously.

Before she could reply, Sloan McCord entered the room. Like his brother, he seemed to fill the chamber with energy and life, as well as a dangerous tension. Caitlin was struck again by how closely he resembled Jake, with his chiseled features and sun-streaked golden hair, although she couldn't imagine this man with his frosty gaze grinning with the boyish charm that came so naturally to his younger brother. Sloan McCord was a hard man, as uncompromising as the Rocky Mountains.

The expression on his lean, handsome face was somber, perhaps even grim, although the spark of hatred Caitlin had witnessed in his cold blue eyes the other day in town seemed carefully banked.

Sloan nodded politely, but did not take her hand or shake Vernon's. Instead he came straight to the point. "I presume you have a reason for wanting to see me, Mrs. Hughes?"

At his brusqueness, Caitlin swallowed the dryness in her throat, telling herself she had no right to expect kindness or even common courtesy from a man who was her mortal enemy. Sloan had suffered in the war more than any of them. But if plain-speaking was what he wanted, she would give it to him. "Yes, Mr. McCord. I was hoping we could work out a deal."

"A deal?"

"I want this senseless war to end, and I'm hoping you do, too."

He was silent for a moment while he studied her. Finally Sloan crossed his arms over his chest, although she couldn't tell if the gesture was belligerent or defensive or merely resigned. "Jake told me that was what you wanted."

From the corner of her eye she saw Vernon give her a questioning glance, but Caitlin managed to avoid his gaze. "If you'll think about it, Mr. McCord, there are major advantages to both sides in putting a stop to all the bloodshed. Not the least of which is financial. It can't be in your best interest to continue losing cattle, while we can ill afford to have our sheep killed. There doesn't seem much point in keeping up this tit for tat, destroying innocent animals and injuring people."

Caitlin leaned forward, her expression earnest.

"Both our fathers are gone. *They* were the leaders of this feud, the ones who promoted the hatred, while we're the ones who suffered. We're the ones left to pick up the pieces. But we can end the insane killing once and for all. Mr. McCord . . . I'm willing to bury the hatchet if you are."

Before Sloan could reply, though, another masculine voice broke in.

"A fine speech, Cat," the amused voice drawled from behind her. "But you ought to come clean. You want to end the feud because you're eager to sell your ranch, and you'll get a better price if the fighting stops."

With a start at those smooth, deep tones, Caitlin glanced over her shoulder to find Jake lounging just inside the door. He stood with his lean body propped against the doorjamb, eyeing her intently. A daub of sticking plaster still decorated his cheekbone, but the bruises from his brawl seemed to be fading

What startled her, though, was finding him holding a baby in his arms, a child perhaps nine months old, with solemn dark eyes and straight raven hair. He didn't look so hard or dangerous, Caitlin reflected in wonder, when he was cradling a child.

The baby's Indian features puzzled her until she remembered that Sloan had lost his Cheyenne wife in the range war. This must be his daughter. Her heart went out to the tiny, motherless child, while memories tugged at her. It wasn't so long ago that Ryan was that age. And while her son had a mother, he had no father.

Jake was watching her intently, Caitlin realized, evidently waiting for her reaction. When she forced herself to meet his gaze, he pressed his lips tenderly against the baby's forehead.

"This sweet little girl is my niece, Janna," he said

softly. "Her mother was murdered by your pa, Caitlin."

Caitlin clenched her fingers around her reticule, knowing it was pointless to argue that the murder had never been solved or that her father's complicity had never been proven. She had little doubt Adam Kingsly had been behind the savage attack on Sloan's wife.

"I'm sorry," she said in a low voice. "Truly, I am. But will dredging up the past do anyone any good?"

"Some things," Sloan responded in a chill tone devoid of all emotion, "just can't be forgotten."

Jake ambled into the room then, and handed the baby to his brother, providing momentary relief for the sudden tension that charged the atmosphere.

"What are you doing here, Whitfield?" Jake asked casually. "You have a financial interest in being here, too?"

Vernon stiffened. "Mrs. Hughes's interests are mine, although I am simply providing her escort."

The tension in the room shot back up as the two men eyed one another. Caitlin was reminded of a fight she'd once seen between two stallions who wanted the same mare.

It would be an unequal battle, in any case. Jake was all hard muscle and intensity, with a deadly skill honed by necessity, while Vernon was a gentleman in the true sense of the word. His quiet strength was no match for Jake's Western-bred toughness.

She was about to speak up when Jake turned to stroll over to the desk. "Reaching pretty low in the barrel, aren't you *Mrs.* Hughes?" he asked lazily, putting an unnecessary emphasis on the 'Mrs.,' "if you're looking for protection from a school-teacher."

"Jake, stop it!" she demanded, her anger getting
the better of her. "I don't need 'protection' from
anyone. And teaching is an honorable profession. I
won't have you belittling it."

"Wouldn't dream of it." He hitched one hip up
on the desk, and half turned to face her. His stance
was casual, but his expression was anything but.
His green eyes burned into hers, capturing her, infusing Caitlin with the same traitorous warmth
she'd experienced two nights ago. It was all she
could do to sit there quietly.

*Remember what it was like between us, Cat? Hot and
wild.*

Caitlin bit her lip hard, but found herself unable
to look away. She'd been determined to remain
calm and controlled, but with a sinking heart, she
realized now how foolish that notion was, how impotent she was where Jake was concerned. She
couldn't escape his presence or the potency of her
memories.

And Jake knew it, too, damn him.

His eyes lifted to hers and crinkled into a lazy,
knowing smile. "You haven't congratulated me on
my new honorable profession."

Her impotence bled into resentment. "What do
you mean?" Caitlin responded with less than civil
grace.

He patted the tin star pinned to his blue chambray shirt. "I've been deputized. Seems like the
marshal thought my experience with a gun might
come in handy in settling things down around
here."

"You must be joking."

Jake feigned a look of hurt. "No joke, wildcat.
Netherson appointed me deputy marshal for the
town. It's only part-time, of course." His eyes
searched hers. "You don't approve? I thought

you'd be pleased that I'm on the right side of the law for a change."

"Pleased?" Caitlin pressed her lips together. "I think it's outrageous hypocrisy."

"How so?"

"Netherson has always sided with the cattlemen against us. And he's a friend of yours besides. By overlooking your notorious past, he's violating the spirit, if not the letter, of the law."

"I thought you said you wanted to forget the past."

"Some things," she retorted, echoing Sloan's words of a moment ago, "just can't be forgotten. Nor should they. You're just a gunslinger, as far as I'm concerned. An outlaw."

A hard smile touched his lips at the scorn in her tone. "I was pardoned by the state of Colorado, remember?"

An expression of distaste claimed Caitlin's features. "Perhaps, but rumor brands you a criminal in New Mexico, wanted for murder during a bank robbery."

"Do you always believe every tale you hear, Juliet?"

Caitlin bristled. Jake hadn't denied his guilt when she'd asked him about the robbery just the other day. And it was just like him, getting her riled and then provoking her further by calling her by a name rife with tormenting memories. "I didn't come here to argue with you about your villainous past, Jake." She was glowering at him, angry color high in her cheeks.

"What *did* you come to argue about?"

"I'm only here to speak to your brother."

A slow grin moved his hard, beautiful mouth. "Don't let me stop you."

"Believe me, I won't." Gritting her teeth, Caitlin

shifted her gaze to Sloan, who had been watching the sharp exchange with an expression something like amusement as he held his baby daughter.

"If we could return to the subject at hand, Mr. McCord," Caitlin said in a strained voice.

To her amazement, Sloan smiled, a genuine grin that held all the formidable masculine charm of his younger brother. "I think maybe you should call me Sloan. If we're going to try to end the feud, there's no reason to stand on formalities. I expect we'll be getting well acquainted."

Disarmed, Caitlin slowly nodded. "And you should call me Caitlin."

"She also answers to Cat," Jake interjected. "And hellcat, and wildcat. Doesn't much care for 'Juliet,' though."

"That's enough, McCord," Vernon broke in angrily.

Caitlin shot Jake a furious glance, while her cheeks flooded scarlet with embarrassment. What would Vernon make of Jake's sly insinuations and pet names for her?

"Sloan," she said, striving for patience, "perhaps we could discuss the matter in private." *Without your brother's irritating interference,* her look said.

"I've got no secrets from Jake. He asked to be part of the discussion. And a man with his reputation . . ." Sloan shrugged his muscular shoulders as he shifted the baby to his other hip. "Well, we try not to rile him."

Caitlin knew she would have to be satisfied with that. With effort, she bit her tongue as Sloan abandoned his position by the hearth. He settled in a wing chair across from her, arranging his bright-eyed daughter comfortably in his lap. Like Jake, he didn't look so angry or cold or intimidating, Caitlin thought, when he was holding his child with such tenderness.

When Vernon settled himself beside her on the settee, she gave him a grateful look. Then, taking a deep breath—and trying to forget the unforgettable presence of Sloan's vexing younger brother—she launched into her proposal for a truce between the opposing sides in the range war.

"Like I said, there would be economic advantages to us all. I want to sell our ranch at a good price, and I can't unless the fighting stops. But a truce would benefit every sheep rancher and cattleman in this territory. If only half the destruction of property stopped, the smaller ranches would prosper instead of barely making ends meet.

"But that isn't even the crucial issue," Caitlin insisted. "Just think what peace would *mean*, Sloan. What it would be like if the reign of terror our fathers started ended. The citizens of this community could live free from fear. Your daughter could have a real future. You could raise her without the threat of some sheepherder bent on revenge making her a target."

"I'm listening," Sloan said slowly.

Caitlin drew a steadying breath, knowing she had his attention. "None of us can have a future here unless we put the past behind us."

"How do you propose we stop a war that's been going on for twenty years?"

She grimaced in frustration. "I don't know exactly, but there has to be a way. No single person is responsible for the violence any longer, but it's out of control. Every week there's an incident where someone suffers. Our two sides can't meet without someone blowing up. The vengeance won't stop by itself, either. We have to *make* it stop. And I think it has to begin with you, Sloan."

He raised an eyebrow, waiting.

"If you wanted to end the violence, you could," Caitlin pressed. "The cattlemen will listen to you. You could talk to them, propose a truce. They trust you enough to follow your lead."

"And as Adam Kingsly's daughter, you could manage the sheep ranchers?"

"I don't know, but I'm willing to try."

"So what do you suggest?"

"If we could all lay down our guns at once . . . Perhaps form some sort of grievance committee, with members from both sides to mediate disputes. . . . "

He *did* seem to be listening, Caitlin noted as she offered possible ideas—listening intently, carefully, and with no small amount of cynicism. That Sloan was bitterly suspicious of any proposal a Kingsly might make was abundantly clear, but he hadn't built a successful cattle empire by being a fool. Adam Kingsly was dead and the opportunity for peace might not come again.

After a short while, Sloan unbent enough to offer them refreshment, and summoned his housekeeper to bring coffee. By the time he returned to his chair, he seemed to have made the shift from skepticism to commitment in trying to end the feud.

While they talked, solemnly and earnestly, Jake watched Caitlin. He applauded her effort to seek a truce, even though part of his reason was selfish. She would never remain in Colorado as long as the feud continued, and he badly wanted her to stay. She belonged here, not teaching in some fancy girl's school back East. The hellion had turned into a fine lady, but her roots were here in the Rockies. With him.

Jake's gaze narrowed on the dandy sitting beside her. He hadn't foreseen danger from that direction until now. It aggravated the hell out of him that she'd turned to a high-browed schoolteacher for help, and he hadn't been able to stop himself from ruffling her feathers a little.

Jealousy seared him when he saw the solicitous Whitfield offer Caitlin a plate of ginger cookies. *He* should be the one sitting beside her, trying to work out a deal to end the range war.

He thought of Cat as his woman, felt it with a bone-deep sense of possession. She was his, even if she refused to admit it yet. He couldn't explain his feeling of need for her, couldn't explain the explosion of passion that happened every time he touched her. But four years apart hadn't diminished his uncontrollable compulsion to have her.

Jake stared down at the top of her head, wanting to reach out to her. The memory was still raw in him, how Cat had turned away from him the other night. He wanted her willing and eager, not pushing him away in fear.

No doubt he was a damn fool to feel as hungry and obsessed as he did, but he couldn't help himself. Every bit of contact with her made him want more. When Cat was near, he felt intensely alive, his senses alert, his loins stirring with anticipation. She filled his thoughts, filled his dreams. And he knew his obsession wouldn't end once he made love to her—and made her love him again.

His competition would be tough, though, if she wanted a fine, upstanding citizen like Whitfield. Jake's glance shifted to the schoolteacher, then back to Caitlin.

He'd managed to get himself deputized, not because he wanted the job, but because he'd thought it would make Cat happy. But she hadn't trusted him, hadn't believed he could change. She'd scoffed in his face, making the achievement seem hollow, leaving him with a discontent that was sharp and bitter.

The discontent turned to ashes when Caitlin asked to hold Sloan's daughter, who'd started to fret. When she began to rock the baby gently against her breast, her soft, crooning voice settled Janna down at once, making the tiny eyelids droop. But the sight sent a shaft of pain streaking through Jake, and made a hard ache settle in his body. She was good with kids, he realized with a gut-deep yearning, thinking of all the time they'd lost. He wanted her to be the mother of his.

The baby had fallen asleep by the time the discussions wound down. Caitlin and Sloan each agreed to approach the other ranchers to suggest a truce, and made final arrangements to meet later in the week to discuss their respective progress. Then Caitlin rose to take her leave.

With a soft smile, she gave the sleeping child over to Sloan's housekeeper, but when she'd thanked her host for the hospitality, Jake stepped in. "I'll walk you to your buggy."

Caitlin gazed up at him warily. "No, thank you, Vernon will see to it."

Without giving her a chance to protest, Jake took her elbow and turned her toward the door.

She gave every appearance of meekness, until they reached the front porch and he bent to whisper in her ear, "Get rid of him, Cat."

"What?"

"The schoolteacher, tell him to back off. I don't want him hanging around your skirts."

She went rigid. "You don't want—How *dare* you think to dictate to me," she whispered back furiously, "whom I can or can't associate with."

Jake gave her a smile that never reached his green eyes. "I'm not dictating to you. I'm warning you. I fight dirty. And I'd dare a lot where you're concerned. You belong to me."

It was absurd how instinctively appealing she found Jake's possessiveness. Absurd and infuriating. Caitlin refused to dignify his threat with a reply.

She kept her lips clamped shut until after Jake had handed her into the buggy and Vernon took his place beside her. "I'll let you know," she said to Sloan, "what the other sheep ranchers say." Then, flashing Vernon a brilliant smile for Jake's benefit, she faced forward.

The two brothers watched the buggy roll away in a cloud of dust that shimmered golden in the early glow of sunset.

In the silence that followed, Jake felt Sloan eyeing him curiously. He took a deep breath, getting a whiff of the familiar smells of home, cattle and horses and sweet summer grass.

"You want to ride into town and get some supper?" Sloan asked. "Maybe find a game at the saloon? Della would be glad to see you."

"I'm not in the mood for a woman."

Chuckling, Sloan slapped his brother on the back. "Like hell you're not. Trouble is, you want a woman you can't have."

"Can't have *yet*," Jake said softly. "But the fight's only just started."

"You've got it bad, don't you, little brother?"

"Yeah." He gazed after the trail of dust the buggy had made. "I guess I never really got over her."

"I can see why." Sloan shook his head. "The sparks you two set off nearly started a brushfire in my study. Reminded me of next week's Fourth of July celebration. But I'm putting my money on you ten to one. And I want a front row seat to watch the fireworks." He draped an arm over Jake's shoulder. "Come on, I'll pour you a drink. You could use one."

Jake nodded, but he wished he felt the same confidence in his ability to win this war. With a final glance after the buggy, he turned toward the house.

He'd spent years wanting Caitlin. He could wait a few days more.

Chapter 8

Once the decision to seek a truce was made, events moved swiftly toward a settlement. Caitlin met with the owners of the largest sheep ranches to discuss their position, while Sloan did the same for his side. Over the course of the next week, terms and methods of enforcement were suggested and negotiated, and eventually a plan was agreed upon: Men from both sides would jointly patrol the countryside in an effort to head off trouble, while a council of ranchers arbitrated any disputes that arose. Because of the schoolmaster's relative neutrality, the warring parties nominated Vernon Whitfield to lead the council and oversee the mediation.

Most of the settlers and townsfolk joyfully welcomed an end to the fighting. A generation of hatred and suspicion couldn't be wiped out overnight, but the time for peace had clearly come—beginning with the Fourth of July celebration the following Wednesday.

The day would be filled with picnicking, horse

races, and baseball games, and after a fireworks display, a dance would take place on neutral ground, supervised by Sarah and Harvey Baxter, owners of the Greenbriar General Store, in order to foster peace between cattlemen and sheep men. The joint venture was a major accomplishment. Until now, the two sides had celebrated the major Colorado holiday separately.

Caitlin stayed busy up until the last minute, acting as chief advocate, prodding and arguing and pleading for peace. It seemed a minor miracle when she finally found herself seated in Vernon's buggy, being escorted to the picnic, which was to begin at noon just north of town.

The site was a perfect place for a reconciliation: a sun-drenched meadow splashed with brilliant wildflowers—Indian paintbrush, columbine, larkspur, and even wood lilies—and bordered by forests of ponderosa pine and Douglas fir and towering blue spruce.

Caitlin had volunteered to help Sarah Baxter set out the food, but when Vernon parked the buggy in the shade, she saw there were already a half dozen women draping the long tables with checkered tablecloths and arranging dishes.

Sarah gave Caitlin a harried smile, but her look of relief was for Vernon. "Thank goodness you're here, Verne. If you could take charge of the children, I'd bless you forever. They're running wild—"

Even as she spoke, a girl of about ten ran shrieking past, chased by an older boy wielding a frog with apparent nefarious intent.

Vernon reached out and grabbed the boy by the scruff of the neck, eliciting a startled yelp. "How many times do I have to tell you, Jimmy, a gentleman doesn't put frogs down a young lady's dress?"

"But Mister Whitfield," Jimmy complained, squirming, "Polly ain't a lady."

Vernon grimaced. "Mind your manners, young man." With an apologetic grin to the two woman, he asked Caitlin, "You want to help me arrange a ball game to keep this fella out of mischief?"

Caitlin smiled. "Certainly, although it's been a long time since I've even seen a baseball game. I may have forgotten the rules."

They gathered up the youngsters and took them to the far end of the meadow to begin play. It was more than an hour later when Caitlin spied Jake and his brother Sloan standing with a group of men on the sidelines.

She felt her heart skip several beats. Jake looked impossibly handsome and starkly masculine in a dark gray, tailored suit. His white shirt boasted a string tie, while his boots and cowboy hat gave him the appearance of a Western gentleman. Even with his elegant attire, though, Jake seemed dangerous. His bruised face had healed, but he wore his Colt six-shooters low on his hips. And with the tin star pinned to his chest proclaiming his position of authority, he looked every inch a man who lived by his gun.

He was watching her, Caitlin realized with a flutter of her stomach. Or rather he was watching Vernon. He gave the schoolteacher a sharp, assessing glance, before shifting his gaze back to her. Absurdly, his lingering scrutiny made her flush. In deference to the warm summer day, she was wearing a calico dress of pale gray with short puffed sleeves, but while it was attractive enough, she was glad she'd brought her blue silk gown to change into for the dance that evening.

Jake didn't approach her then, or any time during the next two hours, yet Caitlin was keenly aware of his presence all the same. And though scolding herself for her foolishness, she was strangely piqued by his indifference.

She hadn't seen him in more than a week—ever since the meeting in his brother's study—and she wondered if Jake had given up his pursuit of her or was merely playing a waiting game. She knew he'd worked every bit as hard as she and Sloan to promote a truce, and she knew his influence mattered. Outlaw or no outlaw, Jake was one of them, and he'd been welcomed back into the cattlemen's community with open arms.

Regardless of whether he was trying to impress her, though, or because he truly wanted peace, nothing Jake could do would make her accept his advances. She knew better than to let down her guard. She didn't trust herself around him.

She didn't dare show him any special attention, either, especially with the entire community looking on. She was no longer the headstrong hellion who'd set gossips' tongues wagging, but the slightest hint of impropriety now would only give credence to the rumors about her and Jake four years ago. There was no way she would take up with him again. She wanted no new scandal to jeopardize her status as a respectable widow, or tarnish her innocent son's name. Just to have Jake openly pursuing her would be inviting infamy, particularly since his own reputation was so ignominious.

She was glad to have Vernon nearby. In the intervening days, her friendship with Vernon had grown. He hadn't pressed her for an answer to his proposal, but seemed content to wait. This afternoon he hovered protectively at her elbow in a way that both reassured her and vexed her; he offered protection from Jake, but it annoyed Caitlin that she even needed it.

She ate dinner with Vernon and the Baxters, although not until most of the crowd had been fed. There was plenty of food—fried chicken and fluffy biscuits, fresh-baked apple and rhubarb pies, with gallons of sweet lemonade to wash it down.

The afternoon was well advanced—with most of the picnickers lazing back on quilts to escape the heat and to give full stomachs a rest—when a commotion broke out near the tables.

Caitlin had taken a turn at the lemonade booth, doling out drinks into tin cups, and so had a clear view of the fight, which began as a shoving match between a cowboy and a herder, and quickly degenerated into fisticuffs.

The two were rolling on the ground when Jake stepped in, grabbing them both by the collar and jerking them to their feet. Both men started to struggle, but when they realized who held them, they froze in obvious respect and perhaps fear.

"Settle down, boys," Jake advised in an easy tone. "Or I'll have to march you down to the jail, and you'll spend the rest of the night locked up and miss all the festivities"—he grinned and cast a glance over at Caitlin—"...and the pretty women."

Someone in the crowd chuckled, and the tension eased.

Watching, Caitlin reluctantly found herself admiring the way Jake had handled the two combatants without violence. Despite the festive air of the picnic, the situation was a powder keg. It would take only a single incident to light the fuse and destroy any chance for peace. She was grateful to Jake for tamping down the sparks.

Yet when she caught his eye, she found herself appreciating more than his methods. Jake had shucked his tailored frock coat, and had rolled his shirtsleeves up to expose muscle-corded forearms. He looked lean and hard and tough as leather, but there was a blatant sensual appeal in every line of his body, and a dangerous allure that called to everything feminine in her.

When the corner of his mouth kicked up in another grin that was pure, devil-may-care Jake McCord, it was all Caitlin could do to make herself look away.

Just then Marshal Netherson came to her table to get his cup refilled. "Seems like it was right smart of me to deputize Jake," he observed pointedly, reminding Caitlin of her earlier objections.

"Evidently it was," she said grudgingly. Jake had never even had to draw his gun, but had quelled the fight with his presence alone. Perhaps his notorious reputation as an outlaw *would* help restore law and order and keep the feuding parties settled down.

She had deplored his violent existence, but in all fairness, Jake did seem to be trying to redeem himself.

Not that it mattered to her. She wouldn't be here to see his transformation if it occurred. Absurdly the thought saddened her.

Caitlin was surprised when Netherson didn't leave, but stood there sipping his lemonade.

"I'm mighty grateful to you, Mrs. Hughes."

"You are?"

"Yep." His narrowed brown eyes scrutinized her. "Seems like I owe you an apology. I thought you were only going to cause trouble, coming back here and all, but you've done your darnedest to stop the feud. Shown a lot of pluck, if you ask me."

She smiled faintly at his praise. "I think perhaps people were just ready to end the bloodshed."

"I don't know. Guess it takes a woman to make us hardheads see the light." Netherson pushed back his hat, exposing his silver hair. "I hear you mean to sell your pa's place."

"If I can find a buyer."

"Seems a shame, you up and leaving when you just got here. Maybe you ought to think about sticking around."

Caitlin shook her head. "My home is in St. Louis now."

"Hmmm . . . me, I can't see why anybody'd want to live in the big city when you could live in God's country." With a thumb he gestured at the magnificent mountains in the distance.

She could have retorted that for the past twenty years "God's country" had resembled Hell; that she would never risk her son's safety by exposing him to the danger of a bloody range war. But she held her tongue.

"Well . . . I reckon you know what you want. In the meantime, though, if you or your woolly boys need something from the law, you just let me know."

"Thank you, Marshal, I will," Caitlin replied, trying to keep the dryness from her tone. This was the first time in her memory that Netherson had ever voluntarily offered to help her side.

He ambled off, leaving Caitlin to contemplate his changed attitude. She was lost in her thoughts when a husky voice broke in.

"You think a thirsty man could get a drink?"

Jake stood there, his hands resting negligently on his hips, his green eyes appraising her. Unable to still the sudden leap of her pulse, Caitlin busied herself by pouring a dipperful of lemonade for him.

"That was well done of you, stopping that fight," she volunteered in a low voice as she handed him his cup.

Jake smiled his grim, enchanting smile. "What's this, a compliment, Cat? I thought you disapproved of me."

"I do—but I still appreciate your effort."

"You're the one who deserves the credit." Jake gestured with his head at the crowd. "None of this would have happened if not for you. I'm proud of your gumption for trying to rope that wild bull."

His praise meant more to her than she would have dreamed, and to her dismay, she found herself flushing. It discomposed her further when Jake leaned forward across the table and she caught the faint scent of bay rum.

"You look mighty pretty, wildcat. Good enough to eat." When she took a defensive step backward, Jake held up his hands. "Don't worry. I plan to behave myself."

Absurdly Caitlin found herself trying to bite back a smile. "That will be the day."

"So . . ." he said lazily, "will you save the first dance tonight for me?"

"Jake . . ." She lowered her gaze, uncomfortable with the subject. "I don't think that's such a good idea."

"Why not? You don't want to be seen associating with an outlaw?"

The question was casual, but she thought there was an underlying edge to his voice. "No . . . yes . . . there's no point in us even discussing it."

"You rather dance with your pet greenhorn, is that it?"

Now she was certain she heard a sharp edge in his tone.

Caitlin stiffened. He had no right to be jealous. "Just because Vernon doesn't run cattle doesn't make him a greenhorn."

"No? He wouldn't even know which end of a gun to hold."

"Perhaps not, but I think that only makes him a better man." When Jake stiffened, she returned his stare pointedly. "Vernon has skills that men prone to violence overlook."

"Such as?"

"Sensitivity, for one. An even temper. Those qualities are appreciated by *some* people at least. Vernon is the one both sides trust enough to lead their council and settle disputes."

"Maybe so." Jake shrugged his shoulders. "But you're changing the subject. Come on, Cat, all I'm asking for is one little dance. You're not afraid of me, are you?"

Warily Caitlin gazed up at him. A slow smile, irresistible in its male charm, crawled across his mouth, making her melt inside and all her nerve endings tingle in alarm. Jake was at his most dangerous when he turned that formidable charm on her. It was all she could do to keep from reaching up to touch that hard, beautiful mouth.

"All right," she murmured reluctantly. "One dance. But not the first. It wouldn't look right."

Jake nodded as if satisfied. "I'll see you tonight, then."

She watched him walk away, knowing she'd been foolish to relent. Granting him a dance was doubtless a huge mistake, since it would only encourage his attentions as well as provide fodder for gossip.

And yet he *was* trying to be reasonable. And despite every logical, proven instinct that told her to run from Jake as far and as fast as she could, she couldn't quell the traitorous yearning to be in his arms one last time. This *would* be the last time, Caitlin vowed to herself. And nothing would happen between them. Not when they were surrounded by a crowd of people.

She was still telling herself that several hours later when the dance began. The fireworks had been pretty although scant, for fear of setting off a blaze in the dry forests surrounding the town. Darkness had fallen, but lanterns stood on the tables and hung from tree branches, providing a soft glow that seemed almost magical. When a fiddler struck up a lively tune, a dozen couples took to the meadow, which served as a dance floor.

Caitlin was standing on the sidelines with Vernon, tapping her foot to the music, when Jake arrived. She had changed her dress for a party gown of deep blue silk the color of her eyes. It boasted a low décolletage, full, elbow-length sleeves, and a bustle in back, while a spray of artificial flowers nestled in her raven hair, which was piled high on her head. Vernon had told her how lovely she looked, but it was Jake's scrutiny that made her truly believe it. His eyes openly approved the bodice, which molded her figure.

When his gaze slowly raked the low neckline, Caitlin felt her breath catch. Jake was strongly, frankly sexual, and his desire communicated itself to her even in a crowd of people. Worse, his look vividly reminded her how he'd stroked and caressed her breasts that night in her kitchen. To her dismay, she felt her nipples involuntarily contract into tight, aching points.

At his hungry, predatory gleam, though, Vernon stepped forward aggressively.

Startled by Vernon's uncharacteristic action, Caitlin caught his arm, wondering in alarm if the two men meant to fight. "Vernon, don't.... Jake, you promised to behave," she murmured urgently.

"I'm only standing here, Cat," he replied, never taking his eyes off the schoolteacher.

She bit her lip. "Perhaps you should ask someone else to partner you."

His green gaze shifted to her, dark and intent on her face. "All right, but I'll be back for my dance."

With a final sharp glance at Whitfield, he turned on his heel and melded with the crowd. Yet Caitlin doubted she'd heard the last of it. One stallion didn't allow another near his mare, and Jake was as possessive and domineering as any stallion.

Caitlin would have been more worried had she been privy to Jake's thoughts. He stood blindly watching the whirling couples, his jaw clenched as he tried to control his anger and savage impatience. He'd waited more than a week for Caitlin to grow accustomed to him being back in Colorado. Yet biding his time had only allowed his rival the chance to win her affection. Jake cursed himself for a fool. Acting the gentleman hadn't worked, either. Caitlin had only tied his hands with his promise to behave.

Behave, hell. How could he behave when all he thought about was carrying her off somewhere so he could have her alone? He hadn't been able to sleep for thinking of her. Every time he closed his eyes, Caitlin's image rose up to haunt him.

Jake stepped back farther into the shadows, shifting his position to make his arousal less obvious. He was so hard he'd have to find some way to disguise it. Seeing Cat in that fancy gown—one that accentuated her curves and heightened her vibrant beauty—had only stirred his fantasies further.

Yet lust wasn't the sole cause of the savage jealousy that was ripping him apart inside.

Go ahead and admit it, man. You're still in love with her.

God, he thought, bowing his head. He'd loved her for years, even if he'd lied to himself about it, burying his feelings under layers of bitterness and resentment. It startled him how very much Cat meant to him. And he couldn't bear the thought of her giving her heart to yet another man.

It was nearly an hour later before Jake trusted himself to approach Caitlin again. He had to get her alone, had to touch her soon or go crazy.

But he didn't get the chance, not then. As he moved toward the sideline where she stood with her greenhorn schoolteacher, a man called out his name.

"Hey, McCord! I hear yo'r pretty fassht with a gun."

Jake came to a halt, trying to place the voice. It was slurred, as if by an overindulgence of whiskey, but it sounded like Lee Hodgekiss, a cowhand from one of the nearby ranches.

"Fast enough," Jake replied slowly, not turning around.

"Lee, c'mon," someone chided. "Don't be a danged fool."

The crowd around Jake suddenly grew quiet while he waited for Hodgekiss to make a move. He'd been challenged before by foolhardy kids itching to prove their manhood, but drunks were twice as dangerous. Drunks drew false courage from a bottle, and sometimes got lucky.

"You sss-scared of me?" Hodgekiss demanded. "You 'fraid I'll outdraw you?"

"When you sober up, I'll be glad to discuss it with you."

"You ain't yeller, are you?"

Jake heard the collective gasp from the crowd. Sensed people moving back. In only an instant a wide space cleared around him. Even the fiddles stopped.

"I hear there's a ree-ward out for you for a murder you done down New Mexico way. Maybe I'll take you in and collect it for myself."

"Maybe you need a little time to think about this."

Jake remained completely still, his hands held lightly at his sides, listening for the quiet rasp that would mean a gun clearing leather. When it came, he was ready. In an instant he'd spun and fired his Colt, his reaction lightning fast. The warning shot exploded into the silence, spurting dirt at the cowhand's feet.

Hodgekiss froze, his revolver half out of its holster. The acrid scent of gunpowder mixed with the warmth of the evening, cloaking the sweetness of the ladies' perfumes.

"Hey, little brother," Sloan said, stepping forward, his voice calm. "No need for fireworks. Lee's sorry he riled you—aren't you, Lee?"

Hodgekiss had gone pale, obviously reconsidering the wisdom of challenging a renowned gunslinger. He nodded slowly, barely breathing.

"Why don't we all get back to the party?" Sloan suggested. When he glanced pointedly at the musicians, the fiddlers struck up a reel.

Ignoring the wary glances of the crowd, Jake turned to Caitlin, his hard face enigmatic. "I believe this is my dance."

Her heart beating too fast, Caitlin simply stared at him. The scene she'd just witnessed had left her shaken. Seeing Jake draw like that had reminded her just how brutal the code he lived by was.

Without a word, without a glance at the school-teacher hovering protectively beside her, Jake took her elbow and led her into the crowd of dancers.

At least the dance was a reel and nothing more intimate. With the lively exertion, Caitlin had time to get her shaky pulse under control. As soon as the dance was over, though, she found herself being urged toward the north edge of the meadow and the forest of pines.

She tried unsuccessfully to pull back. "Jake, where are you taking me?"

"Nowhere. Just away from the crowd."

She had fully intended to refuse, but looking into his eyes, the threat he presented to her reputation and peace of mind suddenly seemed not to matter.

His fingers were rough and warm around hers as he drew her into the wood, where they were swallowed up by the shadows. When a moment later Jake came to a halt, she could scarcely see him in the moonlight that dimly penetrated the branches. Her blood hammering in her ears, she braced herself for his touch.

Wordlessly Jake drew her into his arms, pulling her tight against him. It was a mistake to let him hold her so closely, Caitlin knew. She could feel the graceful strength of his lean body, the ripple of his muscles as he pressed against her ... the hard bulge at his loins that made not a single attempt to camouflage his gender or his obvious arousal. Her breath caught in her throat, yet despite the danger, despite her aversion to his violence and the urgent voice in her mind that warned of scandal, she couldn't pull away. Her own longing stripped her of reason.

The band was playing a waltz, but Jake barely

moved. Instead he swayed slowly to the music, wrapping her in his embrace, holding her a willing captive.

With a reluctant sigh, Caitlin closed her eyes and leaned against him. She'd been lying to herself. This was what she wanted. What her body had yearned for. She was surrounded by Jake's strength and warmth and the subtle male scent of his skin. *Only a moment longer*, she promised herself. Her hands crept up his shoulders, and she pressed her cheek against his chest, revelling in the feel of him.

When the lilting music finally ended, she still clung to him. It was only when she felt his searching lips brush her temple that Caitlin stirred herself to protest.

"Jake . . . we shouldn't . . ."

"I still want you. I want you like hell."

"Don't. This is wrong. Please . . . let me go."

"I can't," he said simply. "Once a man has you in his blood, he can never be free of you."

Her heart ached at the raw pain in his voice, at the savage pain that flowed through her.

She raised her face to his, she couldn't help it.

His kiss was restrained yet determined, claiming her as if it was his right to be so intimate. His possessiveness demanded her surrender, yet his passion seemed to whisper something else altogether, something generous and giving, something she wanted with all her heart.

Caitlin accepted the slow thrust of his tongue as he penetrated her mouth and filled her with his taste. It seemed incredible that a simple caress could give birth to such intense need, intense hunger, yet there were four years of wanting behind their kiss. Four years of thwarted desire.

His leg pressed between hers, his hard thigh rubbing against her womanhood even through her gown and petticoats. Sweet, searing pleasure swept through Caitlin, weakening her even as she desperately tried to fight the feeling. Dear God, how could her body turn traitor this way again?

Her breath was coming in erratic spurts when she finally found the resolution to tear her mouth away. She *had* to get herself under control. "Jake, st-stop." She pressed her hands against his chest, warding him off. "We can't *do* this."

"I want you, Cat, but don't expect me to grovel." The husky words were tauntingly seductive, threatening and promising at the same time.

"I . . . I don't expect anything of the k-kind."

Weakly, she took a step backward, but he reached out and caught her wrist in an easy grasp. "I'm not letting you go back to that greenhorn." His features were shadowed, yet she could make out the taut set of his jaw, could hear the sudden warning anger in his voice.

"Stop calling him that," she replied unsteadily, vexed that Jake kept taunting her about her relationship with the schoolteacher. "Vernon isn't a greenhorn."

"Whatever I call him, he's not for you."

"I hardly think that's any of your concern."

Jake's eyes narrowed at her in the darkness. "Everything you do is my concern. And Whitfield has been sniffing around you long enough. He's just trying to get under your skirts."

"And you're not?" Her cheeks flushing with temper, she raised her chin. "You may have nothing but lechery on your mind, but you've no call to accuse Vernon of it."

Jake gave a snort. "You can't be naive enough to think he's only after your mind. He's trying to get you into bed. Not that I much blame him."

"Jake, let me go," she ordered with forced calm.

"I could tell him what it's like. In fact, maybe I *should* tell your schoolteacher how you and I used to be lovers."

Her heart seemed to stop. "That's blackmail."

"Yeah, it is, isn't it?" The sudden maddening hint of amusement in his tone renewed her ire.

"You say one word to anyone, Jake, and I'll . . . I'll never speak to you again!"

"That's okay. You don't need to talk anyway when you're kissing me."

He tried to pull her closer, but Caitlin resisted his embrace. "Jake, stop . . . I swear I'll call for help."

His mouth curled. "Sure you will. You really want all those fine people to know you're consorting in the woods with a desperado?"

If he was deliberately trying to incite her to mayhem, it was working. Her temper began to simmer. "Will you get it through that thick skull of yours, I do *not* want you?"

"You want me all right. I thought I proved it to you the other night."

He was so damned cocksure, she wanted to punch him—for that and for reminding her of her shameful behavior that night in her kitchen. "You didn't prove anything, you arrogant braggart!"

"You used to like arrogance, if I recall."

When Caitlin gritted her teeth in frustrated silence, Jake's mouth curved in a taunting grin. "What do you suppose your schoolteacher will say when I tell him how good you are in bed?"

"You wouldn't dare!"

"Better than good, in fact," Jake murmured, ignoring her protest. "Best sex I ever had."

"Why you . . ." Caitlin sputtered, incensed by his deliberate provocation, yet more alarmed that he might actually make good his threat to divulge their past relationship.

"What do you think he'll say, hellcat?"

She was conscious of an almost-overwhelming desire to injure him. "I won't discuss this with you any further. I won't be dragged down to your level."

Jake went totally still. "What level is that, Cat?"

"The lowest." With another try, she managed to jerk her wrist from his grip as she lashed out at him verbally. "You're a hired gun, a man without a conscience. A killer."

Her voice dripped scorn and hurt him like he never thought he could be hurt. When Caitlin turned away as if she couldn't bear the sight of him, Jake's jealous fury erupted. He caught her wrist again, this time roughly. "Don't turn your nose up at me like some ice princess."

It shocked her a little, his edge of violence; it dismayed her, how swiftly their discussion had degenerated into such a bitter argument. Could they never be together for two minutes without fighting? Yet she refused to be bullied.

"Damn you, let go of me!" Caitlin demanded in a low, furious voice.

Ignoring her outrage totally, Jake dragged her into his embrace, one arm wrapped around her waist, the other hand tangled in her hair in a fist of hard control. Holding her immobile, he slanted his hard mouth over hers in a sensual, brutal caress that punished and possessed her all at once.

And Caitlin, God help her, was helpless to resist. Her body flared with raw desire, and instead of fighting him, her lips parted to accept Jake's hot, thrusting tongue.

His taste was hot and heady, his mouth fevered. Caitlin shuddered in ecstasy and torment. It was all so achingly familiar. He was kissing her with savage, punishing force, yet all she could do was open to him. Caught in the dark grip of passion, she drowned in the fierce seizure of his kiss.

Her head was spinning dizzily when Jake finally broke off his assault and lifted his head. Shaken, her legs weak, Caitlin could only stare up at him.

"Maybe he's already had you," Jake taunted in a voice savage with jealousy, his rage still driving him. "Maybe you've already spread your legs for Whitfield, the way you used to do for me."

She slapped him then, full in his mocking face, blind to his seething anger. Jake didn't loosen his grip, though one of his hands did rise to his cheek.

When he stared at her with burning eyes, Caitlin ground out defensively, "You deserved that."

"For what? For telling truth?"

"I must have been insane to ever think I loved you."

She could feel him wince. "Maybe so," Jake retorted roughly. "Maybe we were both crazy."

Every muscle stiff with outrage, Caitlin shoved once more against his chest. To her amazement, Jake released her this time, yet his savage questioning continued.

"Tell me, wildcat, is your greenhorn as good between your legs as I am? Does he make your skin burn the way I can?" His narrowed eyes stared fiercely into hers. "Do you flame at his touch the way you do beneath me? Do you rake him with your nails when he plunges inside you?"

If she weren't in a killing rage she might have walked away; it would have been the wisest thing to do. Yet she'd never been wise where Jake was concerned.

Her blue eyes flashed sparks at him as Caitlin gave him a venomous look. "Yes! He's every *bit* as good as you! Better. And furthermore, I'm going to marry him!"

She saw Jake's body go rigid. "Like hell you are," he said with ominous softness.

Her eyes glittered with defiance. "I am so! You can't tell me what to do, Jake. Vernon and I are engaged to be married, and I think he'll make an admirable husband!"

"Do you really mean it, Caitlin?" Vernon asked quietly from the darkness.

Startled, Caitlin jerked her gaze around. Vernon stood only a few yards away holding a lantern, obviously having come in search of her.

She wondered how much he'd heard, yet it was Jake who disturbed her more. His gaze slammed into hers with a look that was almost frightening; burning in his eyes was a savage possessiveness.

"Do you mean it?" Vernon repeated. "You're going to be my wife?"

Caitlin bit her lip hard. She'd made her foolish declaration in a fit of anger, but she wasn't about to withdraw it in Jake's hearing. She would tell Vernon privately, as soon as she could escape. "Any woman would be honored to be your wife," she said stiffly, still seething. "Will you please take me back to the dance now?"

"Sure."

She caught a glimpse of Jake's eyes blazing with fury as she took Vernon's arm, but she refused to give him a second glance.

His heart pounding with rage, Jake stood there long after she'd gone, cursing himself for letting his jealousy burn out of control. In time he managed to swallow the raw panic that had filled him at Caitlin's announcement, but it was a while longer before a deadly calm settled over him.

He couldn't stand the thought of her marrying

another man, but it wouldn't come to that. He wouldn't let it. Caitlin didn't belong with any man but him, and he was determined to prove it to her.

Back at the dance, it took several minutes for Caitlin to stop trembling, and longer still for her heated emotions to calm down. By the time she'd gotten herself under control, though, Vernon had—to her complete dismay—announced to the Baxters that they planned to marry. Sarah professed herself delighted, but Caitlin was horrified. She'd never expected Vernon to publicly declare their engagement. Yet having no wish to contradict him and make him look like a fool, she reluctantly accepted the good wishes of their friends, all the while cursing her wayward tongue—and Jake as well for goading her into this mess.

Caitlin spent the rest of the evening alternately seething and glancing nervously over her shoulder for Jake. She was grateful that he was nowhere to be seen.

She didn't like the feeling of impending danger hanging over her, though; it resembled the strange, charged air before a lightning storm.

It was nearly midnight by the time she and Vernon set off in his buggy for her ranch and she had a chance to speak privately with him.

"Vernon," she said the moment they were alone, "I think I may have misled you. You see . . . I was angry at Jake—"

"I know." In the darkness, he reached for her hand and raised her gloved fingers to his lips. It was a sweet, gentle gesture that tugged at her heart.

"I know you didn't mean to accept me, Caitlin. But I'm not going to let you take it back just yet. Who knows? Maybe you'll come to like the idea of being my wife. Sleep on it, why don't you, and we'll talk about it in the morning."

Strangely she felt tears sting her eyes. Vernon was such a kind man. She didn't want to disappoint him, yet she wasn't certain she could ever respond to him the way he hoped she would—the way she did so effortlessly to Jake's slightest touch.

Vernon delivered her safely to her back door and walked her to the porch. When he pressed her hand and murmured a quiet good-night, Caitlin took a shallow breath and stopped him from turning away with a touch on his jacket sleeve.

"Vernon . . . would you . . . like to kiss me?"

He smiled tenderly down at her. "Of course I would. I just didn't think you'd let me."

How different he was from Jake, Caitlin thought as she raised her lips to his. Never in a million years would Jake have waited for her permission.

Disappointment flooded her at the gentle pressure of Vernon's mouth. His kiss was hesitant, gentle, his embrace tentative as if he thought she might break if he held her too hard. There was affection certainly, yet it was every bit as tame as she'd feared it would be.

Not that it really mattered, Caitlin scolded herself silently for the futile comparison. If she did marry Vernon, it wouldn't be for his kisses, but because he would make a safe husband and a good father.

Drawing back, she lowered her gaze to hide her discontent. "Good-night, Vernon," she murmured quickly.

Her heart twisted at the soft smile he gave her.

Wishing him a safe drive home, Caitlin slipped inside the darkened kitchen. She waited until she heard Vernon's buggy drive off, but even then she didn't move. Instead she stood quietly in the darkness, her arms wrapped around herself, her feelings stirring with renewed turmoil as she remembered the disastrous events of the evening.

She'd thought she was strong enough to face Jake's anger, to deal with his jealousy and possessiveness, but they'd shaken her, raked her emotions raw. Fighting with him had left her drained, while her heart throbbed with a hollow ache.

The silence of the lonely house didn't help. She missed her son. Missed cuddling Ryan's warm little body and hearing his gurgles of laughter. Missed the physical closeness.

If she were honest, she missed Jake, too. She ached for his kisses, for his hard body, the feel of his arms around her. She missed the intimacy, the tender moments she'd once shared with him. The joy of having someone to talk to, someone who understood her dreams and dared her to realize them. Someone who made her feel *alive*, not numb with grief and loneliness like she'd been for so long.

Calling herself a fool, Caitlin gave a sigh and picked up the box of matches to light the lamp. She was too restless to sleep, yet she could change out of her gown and perhaps try to read.

Carrying the lamp, she made her way along the hall to her bedroom. She was three steps inside the room, though, when she halted abruptly in alarm, sensing that she wasn't alone.

"It's about time you got home," a familiar masculine voice said softly from the darkness.

Chapter 9

She nearly dropped the lamp. "Merciful heavens, Jake! You frightened me out of my skin!"

Apparently unconcerned, he clucked his tongue. "Such pretty skin it is, too."

His drawl rekindled her anger. With trembling fingers Caitlin placed the lamp on the dresser so as not to set the house on fire. Then she turned to glower at Jake. He sat in the rocker, unmoving, obviously having waited for her to return home.

"What the devil are you doing here? How did you get in here?"

With his head he gestured at the open window, where a slight breeze stirred the curtains. "I climbed in."

"Get out of my house!"

"I don't think so, hellcat."

She wondered if he'd been drinking. His green eyes glittered in the lamplight. What startled her, though, was the sudden realization that Jake was only half-dressed. Caitlin inhaled a sharp breath. He wore no shirt, and the sparse tangle of golden hairs on the smooth expanse of his chest gleamed in the lamp's glow, his bronzed shoulders and corded arms rippling in a powerful play of sleek muscles. The masculine beauty was marred only by the scars left by her brother's bullets.

"Is this him?" Jake asked suddenly, holding up an object in his hand.

Caitlin blinked, then stiffened as she recognized the gilt-framed daguerreotype. "Him?" she repeated warily.

"Your dead husband."

"How dare you touch that—"

"Is it?" A hint of savagery edged Jake's tone.

"Yes, that was my late husband!"

" 'To my beloved wife . . . Martin,' " Jake read the inscription in the lower corner of the black-and-white likeness.

Forgetting Jake's state of undress, Caitlin marched up to him and snatched the picture from his hand. "You have no right to paw through my things."

"I didn't paw." His gaze skewered her. "It was on your dressing table in plain sight." When Caitlin turned away to replace the picture, Jake observed mockingly, "Seems uncalled-for, keeping that there, since you were only married a short time."

"I do it to honor Martin's memory."

"You never kept any picture of me."

An unexpected flash of pain shot through Caitlin. Unwillingly she met Jake's eyes across the room, seeing the same raw memories shimmering there. "I . . . never had any picture of you to keep."

"Your husband . . . he was a lot older than you, wasn't he?"

"A dozen years or so . . . not that it's any of your concern. And older or not," she added, driven to rile Jake as he always did her, "he was a wonderful man."

Jake clenched his teeth. The bitter reminder of Caitlin's previous marriage coming directly on the heels of her new engagement made him want to explode.

"I told you to leave, Jake," she demanded, putting her hands on her hips defiantly.

"No. I've been patient for days now," Jake observed grimly, "and it hasn't worked worth a damn." He bent his head to unfasten the leather thongs of his holsters from around his thighs.

"W-What are you doing?" she stammered, her voice suddenly high and breathless.

"What does it look like I'm doing? I'm getting undressed. I'm going to convince you that you don't want to marry your schoolteacher."

"What . . . what do you mean?"

He looked up at that, and his green eyes burned into hers. He was obviously spoiling for a fight. "I'm through waiting for you to come to your senses."

"*My* senses! You're the one who's lost his mind—sneaking into my house and getting undressed like you belong here!"

"I haven't lost a thing, Cat," he murmured grimly. "Fact is, I finally smartened up. I should have done this over a week ago."

"A week—I mean it, Jake, I want you to leave! *Now.*"

"No. Not until morning."

Her breath suddenly seemed to stop as she realized exactly what he intended. "I'll . . . I'll scream. Some of the ranch hands are in the bunkhouse."

He surveyed her intently, the corner of his mouth twisting in wry amusement. "You can scream all you want. But it'll be mighty hard to explain, having me here naked in your bedroom."

Caitlin stared at him, panic rising in her throat. Jake was right. She couldn't ask for help from her hired hands, for then she would have to explain what he was doing here. It was an impossible dilemma.

When his fingers went to the buckle of his gunbelt, though, she found enough voice to issue a breathless threat. "I'll get my gun."

His green eyes raked her coolly, stripping her naked and insolently weighing her charms. "It's okay for you to resort to violence, but not me, is that it?"

"That's the only thing you understand, apparently. I'll shoot you only if I have to, Jake."

"A lamb should be smarter than to push a wolf," he said softly.

Caitlin fell silent. She should have fled. Should have turned around and run for dear life. But she stood rooted to the floor. Helplessly she watched as Jake slung his holsters over the back of the chair, her gaze taking in the rippling shoulder muscles and taut torso ... moving lower. The fabric riding low on his hips did nothing to hide the flat planes of his muscled belly.

Then he reached down and slowly unbuttoned his pants.

"Jake, stop this ..." Caitlin pleaded, her voice hoarse.

He paid no attention to her frail demand. Instead he unfastened his underdrawers, slowly drawing the flap open, exposing his flagrant masculinity that was heavy with arousal.

Her gaze locked on his loins and the hot, rigid flesh that sprang from a dark bush of curling hair. The skin was lighter there yet still tanned and golden, making her remember how Jake used to like to bask naked in the sun. Evidently he still did.

Her heart began to hammer wildly. "You can't do this," she said, her tone desperate.

"I can. I'm going to make love to you till neither of us can walk. Take off your gown, Cat."

"You're crazy if you think—"

"Take off your clothes, or I'll take them off for you—and I won't be particular about buttons and seams."

Flames of fury licked at her blood as she glared at him, yet she read the determination in his eyes; the time for reckoning had come. He was going to have her. She could resist him with all her might, but in the end she would be no match for Jake's persuasion.

"Go ahead and fight me, hellcat," he drawled as if he'd read her mind, grinning with a slow laziness. "A good tussle only makes me hotter."

The husky declaration should have been crude, offensive, yet instead it was erotic, sensual, stroking her senses. Caitlin quivered, feeling her body already beginning to throb and come alive for him.

Just once more, a forbidden voice whispered in her mind as she gazed helplessly at him. *Just once more let me lie with him, let me feel him deep inside me, completing me.*

"Damn you, Jake. . . . You're determined to ruin me, aren't you?"

"That's the last thing I want."

"This is a fine way to show it! It was bad enough at the dance, you dragging me into the woods when anyone might see. If anyone but Vernon had found us together—"

"Don't," Jake interrupted sharply. "Don't mention his name. I don't want to hear it. Not tonight."

In the ragged silence that followed, Caitlin took

a steadying breath, knowing she had to keep a rational tone if she meant to reason with him. "Jake ... the scandal ... You'll destroy my reputation."

That stopped him for an instant. "Nobody will know but us."

"*I'll* know. I won't behave like a wanton with you again. I *won't.* You can't make me."

Jake hesitated at the distress in her voice. He didn't want to hurt her. He only wanted to make Caitlin see they belonged together. To make her forget the man who'd been her husband. Make her see that her greenhorn schoolteacher couldn't give her anything like what *they'd* once shared. He wanted to hold her, to touch her, to draw her close and turn her blood to fire. . . .

Needing to touch her, he stepped closer, his eyes blazing with a fiery, restless need she could see. Caitlin took an evasive step backward.

"Jake ... *please* ... if a tussle in bed is all you want, you can get it in any saloon. You don't need me."

"A tussle isn't what I want, Cat." His voice softened. "And you're wrong. I do need you."

He'd sell his soul to have her back in his arms, Jake thought, watching her. He'd had sex with other women, countless times, but he'd only made love to one: Caitlin. She was the only woman he'd ever wanted this way, fiercely, urgently, permanently.

And he was sure she wanted him. The bond still existed between them, and he meant to use it to win her. Maybe it wasn't honorable, turning her own desire against her, but it was the only way he knew to get to her, to break down her defenses.

"You feel the same way," he murmured. "You know you do."

Weakly Caitlin closed her eyes, fighting the savage, pulling ache low in her belly, struggling against the harsh torment of longing. Yet she couldn't ignore the truth. She wanted Jake. She had tried to deny her desires for too long, pretending she could escape a woman's needs, a woman's wants. She needed Jake. She needed to feel part of him, needed him to make her forget the lonely nights of pain and despair, needed a memory to sustain her through the long, barren years ahead. She needed him to ease the empty ache, an ache only Jake could fill.

"Jake, I can't . . ." she murmured weakly, without conviction. "This is insane."

"It's not insane, Cat. It's *right*. And I'm going to prove it to you."

Slowly Jake strode toward her, moving with a noticeably effortless, catlike grace, like a predator, stalking her. At the last moment, she tried to take another step backward, but he caught her shoulders and drew her inexorably into his arms, with the manner of a man who knows he isn't going to stop at a simple embrace.

Fragments of memory struggled for control within her, reminding her how wonderful it had once been between them, how cruel the pain when fate had separated them. Her heart pounded wildly, yet she knew she wouldn't stop him. She wanted his kiss, didn't know how she would survive if she were never to know it again. . . .

Then Jake bent his head.

His mouth was ruthless, his kiss long and hot, a hard sensual caress that took without permission yet seemed to soothe at the same time. She'd been braced for violence, but his ferocity remained leashed, even though the vise of his hand held her head immobile. He kissed her with a hard assurance that beguiled even as it demanded, using his tongue with devastating thoroughness. And Caitlin responded. It didn't seem to matter that his passion might be driven by sheer male possessiveness. This was Jake, her first lover, her only love.

How familiar it all was, Caitlin thought in a heated daze. Almost as if those long years of separation had never existed. The savage pain of those tender memories had vanished, leaving behind only a desperate urgency.

When Jake finally broke off the kiss, Caitlin found herself swaying against him, pressing her body against his, wanting him, feeling the hard bulge of his sex even through her gown.

"You feel it, don't you?" he whispered. "Every bit of the same fire I feel."

Yes, she felt it. She had never, not in four years, felt so alive, so hungry. Sweet mercy, Caitlin thought, cursing herself because she wanted to be with him and she shouldn't, but she was going to do it anyway.

"God . . . Cat, don't send me away," he whispered hoarsely in her ear, his voice shaking.

"Your boots," she said incongruously, her own voice a mere rasp.

With one finger, Jake tilted her flushed face up to his, his green gaze searching. He must have read her answer in her eyes, for his mouth curved into a slow, enchanting grin.

He gave her lips another hard, swift caress, then returned to sit in the rocker. He tugged off his boots one by one. Then his socks. Then his pants. And finally his drawers.

Caitlin caught her breath when he stood naked in all his magnificence. Like his face, Jake's body was lean and hard and possessed of a dangerous masculine beauty, his chest tapering to a flat, rock-hard belly and slim hips. His erection jutted proud and thick from a dark gold bramblebush of hair.

Lithe and naked, he moved toward her, his body fluid and mesmerizing in its natural grace.

The night trembled around them as he reached up to touch her face with gentle fingertips, his tenderness as seductive as a lover's first kiss.

"I dreamed of this for four hellish years," Jake murmured hoarsely.

So did I, Caitlin wanted to reply as she raised her mouth for his kiss.

His heart began to pound, a harsh thud in his tight chest. The softness of her cheeks was sweet against his rough and callused palms as he cupped her face. He felt her warm and trembling against him, felt the quiver of her mouth beneath his that sent little shocks of desire rippling through him. He felt the heat, the pleasure, and the longing for more, so much more . . . the longing for her to fill the empty place in his soul.

"Do you need this as much as I do?" Jake asked, trailing his fingers downward, along her throat to the low neckline of the gown that barely covered her breasts, making her quiver.

"Yes . . ." she whispered.

"No, let me," he ordered when she reached behind her back to unhook her gown. Obediently, she let her hands fall to her sides.

Jake undressed her slowly, beginning with her headdress and the pins that bound her hair up, refusing to let her help. Turning her around, he ran his fingers reverently through the silken skeins. How many times had he dreamed of this?

Caitlin held completely still as he undid the fastenings of her gown. She could feel her heart pounding as he slipped the bodice over her shoulders and let the gown fall to the floor. She felt as reckless as a girl again, flustered and unsure and intensely aware of herself.

Her corset followed, and Jake bent to remove her slippers and stockings. Caitlin stood rigid as he drew down her lacy drawers, leaving her standing in only her thin shift. And then even that went.

Jake held his breath as he drew the filmy garment over her head and bared her slim, lithe body to his gaze. Need slammed into his chest, while blood rushed to his loins.

He had dreamed of this constantly, yet not even his dark, fevered imaginings could ever match reality. Caitlin's ebony hair, shining and glorious, spilling over her naked shoulders. Her body, white and wanton, shimmering in the golden lamplight. Her breasts, firm and high, the taut nipples taunting and beckoning him. The dusky hair curling at her silken thighs.

Jake gritted his teeth against the surge of heat flooding his loins. The want was so damned strong that it was squeezing the breath from his chest. Yet the fear was stronger.

He was scared spitless. It had been so long, after all, and he wanted badly to please Caitlin. The ache of desperation tying him in knots had little to do with lust, though. This could be his last chance to convince her that she belonged to him. The knowledge assaulted him with relentless force. If he failed, he would lose her.

Restlessly, wordlessly, Jake buried his face in the night shadows of her hair, vowing he would win her.

If she sent him away afterward, she'd think of him every time she climbed into that bed without him. When he left, he'd leave his touch on her body, his taste in her mouth, his scent on her skin—and with the act, condemn himself to the same fate.

Sensing his determination, Caitlin shuddered in his embrace, her breasts swelling painfully against his hair-roughened chest, her nipples taut with desire. His flesh felt smooth and hot everywhere it touched her; the muscles of his bare shoulders coiled and quivered reflexively beneath her clutching fingers. The rigid, heated length of his manhood throbbed against the soft yielding of her loins, branding her like searing steel.

She closed her eyes with the sweet pain of it. She wanted to sob at this bit of heaven, at his tenderness that reminded her so much of the past. She wanted to cry, *Love me, Jake, like you used to*. . . .

As though sensing her need, he drew back a little, so that he could see her eyes. His work-hardened hands rose to her bosom, his strong, bronze fingers cupping her pale breasts. Caitlin drew a sharp breath. Jake seemed intent not just on arousing her but on driving her mad with need, his callused thumbs teasing and tormenting by turns, the roughened skin rasping over her swollen nipples as he rubbed and lightly pinched.

"Jake . . . I can't bear it. . . ."

"Yes, you can. . . ."

Then his mouth was on hers again, hard and hot and compelling, letting her feel the sleek rapture of tongue and teeth, giving her nothing but raw pleasure and aching delight. His hands gripped her yielding bottom and ground her against him, moving her hips against his. Caitlin arched feverishly in his arms, pressing closer, as if trying to become a part of him. It had been so long. . . . She couldn't seem to remain still. Her body was hot and tense and untamed. She felt as though she were drowning in need.

"Jake . . . please. . . . "

"I know, Cat. I know. . . . "

In a single, smooth motion, he bent and lifted her in his arms. Carrying her to the bed, he laid her down and stood over her, hesitating. Pale and perfect, her body opened to his heated gaze as she looked up at him trustingly.

For an instant he wondered if he should go through with this, if he was being fair to Cat, using his skills as a lover as a weapon against her. But then she murmured his name, a sweet little sound of pleading that pierced his heart like a honey-tipped arrow. His desperate need to convince her she was his overrode any good intentions of his conscience.

Clenching his teeth, he followed her down, his lips seeking her breast as he bent over her. "I'd forgotten how beautiful you are," he muttered hoarsely.

"I'd forgotten . . . how beautiful you make me feel. . . . " Her voice shattered at his touch. His wet mouth seared her nipple, making Cat arch up off the bed.

Holding her shoulders down, he sucked strongly at her in a hungry, plundering rhythm, his mouth never ceasing its drugging torment while his hard, stroking hands worshiped her naked body. When she was whimpering with need, his hand swept lower, gliding down her sleek skin to touch the vee of her womanhood. Her thighs naturally parted to welcome him, giving him complete access to the moist, satin petals hidden below.

She was wet silk between her legs, Jake realized dazedly, all hot and ready for him. He groaned, a ragged, needy sound that sounded loud and harsh in the hushed room. When he lifted his head, his eyes shone with a heated brightness, emeralds at the heart of a scorching, searing fire.

He wanted her now; he was as hard as a stallion, and so hot he thought he might explode just touching her. Yet he was determined to hold back.

"God, I've waited so long for this," he whispered hoarsely, pushing the hard ridge of his manhood against her soft folds. "I want to make it good for you."

The hungry yearning was so strong, his body trembled with the force of it, but he mounted her with exquisite caution. "No," he whispered when she winced, "open your eyes, baby, let me see your pleasure." He tightened his buttocks and very slowly, very carefully began to enter her.

Caitlin said his name in a raw, shaking voice as she felt his rigid fullness inside her, while quivers of wanting shot through her body.

"That's right, honey, let me feel you move. God, you feel so good . . . it drives me wild when I'm inside you."

He pressed deeper within her, beginning a slow rhythm, keeping his strokes deliberately shallow, the muscles in his arms aching with the strain of holding back. "Say it's good, Cat," he urged.

"Yes . . . oh, God, yes . . . Jake."

His hard face taut with pleasure, he thrust deeper, sheathing himself to the hilt. A ragged sound that was half sigh, half groan rasped from his throat. This was like coming home. This was where he belonged.

Caitlin cried out at the same moment, twisting and surging beneath him, yet it wasn't enough for Jake. He wanted her wild with need. He wanted her clawing at his back and straining savagely to become part of him.

With the violent, pent-up passion of four years,

his hands closed over her buttocks, lifting her hips so he could thrust more deeply inside. Her body spasmed in response. He whispered urgently in her ear, telling her how much he wanted her, needed her, how he wanted her to come apart in his arms. Caitlin's head thrashed from side to side.

Her body felt liquid and hot. She could barely hear the raw sexual things Jake was saying to her. She was beyond words now, beyond thought. He was enormous and hard and fiery hot and filling her to bursting.

She heard a high keening sound and knew it was hers, but then her body soared wildly out of her control and nothing existed in her world but her and Jake and their passion.

Her heels dug into the backs of his muscled thighs, her slim body arching as over and over she drew him inside her. When she gave a wild cry, Jake growled, raw and primitive. He felt the violence of her climax, felt her ripple and convulse in her ecstasy, each tremor burning through him with an exquisite torture.

And then everything inside him shattered. Desperately he sank into her, trying to absorb her body into his, needing even more of her to quell the hunger that went so deep it would never be satisfied.

It was a savage, restless coupling. They were two bodies, writhing and straining together. Man and woman. The bitter past was immaterial; there was only the present, and the fiery need to take from each other, and to give.

When at last it was over, they lay together, panting, unmoving, trying listlessly to recover from the searing pleasure of their joining.

Replete, Jake lay quietly, savoring the experience. For the first time he knew what it was like to make love to Caitlin in the dark and hear her cry his name. For the first time since leaving her, the dark emptiness in him was gone.

Reaching out, his fingers found hers and laced tightly together, as if to confirm he wasn't dreaming. Her hand, the same delicate but strong hand he remembered, felt limp and helpless in his.

He leaned closer, his lips brushing the quivering corner of Caitlin's mouth with tantalizing gentleness. He'd been too rough, he knew, taking her with every bit of passion and hunger and need he'd saved for four years. But he wouldn't change what had happened. She was warm and weak from his lovemaking, just the way he intended to keep her until she became used to his possession. Until she realized she belonged to him.

Wearily Jake closed his eyes and drew her against him. Remembering the feel of that soft, silky body writhing beneath him made the ache start all over again, but he would let Cat rest before taking her again. The next time he might even get around to turning down the covers.

She lay with her cheek pressed against the sweaty silk of his bare shoulder, her legs threaded with the long, corded length of his.

"So this is what it's like," he murmured hoarsely, "having you in a real bed."

She smiled at that remark. His dark voice, so warm with tenderness, caressed her dazed senses. She ought to move, Caitlin told herself languidly. She should be pushing Jake away instead of snuggling against him. Her surrender had been shameful and wanton, yet she couldn't regret his taking of her. Jake had made love to her with an intensity that seared them both, and she didn't want to let him go. Not yet. Just a few more moments of bliss, and then she would make him leave, before his presence caused a scandal she could never live down. She couldn't bear to let him go just yet, though. His fingertips were softly stroking her arm, and she could smell the musky male scent of his body on her skin, could feel the satin-slick dampness of his seed between her thighs—

Caitlin's breath suddenly caught in her chest. "Oh, my Lord . . ." How could she have forgotten the consequences of a rash moment of lovemaking?

"What is it?" Jake asked, concerned.

"I could get pregnant."

He heard the anxiety, the dread, in her voice and pressed his lips against her temple. "Would that be so bad?" he said quietly.

Caitlin pulled back to stare at him. "I can't bear a child out of wedlock. How would I explain a baby without a husband?"

"I told you"—Jake's mouth curved in the semblance of a smile—"I'm willing to make an honest woman of you."

His tenacity only frustrated her. "We've already been over that, Jake. I can't marry you. I won't. I have my son to think of."

Jake reached down to cover the smooth velvet skin of her bare abdomen with his palm. The thought of Caitlin pregnant with his child filled him with awe, yet the last thing he wanted was for her to be afraid to make love to him. "It's too late to do anything about it tonight, but you won't have to worry about it after this. I'll take care of it."

She eyed him with wary confusion.

"There are these little sponges you can use," he explained. "You soak them in whiskey or brandy, and they'll stop a woman from breeding. They go inside you, here." He threaded his fingers through the curls between her thighs. "I'll teach you how to use them."

Gasping, she tried to draw back from his probing

caress. "You'll do nothing of the kind. I'm not a loose woman, Jake, despite your efforts to turn me into one."

"Nobody said you were."

"If you think I intend to do . . . *this* with you again, you're loco."

His emerald eyes filled with amusement. "I reckon so. Loco over you."

"This isn't funny, Jake!"

"Sure it is. You're getting riled about nothing, hellcat."

"Nothing!" Her voice was high-pitched with disbelief. "You sneak into my house, worm your way into my bed, and you call it *nothing?*"

He laughed, a low, sexy chuckle that aroused and raked her nerve endings at the same time. "Well, if you put it that way . . . it's a hell of a lot better than 'nothing.' Best sex I've had in years."

Instead of mollifying her, his declaration only incensed Caitlin. "I suppose I should be *honored,* being compared to all your other women?"

"There's no comparison. You spoiled me years ago. Everything else has just been marking time." He nuzzled his face in the midnight sleekness of her hair. "God, I love making love to you."

Her stiffness told him the battle was far from over. She had been temporarily defeated but not won. "It's been so long, Cat. Haven't you missed it? Haven't you missed *me?*"

"No," she lied, pressing her hands against his bare chest. The very scars beneath her palms reminded her that Jake had killed her brother. "And it's time for you to go."

"Go?" His eyebrow rose. "I'm not about to leave now. We've already wasted too many empty nights."

"You have to, Jake. This has gone way too far. *You've* gone too far."

Perhaps he *had* been ruthless in his tactics, Jake admitted to himself, but he'd been desperate to prevent her from making a terrible mistake in marrying that schoolteacher.

She would fight him, he was certain. She would give as good as she got. But in the end, he would win. He had to.

At the prospect, his loins began to harden as desire heated his body.

He was contemplating what to do about it when Caitlin played her trump. "Have you forgotten I'm engaged to be married to Vernon?"

Jake's good humor abruptly vanished. "I haven't forgotten, but it makes no difference. You're breaking your engagement first thing tomorrow."

"I am not!"

"You are so, Cat. Tell your schoolteacher you made a mistake. That you changed your mind."

Caitlin stared at Jake, amazed at his audacity. Clearly he thought the issue was settled between them, that they would become lovers again. "My only mistake was trusting you to get within a hundred yards of me."

"You don't want to marry that greenhorn, Cat."

Caitlin bristled. She profoundly regretted her rash agreement to wed Vernon, yet it wasn't Jake's place to dictate to her. His high-handed possessiveness infuriated—and alarmed her as well. He was taking shameless advantage of her uncontrollable weakness for him. "Damn you, Jake. It's none of your business if I marry a dozen men."

His eyebrow shot up. "A dozen?"

"You know what I mean!"

"Sure, but I thought I just proved that you don't want any man but me."

"You conceited lout, all I want is for you to leave me alone!"

He smiled tauntingly. "You wanted me, all right. You were all woman, hot and hungry for me. Why can't you just accept it?"

"Because it isn't true!"

"I guess I'll just have to show you again, then . . ." With his hands he reached up to cup her breasts, caressing the sensitive, swollen tips with his thumbs.

Unsuccessfully Caitlin tried to evade the maddening strokes of his circling touch. When she managed to turn onto her back, Jake just rolled over her, pinning her down, one hard thigh thrust between her legs. Despite her gasp of protest, he dipped his head and feasted on her breasts.

Branded, Caitlin felt his mark everywhere. Helplessly she writhed beneath him, trying to escape his tormenting mouth and tongue, cursing him even as she thrilled at the sweet ache he was stirring deep within her.

It was several, long, sensual moments later before Jake finally lifted his head, leaving her wet nipples tight and hurting and painfully sensitive to the night air.

"You ought to be shot," she muttered breathlessly.

"For what?" His voice was lazy and dark. "For taking what you ached to give me? You wanted me, Cat. You were hotter than a firecracker, and if you're honest you'll admit it."

She glared at him with impotent fury.

"You felt every bit of the same fire I feel for you, Cat." Deliberately he caught her hand and pressed her fingers against his throbbing erection.

"Jake, stop it. . . ."

Her feeble protest wasn't enough to keep him

from having her again, but this time he would have every part of her. . . . Shifting his body between her thighs, he eased his thick shaft into her, and reveled in her helpless whimper.

His green eyes were molten as he gazed tenderly down at her. "You really want me to stop?"

She refused to answer, yet she gasped when he thrust deeper.

"Do you, Cat? You want me to leave you alone?" Jake pressed even deeper, filling her completely with his swollen hardness. "Tell me you don't want me inside you, and I'll quit. Tell me to stop, wildcat. . . . "

Withdrawing only a little, he waited, holding himself still inside her, giving her the choice. Yet there really was no choice, Caitlin realized. Not for her. Not now that she had found Jake again. Vanquished, she closed her eyes.

"No . . ." she whispered, and knew with that single word she was throwing away her soul.

Chapter 10

~~~⟨⟨⟨⟨◦⟩⟩⟩⟩~~~

Brushing an errant lock of hair back from her forehead, Caitlin bent over her desk and tried to focus on the columns of numbers before her. Balancing the ranch account books on a beautiful summer's afternoon was the furthest thing from her mind. Instead she caught herself gazing out the study window at the foothills abloom with vibrant color, wondering if and when Jake would return to wreck all her hard-won peace.

It had been two days since the picnic-dance, when, disregarding propriety or even common decency, Jake had forced his way into her bed, determined to prove that she still felt something for him. She hadn't seen him at all yesterday, not since he'd left her in the early hours before dawn to avoid being seen by her ranch hands.

In the interval, Vernon had called on her both mornings to report on the progress of the truce. Defiantly she'd made no move to end her engagement to Vernon—even though she *was* now certain she would never marry him. She couldn't make love so passionately to one man and then settle down in a marriage of convenience with another. Jake had ruined her for any other man. *Damn you, Jake.*

Out of sheer stubbornness, though, she'd resisted telling Vernon of her decision, despite Jake's demand and his threat of blackmail. She refused to be bullied by that arrogant, unprincipled devil. Yet he *had* won the argument. Jake had proved beyond a doubt that there was still an incredible physical attraction between them, that she was still driven by a fierce hunger only he seemed able to fulfill.

She was going insane, Caitlin thought wryly, trying to figure out what outrageous action Jake would take next. He was purposely trying to drive her crazy, making her wait and wonder what he intended. She'd expected him to show up on her doorstep last night, and was almost disappointed when he hadn't even tried. For the past hour she'd accomplished very little. How could she, with every nerve in her body tingling and strumming in nervous anticipation of Jake's appearance?

She didn't think he would stay away much longer. If he came tonight, though, she was adamantly determined not to allow him in the house, even if she had to lock all the doors and windows and stand guard with a shotgun. She would not let his scandalous behavior destroy her respectable life and the peace she'd worked so hard to find.

Her eyes clouded for a moment. After all the bloodshed and pain of the past, she longed for peace. Jake's arms seemed to promise her that, but they lied. He would bring her nothing but heartache and haunting memories. He didn't want what she wanted—for her future or her son's.

If only she'd never loved him, she might be able to resist his ruthless advances now. But she had to forget what he'd once meant to her. She couldn't risk her heart again, couldn't imperil her entire existence for a few stolen moments of reckless passion.

As it turned out, Caitlin was right about Jake's intention to visit her today, but mistaken about the time. A half hour later, she heard the soft chink of a spur. When she looked up with a start, she found Jake watching her from the study doorway, one shoulder propped against the frame.

"How do you manage to look sexy," he asked lazily, "even when you're dressed up like a school-marm, pouring over ledgers?"

"Out!" Caitlin leaped up from behind her desk, pointing beyond him at the hall. "Get out of here, Jake." The brazen nerve of him, showing up at her house in broad daylight!

Jake gave her a bland smile. "I left my horse grazing a quarter mile away. No one will know I'm calling on the Widow Hughes."

"*I* know—and I won't have it! You have no right to be here."

The teasing expression fled from his face, to be replaced by a cool dispassion. "You haven't told Whitfield the engagement's off, have you." It wasn't a question. "Your schoolteacher still thinks you're going to marry him."

"No," Caitlin replied defiantly, "I haven't told Vernon anything—because I haven't made up my mind."

"It isn't like you to keep a man dangling like a hooked fish, Cat."

"I am not keeping anyone dangling!"

"Sure you are. You're never going to be that greenhorn's wife, so you might as well put him out of his misery."

"Blast it, Jake, you aren't going to run my life!"

Casually he crossed his arms over his chest. "I'm warning you, Cat. You tell him or I will."

She stared at him, wondering if he meant it.

His tone was almost gentle when he asked soberly, "What would Whitfield think if he knew what happened between us the other night?"

"You wouldn't dare tell him...."

"I *would* dare, Cat." His assertion was quiet but edged with steel. "If I leave here, I'm riding straight to Whitfield's place. He's going to hear all about the other night. How you were moaning and panting and crying for me to take you. Not once, but four times."

Her eyes shooting sparks, Caitlin glared at Jake impotently. He was obviously determined to force the issue, and there was little she could do to stop him.

"Damn you, Jake...what do you *want* from me?"

His green gaze softened. "What I want, darlin', is everything you have to give."

"I don't have anything to give you."

"I told you I'm willing to make our relationship official."

"I won't marry you, Jake. I have my son to think of."

He shrugged noncommittally. "I guess that's your choice. But married or not, you belong in my bed."

Seething, she refused to dignify his audacious claim with an answer.

At her silence, Jake eyed her speculatively. "I want what I got the other night, Cat. Whenever I want it. I'll have you anytime, anywhere I want you. The same way, hot and willing."

He was serious, Caitlin thought with alarm. He wasn't simply trying to get a rise out of her. "Or what? You'll tell all our neighbors about us?"

"Yep. That's about the size of it."

"I won't let you blackmail me."

"Consider it a swap, then. You want something from me—my silence. And I want something from you."

It was only sexual desire, Caitlin thought desperately. And pure possessiveness. A primitive male drive for a female, a masculine need to conquer. Jake didn't love her. Her body was merely an acquisition to him.

She took a deep breath in a futile attempt to remain calm. "I'm a respectable woman, Jake, trying to give my son a respectable life."

"I don't mean to change any of that."

"No? How do you plan to keep it a secret if you keep sneaking into my house? Everyone will know we're lovers."

"We *are* lovers. You're my woman, and you'd better get used to the idea."

"I am *not* your woman!"

Jake had a hard time repressing a smile at her fury. His wildcat was magnificent when she got riled . . . her blue eyes flashing, color high in her cheeks, her bosom heaving. Too clearly he remembered the taste of those peaked nipples when he sucked them . . . the way her long, slender legs wound around him and took him inside her body. . . . Feeling himself harden, Jake cursed the restriction of his pants.

He'd been half-aroused all day, yet he'd held out longer than he expected, nearly two full days, all the while fighting the need to touch Caitlin, to be with her, to feel her lying against him, moving beneath him.

But the waiting was over.

His heart began beating in a slow steady rhythm

of anticipation as he stepped into the room.

Seeing the determined, sensual look in his eyes, Caitlin knew she wasn't going to escape. He would have her, with or without her permission. The thought sent arrows of excited painfulness shooting between her thighs, even as she took a defensive step backward. "Jake, we *can't*. I told you I don't want to get pregnant."

Fishing in his vest pocket, Jake withdrew a small paper-wrapped packet and held it up. "I brought the sponges."

Her heart skipped a violent beat.

"Come here, Cat. I want to show you how to use these."

Nervously she took another step backward, determined to keep the desk between them. "That's a whore's trick."

A sudden sparkle of humor lit his emerald eyes. "Maybe so, but a useful one. You have any whiskey?"

"No," she retorted exultantly. "I poured it all out after my father died."

"I guess living with a drunk makes you a bit suspect of liquor. No matter. I brought my own."

He reached in his vest pocket and brought out a small tin flask. Sauntering over to the desk, Jake proceeded to douse one of the sponges with whiskey then placed it carefully on one corner of the oak surface, while Caitlin watched in disbelief.

The whiskey fumes that filled the air made her slightly dizzy, but that wasn't what held her spellbound. It was Jake's look. When he captured her gaze with his bright emerald eyes, the current that sizzled between them was like a lightning bolt.

Oh, God, Caitlin thought helplessly. She had vowed to be strong this time, to resist Jake's every attempt to coerce or threaten or seduce her, but she was impossibly weak where he was concerned. She stood rooted to the floor as he moved around the desk to her side.

Wordlessly he closed the account ledger and shoved it to one side of the desk's surface, along with all the other papers and knickknacks.

Caitlin licked her suddenly dry lips. "Jake . . . it's the middle of the afternoon."

His slow grin was brilliant with sensuality. "Afternoon's the best time of the day to make love . . . unless it's first thing in the morning . . . or just before dusk . . . or late at night. In a minute you won't care what time it is, wildcat."

Reaching out, he caught her waist and drew her slowly toward him, into his arms. He kissed her then. A determined, forceful, tender assault that vibrated with desire. She felt his need; the very rawness of his male hunger took her breath away and drained her of any will to resist.

He held her hard against him, one muscled thigh moving between her legs . . . legs that suddenly seemed as boneless as jelly. Overwhelmed by his heat and sexuality, Caitlin swayed against him weakly and heard Jake's husky murmur of approval.

With one arm he lifted her by her waist to settle her on the edge of the desk. "This'll serve as well as a bed."

"Jake . . ."

"Be still, Cat. God, I've wanted to do this all day long. I wanted to pull up your skirt . . . like this . . ." She felt his strong hands venture under her petticoats, his fingers probing for the open crotch of her drawers.

"Jake, no!"

Reflexively Caitlin grasped his shoulders and tried to push him away; modesty demanded that she put up at least a token struggle. But he managed to slide one finger between her thighs and find the open slit of her drawers. Caitlin gasped as he stroked the hot, damp flesh of her woman's mound. She wanted to protest, but it felt too good.

A shudder rocked her as he gently explored.

"Lie back, Cat," he murmured. "I'll take care of you."

He pulled her legs forward and up, forcing her back on the desk's surface, till she lay with her elbows braced behind her, her skirts hiked up around her waist. Then he was opening her drawers and pulling them down over her hips, sliding them off her legs.

"Jake . . . this is scandalous."

"Sure, and you love it. Relax now and let me make you feel good."

She shivered to feel those hot, callused hands sliding up her thighs, opening her to his gaze. Caitlin held her breath as Jake bent down to her. She saw his nostrils flare as he breathed her spicy woman's scent, but was disappointed when he did nothing more than plant a tantalizing kiss on her inner thigh. Instead he picked up the sponge soaked in whiskey.

"Watch me put it in you, Cat."

Dazed, she did as she was bid. Carefully he slid the sponge inside her, yet Caitlin gasped at the chill, burning sensation.

"Does that hurt?"

"No . . . it's just cold."

"I'll warm you up soon enough. See, this goes deep inside you . . . just where I'm going to be in a minute." His fingers pushed deeper, while his thumb gently stroked the tiny nub that was the heart of her desire.

Already aroused, Caitlin moaned, aching for him

to do more than just pet her, but Jake took his time, watching the slow movement of his hand against her silky, shivering flesh.

"Jake, you're torturing me. . . . "

"That's exactly the idea, wildcat."

He stroked her again for the sheer pleasure of watching her response. Then he placed his thumbs on either side of her cleft and spread the lips apart, leaving her slim, silken body open for his pleasure.

"Jake . . . don't . . . please . . . hurry . . ."

"In a minute. First I want to taste you. I want to see how soft and wet you are for me."

He bent his head again, seeking her out. His tongue was scalding hot as it found the delicate nub and flicked her in a lash of pleasure that was almost cruel.

Caitlin shifted her hips restlessly, trying to escape, yet Jake's hands forced her to be still. Sliding his fingers beneath her buttocks, he held a cheek in each hand, palms flat, fingers spread beneath the soft, rounded flesh, gently squeezing.

He was in no hurry. In his mind he was already inside her, enjoying her, feeling her quiver, giving her pleasure.

"I used to dream of doing this to you . . . how you looked . . . how you tasted."

She felt his jaw scraping her inner thighs, felt his lips burning hot on her skin as he trailed soft, tender kisses up her leg. "Jake . . . please . . . I can't bear it."

He hesitated at the crown of her thighs, drinking in the sweet scent of woman rising to his nostrils. Then slowly, deliberately, he put his tongue inside her.

Caitlin nearly arched off the desk.

"God, whiskey never tasted so good," Jake muttered with a sigh of contentment.

He thrust inside her again, showing her with his tongue exactly what he was going to do with his throbbing erection. The little whimpering sounds Caitlin made sent Jake's pulse soaring. His hard mouth curved in a very male, very satisfied way.

"That's good, hellcat, but not good enough. I want you to come again and again for me. I want you panting for me, mindless. . . . "

He shifted his weight, forcing her legs high and wide, and lifted them onto his shoulders. His mouth burned hot against her, nipping softly, tasting her to his ruthless satisfaction, while like a dark fire his tongue flickered and teased. Caitlin moaned out loud, her hips restlessly straining against the velvet torment of his mouth and caressing tongue.

"That's it. I want to hear you, baby. Let me hear how good it feels to you."

She heard the husky triumph in his voice, but she didn't care. She was oblivious to anything but Jake and what he was doing to her. She held his head in place with two tight fists in his hair as his tongue ravished her, arching wildly under the lash of sensation so exquisite it was almost unbearable. Her body was hot and explosive, and she was perilously close to the edge. . . .

She nearly cried out loud when Jake abruptly raised his head.

"Want me?" he growled.

Her answer was a heated whimper.

"Say it," he ordered softly.

She saw the fierce glitter in his eyes, the wetness of his mouth. "God, yes, I want you . . . please . . . don't stop."

His answering growl inflamed her. He bent to finish what he had started, driving her over the edge into an endless, raw pleasure so intense it seared. He held her surging body down, his mouth pressed hard to her as she bucked and clawed at him like a wildcat.

She was unutterably wild and glorious, Jake thought exultantly, urging her to greater and greater heights.

His mouth became gentle and soothing, though, when her climax was done. Caitlin lay panting, her eyes closed, her tongue wetting her dry lips.

Her legs were still draped over his shoulders, but when she felt Jake ease away, her eyelids fluttered open in alarm. She thought he might be abandoning her, but he was only unbuckling his gun belt and unbuttoning his pants, revealing his straining arousal.

His rigid phallus held her gaze. The taut, hot skin was engorged, flushed with desire, Caitlin saw with trembling awe. His lean, handsome face was flushed with passion as well as he moved to stand between her legs again.

"Open for me, Cat," he whispered hoarsely. "I want to feel you tight and hot around me. I can't wait, damn . . ." His voice actually shook, he was so swollen with need. "I'm so hot I'll explode if I don't get inside you."

Fighting the savage heat of his body, he mounted her with powerful thighs, bending close, his aching shaft gliding forcefully inside her in one smooth, long motion. Jake shut his eyes, groaning as her hot, moist flesh tightly sheathed him. "God, you feel so good, so warm and wet and tight. . . . "

Caitlin sighed in contentment, her head falling back in surrender as his body moved in a slow, maddening undulation above her. He was torturing her with exquisitely slow thrusts, trying to drive her out of her mind, exciting and arousing her beyond bearing. Then suddenly Jake's rhythm quickened, as if his renowned control was slipping.

She felt a surge of feminine power when his muscles clenched rigidly, as if he couldn't help himself. His thighs tightened, grinding against her hips, and Caitlin reveled in his helplessness. He *was* losing control. His face was hard and intent, his teeth clenched, his neck corded as he drove into her, yet she welcomed the violent thrusting of his body, the pressure of his straining thighs, her flesh shivering under the slamming thrusts of his loins.

His rough excitement matching her previous frenzy, he lunged into her with a fierceness that made her cry out, but she only wrapped her ivory legs around him. A low, rough groan burst from his throat as he exploded inside her, but she held on to him tightly, absorbing the shuddering convulsions of his shaking body . . . smiling faintly when it was over.

Jake lay sprawled heavily on top of her, breathing erratically, his hard-muscled body pinning her to the desk, grinding the ribs of her stays into her soft flesh, yet Caitlin was content to wait.

"It's all right," she whispered tenderly, stroking his golden hair, wanting to comfort him, to soothe him after the ravaging passion as he'd done for her so often. She could smell the hot musk of Jake's arousal, feel his harsh puffs of breath against her temple as he tried to regain control, and she wanted to laugh in triumph. He'd been as mindless with desire as she.

It was only a moment, though, before her eyes widened. Jake's shaft was starting to swell and throb once again. He was getting hard inside her, she could feel him filling her.

"Jake, no, that's enough," she murmured hoarsely.

"It'll never be enough, hellcat."

Reason suddenly returned at his impassioned declaration. Caitlin closed her eyes, an ache welling in her throat. "Jake . . . this has to stop," she pleaded, wishing she didn't have to be so sensible, wishing she could simply surrender to the reckless craving he aroused in her, and accept the exquisite fulfillment he promised.

Her tone was regretful, almost despairing, but the gravity of it alarmed Jake. He couldn't let it end like this. He had to make Caitlin understand she was wrong.

He took a deep breath and seemed to gather his strength, then lifted her in his arms. He meant to prove to her they belonged together. She was *his* again, bound to him by laws older than civilized man.

Still joined to her at the loins, he turned and headed for the door, making Caitlin gasp in protest. "Where are you taking me?"

"To bed, where else?"

"Jake . . . Haven't you heard a word I've said? I'm a respectable widow! I can't go to bed with you in broad daylight—"

"You don't want your hands to burst in on us like this, now do you?"

"No, but—"

His mouth covered hers, cutting off her desperate objection, robbing her of breath, and, most damning, smothering her will to resist.

Chapter 11

❦

"Still in bed, lover?" a deep, masculine voice prodded, the tone faintly teasing.

Starting awake from a doze, Caitlin opened her eyes to discover Jake standing over her, the glow from a lamp dispelling the night shadows and illuminating his beautiful body.

He was bare-chested, a towel riding low on his lean hips. Evidently he had just washed, for beads of water sparkled in the golden hair on his chest and glistened against his bronzed skin. Beneath the towel she knew he was naked.

Flushing, Caitlin dragged her gaze away and glanced around the room. Her bedchamber was utter chaos. Articles of clothing were scattered everywhere, while the tumbled sheets attested to the strenuous activity of the afternoon. She must have fallen asleep, for now it was evening.

"Come on, sleepyhead, get up," Jake's amused voice urged. "I'm hungry. I'm going to fix us something to eat."

She was about to retort that she'd never given

him permission to make free with her house when he startled a gasp from her. Jake had let the towel drop to the floor and now stood brazenly naked, giving her an eye-level view of his flat, tightly muscled belly and slim hips. Casually turning then, he bent to search for his denim pants, and her gaze ranged over his backside. She knew from experience his buttocks were as tight and hard to the touch as they looked, that his horseman's thighs were strong as steel, that when he was aroused he had the shaft of a stallion. . . .

Caitlin felt an impossible warmth flooding her at the hot, sweet memory of the past few hours. She'd thought after the exhausting pleasure he'd given her all afternoon that she would be numb, yet incredibly, his earthiness and obvious maleness aroused her still. She actually ached to touch him, to run her palms all over him, the way he had done to her for the past several hours. She wanted to feel the virile warmth of his lean body against her skin, to have his muscles rippling beneath her touch, his magnificent body moving between her thighs. . . .

When he stood and saw where she was looking, Jake favored her with an easy grin as seductive as it was dangerous. That grin of his would have stopped any woman at fifty paces.

Flustered despite herself, Caitlin dragged her gaze from his groin and muttered an unladylike oath as she buried her face in the man-scented pillow.

"It's a little late to play at being shy."

It was much too late, Caitlin agreed shamefully, after the intimacy they'd just shared.

Each time he made love to her she told herself it would be the last, and each time he managed to obliterate all her defenses with little more than a caress. He could control her body at will. Her senses turned traitor when he so much as kissed her.

Worse, he refused to leave her house. He was making himself at home now as if he belonged here, and she had no idea how to be rid of him. He had taken over her house, her body, her will.

She was grateful for the rustling sounds that told her he'd put on his pants, but tensed when she felt him settle a hip beside her on the bed. When he tugged the sheet down over her back, Caitlin gasped at the coolness of the night air.

"Come on, get up," Jake repeated, stroking a bare buttock with a callused palm. "I'll start supper while you wash up."

"Can you even cook?" she muttered, squirming beneath his arousing caress.

"I've fended for myself enough to times to get pretty decent at it." With a finger under her chin, Jake turned her face up. Covering her mouth with his, he stole her breath away with a hot, hard kiss. "Get up, or I'll climb back into bed with you, and we'll never get to eat." Rising, he went to the door, but glanced back over his shoulder. "And Cat? Don't take out the sponge. We may need it again."

Caitlin directed another muttered curse at his retreating back, but forced herself to get up. She went to the washstand, her lips still tingling from her lover's warm, hard mouth, and caught a glance at her naked, wanton image in the cheval glass. She looked like a woman who had just been thoroughly pleasured, with her lips passion bruised and her wild, sleep-tumbled hair spilling down her back.

This can't go on, Caitlin thought with a growing sense of panic. Somehow she had to make Jake see that this reckless disregard for all propriety would ruin her. More crucially, she had to make him realize they had no future together.

A short while later, she entered the kitchen, dressed in a modest wrapper. There was nothing modest about Jake, though. Barefoot and shirtless, he wore only low-riding denims, and the expanse of naked flesh he showed was disturbingly brazen, the muscles in his bare, tanned back, coiling and sliding under satiny skin. The bullet scars on his chest were even more disturbing. Would she ever be able to look at his body, to make love to him, without remembering the past? Caitlin wondered.

At least he had closed the curtains for privacy, she saw with relief. The first thing she did was carefully lock the back door. Then she made Jake sit down at the kitchen table. He had started the coffee and begun frying bacon in a huge iron skillet, but she took over the task, as well as that of warming some day-old biscuits, keeping her gaze averted from his distracting presence while she tried to figure out how to initiate a discussion.

Jake sat quietly with his long legs stretched before him, enjoying the homey intimacy, wishing he knew how to make it last. A deep ache settled in his loins as he watched Caitlin fixing his supper. A stronger one lodged in his chest, a yearning that was soul deep. This was what he wanted, he told himself. Just to be with her. If not for his killing of her brother, he could have been sharing this domestic contentment with her for years.

There was no use crying over the past, though. He could only try to change the future. He wouldn't be satisfied until Caitlin was living under his roof, sleeping in his bed. Until his ring was on her finger and her name was Mrs. Jake McCord. He wanted the right to love her, not steal into her house in the night like a criminal. He would never be satisfied with illicit meetings again.

He didn't think Caitlin would, either, after this

afternoon. He'd come a long way toward convincing her she still wanted him as much as he wanted her. God, did he want her.

Silently Jake cursed to himself as he watched her slim hips moving beneath that prim wrapper, the way they'd moved under him. The memory left him restless and aching, made his skin feel hot and tight, made his lengthening erection stiffen beneath his pants. The need was riding him hard, but he told himself to cool down. He couldn't claim victory yet. He'd proved he could possess Cat's body, but he wanted her heart as well.

He watched for a while as she turned the bacon, before saying softly, "I used to have this dream when I was down in New Mexico Territory. About something like this. We had a ranch, a log house here in the hills, and you'd be waiting for me with supper when I came in from the range."

Caitlin froze suddenly in the act of reaching in the cupboard for the plates.

"It's what kept me from losing hope all those years. All those lonely nights I was thinking of you."

She felt a tight ache constrict her throat. She didn't want to hear this, didn't want Jake dredging up painful memories.

"We've never done this before, you realize that? Never even eaten a real meal together. The closest we came was that time we gorged ourselves on blackberries. You remember, Cat?" His voice was wistful.

Her back to him, she nodded. "I got sick later, I ate so many."

"Those were good times."

They *were* good times, she admitted silently, even though they'd been forced to meet in secret. At that age, it had been enough to simply be together, to talk and explore and share dreams and hopes for hours on end.

Shaking her head at the disturbing memories, Caitlin straightened and made herself carry the dinnerware and napkins to the table. She flinched, though, when Jake leaned forward and wrapped his arm around her waist.

"Jake . . ."

He slipped his hand inside her wrapper and cupped her bare breast, making her draw a breath at the tenderness of her nipple.

"Sore?" he asked, looking up to watch her face.

"A little."

He caressed her gently, soothing her bruised flesh. "That feel better?" he murmured.

"N-no," she said, slightly panicked as she glanced nervously around the kitchen. If she let this go on, they would wind up making love and nothing would get said or settled. Vexed at Jake's effortless ability to melt her control, Caitlin pulled out of his arms. She was tightening the sash of her wrapper when he slowly stood up behind her.

"Jake . . ." Her voice was breathless as she felt his warm, arousing lips nuzzle her neck. "This has to stop. We can't keep on this way."

"I know. I agree."

Her gaze probing, she glanced back up at him. "You do?"

"I told you, we should make our relationship permanent."

Stiffening, Caitlin drew away again. "And I told you that's impossible."

"Why?"

Turning to face him, she crossed her arms over her chest defensively. "I can't believe you really want to marry me. You only *think* you do—because you like having sex with me. But you can't build a marriage simply on carnal relations."

"Why not?"

"I'm serious, Jake."

"So am I." His usual charming male grin was a trifle wolfish. "I think sex is a great basis for marriage. For sure it's more than most couples have."

"It's not enough for me."

His features suddenly growing serious, Jake searched her face. "What *would* be enough, Cat?"

The ache returned to constrict her throat. What she yearned for—a man who was gentle and loving, a marriage full of tenderness and sharing and giving, a family that was warm and affectionate and there for each other—Jake could no longer offer her. Once, perhaps, he would have, but they were both different people from the young lovers they'd once been.

When she averted her gaze, he caught her hand and drew it to his loins, where she could feel his hardness. "There's more to us than this, Cat. It's beyond pleasure, and you know it."

She tugged her hand away. "Maybe so. But you only want me because I'm familiar. Because I'm part of your past before it went bad."

"That's not true."

"You never really cared for me."

"You're wrong. I loved you, Cat." *I still do*.

Caitlin stared at him in silence. "You never told me," she said finally, hoarsely.

"I never got a chance before your brother came gunning for me." Jake's mouth twisted in the semblance of a smile. "Or maybe I just never figured it out in time. After that it was too late."

"Couldn't . . . you have tried to find me . . . or at least written? I never heard a word from you. You let me imagine the worst."

He shook his head slowly. "I couldn't have come for you, Cat. Not with a price on my head. I was running for my life, and I couldn't drag you into it."

Distracted, she looked away. Jake was stubbornly determined to ignore all her logical arguments, to cloud her judgment. The devil of it was, she was beginning to doubt her own reasoning as well. It would be so easy to succumb to his seductive persuasion. So enticing to think they *could* have a future together, with nothing but love between them. And when she thought of the long, bitter years of loneliness ahead of her, she felt even more vulnerable. . . .

"Well," Caitlin murmured with a forced shrug, "it doesn't matter. All that's over now."

"No, it isn't over. You loved me, too, and you damn well know it."

"That was . . . a mistake."

"Was it?" Catching her arm, Jake made her look at him, his gaze boring into hers.

Yes, a voice inside her cried silently. It had been a terrible mistake to give her heart to this man. Jake was the wrong husband for her, although years ago she'd been too young and foolish to see it—and too much in love. He called to something wild and untamed in her, when she needed someone safe and stable to curb the restless streak in her. She didn't want wild adventure now, didn't want passion. She wanted peace and safety, for herself and her son. She didn't want to love someone so much she was willing to risk everything, including her son's life, to be with him. That kind of need terrified her.

Pulling away, Caitlin made herself check the biscuits warming in the oven, even though her hands trembled. "It *would* have been a mistake for me to marry you then," she insisted in a low voice as she finished frying the bacon. "My mother married the wrong man and regretted it every day of her life. She was so unhappy. . . . I swore I would never go through the hell she went through. I would never marry a man like my father."

"You think I'm like your father?"

Her hesitation answered eloquently, but she sidestepped a direct response. "I think you're trying to run my life, Jake, just like he did."

"I'm just trying to make you see reason."

"*Your* reason. Which doesn't happen to be mine. I spent most of my life under my father's control, and now that I'm out from under his thumb, I prefer to *keep* it that way."

Picking up the utensils, Jake resumed setting the table. "I'm not about to keep you under my thumb."

She glanced back at him, an eyebrow arched in skepticism. "I'm not so certain about that, but regardless, I'm not ready to give up all my plans and turn my life over to you on some whim."

"It isn't some whim, Cat." His gaze pierced hers. "You can't tell me you don't feel something for me."

"I . . . don't know what I feel. I just know I don't want that old life again. I want nothing to do with it."

Willing himself to calm, Jake settled himself in his chair again. "Seems to me you're running from the past, Cat."

"If so, it's because the past is too painful to live with." She took a deep breath. "Can't you see, Jake? I've put my grief behind me, made a fresh start. I have a peaceful life now, and I want to keep it that way."

"Sounds mighty tame to me. You never used to be lily-livered."

In exasperation, she shook her head. She cracked some eggs in the skillet and set them to frying, then busied herself pouring two cups of coffee. "It's absurd even to discuss this with you. We have nothing in common any longer. Certainly we don't want the same things out of life."

"For instance?"

"For instance . . . if I *were* to marry you, where would we live?

"Here. Where else?"

"St. Louis, that's where. I intend to raise my son there, where he can grow up to be a decent human being, away from the violence of the range war."

Jake was silent for a moment, before saying quietly, "I mean to stay in Colorado, Cat. This is my home."

The conviction in his voice surprised her a little. She understood Jake's reverence for the mountains, his love for his family, but those things had never been preeminent with him before. "You never used to want to settle down here," she observed. "You were always talking about moving on, looking for adventure."

His mouth twisted. "I was young and restless, then. And that was before I had my roots torn up. I guess you never know what you have till you lose it. I was forced to leave once. I'm not leaving again."

A shadow passed over her eyes. Nodding sadly, she turned back to the stove and flipped the eggs over in the skillet. "But it proves my point, Jake," she said quietly. "We no longer have a future together. Mine is with my son, and yours is here in Colorado."

"Dammit, Cat . . . I'm not going to let a three-year-old kid stand between us."

Jake regretted the outburst the minute he made it, even before Caitlin slowly straightened, her blue eyes flashing fire. Just because he was jealous as hell of Ryan and resented knowing she'd choose the boy over him, was no excuse to fly off the handle. He knew he couldn't fight her on that front.

"I hardly think that's for you to decide," Caitlin returned with frost in her tone. "As for where I live, it's really none of your concern."

"I think it is. You're my woman, wildcat, don't ever forget it. You belong with me."

"Do I?" Her chin rose, while her voice dripped cynicism. "I'm supposed to give up my life because you order me to?"

"A woman's supposed to follow her man, not the other way around."

"Vernon said he was willing to move to St. Louis with me."

It was Jake's turn to stiffen; the air suddenly crackled with renewed tension.

"The hell he will," he grated through his teeth. "Are you going to let your schoolteacher know the engagement's off," Jake asked, his tone frigid, "or do I?"

"I'll tell Vernon myself," she replied tightly. "But just because I can't marry him, doesn't mean I'll marry you."

"You think I'll be content, having to sneak around and make do with a stolen hour in your bed now and then, like a thief?"

"I don't expect you to be in my bed at all, Jake! I won't become your whore."

"I'm not asking you to, dammit! I'm asking you to be my *wife*!"

In the taut, angry silence that followed, Caitlin risked a glance at Jake. His expression had hardened, while his green eyes smoldered.

"I've waited four years for you, Cat. That's long enough, to my mind."

Seeing his dark look, Caitlin was suddenly reminded of the man she was dealing with, of the lawless existence he'd led recently. Jake was rawhide tough, hard as nails, and grimly determined to reclaim what had been taken from him. He wouldn't give up easily.

Disturbed by his searing stare, she tried another, less confrontational tact. "Jake, you don't understand. If it were just me, I might—" She broke off, biting her lip. "My son is more precious to me than life. I have to think of him first."

"Nobody's asking you not to think of him."

"*You* are. Ryan wouldn't be safe here. I can't bring him to Colorado."

"Sure you can."

"At what price?" She shook her head. "I won't risk it. I lost my brother to the range war, and when I think of losing my son, too, I get sick inside, physically sick." Caitlin's clenched fingers crept to her stomach. "You've never been a mother, so you don't know how strong the feelings are."

No, he'd never been a mother, or even a father, but he knew about protective feelings. He'd felt the same way about his family, about Cat herself. She wanted to shield her son from the fierce conflict that had killed her brother and warped her father, and he couldn't blame her. Her vulnerability spoke directly to his heart.

"The war is ending, Cat," he said with less assurance than he'd like.

"Perhaps . . . but can you promise me it won't

flare up again?" The peace has held a few days, but that's no guarantee it will last forever." When Jake was silent, Caitlin reached an imploring hand out to him. "I'm afraid for Ryan, can't you understand that?"

Her fears weren't irrational, Jake reflected, gazing at her troubled blue eyes. But he was afraid, too. Not of the possibility of more fighting; he thought he could handle trouble. And certainly if the truce held, there would be fewer incidents of bloodshed to worry about.

His fear went deeper than physical danger. The gnawing terror that Caitlin had loved another man, that somebody else had earned what should have been *his*. He couldn't stop thinking about her lying in her husband's arms, even if the bastard was dead. He couldn't stop thinking about the child she had borne. Ryan should have been *his* child, *his* son.

But if Ryan *had* been his kid? Would he feel any differently about bringing him to Colorado and exposing him to the danger?

"If I thought the risk was too great," Jake replied quietly, "I'd be the first one warning you to keep him away. But the feud is ending, and I intend to make damn sure it stays ended. I wouldn't let Ryan come to any harm."

"How could you possibly protect him?"

Jake forced himself to reply calmly, "There's risk in living anywhere, Cat. Is St. Louis really so safe for a kid? He could get run over by a passing carriage. Or he could come down with one of those epidemic diseases that hit big cities so often. Cholera and smallpox kill thousands of people."

"At least he wouldn't get shot by some vengeance-crazed cowboy seeking to even a score in a range feud." Caitlin bent to take the biscuits from the oven. The eggs were burning around the edges, and she scooped them up onto two plates. Then, the anger draining from her voice, she added less vehemently, "Besides . . . there's more to my concern than just the feud. If I'm to marry . . . Ryan needs a good father."

"I suppose that fellow you married was a damned paragon," Jake observed, a bitter edge to his voice.

Caitlin closed her eyes briefly, regretting the lies she'd told him about her life. "He . . . Martin had some of the qualities I used to see in you."

Jake's eyes narrowed at her. "Are you so certain I couldn't be a good father to Ryan?"

Turning, Caitlin regarded Jake with regret, a hollow ache in her breast as she looked into green eyes that were so like her son's. He would never know Ryan. She didn't dare take the risk. "I . . . I'm not sure you could be. Ryan needs someone who can be a role model, who can teach him right from wrong. You . . . haven't exactly been an upstanding citizen the past few years."

"And whose fault is that, Cat? I seem to recall your pa had something to do with me becoming an outlaw in the first place."

She had to fight down the urge to cry. Jake *had* been terribly wronged, but she couldn't let that matter. "You said yourself you lived by your gun. That you . . . killed for money."

"I'm doing my damnedest to make things right, haven't you noticed?" Jake's mouth curled mockingly. "I've become a model citizen. Hell, I've even been made a deputy."

"Pinning a piece of tin on your chest won't erase the past."

"You could help me change."

Aching inside, she gazed at him with regret. It was said the right woman could bring out a man's softer qualities. Could she help Jake change his violent ways if she tried? If she did, would he take it to mean a commitment on her part, a pledge of forever that she couldn't let herself make? Caitlin clenched her fingers, telling herself to be strong. She couldn't let him assault the walls around her heart that had taken four painful years to build.

"I can't..." she whispered, her voice breaking into a plea. "I can't go back, Jake. What we had... It's over."

He closed his eyes against the anguish and helplessness inside him.

"We... should eat," she said in a shaky voice. "Supper's getting cold."

When she picked up the plates and carried them to the table, he reached out and caught her wrist. "Cat..."

He said nothing more, but the hoarse word held a wealth of emotion... an edge of desperation that she herself felt. When he tugged on her hand, Caitlin moved toward him, drawn by some invisible, compelling force... an unbearable sense of loss.

His arms encircling her hips, Jake bent forward to rest his forehead against her belly. "It's not over, Cat.... I won't let it be over...."

His voice, dark and hoarse, raked deep inside her. A ragged sob escaped her. Her heart ached, for him, for her. She felt his need, his pain, felt her own—a savage yearning to regain the tenderness they'd lost, to find the magic they'd once shared. Her hands clutched in his hair, trying to soothe, but communicating only fierce sorrow and desire.

"Jake..."

"It's not over, Cat."

She could feel the tears slipping from her eyes, feel her heart aching, her defenses against him in tatters.

Oh, Jake.

He was right, Caitlin acknowledged with painful honesty. They might not be able to re-create the past, but it wasn't over between them in the least. The indefinable bond was still there. That was the hell of it.

Chapter 12

❧

She was falling in love with him all over again. That was the bald, frightening truth. How else could she explain the intense feeling of anticipation, of joy, of longing, that flooded her at the merest thought of Jake?

Caitlin stared blindly out the kitchen window the following morning, her breakfast virtually ignored as she tried to come to terms with her dilemma.

Damn you, Jake, she cried silently. *I was over you. I had driven you from my heart.* Now she was fighting a losing battle.

She didn't have the willpower to resist him. She might resent Jake's arrogant, domineering manner, might bristle at his conviction that he could command her life to suit his pleasure, but with each kiss, each stroke, each caress, she became more and more his woman. With every moment that passed, he wore down her defenses further. She was falling in love with him again whether she wanted to or not.

Or maybe she'd just never gotten over him in the first place.

Dammit, she didn't *want* to love him. She'd built a peaceful life for herself and her son in St. Louis. That was what she craved, wasn't it: peace? She'd get no peace with Jake in her life—but then she felt no peace with him gone either. He was always on her mind, preying on her heart. She wanted him with her, wanted his arms around her, wanted to share a future with him, to believe all their dreams and hopes could come true. She *wanted* to belong together.

But then there was Ryan. Was she so selfish as to think only of herself and what *she* wanted, and not what her son needed?

The sound of hoofbeats interrupted her tumultuous thoughts. With a start, Caitlin glanced out the kitchen window, hoping it wasn't Jake.

To her surprise and vague alarm, she spied several horsemen riding swiftly into the yard. Rising quickly, she went out on the back porch, her heart in her throat. She'd never forgotten the day her father had brought home her brother's body, and couldn't stop her imagination from conjuring up all sorts of dread thoughts at the sight of armed men approaching the ranch with such apparent urgency, especially since two of them were riding double.

Her foreman, Hank Spurlock, slowed his mount to a halt before the back steps, the riders behind him following suit.

"Is something wrong?" Caitlin demanded, her gaze taking in the horsemen.

"I'm not sure, Miz Hughes. The boys found this fellow snooping around on Kingsly land. He took a shot at them."

Four of the men were familiar to her—her own

ranch hands as well as cowboys from nearby cattle outfits—but one of those riding double was a stranger. To her consternation, he reminded her of Shorty Davis, the man who'd falsely "witnessed" Jake murdering her brother. He was wiry and weathered, with a brown, leathery face and a gap-toothed grimace that seemed somehow repellent.

Lifting his hands which were tied together in front, he spoke up in his own defense. "I warn't snooping, ma'am. Warn't hurting nobody. Didn't even know it was yore land. Heard tell it was McCord land."

"Our spreads run together on the north border," she replied coolly. "But even if you made an innocent mistake, shooting at our patrols was hardly warranted."

"Didn't know who they was. Cain't be too careful nowadays, bein' wounded an' all. With my horse gone lame, I warn't nothing but a sittin' duck."

Caitlin had noticed his left leg, which was wrapped with a dirty, bloody bandage just below the knee. She'd also noticed the flush of fever on his cheekbones and the greasy pallor of his skin beneath the tan. "You were shot?"

"Few days ago, in Golden. A drunk cowpoke decided to shoot up the town. It pains me mighty fierce, thanks to these boys roughin' me up."

"You want us to turn him over to the marshal?" Hank asked.

For the first time the stranger looked nervous. "Ain't no call for that, ma'am. If you'll jest fetch Deputy McCord, we'll git this little scrap straightened out."

"You know Jake McCord?" Caitlin asked.

"Know him right well. I tole these boys to let me

talk to him, but they paid me no mind. You just fetch McCord. He'll vouch for me."

She glanced at Hank. "Would you have someone ride over to the Bar M and see if Jake can come?"

"I'll go, ma'am," one of the cowboys offered, turning his horse.

"Jest tell him Lew's asking for him," the stranger said. "He'll know who it is."

"What do we do with him, meanwhile, Miz Hughes?" Hank asked, obviously disapproving.

"He can wait in the bunkhouse. He looks as if he should lie down, in any case. Perhaps someone should see to that injured leg."

"Leg's fine, ma'am," Lew insisted.

Caitlin raised a skeptical eyebrow. "It hardly looks fine. Judging from your face, you have a touch of fever and you may be risking gangrene. We can patch up most injuries on the ranch, but if you'd rather have a doctor—"

"Don't want no sawbones pokin' at me. If you'll jest round me up some grub, I'd be grateful. Ain't et too well lately."

Caitlin pressed her lips together without replying. It was an unwritten law in the West to offer hospitality to strangers, yet this man had shot at her ranch hands and the other members of the feud patrol. Besides, something about him made her uneasy.

She left Hank to escort the man to the bunkhouse while she fetched a plate of leftover biscuits and beef and a cup of coffee. Lew was propped up in one of the beds when she entered, his wrists still tied.

He gave her a gap-toothed grin and held up his bound hands. "Do ya mind? Cain't eat, all roped up like a steer at brandin'."

Grimly Hank released his bonds, then hovered

protectively nearby, his six-shooter drawn. When
Caitlin gave Lew the plate, he didn't bother to use
the utensils, but grabbed a chunk of beef and
crammed it ravenously into his mouth.

She was about to leave when he said around a
mouthful of food, "I hear tell McCord's the law
around here now. Musta done some fast talkin',
gettin' hisself a tin star after bein' a wanted desperado."

The observation was no more than Caitlin had
previously made, yet hearing it voiced by this . . .
unsavory man, she felt herself stiffening defensively. "How do you know Jake?"

"Saved his hide oncet. Fact, I'm the only reason
he's alive to this very day. Stopped a bounty hunter
'bout to put a bullet in his back. But he shore musta
pulled the wool over folks' eyes around here."

"Perhaps he's turned over a new leaf."

Lew grunted. "P'raps so. But Jake McCord ain't
no angel, you take my word for it."

"And just why should I do that?" An edge of
steel had entered her voice.

The wiry man gave her a sullen glance. "Folks
alus did treaty McCord like he was somebody high
an' mighty, but he ain't no better 'n me. You ask
him about that kid he killed, if you don't believe
me."

"What . . . kid?"

"You jest ask him. Mebbe I done some things on
the wrong side o' the law, but I ain't never killed
no kid."

"I can't believe Jake would ever harm a child."

The patronizing smirk Lew sent her made her
queasy. "You jest ask him."

With a glance at her foreman, Caitlin decided it
best to discontinue this unsettling conversation.
Murmuring, "I'll be up at the house," she left Hank

to watch over his prisoner and returned to the kitchen, where she waited anxiously for Jake to show up.

When he rode up alone about a half hour later, she went out at once to meet him. His expression was enigmatic, even guarded, as she descended the steps.

"There's a man calling himself 'Lew' who says he knows you."

"The boys told me. Where is he?"

"The bunkhouse. Hank is guarding him."

Jake dismounted. When Caitlin started to follow him, he said, "I'll handle this."

She ignored his implication that she stay out of it. "They were my hands he shot at."

Jake rapped on the bunkhouse door once in warning before entering. He barely gave Hank and his six-shooter a glance, but instead focused his attention on the unkempt man on the bed.

"Well, if it ain't Deputy McCord," Lew drawled. Grinning, he swiped his hat off his greasy head with a feigned show of deference.

"Lew. What's this I hear about you shooting at our boys?"

"Aw, it was jest a warnin' shot, Jake. Didn't mean nothing by it."

Jake studied the man for a moment. "What brings you to these parts?"

Lew glanced pointedly at the armed foreman.

"Will you give us a minute alone, Hank?" Jake asked.

Hank looked to Caitlin first, but when she nodded, he left the bunkhouse.

When he was gone, Lew said seriously, "Got in a little trouble over in Golden, Jake. Thought I might hole up at your place for a spell. Then my danged horse pulled up lame."

"You sure it was Golden? The marshal got a wire yesterday saying somebody fitting your description tried to hold up a bank in Silver City."

Lew grinned. "Now whyever would you think it was me?"

Jake didn't return the grin. "That how you got that bad leg?"

"Mebbe. You don't really 'spect me to admit it, now that you got that star on your chest?"

"All right. What do you want from me?"

"A little money to tide me over. And a place to put up for a time, till things die down a bit."

When Jake didn't answer at once, Lew narrowed his eyes. "You owe me, McCord. I'm calling in the debt."

"I'll loan you a horse," Jake said finally. "And a hundred dollars. But you'll move on."

He ignored Caitlin's sharp intake of breath, but Lew didn't. He eyed her speculatively. "Move on? Don't want me to spoil your thing with the purty lady, that it?"

The warning flash that kindled in Jake's eyes was downright dangerous.

"Okay, okay, I'll move on," Lew said quickly. "But a hundred? That ain't hardly enough to keep body an' soul together."

"It's more than enough for your scrawny body, Alderson. And your soul's long past saving. Take it or leave it."

"I'll take it, I'll take it."

When Jake started to turn away, Lew threw out casually, "Ain't you interested to know what happened to the boys?"

"Not particularly."

"Dolby got hisself killed—shot in the back by one of them marshals who was gunnin' for you. Petey an' Buster was hanged in Sante Fe. Dunno

what happened to Marve an' Hooper. Last I heard
they was working for a big outfit in Texas. Heard
tell Deek made it to Virginee. An' then there's me."
He grinned, his yellowed teeth gaping. "The ole
gang jest ain't what it used to be. Guess you was
right to get out afore you came to a bad end like
the rest of 'em."

Caitlin gazed at Jake in dismay, appalled by this
apparent description of gang members from his
outlaw past.

"I'd like to borrow a horse," Jake said to her, not
acknowledging that he'd even heard Lew's catalog.
"I'll return it later, after I get him fixed up."

When Jake abruptly left the bunkhouse, Caitlin
followed directly on his heels. Hank was waiting
just outside the door, but she scarcely noticed that
he returned to guard his prisoner. She was too busy
watching Jake.

"You aren't going to just let that man go?"

Jake didn't answer, but ducked under the corral
gate to catch one of the horses there.

"You heard him, Jake. He practically admitted
he's running from the law."

"Maybe so. But I'm not going to be the one to
stop him."

"Whatever happened to the oath you took when
you became a deputy?"

Flinging her a glance, Jake returned in a low
voice, "I owe him, Cat."

"Honor among thieves, is that it?"

His jaw clenched at her scornful tone. "Something like that."

He led a chestnut gelding through the gate toward the barn, where the extra saddles were kept.
Caitlin followed.

"Jake . . . you can't just ignore the law. What

about the innocent people he might have hurt when he tried to rob that bank?"

"We have no proof he was involved in that holdup."

"All right then, what about what you said last night? That you wanted to change your ways?"

"This has nothing to do with me, or you."

"It has *everything* to do with you and me! How can I possibly consider marrying you? Did you *hear* what he said about all those men you used to know—how they all died? How can I risk exposing my son to those kinds of criminals?"

"I told you, that's all in the past, Cat."

"It isn't past! Lew's here, isn't he? Right here and now. And you're about to commit a crime by helping him get away!"

When Jake wouldn't answer, Caitlin demanded in a unsteady voice, "Is it true, what he said about you killing a child?"

Jake froze in the act of tightening the saddle cinch. He wouldn't meet her eyes when he answered quietly, "Not quite a child, but close enough. He was fourteen."

Caitlin recoiled in sick disbelief. Jake had admitted killing grown men, true, but in self-defense. To hear him state so baldly that he'd killed a boy . . .

"W-What . . . happened?"

Jake shrugged. "What difference does it make? I have no excuses."

"There must have been *some* reason. You wouldn't just shoot a boy down in cold blood."

The green eyes pinned her. "So now you finally believe I'm not a murderer?" The soft bitterness in his tone was accusing.

When she stared at him with a look that was pleading and uncertain, Jake cursed under his breath. "It was part of my job as a hired gun to

run a squatter off my outfit's land. I wounded the
father and the kid came gunning for me. I had to
shoot him."

"So you . . . were defending your life . . ." Caitlin
murmured hoarsely.

"Hell, yes!" The retort was almost savage. "But
I aimed too high. I wish to God I could take back
that bullet."

For a moment he bent his head. His face was
hidden from Caitlin, but she could see his pain, felt
it herself. She had the sudden urge to put her arms
around Jake and hold him. She hurt for him, hurt
too badly to cry.

Oh, Jake, she thought. *What happened to you?*

Her throat aching, she drew a slow, shuddering
breath, gathering her courage. "Jake . . . if you go
through with this, if you let that man go . . . it's
over between us. For good."

"I have no choice, Cat," he returned in a low
voice.

"Then . . . I have no choice, either."

His head came up. "Cat, listen to me—"

"No! I won't listen." Her voice trembled. "I'm
through listening. You don't want to change—
you've made that perfectly clear."

Jake swore in frustration, helplessly torn between
wanting to shake Caitlin and drag her into his arms
to make her see reason.

Something of his intention must have shown on
his face, for when he reached out to her, she
flinched in alarm and took an abrupt step back.
"Don't touch me."

"Dammit, Cat. You don't have to be afraid of
me."

"I . . . I'm not afraid of you. I'm afraid of the violence in your life. I'm afraid it will spill over into
mine and harm Ryan."

"I told you, I won't let it."

"No? How could you prevent it?" Caitlin swallowed a sob. She didn't want to hurt Jake. Couldn't believe he was a bad man at heart. But four years had changed him, hardened him, made him dangerous. And he couldn't even see it.

"You couldn't stop it, Jake," she insisted, her voice husky and low with tears, "even if you really wanted to. Don't you see? You could be the target for any lawman or bounty hunter looking to make a quick dollar, or any trigger-happy drunk wanting to challenge your reputation as a fast draw. Someone from your past could show up anytime, just like that Lew person did today. I can't *live* like that, Jake! Not with the threat of killing and death hanging over my head. I endured that violent existence with my father for eighteen years. I won't go through it again—and I absolutely won't subject my son to it. Not even for you."

"I'm nothing like your father, Cat."

"Yes, you are. . . . You're every bit as violent as he was."

A sharp pain flared in his eyes, as if she'd struck him.

Aching, Caitlin stared at him, wanting to take back her cruel words. But cruelty was the only way to make him see reason. And whatever love she felt for Jake didn't change the fact that he'd lived a violent, lawless existence. That his soul had been darkened by his past. That he was no longer the brazen lover who had once stolen her heart.

She had no future with this man. She couldn't let herself.

With an inarticulate sob, she shook her head blindly. "I n-never want to s-see you again," she choked in a ragged whisper. Clasping a hand over her mouth then, she turned and ran for the house.

Watching her go, Jake balled his hands into fists. He squeezed his eyes shut, remembering the look she'd given him, her unbearably sad eyes . . . She had loved him once. . . . If he was to have half a chance of regaining her love, he had to convince her he wasn't the violent man she feared. Somehow he had to make her see that he could change. That he wasn't ruled by his past. Even if her lack of faith galled him.

He wasn't going to let her go, Jake vowed silently, or stop trying to prove to her that they belonged together.

For the second time that morning, Caitlin stared out the kitchen window, her eyes blurring with tears as she watched Jake ride away with his former cohort in crime, yearning to call him back.

When his distant image finally faded, she bowed her head. She felt helpless, frantic, desperate. Somehow she had to escape Jake's overwhelming influence before it was too late. That possessive streak of his was bone deep. He wanted her, and he was coming after her with the full intention of getting what he wanted.

There was only one decision she could make to protect herself. She had to leave Colorado altogether. Now, at once. Even before the ranch was sold. She had to return to St. Louis for good. It was the only way she would be free of Jake.

Caitlin gave a start when she heard a horse snort outside the kitchen window. It was Vernon. Rising reluctantly from the table, she nervously smoothed her skirts, feeling unprepared to face him so soon after her bitter argument with Jake.

She went to the door, where she greeted Vernon calmly enough and invited him in. When she offered him coffee, he accepted, but to Caitlin's chagrin, he settled in the chair Jake had used last evening.

Averting her gaze, Caitlin poured Vernon's coffee and took the seat next to him, hoping she didn't bear any outward marks of a wanton.

"There's been trouble on the range," he said solemnly. "But then we never expected total peace at the start. The question is, can we patch up our differences. . . ."

She was almost relieved when Vernon started telling her about two incidents of fighting between sheep ranchers and cattlemen, both violations of the truce. Apparently he hadn't yet heard about Lew Alderson and his connection to Jake.

The newly formed council was to meet that evening, Vernon said, and test the system the ranchers had devised to resolve disputes.

When that topic was exhausted, however, Caitlin knew she couldn't put off telling him of her decision any longer.

"Vernon," she began in a low voice, before she lost her nerve, "I've done a great deal of thinking the past few days . . . about your marriage proposal."

His kind brown eyes focused on her face. "And?"

"And . . . I'm very flattered, but . . ." She faltered, searching for words.

"You don't want to marry me."

"That isn't it, exactly. . . . You're the kind of man any woman would be honored to have for a husband. . . . But I have to say no. I'm sorry—"

"It's McCord, isn't it?" Vernon demanded without giving her time to finish. "You're turning me down because of him."

"No, that's not the reason—"

"You're stuck on him," Vernon insisted, his tone

more sad than accusing. His gaze suddenly sharpened on her. "Good God, you're not thinking of marrying that devil, are you?"

Caitlin flushed. "No, of course not. I don't want anything to do with Jake."

"Don't do it, Caitlin. He's a murdering bastard."

Her eyes widened in shock. She'd rarely heard Vernon curse before, or even seen him lose his temper. Perhaps he was upset that she'd refused his offer, but that was no call to condemn Jake in such terms.

"I debated whether to show you this." He pulled an aged piece of paper from his vest pocket. "Look at this." Unfolding the handbill, he laid it flat on the table in front of her and smoothed out the creases.

It was a wanted poster from the New Mexico Territory, Caitlin saw with dismay as Jake's image stared back at her. Her lips moved silently as she read. *WANTED: One Jacob McCord, member of the Outlaw Dolby Gang, for the Vicious Murder of a teller during a bank holdup in the town of Los Marinos. A five hundred dollar REWARD is offered for his capture, DEAD or ALIVE.*

Caitlin stared at the handbill in horror and disbelief. Were the rumors really true? Had Jake not only joined an outlaw gang, but been an accomplice in a bank robbery and taken part in the killing of a clerk?

"This m-must be a mistake. . . . " she breathed.

"It's no mistake. McCord is a fugitive from justice."

"But . . . Jake wouldn't rob a bank."

Vernon's gaze pinned her. "Are you so sure?"

Caitlin shook her head at the invidious doubt that had crept in. She *wasn't* sure any longer, not after hearing what Lew had told her just this morn-

ing. Jake *had* been part of the Dolby gang,
something she never would have believed him capable of only a few hours ago. And there was no
disputing he'd turned to a life of violence after
leaving Colorado. . . .

Panic suddenly clutched at her. Dear God, Jake
still had a price on his head! He had to run, to
hide— But then Caitlin forced herself to take a
deep breath. Maybe no one knew about this but
Vernon.

"How did you get this?" she asked unsteadily.

"I have a friend in Denver—a federal marshal. I
wrote him when Jake first came back. This arrived
by stage yesterday."

"A federal marshal?"

Vernon nodded. "He doesn't have time to go
after Jake himself and return him to New Mexico,
but . . ." The schoolteacher seemed to choose his
words with care. "I know of a bounty hunter who
could do the job. I mean to summon him—"

"No, Vernon, you *can't!*"

"You mean to let McCord get away with murder?" Vernon's tone was suddenly fierce. "You of
all people, Caitlin? After he killed your brother, I
should think you'd at least want to see him in jail."

"But a bounty hunter . . ." Caitlin shook her
head. *Dead or alive.* A bounty hunter could kill
Jake—and many of them *would.*

She couldn't coldly watch him be turned over to
such a man, no matter what he'd done. She
couldn't bear the thought of Jake in prison, or
worse.

"Vernon, you can't. *Please.*"

His mouth twisted scornfully. "The marshal here
certainly can't be trusted to arrest McCord, since
he's the one who made him a deputy."

"Vernon, please. . . ." She reached out and cov-

ered his hand imploringly. "Whatever Jake's done
. . . I couldn't bear to see him hanged for it. Promise
me you'll forget the idea, that you won't bring in
a bounty hunter."

He held up the handbill. "What about the murder he committed?"

"Does anyone really have to see that poster?"

Vernon stared at her a long moment, frustration
evident in his expression. "I guess no one has to
see it. But, darn it, Caitlin, you can't possibly think
of marrying McCord after seeing this."

"No, of course not." She breathed a shaky sigh
of relief. "I'm not planning to marry anyone. In fact
. . . I've decided to return home to St. Louis. I have
to arrange the sale of the ranch first, but I'll be leaving in a few days, as soon as I can find someone
to act as my agent. I could ask a bank to do it, but
it's Ryan's inheritance. I'd rather not leave so important a transaction in a stranger's hands."

"I'll handle it, Caitlin. You know I will. But I
wish you would reconsider leaving. Especially just
when the truce is beginning to work."

With a sad smile, Caitlin shook her head. "I can't
stay here. There are just . . . too many painful memories." *And too many painful conflicts to the future.*

Her gaze dropped once more to the wanted
poster, where Jake's hard eyes stared back at her.

She had made the right decision to leave Colorado, she thought with a deep ache raking her
heart. They had no future together, a gunman with
an outlaw past and a widow with a young son to
protect. She could never share a life with a wanted
criminal. And even if she *were* willing to make such
a sacrifice to be with Jake, she couldn't condemn
her son to such an existence.

Chapter 13

❧

The nearest train station was located in Denver, but after having a word with her foreman, Caitlin drove into Greenbriar that same morning to check the departure schedules for the Kansas Pacific. She sent a telegram requesting a reserved seat on the train, arranging to leave the day after next from Denver. Then she completed a few errands and picked up some supplies for the ranch at the general store.

The talk at the store was all about the wounded stranger. Word had traveled like lightning about the patrol's run-in with Lew Alderson, and Jake's acquaintance with him.

"Was that man really a member of the gang Jake used to ride with?" Sarah Baxter asked Caitlin the moment she walked in.

Caitlin forced her eyes to widen innocently. "Whatever gave you that idea?"

Sarah gestured at the old-timers sitting around the cracker barrel in the rear corner. "They're saying he was hiding out from the law."

One of the old men called out to her, "Heard tell that fella stuck up a bank t'other day, an' Jake helped 'im get away."

Caitlin made herself laugh. "You can't believe Jake McCord would help a criminal when he's just been made a deputy. No, the real story is that man was just a cowboy down on his luck. He and Jake worked at the same outfit a few years ago. Texas, I think it was."

When the old-timer nodded slowly, Caitlin breathed easier. It irked her, being forced to defend Jake when she herself had doubts about his innocence, but she meant to keep both her knowledge and her suspicions to herself. Aiding and abetting an outlaw would threaten Jake's newfound status in the community, even with these staunchly loyal cattlemen.

She clung to her resentment all during the drive home, though. Cursing him at least kept her from dwelling on her despair over his refusing to sever ties to his lawless past, and the savage pain of leaving him.

She had nearly reached the ranch yard when Caitlin drew back sharply on the reins, abruptly slowing the buggy. Even from a distance, she recognized the tall, lean cowboy waiting for her. His arms crossed over his muscular chest, Jake was lounging against the hitching rail by the back porch, two saddled horses beside him.

Caitlin snapped the reins and sent the buggy lurching forward, saying in a tight voice as she halted the vehicle beside him, "I believe I told you I never wanted to see you again."

"I returned your horse."

Her despairing gaze searched Jake's. "You helped him get away, didn't you." It wasn't a question.

"I sent Alderson on his way, yeah."

"Then I have nothing to say to you."

"Well, I have something to say to you." Jake tipped his hat back, giving her a view of narrowed green eyes. "I hear you mean to leave Colorado."

Caitlin regarded him cautiously, surprised as she was wary. "How did you find out?"

Jake shrugged. "Word gets around. Isn't there something you're forgetting, though?"

"What's that?"

"Me."

The word was soft, lazy . . . menacing.

"You know I always meant to return to St. Louis," Caitlin said defensively.

Slowly Jake pushed off from the rail. He'd heard about Caitlin's impending flight from one of his ranch hands, who'd heard it from one of hers. The news had left him raw, exposed, bleeding as if he'd been gutshot. He'd thought he'd have more time.

Now he was desperate.

Toughening his heart, roughening his voice, he reached a hand up to her. "Let's go. I have your things packed."

"Go? Go where?" Her gaze shifted to his horses, one of which was the chestnut she'd loaned him. Both saddles were loaded with bedrolls and other gear. Her carpetbag hung from one of the saddle-horns. "What things?"

For a brief instant, Jake's mouth twisted in a smile. "I didn't include a nightdress—I figured you wouldn't be needing one. But I brought your coat. It gets cold at night where we're going."

"What are you talking about?" Caitlin asked, bewildered.

To her shock, Jake casually reached down and drew out his Colt six-shooter, aiming the muzzle at her.

Her heart gave a violent leap. "W-What are you doing?"

"What does it look like?"

"It looks like a holdup," she snapped.

"Now why would you think that?"

"I saw the wanted poster, Jake. The one from New Mexico that says you murdered a bank teller."

Something flickered in his eyes—a dark emotion that looked like pain—but his intense gaze never wavered. "If you think I murdered that poor devil, then you know I don't mind using this gun."

"You mean to *shoot* me?"

"Not if I don't have to."

The sudden hint of amusement that crept into his eyes made Caitlin bristle. "Damn you, Jake! This isn't at all funny."

"I know. It's not a holdup either, Cat. I'm arresting you."

"You're *what*?" She stared at him. "What in God's name for?"

"I don't know yet precisely, but I'll think of something."

"You don't *know*—" she sputtered in disbelief.

"Come on, get down. You're coming with me."

"Have you lost your mind? I'm not going anywhere with you!"

"Sure you are." He waved his gun, gesturing for her to step down from the buggy.

Caitlin felt her rage rising. "You are *not* going to abduct me in broad daylight."

"It's not an abduction, precisely."

"No?" Her voice dripped scorn. "What do *you* call forcing me to accompany you—at gunpoint, no less?"

"I told you, I'm putting you under arrest." He

patted the silver star on his chest. "Being a deputy has its advantages."

"Like using the law for your own foul purposes?"

"Yep, like that."

Her look was murderous. When he chuckled, she could have shot him. "Jake, if you go through with this, I swear I'll . . . I'll see you hang!"

"Well then . . ." To her alarm and complete dismay, he holstered his revolver and climbed up beside her in the buggy. "What's the old saw? I might as well be hanged for a sheep as a lamb."

Catching her around the waist, he bent his head and captured her resisting mouth with his.

At his brazen assault, Caitlin made an explosive sound of rage and shoved furiously at his chest, but Jake only held her more tightly, refusing to release her. Her blood began to boil at his audacity. He was kissing her in public where any one of her ranch hands could see. And the way he was doing it was scandalous . . . one hand on her hip, the other covering her breast, while he used his tongue in the most blatant imitation of copulation.

It was seductive, sensual, overwhelming, but Caitlin was determined not to relent. She was still struggling in his arms when Jake drew away.

"Stop fighting me, Cat," he murmured huskily.

Instead of obeying, she slapped him. Hard. "How dare you touch me like that!"

Rubbing his offended cheek, Jake grinned ruefully. "It wasn't anything I haven't done a hundred times before."

"Not in public, you haven't!"

"Sheathe your claws, hellcat, and listen to me."

"Why in blazes should I?"

"Because I'm not going to give up until you do. And you don't want to create a scene that would lead to questions you don't want asked."

Seething, Caitlin fell silent, knowing she had little choice. Jake's implied threat to expose their relationship was one more of his despicable acts of blackmail, but she dared not risk challenging him. Jake was accustomed to taking what he wanted, and he obviously intended to get his way this time.

"All right," she muttered. "I'm listening. What do you want?"

"I want you to come with me."

"Why?"

"Because you need to realize what you'll be missing if you leave Colorado . . . if you leave me."

Suddenly breathless, Caitlin stared at him. "What are you talking about?"

"I mean to show you the life we could have together. As husband and wife."

She felt a surge of panic rising within her. She didn't want to know what it would be like, living with Jake as his wife. She'd spent four years trying to banish that dream from her heart.

"No," she whispered, fighting the fierce urge to give in.

His green eyes were very bright. "I'll make a deal with you, Caitlin. Stay with me for a week. Then, if you still insist on leaving, I won't try to stop you. Hell, I'll even drive you to Denver myself."

She bit her lip, refusing to respond.

"Cat . . . if I can't convince you in a week's time that I'm the only man for you, I swear . . . I'll leave your life forever."

"I . . . I couldn't possibly do something so scandalous."

"No one will have to know about it."

"I still can't."

"Sure you can. It's only for a week."

"One week?"

"One."

"And then you'll leave me alone forever?"

"I swear it."

She searched his hard, handsome features, her thoughts whirling. Could she trust Jake to keep his word? Could she possibly manage to keep her heart safe for that long? His "deal" was a ploy to keep her from leaving, true, but could she afford not to go along with Jake? What outrageous stunt would he pull next if she didn't?

Don't do it, she chastised herself. *Don't even think it.*

Yet an anguished voice within her pleaded to be heard. *You don't want to pass up this chance. You can't.* Jake was offering a week of heaven, when she had only a bleak existence to look forward to once she left . . . years of loneliness. She would have to spend the rest of her life without him, never knowing the joy of waking beside him each morning, of falling asleep in his arms each night.

And it was only for one week. Was that too much to ask?

Fool. You'll only be setting yourself up for worse hurt. Besides, what kind of wanton creature would live in sin with a man—a lawless gunman wanted for murder, at that?

Squeezing her eyes shut, Caitlin tried to ignore the restless streak calling to her, urging her on, arguing with her conscience. Didn't she deserve a small taste of happiness? For four years she'd led an exemplary life, taking on her responsibilities without complaint. And the truth was, she would rather cut out her heart than leave Jake now. He was offering her a reprieve—

No, she was mad to even think of accepting. Those dreams were dead.

Husband and wife.

"I've already reserved a seat on the train," she said lamely.

"There'll be other trains."

Distracted, she was scarcely aware when Jake leaned forward to kiss her gently. "Come with me, Cat," he whispered, pulling her dewy lower lip between his teeth and nipping at the soft flesh.

She drew back, not trusting herself to be so close. She opened her mouth to refuse . . . and was faintly shocked to hear herself agreeing. "All right, damn you. One week. And then I'm going back to St. Louis, no matter what."

Jake gave her a grin that made him look all boy, all man. "I thought you'd see it my way."

When he turned to climb down, she caught his arm. "Not so fast. There are conditions."

"What conditions?" he asked warily.

"You'll keep your hands totally to yourself, for one."

"That won't be living like husband and wife."

"Then I'm not going." Caitlin folded her arms across her chest mutinously.

"Okay. I won't touch you." Jake grinned. "Not unless you want me to."

"Jake, I mean it—"

"I said okay. I promise."

"And you aren't to keep harassing me and trying to wear me down."

"It's a deal. I won't say a word. Come on, let's go. We're wasting time."

"This is insane," Caitlin muttered as he helped her down from the buggy. She followed Jake to the horses, but then stopped abruptly. "Wait! I can't just ride off. I have to tell someone—"

"I left a message with your foreman. Said you

would be visiting some friends and would be back next week."

"You *what*?" The arrogance of the man, thinking he could make such decisions for her! "You were pretty darn sure of yourself, I'd say."

Ignoring her bristling look, Jake tossed her into the saddle. "You're right. You'd better talk to your foreman yourself before we leave. Confirm that you're going of your own free will. He's likely to send a posse out after me, otherwise."

"Where are you taking me?"

"You'll know soon enough."

"Jake . . ." Caitlin said warningly.

"Up into the mountains. You'll love it there. Sloan will know how to find us if anything comes up."

Only slightly mollified, Caitlin shook her head. "Maybe so, but I'm telling you, Jake, I won't change my mind about going back to St. Louis."

We'll see, Jake murmured silently to himself— and prayed to God he *could* make her see.

They rode for hours, traveling west and south through the foothills of the Rockies, following a rugged, little-used path, steadily climbing. The scenery was spectacular, even before they reached the higher elevations. Lofty peaks, jeweled meadows, and deep canyons created a grandeur that was changeless, imperial, timeless. The magnificence took Caitlin's breath away, despite the increasing danger of the terrain.

"You can't tell me they have anything like this in St. Louis," Jake said pointedly, watching her when they paused to view one dramatic vista.

Caitlin shook her head in awe.

They negotiated high, precipitous summits, weaved in and out of narrow passageways, between walls of sheer rock, shadowed by rugged cliffs and scarps. Ponderosa pines and scrub oak gave way to towering evergreens; the slopes became cloaked in spruce and fir and thickets of white-trunked aspen.

"God's country," Jake murmured reverently, and she had to agree.

A growing sense of unreality crept over Caitlin as they left civilization farther behind. The dryness and purity of the thin air, the clarity of the azure sky, only added to the enchantment. The sky was a vast vault of blue, the bright sunshine a glittering contrast to the shady, cool depths of the forests they passed. Here and there they came across hidden meadows carpeted with summer's brilliant color—mountain pinks, painter's brush, harebells, and buttercups, as well as delicate columbine— frail, aristocratic, vividly blue.

It was a day of pure magic, and she could almost believe they were the only two people in the world.

Jake, too, became caught up in the beauty, feeling his fear easing with each mile they put behind them. He had gained Caitlin's agreement to stay with him for one week. Maybe by then he could convince her they belonged together. If not ... He didn't want to think about the consequences of failure. But he would have to let her go. He had given his word.

It was almost evening when they arrived at their destination. For some time they'd been riding alongside a swift mountain stream, where willows and alders grew along the banks, and the air had grown cool with the coming dusk. When they came to a clearing, Jake slowed his mount. Caitlin could see a small, rough log cabin nestled in a glade of splendid blue spruce.

Drawing his rifle from its scabbard, Jake rode

cautiously forward. "Wolf?" he called out when he reached the cabin.

Silence met his query.

"He must not be here."

"Who?" Caitlin asked in a whisper.

"A friend of mine. He owns this place, but he doesn't stay here often nowadays. I don't think he'll mind if we use it."

Jake swung down from his horse, choosing not to enlighten Caitlin further, certain she wouldn't appreciate the irony. This was the cabin where he'd recuperated from his wounds after the gunfight that had killed her brother. The place where he hoped he could heal his vast rift with her.

Less eager to dismount, Caitlin remained immobile, aching and stiff after so many unaccustomed hours in a man's saddle.

Jake took full advantage of her hesitation. Reaching up, he lifted her down from her horse, letting her body slide slowly down his . . . bringing back a sharp, poignant memory of how he used to greet her in their secret glen that last, magic summer. Now, as then, Caitlin felt the contact like a sizzle of heat lightning between them.

"Jake . . . you *promised*," she protested breathlessly.

"I know." As soon as he set her on the ground, he held both hands up guilelessly and stepped back, flashing his charming, heart-melting grin. "I won't touch you unless you want me to."

When he turned to climb the two steps to the cabin, Caitlin gazed after him uncertainly. That was precisely what she feared: she badly wanted Jake to touch her. And she wasn't at all confident that her willpower could hold out for long.

Chapter 14

Jake kept his promise not to touch her, at least for the remainder of that evening. Surprisingly, there was no awkwardness between them, and scarcely any strain. They might have been any long-married couple as they worked in companionable silence, sharing chores and settling in.

The cabin was filled with placer miner's gear and layered with dust after standing so long in disuse, so Caitlin spent the first hour sweeping and cleaning, while Jake took care of the horses, unpacked the supplies he'd brought, and fixed supper. They both washed the dishes. Weary from the long ride, then, Caitlin turned in early, claiming the narrow cot as hers and leaving Jake his choice of bedrolls.

That was when the tension began. Regrettably, her mind wouldn't stop working. She kept remembering what it was like to share a bed with Jake— his warmth, his hardness, his passion. She lay awake for hours in the peaceful dark, refusing to glance across the room where he lay alone on the floor, wondering if he was as sleepless with longing as she.

To her continued surprise, Jake kept his hands to himself the entire next morning, without any prompting. He was already up, Caitlin saw when she woke stiff and aching. A cheery fire in the hearth took the chill off the mountain air and gave the cabin a cozy warmth, but she was reluctant to leave the dubious comfort of her bed. She started to roll over—and then groaned in pain.

"What's wrong?" Jake asked, coming over to her.

The muscles of her inner thighs were on fire, that was what was wrong. "Too long in the saddle yesterday."

Jake grinned sympathetically. "I know just the cure."

"What?"

"What you need is a good rubdown."

Pitilessly he tugged the covers off her. She had worn one of his shirts to bed since he'd neglected to bring her nightdress, and her legs were completely bare. Jake was reaching for her right thigh when he caught himself. He cleared his throat huskily. "On second thought . . . maybe you better just get up and move around."

Shivering, Caitlin muttered a curse under her breath. She had set the rules, and Jake seemed determined to stick by them: he wouldn't touch her or make love to her unless she wanted him to. But his restraint might prove a worse torment than dealing with his overwhelming passion.

To her further dismay, the companionship she'd enjoyed the night before was nowhere in evidence as they made breakfast. She was all too aware of Jake, even to the point of flinching when he passed her a serving plate.

For a moment of strained silence, Caitlin stood there powerlessly, her eyes locked with his. Their bodies weren't touching, but for her, his proximity was nearly as potent as actual contact. Then his green gaze dropped to her breasts, lingered. Caitlin felt her nipples tighten to sudden painful peaks . . . before Jake deliberately shook his head and turned away, leaving her with a hollow, achy feeling of incompleteness and regret.

Her mood sweetened after breakfast, though. They explored their surroundings, and she discovered a jewellike lake a short distance from the cabin, which was fed by the crystal-clear waters of the stream. Jake found a hook and line in the cabin, and they spent the rest of the morning in lazy harmony, fishing for trout.

Caitlin fried the two fish they caught for lunch, and later, Jake went out back to chop wood, while she prowled the cabin with a growing restlessness.

The situation couldn't last much longer, Caitlin was coming to realize. When she'd agreed to stay here with him, she'd thought she could control her physical desires as long as Jake kept his own lusts to himself. But their relationship could never be just a simple, uncomplicated bond between two friends. Physical intimacy had been too much a part of their past to pretend it didn't exist now.

That lesson was driven home when Jake came in from cutting wood. He had removed his shirt, Caitlin saw with dismay, drawing a sharp breath at the sight of his lean, muscular torso. When she caught the sweet, tangy damp smell of his sweat, the muscles in her body clenched with desire.

Jake intercepted her look and froze. They stared at each other a moment, neither speaking. The tension was back in the air; the need, the want between them, was palpable.

"I'm going to take a swim in the lake and cool off," he muttered huskily.

Caitlin nodded, knowing it wasn't his earlier exertion or even the bright July sunlight that was overheating his blood . . . or hers.

For long moments after Jake left, she paced the floor, every nerve on edge as she battled with herself and her helpless yearning for him. She counted to a thousand. She put up the breakfast dishes they'd left drying on the table. She swept the spotless floor. She needlessly smoothed the blankets on the cot. She picked up the pillow Jake had slept with last night and buried her nose in the softness, catching his masculine scent. . . .

It was then that she gave up the fight. Swearing under her breath, Caitlin let herself out of the cabin and followed the path he'd taken to the lake; she couldn't help herself.

The sun-splashed scene nearly took her breath away . . . the clear, blue, glacial waters . . . the towering evergreens and aspen . . . the man who was her lover.

He was naked . . . gloriously naked and gloriously masculine.

Her mouth went dry. Jake had his back to her as he stood at the water's edge, poised above the rippling surface of the lake as if prepared to dive in again. Streaming wet, his beautiful, lean body glistened in the strong sunlight.

From his sudden stillness, she knew he was keenly aware of her presence.

She moved toward him silently, drawn by a force more primitive and powerful than she could defy.

Water was dripping in rivulets down his smooth, bronzed back, over the seemingly endless rippling of supple muscles, down his shimmering, taut buttocks to his powerful thighs with their dusting of golden hair.

Hardly aware of her actions, Caitlin reached out to touch his beautiful bare body, caressing the broad, wet expanse of his back . . . trailing lower over the slick, silken skin . . . lightly brushing the tightly contracted buttocks . . .

"Cat . . ." Jake muttered hoarsely as he slowly turned to face her. "What in hell are you doing?"

She was making love to him, that was what. She was foolishly surrendering to her wanton desires.

She'd lost the struggle with herself. It didn't matter how many times she told herself she had no future with this man, that her heart would only break in smaller, more painful pieces when she had to leave him. She had only a short time left with Jake—precious little time—and she wanted to make the most of every remaining minute.

His eyes were very green as he stared down at her; his bare body was stunningly beautiful. Sunlight glistened on wet, bronzed skin, turning the glittering beads of water that clung to him to golden diamonds. Caitlin wanted, needed, to feel that magnificent, jeweled body against hers.

Wordlessly she raised her mouth to his, craving to feed her hunger for him.

To her surprise, Jake responded coolly to the pressure of her lips. For some frustratingly unfathomable reason he seemed to be holding back, resisting her. She recognized the deliberate, almost-studied sensuality of his openmouthed kiss.

She drew back to eye him doubtfully. "Is something wrong?"

"You made me swear I wouldn't touch you."

"Well, I made no such promise," Caitlin retorted lightly.

Deliberately she trailed her hand down his lean,

furred chest, over his flat belly to his groin. When her fingers closed over him, the thick length surged in her hand. Jake shuddered, his lean hips rocking against her.

"What's wrong, Jake?" she taunted softly. "Are you losing control?"

"Dammit, Cat, I'm not made of iron."

She smiled softly. "Good. I was beginning to wonder."

His erection was enormous, throbbing, burning hot, and quivering in her hand. She wanted to taste it, to drive Jake mad with lust the way he always did her.

Sinking to her knees before him, Caitlin leaned close and kissed the hard, velvety smooth shaft of his flesh. When Jake made a rough sound deep in his throat, she gave a feline smile and traced the pulsing length of his manhood deliberately, delicately, with her tongue.

"Cat," he said hoarsely, warningly, his face contorted with pleasure and pain. "You're going to get more than you bargained for."

In answer, she closed her lips around him and sucked gently.

Jake groaned, his muscles contracting with desire. The hot feel of her mouth was driving him insane. He gritted his teeth, but the sweetness of her slowly stroking tongue destroyed any remnants of his shaking control.

Suddenly he couldn't wait any longer. Roughly clutching her shoulders, he sank to his knees before her and pushed Caitlin back to lie on a patch of grass. Shoving up her skirts, her ripped the slit in her linen drawers to give him greater access and, with a suddenness that made her gasp, thrust into her.

Striving to catch her breath, Caitlin gazed up at

Jake in triumph. His eyes were fierce, his face so hard and intent that he looked brutal, but that was exactly what she wanted . . . Jake hungry, shaking, helpless with desire, with need for her. Deliberately she rocked her hips against him.

He lost all his vaunted control then. With the greediness of a man dying of thirst, he seized her hips with feverish hands and plunged deep into her, again and again.

He rode her hard, groaning out his need, oblivious to whether she was deriving any pleasure from their savage coupling. But Caitlin became just as caught up in his frantic urgency. Reveling in the power of his body as he drove into her, she thrashed wantonly beneath him, the pleasure so intense, she sobbed with it. Matching his frenzied abandon, she clawed at his back, convulsing in a shattering climax just as Jake exploded. A hoarse, primitive cry burst from his throat as he furiously pumped his seed into her, in a bonding fierce beyond anything he had ever known.

Stunned by the force of his violent release, his entire body vibrating from the aftershocks, Jake collapsed on her, panting in exhaustion.

"No," Caitlin murmured weakly when at last she could speak, "I don't think you're made of iron."

He chuckled helplessly, but it was a long while before he found the energy to raise his head. As he gazed down at her, her eyelids fluttered open, and she smiled languidly.

He felt his heart contract. He would always remember Cat this way . . . her blue eyes soft with desire . . . her ebony hair streaming across her beautiful, passion-flushed face . . . If he had to lose her, this image would stay with him always. If he lost her . . .

Refusing to even consider the unthinkable, determined to focus only on the present, Jake lowered his head to taste her lips, kissing her with a tenderness as devastating as the wild loving had been, while his fingers went to the top buttons of her shirtwaist. Needing desperately to feel her naked warmth against him, he began to undress her, the way he should have the first time.

Caitlin had given up her absurd demand for celibacy, and he was damned well going to make use of it. His body still hungered with a fierce ache that passion hadn't been able to sate. His heart still hungered with a deep need only she could fill.

The week was magical and bittersweet for them both. They played and worked, they laughed and fought, they made love with a searing sensuality that became more intense with time. They were young lovers again, savoring, remembering, experiencing the sweet thrill all anew, rapt with the rare, fierce splendor they'd found. Their mountain hideaway became their own special world, where nothing mattered but the moment.

They spent hours tangled together in heated passion and in simple pursuits. The enforced intimacy drew them closer together, even though their lovemaking was underlaid with a hint of desperation. By tacit agreement, they avoided the difficult subject of their relationship and Caitlin's impending departure from Colorado. And yet she was achingly aware this might be the last time they would ever be together.

Caitlin wished it could last forever. They marked the passage of time with quiet moments of beauty: a glorious sunset, the brilliance of a clear, Rocky Mountain dawn, a magnificent night with stars blazing in a cool, deep sky.

Jake touched her however and whenever he

liked, and he liked it often. He sated himself with her, yet never felt as if he had enough. Instead of abating, the hunger only intensified. She was a wildcat in bed as well as out, giving as fiercely as she took, but his greatest pleasure was making her take more, feeling her shivering around his hardness while he murmured raw, sexual things in her ear, urging her on, higher and higher, till he felt her shattering release deep inside.

To Caitlin's sorrow and dismay, the magical interlude only made the decision to leave him a thousand times harder. Jake had succeeded in his aim, damn him. After this she wasn't certain she could ever find the strength of will to walk away. If things were different . . . but they weren't.

They didn't speak of their relationship except once, by accident, after a particularly exhausting bout of lovemaking while they lay tangled together on the narrow rope bed.

"God, what you do to me. . . . " Jake rasped as his lips nuzzled her flushed face. "You drive me crazy, you know that?"

"Mmmm," Caitlin murmured weakly. "Crazy with lust."

His features suddenly growing serious, Jake slowly raised himself up on one elbow. "It's a lot more than lust, and you know it."

When she averted her gaze, not replying, he said with quiet insistence, "You know it is, Cat."

"Do I? You want me, Jake, but you don't really love me."

"The hell I don't." His eyes narrowed. "Why do you think I've been acting like such a damn fool over you for the past several weeks?"

She stared back at him uncertainly. This was the first time Jake had ever admitted it to her directly. "You . . . love me?"

"Didn't I just say so?"

"No, you didn't just say so!" she retorted in exasperation. "Not in so many words. You never have."

"Well, it's true." Jake smiled down at her flashing blue eyes. He'd thought she knew what he felt. He hadn't realized he needed to explain, to express this feeling that filled his heart to bursting.

He reached up to touch her cheek with the back of his knuckles, a gesture as possessive as it was gentle. "Don't tell me you couldn't tell."

Caitlin briefly close her eyes. She could feel it, the love in his touch. "Maybe, but . . . a woman likes to hear the words."

He lowered his head and gave her a swift, hard kiss. "Caitlin Kingsly, I love you . . . I love you like crazy. And I very much want you to be my wife. There, is that good enough?"

When she didn't respond, Jake stroked her silky arm tenderly. "I think you love me, too, Cat."

She gave him a troubled look, and to her horror, felt her eyes blurring with tears.

"Now what's wrong? What the hell have I said?"

Mutely she shook her head. For years she'd longed to hear those simple words from Jake, but it only made her dilemma worse.

Her heart twisted in anguish as she searched his hard, handsome face. Was love enough? Caitlin wondered. His loving her couldn't change the stark truth—that a man with his lawless past would be the worst possible father for her child.

When he bent to kiss her again, she flinched. "Don't . . ."

"You're still afraid of me," Jake said slowly as he drew back.

"No, I'm not."

His soul-destroying green eyes captured and

held hers. "You are. You're terrified of what I make you feel."

With great effort, Caitlin tore her gaze away. "I'm afraid of your past. Of the violence."

Absently fingering a lock of her raven hair, Jake gave a sigh. "I can't change the past, Cat. Only the future." He paused. "You could help me. I need you, Cat—have you thought of that? I need you to keep me on the straight and narrow."

"You need me?" she whispered.

"More than I've ever needed anyone in my life," he replied softly.

Caitlin squeezed her eyes shut. She needed him, too. She wanted this man, all of him, for always.

"I want to be with you, Caitlin. And I think you want to be with me."

"If only it were that simple."

"It *is* that simple."

Was it? Caitlin wondered despairingly, her eyes searching his for the answers. Which would be worse? To live without Jake? Or live with him and risk endangering her son?

That conversation gave her more food for thought than she ever wanted during their final days at the cabin, and filled her with burgeoning hope. Here in this magical place it was easy to believe that the future would work itself out, that all her fears and misgivings were unfounded.

The issue came up again, late one evening. They had walked to the lake to sit on the shore and were wrapped in a blanket, watching the light from a brilliant moon shimmer on the placid surface. Snuggled in Jake's arms, Caitlin felt filled with a profound peace.

"It should always be like this," Jake murmured, his tone wistful.

"Yes," she agreed, leaning back against him, savoring his warmth.

Silently he caught her hand, interlacing his fingers with hers.

A moment later he said more quietly, "I used to do this down in New Mexico . . . lie outside and stare at the moon. I'd think about home and all I was missing."

At his unexpected admission, Caitlin felt a sudden ache well up in her throat. "I'm sorry, Jake," she whispered. "For what my father did to you."

She felt his slight shrug. "My biggest regret is that I wasn't around when my pa died. I never got to say good-bye to him. It was months before I even got word he was gone."

She heard the quiet grief in his tone, and realized Jake had never really talked about what had happened to him during all those years. Maybe he needed to talk . . .

"It must have been hard, being cut off from everyone you knew," she said softly. "You must have had other regrets, too."

"The worst part was being hunted like an animal." His voice sounded distant, bitter. "I remember once . . . there was this bounty hunter after me. I couldn't shake him. He dogged my trail across the whole New Mexico Territory. He was about to put a bullet in my back when . . . when Alderson stopped him."

She understood Jake's brief hesitation. He hadn't wanted to remind her of his outlaw friend, or the conflict Alderson's unexpected appearance had created between them. But now that he had, she couldn't simply forget about it. It was several moments later, though, before Caitlin found the courage to broach a subject she desperately wanted to know about.

"May I ask you a question?" she said quietly, turning her head to look back at him.

"If you want."

"Why did you join that outlaw gang?"

Drawing away a little, Jake gave her a sharp glance, wondering if she wanted the truth. Wondering if *he* even knew the truth. Or if he could express it in terms that would make sense to her. The layers of bitter reserve he'd built up over the years were hard to overcome, even with Cat.

Finally Jake sighed. "Several reasons, I guess. Mainly because I was a damned fool." He gave a humorless laugh. "I guess you could say I was rebelling against fate. I'd already been branded a murderer with a price on my head. It didn't seem to matter anymore what I did. And I figured there was safety in numbers. By then I'd had my fill of men hunting me down like a wild animal. It felt safer, riding with others who were on the run." He hesitated, his voice dropping to a murmur. "I know now it was the biggest mistake of my life."

"What made you leave?"

Jake gazed off in the distance, at a high mountain peak that was silvered by moonlight. "One day I just woke up to what I was doing. I wasn't a criminal, and I didn't want to live like one. And then . . . there was you." Jake turned to look at her, his eyes dark and intent. "I knew I couldn't face you if I kept up that life. I'm not excusing what I did, Cat. It was wrong. But that part of my life is over. And I'm not looking back."

Her throat aching with tears, Caitlin fell silent, contemplating what he'd said. She felt like crying. "What . . . about that wanted poster I saw? It s-said you killed a bank teller during a holdup."

The quiet question was like a knife twisting in his gut. "You think I'm a murderer?"

"N-No . . . but you might have had to shoot him . . . to get away . . . just like when you had to kill that boy."

Jake felt his jaw clench, but he remained stubbornly silent. Maybe he was a damned fool, but he shouldn't have to prove his innocence to Cat. She should love him enough to take him on faith.

Catching her chin, he made her look at him, willing her to believe him. "I'm not a murderer, Cat."

"I . . . I kn-know that."

"I would never do anything to hurt you. Or your son, either."

She didn't pull away, but neither did she answer.

"Can't you trust me?"

"It's . . . not a matter of trust—"

"Isn't it?" Jake demanded, his tone holding an edge of anger.

"Please . . . let's not fight."

Jake was the one to look away this time. Caitlin heard him take a deep breath, as if striving for control. "I don't want to fight, either," he murmured finally, pulling her to lean against him.

She gave a sigh as she felt him press his mouth against her hair. It wasn't a matter of whether she trusted Jake. She did. But was she willing to risk the danger simply so she could be with him?

But perhaps there was another way. . . .

"Jake . . . what if you were to come with me . . . to St. Louis?"

"You mean live there with you?"

"Yes. You could start a new life there—"

"I told you, Cat. I'm through running."

"It wouldn't be running exactly."

His tone was grave when he replied, "You think it's fair to ask me to leave my home again?" When she didn't answer, Jake added quietly, "I want permanence after so many years as a fugitive, Cat. I want a place to call my own."

"I understand that," she said, trying to keep the frustration from her voice, "but you could have a place in St. Louis."

"Not like here. My roots are here, and so are yours, whether you admit it or not. Besides, I don't know anything about big-city living. I couldn't support you in St. Louis."

"I still have my teaching job. It isn't much, but after I sell the ranch, we could take the money and invest it in another business for you. Or we could buy another ranch somewhere else—"

She felt Jake go rigid. "I'll freeze in hell," he vowed, his voice soft and deadly, "before I'll live on Adam Kingsly's money."

"I'm sorry. It was a stupid idea. All right then, maybe you could sell your interest in your family's ranch."

"Not without leaving Sloan in a bind. He couldn't come up with the cash to buy me out without selling off a good part of our herd."

"Are you just trying to be difficult? Are you so stubborn you won't even consider moving back East with me?"

Jake sighed. "If I thought that was the answer, Cat, I'd live with you anywhere you wanted. But my past could catch up with me in St. Louis, or anywhere else, have you thought of that?"

Caitlin fell silent, realizing he was right. Moving to another state wouldn't prevent the very thing she feared most: that Jake's past would always be a danger to her son.

She was still struggling with the same tormenting questions at the end of their agreed-upon week. On Saturday, the last morning of their enforced intimacy, she awoke to the feel of Jake's hard arms curving around her body and a deep ache in her heart. After today they would be back among civilization, and she would have to choose between Jake and her son.

Caitlin shivered.

Almost at once she felt Jake's strong arms tighten around her while his lean, hair-dusted thighs brushed hers from behind.

"Cold?" he murmured in a raspy, early-morning voice. "I'll get you warm."

The stubble on his jaw scraped the tender skin of her nape and set it tingling as he pressed closer, stroking the velvet-sheathed hardness of his morning arousal against her yielding bottom.

"Jake . . . no." Caitlin took a deep breath and forced herself to say what must be said. "Jake . . . I want you to take me back."

"Back where?"

"To my ranch."

He went totally still. "You're returning to St. Louis." His voice was low, without inflection.

"I . . . don't know. I haven't made up my mind. I can't make such a decision . . . not here. I can't think when you're near."

"Maybe that's not such a bad thing, you not thinking so much."

"No, Jake. I have to go. I need time . . . time alone. I'm not the only one involved in this decision. There's my son to consider."

Caitlin held her breath, wondering if Jake would argue and try to convince her she was wrong to put Ryan's needs ahead of her own.

For a dozen heartbeats, he remained silent. She could feel his heat at her back, seducing her, melting her fears—which was much of the trouble. Jake's protective arms made her feel safe and cherished, made her forget how dangerous the world around them was. Once she was away from him, though, perhaps her sanity would return—

They both heard the slow tread of bootheels on the steps outside the cabin. The noise was muted, but after so many days of being alone, it sounded as loud as a gunshot.

Alarmed, Caitlin clutched the covers to her naked breasts, while Jake reacted even more swiftly, lunging for the six-shooter he kept beside the bed.

He swung the gun in the direction of the entrance, cocking the hammer, just as the door creaked open.

A man stood on the threshold, his stance quiet but watchful, the alert silence of a wild animal.

"Wolf . . ." Jake said in a voice thick with relief. "Jesus, were you trying to turn my hair gray?"

Her heart pounding, Caitlin stared at the intruder. His striking features were almost beautiful—the high cheekbones and forehead and sharp, chiseled nose bearing strong evidence of Indian blood. His raven hair and bronzed skin looked Indian, too, though he was dressed as a white. His eyes, black as midnight, held an intentness that seemed almost dangerous as he regarded the revolver pointed at his chest.

Shaking his head, Jake lowered the gun and gently released the hammer.

The striking features seemed to relax. The stranger's look was curious as it shifted from Jake to Caitlin, the black eyes speculative. "Am I interrupting anything?"

Jake muttered an expletive. "Wolf . . . I know this is your place, but would you kindly get the hell out of here?"

A slow grin curved the chiseled mouth, while a gleam of amusement lit the black eyes, making Caitlin want to bury her head beneath the covers. "I reckon I could. You want to introduce me to the lady first?"

Chapter 15

It was several hours later when Caitlin found herself alone in the cabin, packing what few belongings she'd brought with her in preparation for the trip home. Jake and his friend, Wolf Logan, had disappeared together—where, she wasn't certain.

She wasn't startled as badly this time, though, when Wolf entered the cabin, for he rapped first on the door and waited for her to call "Come in." She was fully clothed this time as well, but being alone with a Cheyenne half-breed in so confined a space unsettled her. Wolf looked a little savage with his dark, piercing eyes and bronzed complexion and long, shining hair, even though he wore the familiar clothing of a workingman—leather vest and chambray shirt and denim trousers.

"Where's Jake?" she asked somewhat nervously as Wolf dropped his gear on the table.

"Seeing to the horses." When the half-breed caught her eyeing him, one corner of his mouth curved wryly. "You don't have to worry that I'll attack you and steal your scalp, Mrs. Hughes. Despite appearances, I'm well acquainted with the white man's ways, and my manners are at least as good as Jake's.''

Ashamed by her suspicions, Caitlin felt herself flushing. "I'm sorry. I haven't met many people of . . .''

"Indian blood? Most whites haven't.''

She cleared her throat. "I'd like to thank you for the use of your cabin, Mr. Logan.''

"Call me Wolf. And don't mention it. Jake's a good friend, as well as family. His brother married my half sister.''

"Sloan McCord married your sister?''

"Yep. They met while Sleeping Doe was keeping house for me. I brought her here to get her off that pigsty of a reservation where the government keeps the last of the Southern Cheyennes penned.'' An edge of hardness had crept into Wolf's voice. "I never figured she would die at a white man's hands anyway.''

When he gave Caitlin a narrowed look from his penetrating black eyes, she turned away, ashamed. Her own father was rumored to have murdered Sloan's Cheyenne wife, Caitlin remembered. Did Wolf blame *her* for his sister's death?

"I'm terribly sorry about your sister.''

His jaw hardened, but otherwise he didn't reply as he began sorting and unpacking his gear. Caitlin returned to the bed, where she resumed filling her carpetbag.

They worked in silence for a moment, until she suddenly recalled that Wolf had addressed her by her married name. "Jake told you about me?''

"Yeah, he told me. Four years ago, in fact. Couldn't stop talking about you. 'Course, he was half out of his mind with fever at the time.''

Startled, she turned to eye Wolf in surprise.

"You're the man who saved his life," she said slowly, putting the pieces together.

"I dug your brother's bullets out of Jake, yes. He nearly died." Wolf gave her a penetrating look. "He said you didn't believe him when he claimed your brother shot first."

"I . . . I didn't know what to believe," she replied, uncomfortable with the turn of the conversation. "Jake left without a word. And there were witnesses. . . ."

Wolf made a scoffing sound deep in his throat. Although he said nothing further, she felt his unspoken censure as keenly as if he'd called her a traitor outright. And honestly, she couldn't blame him. She should have had more faith in the man she'd professed to love.

"So, what do you believe now?" Wolf asked pointedly.

Caitlin felt a brief moment of sadness as she remembered her brother. "I believe Jake acted in self-defense. That he had no choice."

Wolf's hard features seemed to relax, and he nodded in approval. "Jake got a raw deal from your pa," he observed soberly.

"You seem to know a lot about his affairs."

"We stayed in touch."

"After he recovered from his wounds, you mean?"

"Yeah, afterward."

"I thought Jake headed down to New Mexico Territory."

"He did."

"Did he tell you about what he did all those years?"

Wolf shrugged his lean, muscular shoulders. "Jake doesn't talk much about himself. I guess maybe he just wants to forget that part of his life."

Even so, Caitlin reflected, Wolf evidently knew far more about Jake than she did, which was partly her fault. She hadn't questioned him much about his past. Truthfully, she hadn't wanted to know any more about his life as an outlaw.

But now she did. Intensely.

"Do you know what happened to him afterward?"

"He lay low for a time."

"Jake told me he . . . he became a gunslinger."

"That's right. He learned how to draw mighty fast. He had to in order to fight off bounty hunters. It was either that or be killed."

Caitlin bit her lip. "He wasn't entirely innocent, though. I've seen the wanted posters."

Wolf nodded in agreement. "He wound up in some bad company. Took up with an outlaw gang."

"No one made him join, did they? It was his choice."

"Likely it was. But maybe you shouldn't be so quick to judge him. You don't know what it's like living on the run. Surviving day to day, with a price on your head."

"No," she conceded quietly.

"Seems to me, too, Jake ought to get some credit for wising up. He quit the Dolby gang after a few months. At any rate, he repented."

Caitlin's look grew troubled as she recalled Jake's refusal to disassociate himself from his former outlaw acquaintance. "How can you be so sure he's repented?"

"Call it gut instinct. Or maybe I just trust my eyes. I visited Jake in New Mexico Territory last year. Rode down to tell him his pa had been killed." Wolf gave her a piercing look. "You know what he was doing when I found him? Studying the law."

"The law? What for?"

"He was looking for a way to prove his innocence in your brother's murder. Would a guilty man put any faith in the law?"

Caitlin shook her head. It was hard to think of Jake poring over law books. Then she remembered the legal tomes she'd seen spread out on the desk in Sloan McCord's study. Had those belonged to Jake and not his brother? How much more had Jake neglected to tell her about himself? How much had she neglected to ask?

"Jake's been trying to turn his life around, Mrs. Hughes."

"Please, call me Caitlin," she said absently.

"Okay, Caitlin. I've got one thing I want to say, and then I'll hold my peace. I think you ought to give Jake a chance to prove himself to you."

"That . . . isn't the problem."

"Isn't it? Seems to me you can't get beyond his past."

That much was true, she thought wistfully. "Perhaps not . . . But I'm not certain Jake can get beyond it, either. He's finding it isn't as easy as he thought to walk away from what he's done."

"But he's trying. Okay," Wolf said when she remained silent. "Just answer me this. If Jake was truly bad, would you be here now?"

Unable to meet his piercing gaze, Caitlin looked away. "No." Jake wasn't a bad man, she knew that. He might have done some bad things, either by choice or because he'd been driven to it, but deep down, he had a good heart. She could even admit that for her own self-protection, she'd magnified his sins so she wouldn't have to face this very dilemma. Had she magnified the potential danger, as well?

"You care for him, don't you?"

At the bald question, Caitlin nodded. This past week with Jake had only proven to her how greatly she still cared. She was hopelessly in love with Jake. And now she had to decide what to do about the man who possessed her heart.

"Seems to me he cares for you, too," Wolf mused. "So I don't see what the problem is."

"It's . . . it's my son. How can I give my child an ex-outlaw for a father?"

"Well . . ." Wolf said softly, "if I know Jake, he won't give up easily. He's like my namesake. The wolf mates for life. And Jake thinks of you as his mate."

The sound of bootheels interrupted whatever answer Caitlin might have given. Frustrated to have their conversation cut off, she pretended to be busy with her packing when Jake walked in. Yet he evidently sensed something odd about the silence. He looked from one to the other of them, an eyebrow raised quizzically.

Caitlin was relieved when Wolf asked if the horses were ready.

She wasn't so relieved a short while later, though, when Wolf Logan followed them outside in order to say good-bye. She thought he meant to help her mount, but much to her startlement, he took her hands in his lean, strong ones and stared down at her with his striking dark eyes.

"The Cheyenne have a saying," he said softly. "Only when you understand your heart can you know true peace."

Caitlin gazed back at him a long moment, mesmerized by the intent look in the luminous black depths. Finally managing an uncertain smile, she turned to mount up.

"What was all that about?" Jake asked when they'd said their farewells and had ridden a short distance from the cabin.

"Nothing..." Caitlin murmured, hoping he wouldn't press her.

Thankfully, he didn't. In fact, during the long ride home through rugged terrain, Jake kept silent, pondering his own thoughts. He didn't mention the possibility of Caitlin leaving Colorado, even though it was uppermost on his mind.

This past week had only proved to him beyond a doubt what he'd suspected for weeks. He belonged with her. She was everything he wanted or needed—he, who'd never needed anybody until her. Cat made him remember how to dream, how to hope. With her in his arms, he could vanquish the endless emptiness that had nearly destroyed his soul.

Yet it had to be Caitlin's choice to stay with him. He wanted her to feel as if her life was incomplete without him, because his was empty and bleak without her. Cat had to stay with him because it was right. Because her heart wasn't whole without him.

It wasn't until they were nearly home that Jake finally voiced the question that had kept his guts tied in knots for days, unable to help himself.

"So, are you going to put me out of my misery, hellcat, and let me know what you've decided?"

She gave him a troubled frown. "I haven't decided. I... don't know if I can marry you, Jake, but ... I won't leave Colorado just yet."

His sudden grin was like the sun bursting through the clouds. Then he let out a whoop that startled both their horses. Reaching out to grab her around the waist, Jake hauled her off her horse and onto his lap, his mouth covering hers in a fierce kiss.

"Jake, stop that!" Caitlin ordered breathlessly when she finally was allowed to speak. "Let me go!"

Still grinning, he set her back on her horse obediently, but then he spurred his own mount into a gallop and raced off, waving his hat in the air, only to return and circle around her like a marauding Indian. Shaking her head in exasperation, Caitlin told him to behave or she *would* make up her mind.

She hadn't quite gained her composure from his devastating kiss, though, when she was rudely wrenched back into the real world.

One of the patrols that had been formed to aid the truce met them on the road, armed to the teeth. Jake was instantly all alertness. "What's up, Roy?" he asked the leader.

"A half dozen head of Lee's beeves were shot last night. We're looking for the culprits. Tracks went off this way. You see anybody up in the hills?"

"Sorry, no." Jake's gaze shifted to Lee Hodgekiss, who was eyeing him hostilely, evidently recalling the incident at the Fourth of July picnic-dance where he'd been foolish enough to challenge a skilled gunman.

After a moment, though, the cowboy's gaze skittered away. "This," Hodgekiss muttered sullenly, "is what comes o' gettin' in bed with those stinkin' woolly boys."

The two sheepmen in the patrol stiffened. "Who you calling stinkin'?" one of them demanded.

Roy broke in before tempers grew hotter. "Settle down, boys. Lee's riled about his beeves, and you can't blame him. But for all we know, it could be a cowman trying to commence the feud again. We'll sort it all out." He inclined his head toward Jake. "We could use an extra gun, if you got time to spare."

Jake glanced at Caitlin, who sat her horse, grimly silent. Shaking his head apologetically, he claimed a prior obligation but wished them luck.

He and Caitlin rode on, but both their moods had sobered to the point of moroseness by the time they reached the Kingsly ranch yard. The magic was over. The world of violence and guns, of life-and-death issues, had once more intruded to tarnish their dreams.

Somberly, Caitlin drew her horse to a halt before the back porch, just as the kitchen door opened and a plump, gray-haired woman came bustling out.

"It's about time you got home," Winifred said, wiping her hands on her apron.

Taken aback, Caitlin stared down at the elderly matron in shock. "Aunt Winnie, what on earth are you doing here?"

"I know what *I'm* doing here. I arrived on the train yesterday. Had to drive all the way from Denver by myself, too. The question is, young lady, where have *you* been?"

Caitlin ignored the question as fear struck her heart. "Dear Lord, has something happened to Ryan?"

"No, he's fine. He's inside playing."

"But . . . you weren't supposed to bring him here," she declared, dismounting at once so she could seek out her son. "Didn't you get my telegram?"

"He missed his mother. I figured that was more important than any feud."

"Aunt Winnie . . ." Caitlin had started toward

the house, but she paused to address her aunt. "I *told* you how dangerous it is here."

"Humph, a fine welcome this is, after we came all this way to see you."

Caitlin closed her eyes in dismay. Her headstrong aunt had totally disregarded the telegram warning her *not* to bring Ryan to Colorado. Winnie was Adam Kingsly's sister, and while she was as different from her late brother as sunshine from darkness, she possessed the same stubborn will.

"I'm sorry," Caitlin replied unrepentantly. "Of course you're welcome. It's just that—"

Even as she spoke, a small, ebony-haired missile came hurtling out of the house and down the porch steps, exclaiming in excitement, "Mama, Mama!"

"Ryan, no, be careful, you'll fall!" In an instant, Caitlin had leaped forward and scooped her son into her arms, holding him tightly. His small arms squeezed her neck in a choking hold, but she didn't mind. When he began planting wet, smacking kisses on her face, she laughed in delight and kissed him back.

"Where did you go, Mama? I missed you and missed you."

"Oh, darling, I missed you, too. Dreadfully."

"So this is the fellow," her aunt mused out loud. With a start, Caitlin realized Aunt Winnie was eyeing Jake curiously.

Cold fear suddenly gripped her heart. Dear God, she'd forgotten about Jake. She'd always wondered if this day would come. . . .

"Come on, darling," she whispered in a shaking voice. "Let's go inside." Trembling with unexpected panic, Caitlin turned to mount the porch steps, but Jake's low voice stopped her in midstride.

"Aren't you going to introduce us, Cat?"

For a moment she stood paralyzed, her heart pounding against her ribs. Then, with a hopeless feeling of dread in the pit of her stomach, she turned back slowly, a look akin to fear on her face.

"Th-This . . . is my aunt, Mrs. Winifred Truscott. Aunt Winnie, this is Jake McCord."

Absently Jake tipped his hat to the older woman, but he was frowning down at Caitlin.

"So this little fellow is your son," he said softly.

Ryan pointed a grubby finger at him as he swung a leg over the saddle and dismounted. "Are you a *cowboy*?"

Jake forced a grin as he moved forward. "Sure am. Hello, pardner."

He reached out to grasp the child's small hand, and suddenly froze. Dimples flashing, the boy was beaming innocently up at him. But it was the eyes that startled him beyond speech.

Jake found himself staring into brilliant green eyes the exact shade of his own.

Chapter 16

Jake felt as if he'd been kicked in the gut by a wild bronc. He could remember every word that Caitlin had told him about her son.... *He has my hair and his father's eyes....*

Jake's head whirled, while a single dazed thought roiled in his mind. Stunned, numb with shock, he stared down at the young boy with the bright green gaze so like his own.

His father's eyes.

And Caitlin... she was watching him with a look of fear on her face—as well she should, Jake thought with sudden fury.

"Cat, I want to talk to you. *Now.*" The grim command brooked no argument.

He knows, Caitlin realized, panic still knotting her insides. She wasn't at all prepared to face this just now. "Can't it wait? Ryan and Winnie just got here—"

"No, it can't wait."

Reluctantly, she handed Ryan to her aunt, while Jake stared at the child. Other than the eyes, the resemblance was minor, but he had no doubt the boy was his. He knew it in his gut, a gut that was still churning with shock.

In a shaking voice, Cat was apologizing to Ryan for having to leave so suddenly, telling him not to worry, that she would be right back. She went meekly when Jake's manacle grip took her arm. Without another word, he tossed her up on her horse and mounted his own. For privacy, they rode toward the hills, maintaining a taut, brittle silence all the while.

Once, when Caitlin found the courage to steal a glance at Jake, she quaked at the relentless set of his features. Her stomach felt tied in knots, while guilt and dread warred within her. Jake would never forgive her for keeping such a secret from him. Had she been wrong not to tell him of the child they had made together?

It was almost a relief when they halted their horses in a high meadow and Jake finally spoke.

"Ryan's mine, isn't he." The hoarse demand wasn't a question.

"Jake . . . you d-don't understand—"

"*Dammit*, Cat! Answer me!" Jake's gaze narrowed savagely on her. "Tell me the truth. You said your son was 'almost three,' but he's older than that, isn't he?"

"He's big for his age, but—"

"Goddammit, you've *lied* to me all this time."

She flinched at his savagery, wishing she could deny his accusation. Jake looked angry enough to strike her; his jaw was clenched rigidly while his gloved fingers flexed on the reins as he fought for control. But oh, the pain in his eyes . . .

"He's my son, isn't he?" he asked in a ragged voice.

"Yes," she admitted, her own stricken voice barely audible.

But Jake heard. Shaking his head in dazed disbelief, he swung down from the saddle slowly, unsteadily, feeling as fragile as glass, as if he might shatter if someone so much as touched him.

He stood there with his back to her for a long while. "I never knew," he whispered, shaken.

He had fathered Caitlin's child, a son he'd never even known existed. A son he'd been rabidly jealous of for commanding Cat's love and devotion. It was only by sheerest accident that he'd even laid eyes on Ryan. If her aunt hadn't taken it into her head to bring the boy to Colorado, he might never have discovered the secret Caitlin had kept from him for four, hell-filled years.

He squeezed his eyes shut as a wave of pain and raw betrayal threatened to swamp him. Cat had *lied* to him all this time. . . .

Bewildered, hurt, furious at her deception, Jake abruptly turned to gaze up at her. "*Why*?" he asked in anguish. "Why didn't you tell me? Why did you keep my son from me?"

The rawness in the tormented words raked at her. Unable to bear the savage pain she saw in the green depths, Caitlin looked down at her hands. "I . . . I'm s-sorry, I . . ." She faltered, her voice breaking. Swallowing the savage ache that constricted her throat, she made herself go on. She had to tell him this. Had to make him understand her reasons.

"I'm sorry, J-Jake, truly I am. I didn't want to hurt you, but I had no choice. . . . I was afraid for Ryan. I only wanted to protect him—"

"Protect him from *me*?"

"Y-Yes. . . . " Unheeded, tears began to slip down her cheeks. "Please, can't you try to understand?"

"Right now I only understand one thing." His

features darkened with renewed fury. "Dammit, Cat, you had no right to keep him from me. I missed three years of my son's life! How can you possibly justify that?"

She couldn't hold back a sob. "You weren't *around*, Jake! I thought you had murdered my brother."

"You've known for weeks I was innocent! What the hell kept you from telling me the truth all that time?"

"The . . . the same reason I couldn't m-marry you." She was crying openly now. "I didn't dare risk it, Jake. Ryan needed better than a former outlaw for a father. And then there was your past . . . I was afraid you couldn't renounce the violence, even if you wanted to."

"Damn you, Cat . . . he's my *son*. My flesh and blood."

His hurt reached inside her, tearing at her heart, tormenting her with guilt. She understood what Jake must be feeling. If someone had taken her child from her, she would have been devastated— and she would have lashed out at anyone who stood between them. Jake blamed her for denying him his son. He thought she'd betrayed him, when she'd only been protecting their child. His eyes held such pain that she reached a trembling hand down to him. . . .

But he didn't want her comfort. He couldn't bear it anymore, her nearness. He moved sharply away from her, turning his back to her. Desolation tightened his chest, squeezing his heart like a vise as the full impact hit him: the price he'd paid was greater than he'd ever realized.

"God, to think of the years I've lost," he whispered hoarsely. "I never saw him grow up. . . . "

He wanted to cry out with bitter rage, wanted to

weep. He'd thought hell was the past four years of dark emptiness . . . a rootless, lawless existence that held nothing but blood and violence. But *this* was hell. All this time he'd had a son. Jake felt a deep wrenching inside, a shattering in his soul.

Closing his eyes against the pain, he drew a ragged breath, yet the sob he'd been battling to repress broke free, tearing itself from the depths of his chest.

Caitlin saw his shoulders heave, heard the harsh, choked sound he couldn't hold back, a strong man struggling for control.

Tears rose to strangle her. She felt as shattered as Jake looked. Weeping, aching savagely for him, she slid off her horse and went to him, her fingers hesitantly reaching out to touch his arm. He flinched and jerked his arm away.

"Damn him." The jagged curse trembled with rage, while Jake's hands curled into fists. "Goddamn that bastard. If he wasn't buried in his grave. . . . "

Caitlin squeezed her eyes shut against the grief, knowing he was speaking of her father. Jake had every right to despise Adam Kingsly for the years that had been stolen from him. The loss of his son was only one more cause for bitterness.

Anguish and regret stabbed at her heart, yet she didn't know how to express it, or how to ease the hurt Jake was feeling. Or if he even wanted her to. "Jake . . . I'm sorry," she whispered, her voice low and ragged.

He heaved a shuddering breath. After a moment he raised a hand to cover his eyes, pressing his fingers into the sockets.

"Did your pa know?" he asked finally, the quiet question surprising her.

Roughly wiping at her damp cheeks, she drew a

quivering breath, trying to regain her composure. "That I was pregnant? Yes, he knew. I had to tell him. A month after you disappeared, I realized I was to bear your child. . . . Papa was furious, to say the least."

"He didn't hurt you?" Jake demanded in a dangerous tone, his gaze slicing to her.

"No . . . he never hurt me. He only disowned me and sent me to St. Louis to live with his sister. Aunt Winnie took me in . . . without judging or condemning. She knew the truth, but I . . . I told everyone else I was a widow and invented a last name to protect my reputation and my unborn child's future. My baby was innocent of any sin I might have committed, and he didn't deserve to suffer for it. It . . . it wasn't difficult to pretend my husband had died. You were as good as dead to me anyway. I never expected to see you again."

Jake turned to stare at her, his eyes shadowed. "You were never married?"

"No."

"So . . . you didn't love another man?"

"N-No. There was never . . . anyone but you."

Jake's heart seemed to stop beating at her quiet admission, at the look she gave him. The gaze Caitlin lifted to his was so filled with pain that he took a step toward her. He hadn't considered what she'd been through, how alone and afraid and grieving she must have been. He'd thought only of his own feelings of pain and betrayal. "That portrait I saw of Hughes, the one you keep on your dresser . . ."

"I f-found it in a shop in Denver, but he was just a stranger. I made up a story about him before I ever reached St. Louis. So I could give Ryan a name. So he wouldn't be branded a . . . a bastard."

Jake's jaw clenched reflexively. A moment later,

though, a quiet light of wonder softened his hard features.

"*My* son . . ." he murmured in a hushed undervoice. He startled her by reaching out cautiously to cover her stomach with his palm, pressing almost reverently. "What was it like, having my baby?"

Caitlin forced a tremulous smile as she remembered the difficult labor she'd endured. "It was painful, actually. And miraculous. I couldn't believe I'd given life to this tiny creature. And he was . . . part of you . . ." Fresh tears misted in her eyes as she gazed sorrowfully up at Jake. He'd never known the child of his passion, the child of her heart.

"I should have been there," he whispered. Jake reached up to brush her tear-stained cheek with his fingertips, a tender gesture that tore at her soul.

"I wish you *had* been there."

"Well . . . that's all in the past now. You're going to marry me, just as soon as I can find a preacher."

Caitlin went still, a bleak look suddenly claiming her features. "Jake, I . . . I don't see how that will solve anything."

"What are you talking about?"

"Your . . . past . . . It's still a threat to our son's safety. The violence . . ."

He looked as if she'd struck him. "You can't possibly think of keeping Ryan from me now."

She wanted to back away, not from Jake, but from the pain she'd given him. "I don't want to, but . . . nothing has really changed—"

"The hell it hasn't. I know about my son now."

"Even so, I have to think of what's best for him, don't you see? He'll be safe in St. Louis. . . . "

Jake's jaw hardened. "This isn't negotiable, Cat. My son is going to have my name. I'm his pa, and I won't miss any more time from his life. You're going to marry me, and that's the end of it."

Caitlin drew a shaky breath. It was just like Jake to take that domineering, arrogant tone with her, thinking he could command her to marry him and she would jump to do his bidding. She even understood his urgency, his pain. She *hurt* for him. But that didn't mean she would be rushed into a decision that would be harmful to Ryan. She might love Jake with all her heart, but she couldn't put his needs or her own ahead of their son's.

She cast him a look of entreaty. "There, you see," she said imploringly, "this is just what I was afraid you'd do—ride roughshod over me, regardless of the consequences. That's why I didn't dare tell you the truth about Ryan. Because then you might insist on becoming part of his life—"

"You're damn right, I'll insist! I want my son, and no one's going to keep him from me. You'll either marry me, or I swear to God, Cat, I'll take Ryan and disappear. You'll never see either of us again."

She felt the color drain from her face. Fear ripped through her at his threat—fear and hurt—for she knew Jake meant every word.

Stepping back in alarm, Caitlin clenched her fists. Her blue eyes flashing defensively, she looked every inch the lioness protecting her cub. "If you *dare* harm one hair on Ryan's head," she declared hoarsely, "I swear, Jake, I'll . . . I'll shoot you myself."

He flinched. "Harm him?" Staring back at her, Jake shook his head. "You can't think I'd hurt my own son."

"You just threatened to kidnap him! To steal him away from his own mother."

Jake forced himself to take a deep breath, fought down an angry reply. "Hell, Cat, you know I didn't mean it. I was just afraid of losing Ryan again."

"Well, I'm afraid, too! Afraid for my *son*. You c-can't possibly be concerned with his best interests, or you'd never consider letting him live here, subjecting him to constant danger."

The anger drained from Caitlin's voice then, breaking into a million, tearful pleading pieces. "I k-know you want him, Jake. I know it isn't fair to keep him from you after all you've endured. But you weren't the only one to suffer because of the past. I lost, too. I lost the man who should have been my husband. I had to raise a child alone, and if you think that was easy . . . I lost my brother to a stupid, vicious range war, and my father, too, for that matter. And I'll f-fight hell itself before I allow Ryan to follow in their footsteps!"

With a sob, Caitlin spun on her heel and caught up her horse's reins. Before Jake could stop her, she had dragged herself up into the saddle.

"Cat . . . dammit, wait! I wasn't just thinking of me. I was thinking of Ryan, too. A boy needs a father—"

"I *know*. But not one who will put his life in danger."

Jake ground his teeth, but he stopped short of giving vent to his explosive rage. "Maybe not," he forced himself to say grimly. "But I'll tell you right now, no other man is going to be Ryan's pa but me. You aren't marrying anyone else."

"I don't *want* to marry anyone else!" Caitlin glared at Jake through a blur of tears. "I'm taking Ryan back to St. Louis just as soon as I can arrange it! Maybe we should talk about you coming with us—but I don't have time to discuss this any longer. Right now I need to get back to my son. I haven't seen him in *weeks*, and he misses me. You can come by the house tomorrow—*if* you promise not to say a word to Ryan about being his father. And *if* you leave your guns behind. I won't have my son exposed to the violence that is so much a part of your life. You can become acquainted with him then—as a friend, nothing more. We can talk about our future then."

She jerked on the reins, leaving Jake to stare after her grimly, a dozen savage emotions warring within him. Fury was the strongest: at Cat for keeping such a secret from him and for even thinking of denying him his son now. At himself for voicing threats he didn't mean. Pain was another fierce emotion: anguish at discovering something else so precious had been stolen from him. But there was also disbelief and joy and incredulous wonder.

Shaking his head, Jake closed his eyes and drew a shuddering breath, still dazed by his discovery.

He had a son. A son whose existence he'd never even known about until today.

Chapter 17

"So," Winifred said, "are you going to tell me about this Jake fellow of yours, Caitlin?" Ryan had been put to bed directly after supper and both women were sitting at the kitchen table, sipping coffee.

"Why don't you tell me about what's been happening at home, instead?"

"That can wait till after you come clean."

Caitlin sighed. Aunt Winnie was sweet-natured but iron-willed, and sooner or later she would get her way. "All right. What do you want to know?"

Her blue eyes held a lively curiosity. "Well, first of all . . . are you going to marry him?"

"I don't know. I'm not sure I should."

"Why not? You love him, don't you?"

"Yes."

"Does he love you?"

"He . . . says he does."

"Then that should settle it."

Caitlin shook her head. "Love isn't always enough, Aunt Winnie."

"Well, passion is nice, too," she acknowledged with twinkling frankness. "But your Jake looks like a man who could do quite well in that regard."

Caitlin felt her cheeks flushing. Jake did much better than "well" at passion. She couldn't help remembering how he'd made love to her at this very table, turning her body to molten flame. "That *isn't* what I meant. I was thinking of my son. I have a responsibility to do what's best for Ryan."

"Sure you do, but don't you have a responsibility to yourself, too?"

"What do you mean?"

"Caitlin, you know I'm not one to meddle, but I have to say something before I burst. I think you'll be making a huge mistake if you don't marry that Jake of yours. No"—she held up a hand—"let me finish. Love doesn't come to many of us. I was lucky. When Truss passed away, I thought my heart would break, but eventually I came to realize I should be grateful for the time we had together. We're on this earth too brief a span not to make the most of the chances we're given. And you've been given a second chance with the man you love. Life's too short for you to let that slip away. Think of all those years you could have been with Jake if your father hadn't framed him for murder."

"I know." Her throat aching, Caitlin rose and began clearing away the supper dishes, needing something to do.

"And think of Jake himself. He's Ryan's father. Don't you think he deserves a chance to know his son?"

Caitlin swallowed hard. "I don't want to deprive him of his son, or Ryan of his father, but . . . that doesn't mean a man with Jake's past is the best model for a parent."

"Why not?"

"Why not?" she repeated in exasperation. "I could give you a dozen reasons." Her voice dropped to a low murmur. "You don't know what Jake's done."

"What *has* he done?"

The gaze she turned to her aunt was bleak. "He killed my brother, for one thing. I know he never meant to, but there were others afterward. . . . Jake made his living as a *gunslinger*, Aunt Winnie. He shot a child who accidently got in his way. And he's wanted for killing a bank clerk during a robbery. He ran with an outlaw gang. . . . There might be a dozen more reasons I don't even know about. Is that the kind of man my son needs for his father?"

Winnie pursed her lips thoughtfully. "Ordinarily I'd say no. But if Jake is as wild as you say, maybe you could do him some good. I've always thought a strong woman could change a man if she put her mind to it. I did with Truss. I had to work hard at it, too, let me tell you, but I managed to unearth his finer qualities under that rough exterior. My guess is your Jake has some good traits or you never would have loved him in the first place. Am I right?"

Caitlin gave a murmur of assent. When she'd invented her imaginary husband, she'd patterned him exactly after Jake. The *old* Jake, who'd been gentle and strong and loving, full of devilment and laughter.

"I expect if Jake loves you," Winnie insisted, "he'll change his ways."

Her niece shook her head skeptically. "Even so, how can I be sure his past won't catch up with him? Some of his friends are hardened *criminals*. One of them showed up just the other day, claiming Jake owed him. He was suspected of holding up a bank, but Jake refused even to turn him over to the marshal!"

"Caitlin," Winnie said firmly, "don't get so wound up. Put that skillet down and come sit with me. We can't have a serious talk if you're up to your elbows in dishwater."

In spite of herself, Caitlin smiled wryly. She did as she was told, resuming her place at the table beside her aunt.

Winnie reached out to cover Caitlin's hand with her aging one. "The good Lord never blessed me with children, but He gave me you and Ryan. You've been like a daughter to me. And watching that precious baby grow has been pure joy. I don't want to lose either of you, but I *can't* sit by while you throw away this chance for happiness. My brother, God rest his departed soul, did his best to ruin your life—and Jake's, too. But it doesn't have to stay that way forever."

When Caitlin remained silent, her aunt took another tack. "There's something else you should consider. You don't want Ryan to grow up a mama's boy, do you?"

"No, of course not."

"Well, he might if you don't watch out. A boy needs a father in his life, to teach him how to be a man. Don't you think Ryan deserves that chance?"

"Yes, certainly he does," Caitlin said in frustration, torn between her own heartfelt longings and what she believed was best for her child. "But I'm still not sure Jake would make a suitable father. Maybe it would be best for Ryan if Jake just settles for knowing him from a distance."

"You think that would be good enough? A boy needs someone to show him how to survive, especially out here in the West."

"Perhaps so, but Ryan won't be living here."

"Why not?"

"Because it's too dangerous with the feud. I won't let him stay in Colorado."

"You can't tell me you'd rather live in St. Louis."

"Yes, I can. I've always hated this place—"

"I don't think you really mean that," Winnie stated flatly. "You hate the bloodshed, certainly. But I hear that's ending. And really, you do belong here, Caitlin."

"Why do you say that?"

"Because you were born and bred here. Be honest with yourself. You've never thought of St. Louis as home. I've heard you talk about these mountains. You love it here. Your roots are here, and so are your son's. *This* is your home."

Caitlin turned to gaze wistfully out the window where the setting sun had gilded the rugged hills gold and red. She did love this majestic land. It was part of her, buried deep in her soul. Yet she'd tried not to let herself become reattached to it, not daring to think of having a future here.

She bit her lip. "There's too much violence here. I'm not going to let Ryan be hurt by it," she murmured, but with less conviction than usual. "I plan to take him back to St. Louis as soon as your visit is over."

"I expect your Jake might have a thing or two to say about *that*," Winnie observed dryly.

Caitlin's answering smile was thin. "However did you guess?"

"There's also something else." Her aunt frowned. "If you do go back, you might have another problem."

"What?"

"We haven't had time to discuss it yet, but things haven't been so good for Heather lately. There's been some trouble at the school since you left."

"What sort of trouble?"

"Heather wouldn't say exactly. You know her, she's too proud to admit she needs help. But I'm afraid it has to do with her father's debts and that railroad millionaire who's been after her. The bank's threatening to foreclose on the mortgage, and she's worried she might have to shut down the school. If she does, Caitlin, you wouldn't have a job."

A look of dismay crossed Caitlin's features, not only because of the possibility of losing her teaching position, but because Heather Ashford was a dear friend as well as her employer. "Isn't there something we can do for her?"

"I don't know. Maybe. But my point is that St. Louis isn't the haven you think it is."

"It's safer than Colorado."

Winnie patted her niece's hand. "I can understand you wanting to keep Ryan safe, but it seems to me Jake would be more capable than most at protecting his family."

Caitlin couldn't disagree. There was no one she would rather have on her side in a fight than Jake.

"And I think he would give his life for that boy. I saw the look on his face when he figured out Ryan was his. It was a *hungry* look, Caitlin. Like he'd been given a glimpse of heaven. And Jake *is* Ryan's father. He cares for the boy already, even if they're strangers. You three belong together. You think about that, will you?"

Caitlin nodded solemnly. She'd done nothing but think about it for weeks now, and doubtless she wouldn't stop thinking about it, even after she came to a decision. "I haven't refused Jake outright," she said in a low voice. "In fact, I asked him to come with us, but he wouldn't even consider it. He intends to stay here."

"Because this is his home. Just as it's yours. Now, there . . . I've said my piece," Winnie announced, patting her hand. "I'm going to play your lazy guest for another day and go read in the parlor while you finish the dishes. A privilege of old age. You come join me when you're through."

Caitlin smiled faintly and rose to her feet when Winnie did, impulsively giving her aunt a fierce hug. "You're welcome to be lazy for as long as you like. And whatever happens, Aunt Winnie . . . I'll never forget how good you've always been to me."

"It was the least I could do to make up for that terrible brother of mine. But enough of the past. You just figure out what's most important in your life."

Caitlin finished cleaning up slowly, her thoughts wrapped around Jake and Ryan. Too restless to sit still then, she went to her bedchamber and gazed down at her sleeping child, who was snuggled in the lower right corner of her bed.

Her heart swelling with love, Caitlin straightened the tangled sheet and tenderly brushed back a tousled lock of black hair from Ryan's forehead. He was such an appealing child. His cheeks were flushed with the warmth of the summer's night, and, although they were closed at the moment, his bright, beautiful mischievous eyes so like his father's held a delightful charm that would be the bane of many a female heart when he was older. She loved him more than her own life.

She loved Jake that way, too, Caitlin reflected wistfully.

The question was, was there room for both of them in her future?

She woke early the next morning to the vague sensation that something was wrong. Ryan wasn't lying in bed beside her, nor was he even in the room. More than likely Aunt Winnie was fixing his breakfast in the kitchen, Caitlin knew, but she rose and drew on a wrapper anyway.

The house was quiet, disturbingly so. Aunt Winnie was sound asleep in her bedchamber. Worse, there was no sign of Ryan in the kitchen—or anywhere else in the house, though Caitlin searched every conceivable nook and cranny.

Trying to quell a feeling of panic, she retraced her steps to the kitchen and went outside. A fresh, early-morning breeze teased her unbound hair as she hurried across the yard to the bunkhouse. None of the ranch hands were around; most likely they were all out seeing to chores. But a swift search of all the outbuildings still turned up no sign of her son.

For a moment, Caitlin stood in the yard wringing her hands, feverishly debating what to do, but then she saw a lone horseman down the road, riding toward her at a lope. Her heart gave a leap when she recognized Jake's familiar, lean form. Even in her fear, though, she realized something was different about him. He wasn't wearing his guns.

She stood frozen as he reined to a halt before her. He'd raised an eyebrow at finding her outside in her nightclothes, but her expression must have given her away, for he frowned at once and asked sharply, "What's wrong?"

"It's Ryan . . . I can't find him." There was a note of panic in her voice she couldn't suppress.

"He's not in the house?"

"No. Nor anywhere out here."

Jake's gaze narrowed thoughtfully. "Did you check the barns? Young boys like to play in hay."

"Yes . . . the lofts, the warehouse . . . everywhere. Jake . . . he's not here!"

"Calm down, Cat. We'll find him." He reached a hand down to her. "Climb on. We'll search faster mounted."

Obediently Caitlin let Jake pull her up behind him on his horse. Grateful for his steadying presence, she clutched his waist and hung on tightly. It was only when he headed toward the hills in back of the ranch that she shook herself from her distraught state. "Where are we going?"

"Up there. If I were a kid who'd never seen mountains, that's where I'd go."

It made sense, she thought hopefully.

"Don't worry, Cat. We'll find him, I promise."

The grim edge of determination in his voice reassured her even more than his pledge. Jake had said they would find their son, and she was certain he would move mountains if he had to. Weakly Caitlin pressed her cheek against Jake's muscular back, thinking how comforting it was to have him share her burdens.

They found their son a short while later, twenty yards off the trail in a meadow where a flock of sheep were grazing. He was sitting forlornly on the ground and sobbing, surrounded by three ewes.

Caitlin cried out to him and nearly jumped off the horse, but Jake stopped her by grasping her arm.

"Will you let me do this?" he asked quietly.

She saw the vulnerable, imploring look in his green eyes and nodded.

Jake swung his right leg over the pommel and dropped to the ground. Caitlin watched fretfully, with every motherly instinct screaming. It was all she could do to remain mounted while he casually strode over to his weeping son.

"Hey, pardner," Jake murmured as he hunkered down beside the child. "What are you up to?"

Abruptly, Ryan lunged for Jake's leg and clung for dear life.

Jake rubbed the wailing child's back soothingly and asked, "What's wrong, fella?" even though it was clear the boy was terrified of the sheep. "These woollies bothering you?"

Ryan only crammed his fingers in his mouth and wailed harder.

"They won't hurt you, you know."

After a moment the boy gulped back his sobs and pointed to one of the ewes. "It b-bit m-me."

"Did it, now? You know, I'll bet it nibbled on you, looking for food, but it figured out you didn't taste as good as grass. It really won't hurt you, though. You see, sheep are kinda dumb. In fact, you're a lot smarter than they are."

"It *sceered* m-me," Ryan insisted, though his sobs lessened as he peered around Jake's leg at the ewe.

"I can see why. Yep," Jake agreed, scrutinizing the animal solemnly, "that old lady is so ugly, she would scare a coyote. But I've something to show you that I bet you'll like. Will you come with me?"

When Ryan nodded tentatively, Jake scooped the child up in his arms and strode toward the main flock. Ryan clung fearfully until Jake came to a halt and pointed down.

"Look at that cute little fellow. He's more your size."

A black lamb was chasing a yellow butterfly across the grass. Ryan stared, fascinated.

"He's not so scary, is he? He even looks like you. His coat is curlier than yours but every bit as dark." Jake ruffled the boy's raven hair and earned a hesitant gurgle of laughter. "Maybe we should call him Charcoal. You think that's a good name for him?"

Just then the lamb stopped, spun around, and

ran straight at the man and boy. Impulsively Jake reached down and caught the small animal with one arm and held it up for Ryan to see. The two youngsters stared at each other with wary curiosity.

"Ryan, this is Charcoal. Go ahead, you can pet him. A lamb won't bite. He's probably wondering about you the way you are about him. Be gentle, now."

Cautiously, the child reached out to touch the soft, woolly black head—and jumped in startlement when the lamb gave a bleat. When it began to struggle, Jake set the lamb on the grass and watched as it ran crying for its dam. "See, he wants his mama . . . which reminds me. Your mama's waiting for you. You ready to go back to the house now, pardner?"

The boy nodded, but not eagerly; he was still eyeing the lamb with something akin to wonder.

Shifting his hold, Jake lifted Ryan to ride on his shoulders and headed back toward Caitlin. "What brought you here, by the way? I figure you were curious, is that it?" Jake felt rather than saw Ryan's nod. "You know, you gave your ma a scare, heading up here without telling her where you were going. But I'll bet you won't do that again, will you?"

Ryan shook his raven head emphatically.

"That's good, since you could get hurt up here on your own. It's better to come with a friend. Tell you what, I'll make a deal with you. Anytime you want to go exploring, you just ask me and I'll take you, or we'll find someone who can. Do we have a deal?"

"Uh-huh," Ryan replied, but then called out excitedly, "Mama, I petted a lamb!"

"I know, darling, I saw."

Jake handed the child to Cat, who tried hard not to smother him in a crushing hug or scold him for frightening her out of her wits.

Really, Ryan had never been in any real danger. And Jake had handled the situation adroitly, talking man to man with his son yet making allowances for his childish fears. Truthfully, she was grateful Jake had been there. Without him she would have been hysterical with worry.

She pressed a kiss on the top of Ryan's head, hugging him tightly, and murmured a quiet "thank you" to Jake. Their eyes met in a smile before he turned the horse and began leading it down the trail toward home. Almost at once Ryan's delight over petting the lamb turned to excitement about riding a horse.

Winifred was fixing breakfast in the kitchen when they returned. With the remarkable resilience of children, Ryan immediately began boasting to his Aunt Winnie about his adventures, forgetting entirely how frightened he'd been only a short while before. When he told about meeting Charcoal, Caitlin had to smile at the memory of Jake introducing their son to the lamb. Jake *hated* sheep, and his gentle restraint was an irrefutable sign of the lengths he was willing to go for his son.

Jake stayed for breakfast, and it seemed natural to be sitting around the kitchen table like a family. All during the meal Caitlin watched Jake watching Ryan. He couldn't seem to take his eyes off his son.

And Ryan hung on Jake's every word, even going so far as to copy his actions. If Jake hooked his thumbs in his belt, Ryan did the same. If Jake leaned back in his chair, Ryan followed suit.

It was only when the conversation turned to livestock that Caitlin grew uncomfortable.

"If you like lambs," Jake was saying to Ryan,

"we'll have to show you my ranch. Calves are a lot better than smelly old woollies. You'll have to get to know both so you can decide whether you want to be a cattleman or a sheep man when you grow up."

Stiffening, Caitlin frowned disapprovingly, but Jake merely grinned with roguish mischief, the deep creases in his cheeks reminding her of where her son got his dimples. "Jake . . ." she said warningly. "He's too young to be talking of ranching."

"It's never too young to start." Jake's look was one of pure, devilish charm. "Just watch. I'll make a cattleman of him yet."

"Jake. . . ."

"First he'll have to learn how to ride a cow pony, of course. What do you say, pardner? Would you like me to teach you to ride?"

"Mama, can I?" Ryan jumped up and down in his chair. "Can I ride a pony?"

"May I," she corrected.

"May I, may I?"

"Oh, very well," Caitlin conceded in exasperation at Jake's underhanded tactics, knowing she couldn't possibly deny the child such a treat now.

They spent the entire day together. Caitlin worried that Ryan was becoming too attached to Jake, which would make separation that much harder if they returned to St. Louis alone. And yet father and son seemed so natural together. In fact, Ryan was already well on his way to developing a strong case of hero worship.

And that was *before* his first riding lesson.

Jake took him out to the corral and found a gentle old mare for Ryan to climb on. Wide-eyed with excitement, the young boy listened and obeyed Jake's every word—something he rarely did with her.

Perhaps Aunt Winnie was right, Caitlin thought pensively as she watched them from the back porch. Maybe Ryan *did* need Jake for his father. Perhaps they needed each other. There was already a potent bond between them that couldn't be explained even by blood ties. The tender look in Jake's eyes was . . . loving, there was no other word for it. Loving and gentle. A gentleness sharply at odds with his dangerous reputation.

Despite his lawless past, she knew Jake would be a positive influence on her son. And he could teach Ryan so much more than she ever could, like how to be a man, how not to be afraid of life's trials. She couldn't provide her child with that perspective on life. Unless she married. And even then she couldn't be certain any man would care for Ryan half as much as Jake already did.

She was frowning thoughtfully when Aunt Winnie joined her on the porch.

"You worry too much about that child," Winnie said with her usual perceptive candor.

Caitlin sighed. "I suppose so."

"There's no supposing about it. And it's not good for him, Caitlin. You have to realize you can't keep Ryan tied to your apron strings forever. It's better to start loosening them a bit now. You have to let him grow up, make his own mistakes. You can't live his life for him."

"I . . . I know. But he's so . . . *young*. So defenseless. I just want to keep him safe."

"There's such a thing as smothering a child with love."

Caitlin nodded, knowing her aunt was right about her obsessive fears. She wanted to protect and shelter Ryan the way she never could her brother Neal.

But she would have to get over her phobia. She'd

have to accept the fact that she couldn't be with Ryan every minute of every day, hovering over him possessively. She couldn't keep him wrapped in a cocoon until he grew to manhood. It would do him more harm than good, no matter how much she loved him.

She gave her a wry glance. "I thought you said you didn't like to meddle, Aunt Winnie."

"Well, there's meddling, and then there's *meddling*. And sometimes a hard-headed Kingsly needs a little of the stronger kind."

The two women shared a smile of accord before turning to watch Jake with his son.

Supper was a merry meal. Aunt Winnie just naturally assumed Jake would stay, and without discussion, set a place for him.

Afterward, Ryan delightedly perched on Jake's knee, pretending he was mounted on a horse, while Jake told stories about riding the cattle trail.

Finally, though, the child's acute level of excitement wore him down. When Ryan began nodding off, Jake smiled tenderly. "Come on, pardner. It's bedtime for you."

He tossed Ryan up on his shoulders, which earned a sleepy giggle, and carried him from the kitchen. Caitlin followed with a lamp and watched as Jake tucked Ryan into the same bed where he'd made love to her so passionately only a few short weeks ago.

Sitting on the bed, he brushed back a raven lock of hair and won a drowsy smile. "'Night son."

"'Night, Jake," the young boy mumbled before his eyes fell shut.

Jake joined Caitlin at the door, but turned back to gaze at his son, the look of yearning on his face so strong it was painful to watch.

Caitlin felt her heart turn over. She couldn't possibly think of separating the two of them now. There had to be some other way to keep their son safe. . . .

"No, leave it open," she whispered when Jake began to shut the door. "I want to be able to hear him if he calls out."

"He's a great kid," Jake murmured as he followed her out to the dimly lit hall.

"You were good with him," Caitlin admitted.

"Does that surprise you?"

"I didn't think you knew much about children."

"I don't, but I grew up in houseful of men after my ma died. And I know what it's like to be a boy."

That experience was something else she couldn't give her son, Caitlin reflected silently.

"You're good with him, too," Jake said softly. "Ryan's damned lucky to have a mother like you."

Absurdly she felt herself flushing at the praise. "I suppose I worry too much about him."

"I think maybe you do—but at least now I understand why you're so protective of him. It's something you feel in here about your own kid." He raised a hand to his heart.

Catilin smiled briefly in agreement, but her expession sobered as she gazed up at Jake. "Does that mean you forgive me? For not telling you about Ryan?"

"I wouldn't go *that* far. But I'm trying damn hard, Cat."

"I know you are," she acknowledged, heartened by his light tone.

When she started to turn away, Jake touched her arm, making her stop and look up at him. "I'd like the legal right to worry over him, too, Cat. I want to be his pa for good. I want you to marry me."

An ache rose in her throat. "Jake . . . please . . . I can't make such an enormous decision just yet."

"Okay. . . ." A muscle flexed in his jaw, but then he let out a sigh. "I won't press."

And yet he belied his own words and drew her into his arms. Instantly Caitlin felt a spark of tender desire arcing between them. And from the way his eyes kindled, she could tell Jake felt the same fire.

"I've missed you, wildcat," he murmured huskily.

She'd missed him, too. Keenly. She'd lain awake last night aching for his touch, his warmth.

"I wish like hell I didn't have to go," he admitted. "I wish I could stay here and be your husband and share your bed."

"Jake . . ." When he started to lower his head for a kiss, Caitlin averted her face and glanced over her shoulder at her bedroom door. "We're not alone. Ryan . . . my aunt."

"Your aunt's no prude, Cat. And it won't hurt Ryan to grow up in a house where hugging and touching is natural."

Her mouth curved in a wry smile. "I wouldn't worry if I thought you would *stop* at just hugging and touching."

Jake grinned his boyish, devastating grin, but then his smile slowly faded as he found himself unable to keep up the pretense of nonchalance. His very life hung in the balance.

"Cat . . ." He pressed his forehead against hers and squeezed his eyes shut.

She drew a shaky breath. "Jake . . . I need time."

"Okay, you have it. But Cat . . . I swear my old life is over. You don't have to choose between the two of us. We can work it out somehow."

Chapter 18

❧ ∽○C ❧

Caitlin thought she had time to make a decision. She thought that a careful analysis of the risks and advantages would help her decide the right course. She wanted desperately to believe that marrying Jake would be best for Ryan.

But time ran out the following morning, while her optimism shattered.

Marshal Netherson showed up at the Kingsly ranch just after breakfast with alarming news. Standing at the kitchen door on the back porch, he tipped his hat to Caitlin. "Sorry to bother you, Mrs. Hughes, but have you seen Jake?"

"No, not today. Should I have?"

A troubled frown creased Netherson's brow. "I thought he might be here. Word is he's been spending time out here, courtin' you."

Caitlin had difficultly keeping a flush from her cheeks. "I haven't seen him. Is something wrong, Marshal?"

"I don't know. Maybe. Something's come up he ought to know about. There was a stranger in town last night, asking about him. Man by the name of Ethan Grimes. Seems Grimes is a bounty hunter."

She felt her heart give a lurch. "A b-bounty hunter?"

"I've heard of this particular fella. He's gotten rich off collecting rewards for wanted men. Takes 'em dead or alive . . . but mostly dead. He could be dangerous for Jake."

"Does Jake know?" she demanded as cold fear swept through her.

"Not yet. I called at his place a while ago, but he wasn't home and neither was Sloan. I left word with that housekeeper of theirs, but I'd feel better if I could tell Jake myself."

Drawing a shaky breath, Caitlin raised a hand to her temple, trying to think in the face of her rising panic.

"I understand Grimes rode out to Verne's place last night," the marshal added.

"Vernon Whitfield?" Her voice was a hoarse rasp, while her thoughts spun. Had Vernon sent for a bounty hunter after all? She hadn't seen the schoolteacher in more than a week, not since turning down his marriage proposal and riding off to the mountains with Jake, but he'd *promised* not to take any action regarding the wanted poster with Jake's face on it, the one of the bank robbery in the New Mexico Territory where a clerk had been murdered.

"Thank you for telling me, Marshal," Caitlin murmured weakly. "If Jake comes by, I'll surely let him know about Grimes."

The instant Netherson had gone, Caitlin sought out Aunt Winnie and asked her to look after Ryan. Then she saddled a horse and rode swiftly over to Vernon's homestead.

She was surprised to find him at home, and relieved that there was no immediate sign of the bounty hunter named Grimes. Vernon's expression, however, as he greeted her at his back door, was one of wariness—which convinced Caitlin he knew why she'd come.

"Vernon," she asked at once after declining his offer to come inside the house, "you didn't go back on your promise, did you?"

"What promise?"

"You said you wouldn't send for a bounty hunter to apprehend Jake, but Marshal Netherson thinks one is here looking for him."

"I never promised anything of the sort, Caitlin, but—"

"Vernon, how *could* you?" Her distraught gaze turned bitterly accusing at his betrayal.

"Just a minute, you've got it wrong! I didn't send for any bounty hunter. In fact, I telegraphed the federal marshal who'd sent me the handbill and said I was mistaken about McCord being here."

"Did you?" She searched Vernon's face doubtfully. He looked so angry at her accusation, she didn't think he was lying.

"I didn't send for anyone," Vernon repeated. "Grimes came here on his own."

"But he paid you a visit."

"Yes, last night."

"Did you tell him where to find Jake?"

"No, blast it, I didn't. I said I thought McCord had moved on. But I'm not sure Grimes bought it. He's after the reward. There's five hundred dollars in it for him if he apprehends McCord and takes him back to New Mexico Territory."

Dead or alive. Cold fear gripped Caitlin at the thought. Grimes wouldn't be interested in keeping Jake alive. "Dear God, he'll be killed. . . . "

Vernon's jaw hardened. "Maybe that's what McCord deserves. He's a criminal—"

"No." Her whisper was anguished. "That isn't true."

"He's wanted for murder, Caitlin."

"Jake didn't murder anyone!"

"How can you be sure?"

"Because I *know* him." She knew Jake as well as she knew herself; he was part of her. Not even if she were faced with incontrovertible proof would she ever believe he'd intentionally killed someone. But perhaps he'd had no choice. . . .

"He's still wanted by the law," Vernon pointed out, echoing her tormented thoughts. "He's still a fugitive from justice." When she couldn't reply, Vernon gently took her gloved hands in his. "Caitlin, I know you think you're in love with him, but you're making a huge mistake. Don't throw your life away on an outlaw."

"Don't call him that." She pulled her trembling fingers from Vernon's grasp. "Just tell me where Grimes is now."

"Why?"

"Because I have to stop him."

"Caitlin . . . Even if you could manage it this time, what about the next? How will you keep other bounty hunters away in the future?" His tone grew sharp with impatience. "McCord will never live down his past. There'll always be somebody gunning for him."

She gazed at Vernon in agony. "I can't worry about the future! I have to do something *now*. I can't let that bounty hunter take him. Jake could die."

"Well then . . . you'd do better to persuade him to turn himself in to Marshal Netherson."

Caitlin shook her head adamantly. If Jake were

found guilty he would *hang*. She bit back a sob—God, she was wasting precious time. She couldn't stand here arguing when Jake's life was at risk. "Vernon, you have to help me."

"Help *you*? You mean help McCord," he retorted with an edge of bitterness.

"All right, then, help Jake."

"I don't want to help him, Caitlin! He's my competition."

"Vernon, please. . . . Where did Grimes go?"

Clenching his teeth in frustration, Vernon took a long time in answering. "I think he headed back to town. He said he'd taken a room at the saloon—"

Abruptly she turned away.

"Where are you going?" Vernon demanded as Caitlin ran down the back porch steps.

"To town. I have to find Grimes."

"Are you mad? The man's dangerous!"

"I *know*. That's why I have to find him."

"Wait, Caitlin, I'll come with you. Let me saddle my horse—"

"I don't have time to wait!"

She heard Vernon curse under his breath, but she mounted her chestnut without pause. Whirling the animal toward town, she spurred it to a gallop, leaving Vernon to fetch his own horse and follow her if he would.

She tried to plan. She tried frantically to think what to do on the mad ride into town. But all she could focus on was that she had to save Jake. Grimes wouldn't care if he were innocent or guilty of murdering that bank teller.

At the very least, she had to get Grimes off his trail. She couldn't bear for Jake to be hunted down like an animal, but that concern paled in comparison to the threat on his life. Somehow she had to gain Jake time to run.

Her horse was lathered and breathing hard by the time she reached Greenbriar's main street and pulled up before the Stirrup & Pick Saloon. She'd never been inside before. Ladies didn't frequent such low establishments, and her reputation would likely suffer for it now. If it were only her own good name at risk, she wouldn't worry, but she'd fought for four years to keep her behavior from tarnishing her child with scandal. Even so, she couldn't fret about such things now. Jake's life was in danger.

A raven-haired woman stood behind the bar, wiping the countertop. Her brown eyes opened wide when she spied Caitlin gazing around the empty saloon uncertainly.

"Can I help you?" she asked curiously.

"I'm looking for a man . . . a stranger by the name of Grimes. Perhaps you've seen him?"

"I've seen plenty of men in my time, sugar."

Caitlin recognized her reply for an evasion, but suspected the woman was only protecting her clientele. "I was told Grimes had a room here."

"I guess it depends on what you want him for."

"My business is . . . personal."

"Did he run out on you?"

"No . . . it's nothing like that."

The woman's dark eyes scrutinized her. "Ain't you Adam Kingsly's daughter?"

"Yes," she answered impatiently, "I'm Caitlin King . . . Hughes, but . . . I'm in something of a hurry."

"I guess you're the one, then."

"The one, what?"

"Jake said there was a girl who'd turned him

down. You're the one who muddled his head and tied him up in knots."

Caitlin stared, taken aback. "You know Jake?"

The woman smiled rather sadly, showing a chipped front tooth. "Everybody knows Jake, honey. The name's Della. Della Perkins."

A surge of jealously she couldn't repress spread through Caitlin, although strangely, she thought Della might be experiencing the same possessive sentiment. Immediately Caitlin chastised herself for overreacting. She'd never expected Jake to live the life of a monk. She'd always known that other women found him devastatingly attractive. But still, the thought of him making love to this faded beauty made her ache inside.

"Funny," Della said with a faint laugh, "you don't look like a fool."

Uncertain how to respond to the insult, Caitlin frowned. "I beg your pardon?"

"Only a fool would think of turnin' Jake down."

Caitlin felt herself stiffen defensively. There really was no reason to justify her decisions, especially to this strange woman, and yet she found herself wanting to explain why she'd turned Jake down, why she was still afraid to marry him. Because she could never be certain when his violent past would catch up with him. Like now. With a bounty hunter gunning for him, Jake would have to flee for his life.

Grimes's arrival was a stark reminder of reality—and why she couldn't let herself believe Jake's argument that the future would work itself out.

Della was eyeing her searchingly. "Sugar, if Jake asked me to marry him, I'd follow him clear to China."

Caitlin shook herself. She didn't have time to debate her possible marriage. "If you're a . . . a friend of Jake's, then I'd think you would be concerned about Grimes being in town. He's a bounty hunter."

The brown eyes widened again. "Oh, Lord . . . he's not here after Jake?"

"Marshal Netherson thinks so. And if someone doesn't stop him, Jake may be a dead man. I'd like to speak to Grimes. Is he here or not?"

"Come on, honey, I'll take you upstairs."

Vernon pushed through the swinging doors just in time to hear Della's offer. To both women's surprise, he was wearing a six-shooter strapped to his right thigh.

"Caitlin, you can't go up there," he said at once.

"All I want is to talk to Grimes," she insisted.

"It won't do any good."

"Perhaps not, but I have to try and stop him."

"Well, at least let me go with you."

She nodded, knowing she would feel safer with Vernon's presence. When she turned toward the stairs, though, he stopped her.

"Wait a minute. You need to have a plan. What are you going to say to him?"

"I'm going to offer to pay him to leave town."

"Bribe him, you mean?"

"Yes. I'll match the reward for Jake's capture if Grimes will agree to leave him alone. He can ride away and forget he ever heard of Jake."

Della frowned. "I don't know if that'll work, honey."

Caitlin wasn't sure it would either, but she was desperate. Buying Grimes off was the only way she knew to protect Jake and avoid the bloodshed that would result from a showdown.

"It *won't* work, Caitlin," Vernon stated flatly. "You can't expect Grimes to honor his word.

What's to keep him from taking your money and
still going after Jake?"

"The money doesn't matter, not if I can just get
Grimes out of town long enough to warn Jake."

"You'd do better to offer him an additional reward for capturing Jake. He'll be more likely to
believe you."

"*Capture* Jake?" The question held alarm.

"Tell him you want him to find Jake for you.
That you desire justice for your brother's murder.
We can send him off on a wild-goose chase. In fact,
I'll say I got word McCord was spotted in Denver."

"But ... Jake was pardoned for my brother's
murder."

"Grimes doesn't know that."

Caitlin hesitated in an agony of indecision, but
Della took her elbow and propelled her briskly
across the saloon. "Listen to Verne, honey. He
knows men better'n you do. Fellas like Grimes got
suspicions about their own kin. And you'd best put
on a good act if you want him to believe you. Don't
seem so anxious. Look riled, like you want Jake
dead."

"And for God's sake," Vernon added, "don't offer Grimes the entire amount now. He'll smell a
skunk. Tell him you'll give him a hundred now,
and the rest when he brings Jake back from Denver
alive."

Caitlin drew a deep breath and nodded, trusting
they were right, praying she could pull it off.

Vernon accompanied the women up the stairs
and down the narrow corridor. Pausing before
Room Number 7, Della rapped on the door and
called out, "Mister, it's Della. There's a lady to see
you."

A moment of silence ensued, followed by the
sound of a key being turned in the lock. When the

door swung open, a large, unkempt man with several days' growth of dark beard stood there frowning, his revolver drawn.

Shaking inwardly, Caitlin stepped forward. "Mr. Grimes?"

"Who's askin'?"

"I'm Mrs. Hughes. May I speak with you? I'd like to discuss a . . . a lucrative proposition with you, if you have a moment."

He stared at her for the space of several heartbeats while Caitlin didn't dare breathe.

Grimes's suspicious gaze swung to Vernon. "You bring her here?"

"She brought me. I think you should talk to her."

Grimes suddenly broke into a grin, his teeth flashing white in his swarthy face. "Always willing to oblige a pretty lady."

Holstering his gun, he waved his hand in a sweeping gesture, inviting her inside. Vernon followed hard on her heels, while Della hovered outside in the hall till the door was shut in her face.

The room was just as untidy as Grimes's person, but he made an effort to straighten it. Snatching his hat off the only chair, he offered her a seat, but Caitlin preferred to remain standing.

"Mr. Grimes," she began with far less confidence than she felt, "I understand you're a bounty hunter."

"I reckon so."

She forced a smile. "I also understand you've come here looking for Jake McCord."

"Maybe I am."

"If you are . . . then we have something in common. I want him found, too. And I'm willing to make it worth your while."

"What'd you have in mind?"

"There's a five hundred dollar reward offered for

a murder he committed in New Mexico during a holdup, but I'll go better than that. I'll pay you a thousand if you'll find McCord and bring him back here to Greenbriar for trial."

"Did I hear you right, ma'am?" Grimes asked in obvious surprise.

"Yes."

"Why are you so interested in McCord?"

"Because he killed my brother, and I want him brought to justice." When the bounty hunter hesitated, Caitlin pressed on doggedly. "McCord fled yesterday when he heard you were in town, but he was seen headed for Denver. If you hurry, you could track him down."

"I could put a bullet in him easier than hauling him back alive."

With effort Caitlin held back a gasp and forced her lips into an angry smile. "It's no more than he deserves, but I don't want him murdered, Mr. Grimes. I want the law to deal with him. If he hangs for his crime, then his death won't be on my conscience."

"Why'd it take so long for you to get this itch for justice if McCord's been holdin' up here?"

She saw Vernon's warning look and was grateful when he answered for her. "I told you McCord was in deep with the cattlemen around here. Mrs. Hughes never could get the marshal to arrest him. But if you bring him back for trial, Netherson will have to act."

"I'm willing to pay you a hundred dollars now," Caitlin added, "and the rest when you bring him in. Alive, Mr. Grimes."

"Forgive me for askin' ma'am, but do you have a thousand dollars?"

"I have it, yes, from the recent sale of my wool. I'll have to visit the bank first, but I can get the first hundred for you this morning. And you can be on your way to start looking for him."

Grimes grinned again, his startlingly white teeth flashing. "Make it two hundred, and I think we can do business, ma'am."

Relief flooded Caitlin as she rode swiftly home, along with a dismal ache that slashed at her heart. Grimes apparently had believed her, for he'd accepted her offer, and together she and Vernon had watched the bounty hunter ride out of town. Yet the danger to Jake wasn't over by a long shot. He couldn't remain here any longer, not and risk being hunted down as a criminal. Too many people knew where to find him.

Grimes would be back, Caitlin had little doubt, and he wouldn't be handled so easily when he returned from Denver empty-handed. And if he should discover Jake had already been pardoned for her brother's murder . . . Even though she would gladly pay the bounty hunter every penny she'd promised him, he would know he'd been tricked and would be out for blood. Jake could be apprehended or even killed.

No, Jake would have to leave, and at once, Caitlin knew—although convincing *him* of that might be impossible now that he'd discovered his son.

She and Vernon had split up to search for him, with Vernon riding out to the McCord ranch, while she went home and Della stayed in town in case he showed up there.

One of Caitlin's prayers was answered, at least, when she found Jake at her ranch, giving Ryan another riding lesson in the yard.

"Where have you been?" he asked casually as she brought her mount to a plunging halt beside him.

"I have to talk to you," she replied, her tone edged with urgency as Jake helped her dismount. Evidently he was unaware his past might be closing in on him. "Ryan, it's time for lunch. Will you go inside and get Aunt Winnie to fix you a sandwich? There's some ham left over from supper."

"Mama, no," the child said plaintively. "I wanna ride with Jake."

"Ryan," Caitlin snapped, her voice sharper than necessary. "I would like you to go inside." When Jake gave her a piercing look, she took a calming breath. "Please, darling. I need to talk to Jake alone. You can ride some other time."

"Come on, pardner," Jake said, reaching up for Ryan. "A gentleman always does what his ma says."

"Aw, Jake. . . . "

Lifting the child down from the mare's back, Jake ruffled his dark hair. "Go on, now. No arguments."

Pouting, Ryan nevertheless obeyed and ambled across the yard to the back porch, his small booted feet dragging.

"Now, what's so all-fired important that you had to disappoint him?" Jake demanded the moment the back door closed.

"Your life, that's what," Caitlin retorted.

"What are you talking about?"

"There's a bounty hunter looking for you."

He shrugged his shoulders as he led her horse toward the corral. "So what else is new?"

"I *knew* you would say something like that!"

"Well, what am I supposed to say?"

"Jake . . ." Caitlin exclaimed in frustration. "Are you insane? Or merely thick-witted? You have to get out of here!"

"Why?"

"Because I don't want to see you get killed!"

Jake smiled faintly as he began to unsaddle her horse for her. "That's nice to know, Cat. A few weeks ago I wouldn't have bet good money you gave two figs what happened to me."

"Stop it! Just stop it!" She was astonished to feel tears fill her eyes, while Jake grew alarmed.

"Hey . . . wildcat, what's wrong?" Forgetting about the horse, he reached out and drew her into his arms. "You don't have to worry about me."

Fighting back sobs, Caitlin pressed her forehead against Jake's chest. "I do so have to worry. I can't help it, Jake. . . . I couldn't bear it if you died."

"I'm not going to die. Nothing's going to happen to me."

"*This* time, maybe. But only because I offered to d-double the reward if Grimes would go to Denver to look for you."

"What reward? Who the hell is Grimes?"

"The bounty hunter who's after you."

"Ethan Grimes?"

"Yes."

"I've heard of him. What reward?"

"The one the wanted poster was offering for your capture. For the m-murder of the bank clerk."

It took the space of several heartbeats for comprehension to sink in. When he drew back, Jake's face had darkened like a thundercloud. "You did *what*? . . ."

"I promised him a thousand dollars if he would—"

"Dammit, Cat!" Jake grasped her upper arms, his features taut with fury and bitter hurt. "Did it never once cross your mind I might be innocent of that murder?"

She stared at him in anguish. "Of course it did, but the poster says—"

"Damn the poster! I didn't murder anybody.

And you sure as hell might have had a little more faith in me!"

A sob escaped Caitlin as she shook her head. "It doesn't matter what I believe. You're wanted by the *law*, Jake! Grimes thinks you're guilty, and so will anyone else who sees that poster. You *have* to leave now if you want to stay alive."

Jake locked his jaw. "I'm not leaving my son."

She'd known he would say exactly that. She drew a trembling breath, bracing herself to play her desperate trump card. "I'm afraid that's not up to you. I've reached a decision, Jake. I can't marry you."

He went white about the mouth, while his green eyes fixed on her with blistering force. "Why the hell not?"

"Because it wouldn't be best for Ryan."

"God*dammit*, Cat—!"

"No, I mean it. This is exactly what I was afraid would happen—you not being able to live down your violent past. Your very presence puts Ryan in danger, can't you *see* that?"

If Jake was angry before, he was seething with rage now. "If you think for one minute," he began in a vehement undertone, "that I'll give Ryan up—"

The bullet came out of nowhere. The explosion of gunfire startled them both, making Caitlin freeze and Jake react with desperate instinct. As her saddlehorse bolted for the barn, he grabbed Caitlin and shoved her to the dirt, knocking her breathless when he covered her with his body. At the same instant he reached for his revolver—which wasn't there.

Jake cursed savagely under his breath. The horses in the corral shied nervously as his narrowed eyes searched beyond the enclosure for the shooter's hiding place. The most likely location looked to be behind the large cottonwood lining the drive. He caught the glint of sunlight off metal—a rifle barrel, no doubt—just as a man's voice called out.

"McCord, that was just a warning shot! Next time I won't miss."

"Who the hell are you?" Jake shouted back. "What do you want?"

"It's Grimes . . ." Caitlin breathed in bewilderment. "The bounty hunter . . ."

"I'm here to take you in!" Grimes called again.

"Damn him, he *promised*," Caitlin exclaimed. "I paid him two hundred dollars. He should be halfway to Denver by now!"

Jake clenched his jaw as he cast her a withering glance. "Yeah, well it looks like he didn't fall for your trick. He double-crossed you."

Not only double-crossed her, Caitlin realized in despair, but he must have doubled back to follow her. Grimes had trailed her from town, and like a stupid fool she'd led him straight to Jake.

"He has a rifle," Jake murmured while she cursed herself for her naïveté in trusting such a man. "Cat, I want you to take cover. Get inside the house and lock the doors. Go around to the front . . . stay low and keep the corral between you and him."

"But what are you going to do?"

Jake's mouth twisted in a grim smile. "Keep my head down and pray like hell."

Chapter 19

❧∽❁∽❧

"Cat, do as I say," Jake demanded, his voice low and urgent. "Get inside the house."

She looked at him as if he'd lost his mind. "You can't believe I'd leave you like this!"

"I'll be all right if I can get to a horse. Go on, *please*. I don't want to have to worry about you."

"What do you mean to do? Maybe I can help."

"I don't want your help. I need to know you're safe."

"Well, I need to know *you're* safe."

"Dammit, Cat. . . . "

"What will you do?" she repeated insistently.

"I'm going to ride out of here and hope Grimes follows. I've got to draw him away. You're right. You and Ryan are in danger as long as I'm here."

Caitlin's blue eyes widened in horror. "You're going to act as bait to make him follow you? Jake, he'll shoot you!"

"I'll be all right—"

"No, you won't!"

"Dammit, Cat, get out of here!" he growled.

"No!" she spit back.

"McCord!" Grimes yelled from behind the cottonwood. "Toss your guns aside and come out with your hands up!"

"At least he doesn't know I'm unarmed," Jake muttered under his breath.

Caitlin felt another wave of dismay. *She'd* been the one to insist Jake leave his revolvers behind when he visited Ryan, and now it might very well cost him his life.

Yet there should be a loaded rifle in the bunkhouse, she remembered desperately. One was always kept there in case of trouble. She glanced over her shoulder, gauging the distance to the bunkhouse. Realizing it was too far, she placed an imploring hand on Jake's arm. "Jake, please . . . why don't you just surrender? Grimes won't hurt you if you turn yourself in."

"Can you be so sure of that?"

She bit her lip, knowing he was right. Grimes had far too few scruples to be trusted.

"I'm not surrendering to him, Cat. Even if he doesn't decide I'd be easier to deal with dead, he'll want to take me down to New Mexico, and I'd have to stay there till I could clear my name. I'm innocent, and I'll be dammed if I'll lose any more time from my life trying to prove it. Now, get the hell out of here. He's not going to wait forever."

Caitlin wanted to scream with frustration, fearing Jake's stubbornness would get him killed.

"McCord! Are you gonna come peaceably? Or do I have to come get you?"

When Jake shifted his body, edging toward the corral, she caught his arm. "Jake, please . . . not that way." Caitlin's voice broke on a sob. "You could die."

Glancing back at her, Jake gave her a long, level

look that held an edge of bleakness. "If I can't have you and Ryan, what's the use in living anyway?"

His grim appraisal shocked her. Pain, like a sharp knife, twisted inside her, yet it galvanized her into action. Turning on her stomach, Caitlin started crawling toward the bunkhouse to fetch the rifle there.

Jake swore when he realized she was heading the wrong way, but he couldn't go after her without putting her in more danger. Rolling under the corral fence, he rose to a crouch and caught the mane of the first horse he came to. He swung himself up on the bay gelding and ducked low over the horse's neck, just as a bullet whizzed over his head. Spurring the bay sideways, he reached the corral gate and bent lower, fumbling for the latch.

He hadn't quite managed to release it when a gunshot rang out from the direction of the bunkhouse—followed by a cry of pain from behind the cottonwood.

Jake stared as Grimes staggered out from behind the tree and fell to the ground, clutching his shoulder and groaning. When Jake glanced back, he saw Caitlin standing there defiantly in the yard, her smoking rifle trained on the fallen man, her eyes flashing fire, her jaw clenched in grim determination. At the sight, Jake felt his heart contract, while a tumultuous wave of emotion hit him: relief, fear, admiration . . . pride in Caitlin's strength and courage and loyalty to him.

"Looks like you got him," Aunt Winnie declared with satisfaction as she stepped off the back porch, her own rifle raised.

Caitlin gave a start and shook her head, as if jolted from a daze.

Bent low, the elderly lady crossed the yard to her niece, all the while keeping her own rifle aimed at the fallen man beyond the corral. "Fine shot, Caitlin. If you hadn't fired, I would have—though my eyesight isn't what it used to be."

Caitlin blinked. "What . . . are you doing with a gun?"

Winnie's blue eyes twinkled. "Did you think St. Louis was always a bastion of civilization? Back when I first lived there, it was as wild and woolly as any town out West. I could singe the hair off a buffalo at a hundred paces."

Jake chuckled weakly as he slid off the bay horse and ducked under the gate.

"Of course," Winifred added, "I didn't have rough characters like *that* gunning for me. You ought to choose your friends with more care, Jake."

He bent and kissed the lady's wrinkled cheek. "Thanks, Winnie. I'll try to take your advice." She blushed at his forward gesture, while Jake turned to Caitlin.

Taking the rifle from her, he drew her into his arms. She leaned against him, shaking.

"You saved my life, wildcat," Jake said softly.

Caitlin shook her head—in denial or disbelief, she wasn't certain. She was still shocked by her own savagery, by the murderous rage that had taken control of her, body and soul. Until this moment she hadn't realized she was capable of shooting a man with every intention of killing.

She felt her aunt pat her arm gently in understanding. "You did what you had to do, Caitlin. Sometimes you have to commit violence in order to protect the ones you love."

Still trembling, Caitlin nodded slowly. "W-Where's Ryan?" she asked, her voice unsteady.

"In his room," her aunt answered, "where I ordered him to stay if he ever wanted to ride a horse again in this lifetime. Perhaps you should check on that trigger-happy fellow before he comes to his senses, Jake."

With a nod, Jake hefted Caitlin's rifle and moved cautiously past the corral, across the open space to the cottonwood, where Grimes lay groaning. The bounty hunter was wounded in the shoulder, Jake saw when he hunkered down beside him. Opening the man's shirt, Jake drew off Grimes's bandanna and pressed it against the bleeding flesh.

Just then he caught the sound of horses' hooves pounding in the distance. Jake looked up to see a group of horsemen galloping hell-for-leather up the ranch road. He recognized his brother Sloan in the lead, followed directly by Marshal Netherson and Della Perkins, all three of them armed.

They brought their lathered mounts to a skidding halt beside him and stared down at the wounded Grimes.

"You okay?" Sloan demanded of Jake.

"I'm fine."

"What happened to him?" Netherson asked.

"He had a little accident."

Sloan's mouth curved in a grin. "I thought you might need rescuing, little brother, but I should have known you could handle it."

"I couldn't have without help," Jake answered, gesturing with his head at Caitlin and Winnie, who were walking toward them. "Have you met Caitlin's aunt, Mrs. Winifred Truscott?"

"I don't believe I've had the pleasure." Sloan tipped his hat to the elderly lady, his slow, brilliant smile holding all the McCord charm. "How do you do, ma'am?"

Winifred stared back frankly, sizing him up. She must have liked what she saw for she nodded graciously. "Very well, young man. But I understand now what my niece was up against. It's a wonder any of the female population is safe with *two* of you around."

Blushing, Caitlin interrupted and finished the introductions Jake had started. Winifred smiled pleasantly at both Luther Netherson—who was showing a definite masculine interest in the attractive widow—and at Della Perkins—despite the paint on her face proclaiming her trade.

"What made you think I needed rescuing?" Jake asked.

"A cowboy came into the saloon," Della explained. "Claimed he saw Grimes headed out this way. I came to warn you and met up with Sloan and the marshal on the way."

"I guess we better get him to the doc," Netherson said of Grimes, who was sweating and gritting his teeth.

After a glance at Caitlin, Winnie took charge. "You can bring him to the bunkhouse. I'll patch him up so you can move him in the buckboard."

"Just a minute," Jake said. Fishing inside Grimes's pockets, he discovered a wad of bills and handed it to Caitlin. "Two hundred dollars. I think this money belongs to you."

"I believe it does," she said tersely, giving Grimes a look of scorn.

Netherson and Sloan dismounted then, and bent to pick up the wounded man.

"Stop!" Grimes rasped. "Marshal, you're not just gonna let McCord walk, are you? It's your duty to arrest him."

"Now, I don't see why," Netherson replied.

"He robbed a bank and killed a man down in New Mexico." Weakly, Grimes fumbled in his vest pocket and pulled out a crumpled piece of paper. Taking it, the marshal unfolded the handbill and scrutinized it for a long moment. It was the wanted poster with Jake's picture on it, Caitlin saw with alarm.

Netherson's look was troubled when he finally glanced at Jake. "Seems he's right, Jake. As an officer of the law, I'll have to take you in."

"No, you can't!" Caitlin cried in dismay, while Sloan took a protective step forward.

"Of course," Netherson added slowly, "I'll be tied up for a while, seeing to this fella's wounds. It'll be some time before I can get around to taking care of my duty."

Everyone present understood he was giving Jake a chance to run—an understanding that made Grimes curse savagely.

"I'd advise you to shut your mouth, mister," the marshal warned. "You're in the presence of ladies."

"There's no need to wait to arrest me, Luther," Jake replied coolly. "When you've patched him up, I'll ride into town with you."

Caitlin drew a sharp breath, but Sloan caught her eye and shook his head. "Mrs. Truscott, if you'll lead the way?" Sloan prompted.

The two men bent again. Picking up the wounded Grimes, they followed Winifred to the bunkhouse, leaving Caitlin and Jake alone, except for Della Perkins.

Della looked from one to the other, but neither was paying her the slightest attention. Jake was eyeing Caitlin grimly, while Caitlin was staring down at him in dismay.

Awkwardly Della cleared her throat. "Well, I guess I'll be going now. I just wanted to make sure you were okay, Jake."

Tearing his gaze from Caitlin, Jake flashed a smile up at her. "Thanks for coming to my rescue, Dell. It's nice to know I have friends."

Shaking herself, Caitlin stepped forward and gave Della an earnest smile. "Yes, thank you for coming. It's nice to know *someone* is interested in saving his wretched hide, even if he's not."

"Well, I'll leave you to try to talk some sense into him," Della said with a grin. She started to turn her horse, but then hesitated. "I think maybe I was wrong, Miz Hughes. I can see why Jake fell for you, but maybe it wasn't such a fool thing, turning him down. You stick to your guns, honey. These men get too big for their britches sometimes, and it don't hurt 'em none to have a woman set 'em on their ears."

With a conspiratorial wave then, Della turned her horse and rode away.

A taut silence followed her departure, the air vibrating with tension. Jake didn't rise from his position on the ground. His smoldering gaze bored into Caitlin relentlessly, while she glared back at him in despair and frustration.

The fear of the past hours had taken a toll on her. She was terrified to think Jake could have been killed, to know he might be imprisoned and hanged now. Her nerves felt as if they were shredded raw.

She knew he was seething at her, but she went on the offensive first. Her hands balling into fists, she said in a raw voice, "Are you out of your *mind*, telling Netherson you'll go with him?"

Jake leveled an arctic stare at her. "You always say that whenever I don't agree with your aims."

"Jake, damn you—turning yourself in to the marshal is crazy! You can't! He'll put you in jail!"

"I expect so."

"Jake . . ." She took a deep breath, striving for patience. "You have to leave, don't you see that?"

"You want me to go into hiding, is that it?"

"Yes!"

His jaw hardened. "Sorry, Cat. I'm not going anywhere."

"Jake, *please*, you aren't safe here. I don't want to see you in prison, any more than I want to see you dead."

"I don't want to see me in prison, either. But, I'm not running, Cat."

When she gazed at him helplessly, he stared back at her in grim silence, his eyes betraying a quiet fury. "You never really have trusted me, have you?"

"That's . . . that's not true."

"Sure it is. You believed your father when he claimed I murdered your brother. And you think I murdered that bank teller."

"No, I don't—"

"You were willing to pay Grimes a thousand dollars to get him off my trail."

"Jake . . . you don't understand. . . . "

He skewered her with his eyes. "Then explain it to me."

He couldn't remember ever being so livid, couldn't remember ever feeling such bitter resentment. He was spitting mad and aching—because Caitlin hadn't trusted him, because she'd decided to take care of Grimes on her own, because she'd believed the worst of him and convicted him without a trial. . . . But among her catalog of sins, by far the worst was that she wanted to deny him his son.

Jake closed his eyes with the pain of it.

"Jake . . ." Her pleading tone penetrated his bitter thoughts. "I know you're not a murderer. I was afraid for your life! I couldn't allow it to matter whether you were guilty or not. You're wanted by the law, dead or alive—and I was afraid it would be dead."

A muscle worked in his jaw. He could have eased her fears, but he refused to respond. *Let her stew a little,* Jake thought harshly. He was through defending himself, through giving excuses. If Cat couldn't take him on faith, then he was damned if he would grovel.

"I shouldn't have to prove myself to you," he said in a deadened voice.

"You don't have to prove yourself, Jake."

"The hell, I don't. I've been on trial since the minute I came back to Colorado. I've had to fight you every step. You still think I'm not fit to be Ryan's pa—"

"No . . . I know you'll be a good and caring father."

"You intend to keep Ryan from me. You told me so not a half hour ago."

"I didn't mean it, Jake. I was scared out of my mind when I said that. I was just trying to make you leave—"

"I'm not leaving, dammit."

"Jake, you have to. . . . "

Caitlin stared at him impotently, wishing she knew how to get through to him, to make him see the danger he was in. She'd never been more terrified in her life than a moment ago when Grimes was shooting at him. It had stunned her, how fierce her need was to protect Jake, to keep him safe. She would have committed murder if it meant saving his life. She would have died herself. The violent rage inside her still hadn't completely faded. How ironic, she thought humorlessly, when she'd protested so vehemently against the violence and bloodshed of the feud. But there *were* some things worth fighting for. Worth dying for. Like family and loved ones. Like Jake.

Caitlin squeezed her eyes shut, realizing exactly

what she was admitting to herself. For weeks now she'd been deluding herself about the strength of her feelings for Jake, thinking she could simply walk away from him when the time came, hoping they could rekindle old passions with no devastating consequences. But her love for him was stronger, far deeper than passion. She would give her life for him if need be. She couldn't bear to lose him again, whatever the cost.

The ache of tears clawed at her throat as Caitlin dropped to her knees beside him. It was all she could do not to throw herself into his arms and weep, begging him to listen. "Jake, you have to go. You *have* to. If you're found guilty, they'll *hang* you."

Despite his fury, her fervent plea affected Jake deeply. With one hand he reached up to brush a tear from her cheek with his knuckles. "I'm not leaving you, wildcat. Not ever again. I've had four years of living without you, and it was pure hell."

Forcibly swallowing the ache in her throat, Caitlin made herself meet his gaze. "You won't have to leave me, Jake. You won't have to go alone. Ryan and I will go with you."

A flicker of some unfathomable emotion shone in his green eyes. "You'd really do that? Live with me as an outlaw?"

"Yes . . . if that's what it takes to keep you from being killed. I'll marry you, Jake—today if you want. I'll live with you wherever you want."

He smiled at her with painful tenderness; his chest felt tight. Caitlin's willingness to sacrifice for him touched him to the core.

"I thought you considered me a desperado."

"No . . ." Her voice quavered. "You're a good man, Jake."

"I've killed for a living, Cat."

"It doesn't m-matter. I love you. And I don't want to live without you."

He'd waited four hellish years for that simple admission. He felt the tension uncoil within him—a tightly wound knot unraveling. "What about Ryan? Aren't you worried he'll come to harm?"

"Yes, I'm worried sick, but . . . I'm willing to risk it. You can protect him, if anyone can."

Jake shook his head slowly. Her offer to go into exile with him made her capitulation after so many weeks all the more precious, but he couldn't accept it. "You may be willing to risk it, Cat, but I'm not. I don't want to expose you or our son to a life on the run, any more than I want to live it again. I'm not going back to being a hunted animal."

She made another desperate bid. "But we can go East, Jake," she said hopefully. "It doesn't have to be St. Louis, just someplace where no one knows about your past. Where Ryan can have something resembling a normal life."

He shook his head. "We've been over this before. My past would catch up with me eventually."

Caitlin clenched her fists to keep from crying or screaming. "Jake . . . "

"No, Cat. Running is cowardly. I'm not going to teach my son to be a coward. I'm making a stand here. Besides," he added more gently, "it's better to stick with family. You saw how your aunt came to our rescue. And my brother. This is my home, where I belong. I'm not running."

The tears in her eyes threatened to spill over, but she held them back, knowing she could argue and plead till she was blue, and he still wouldn't listen. "Damn you, Jake . . . I've n-never known anyone more foolishly stubborn."

"Except you." Jake flashed his devastating, heart-rending grin. "You have me beat by a mile."

She stiffened at his reckless humor. When she started to rise, though, he caught her upper arms, his hold tender. "Cat, I want you to trust me this time."

She gazed back at him in silence, her eyes shimmering.

He brushed a light, gentle kiss across her trembling mouth. "I'm through being on the wrong side of the law. I'm turning myself in to the marshal, Cat. I'm going to jail, and I'm not coming out until I either hang or I clear my name."

Chapter 20

The jail cell was barely large enough to hold a man, while the lumpy cot squeezed between rough log walls was too short to fully accommodate someone of Jake's height.

His muscles stiff after a cramped night of tossing, Jake clenched his jaw and contemplated the imprisoning iron bars. Even though Netherson had left his cell door open, even though a bright shaft of morning sunlight streamed through the barred window and lightened the oppressive atmosphere, he still felt as if the walls were closing in on him.

He'd sworn he would never face the inside of a cell again, not after spending two months in a sweltering, stinking New Mexico jail last year while waiting for his trial to start. He sure as hell didn't want Cat seeing him here. But he'd had little choice if he wanted to clear his name and avoid the indignity and peril of being apprehended by a trigger-happy bounty hunter. And so he'd insisted on turning himself in to the marshal.

According to Netherson, Grimes had been

patched up by the Greenbriar doctor and was laid up in a room above the saloon, with Della acting as nurse. Marshal Netherson had sent a telegram to the territorial judge in New Mexico regarding the wanted poster and the murder Jake had allegedly committed during the bank robbery.

Now all he could do was wait. And think. And consider. And search his soul as he questioned his own motives.

Was he wrong to want Caitlin as his wife? Wrong to want to be a part of his son's life? Cat was correct in one respect, Jake knew. His very presence put her and their son in danger. Was he being selfish, wanting them so badly he was willing to risk their safety for a future with them? Maybe his best course was just to leave, to get out of their lives for good. It would be like ripping his heart out, but that was better than having them come to harm because of him. On the other hand . . . Ryan needed him. A boy needed a masculine influence in his life. Needed a father to love him and look after him.

Cat needed him, too, for that matter. She was a woman made for loving a man. Cat needed *him*. She was his woman. His soul mate. But just when he'd finally made her see it, he was no longer so certain that was all that mattered.

She loved him, Jake knew. When she'd shot Grimes yesterday, defying the danger and risking her own life to protect *him*, any lingering doubts he'd held had shattered. He felt awed and humbled to have so courageous a woman at his side, one who would stand by him with loyalty and strength and heartfelt conviction, one who would brave the future with him despite the risks. Yet he was no longer certain he deserved Caitlin, or that he had the right to ask it of her.

He must have dozed, for the next thing Jake knew, Caitlin was bending over him, her blue eyes soft with dismay.

His heart contracted at the concern he saw on her beautiful face. "I told you," he muttered in a husky rasp as he cleared the sleep from his throat, "I didn't want you coming here. You don't belong in a rathole like this."

Biting her lip, Caitlin sat beside him on the narrow cot and surveyed Jake's hard, handsome features. His jaw was shadowed with a stubble of dark whiskers, but his tawny, sleep-rumpled hair made him look years younger, a little like their precious son after a nap. A maze of emotions rose within her: fierce tenderness. Bittersweet love. The need to keep this man from harm, to cherish him always.

She'd done a vast amount of soul-searching during the long hours of last night. At first she'd been distraught and furious with Jake for refusing to flee and save himself. But gradually she'd come to realize he couldn't keep running for the rest of his life. He had to make a stand somewhere. And this time she meant to be by his side. Even if it had taken every ounce of fortitude she possessed to come here this morning.

She hated to see Jake locked up this way, sensed his shame at having her view him like this, but her fear was stronger than her regret. She was terrified to think what might happen if he couldn't prove his innocence in the bank clerk's murder.

"You don't belong here, either," Caitlin replied softly.

Pushing himself up to a sitting position, Jake propped his back against the wooden wall and braced himself for another argument. "I told you,

Cat, I'm not running. I'm going to stay within the law and clear my name."

"I know. And I think you're right. I don't want you to run."

When Jake regarded her skeptically, she glanced at the iron-barred door that had been left ajar and forced a smile, trying to put on a brave face. "The marshal can't be too concerned that you'll escape. Whoever heard of a prisoner being held in an un-locked jail?"

His mouth twisted wryly. "I think Luther wishes I *would* go. It would save him the trouble of having to deal with me."

"It would spare his conscience, certainly. He doesn't like having to lock up a fr-friend." When her voice broke, she swallowed hard and took a deep breath. "I brought you some breakfast, by the way." Feeling helpless at the inadequacy of such a small comfort, she handed him a cloth-covered tin plate. "Aunt Winnie made strawberry muffins. They're Ryan's favorite, and he wanted you to have some."

"You didn't tell him I was here?" Jake asked sharply.

"Of course not," she replied, striving to keep her hands from trembling as she unwrapped the cloth. "But he was asking for you."

"Don't bring him here. I don't want him to see me in jail."

Caitlin fell silent as she stared down at the plate, not voicing the dreaded question that was foremost in her mind: *What if you can't clear your name?*

"Jake," she said, her voice unsteady, "I've been thinking about this. . . . "

"I've been thinking, too."

"I want us to get married right away."

He stared at her. "Why?"

"Because you should have a family if . . . if s-something should happen to you."

"If I'm found guilty of murder, you mean."

"Y-Yes."

To her surprise, she saw his jaw harden. "I asked you to trust me, Cat."

"I do. I . . . I believe you're innocent. But I'm afraid the law won't."

It was a moment before Jake replied. "I think maybe you and Ryan should go back to St. Louis."

Caitlin's brows drew together in confusion. "You want us to just leave you here?"

"No, I don't want you to leave. But you'll be safer there."

"You intend to come with us, don't you?"

"No."

She rose abruptly to her feet. "What do you mean to do if we go?"

"I don't know. I'll be out of this cell soon—"

"Will you?" Caitlin interrupted, despair almost choking her. "How can you be so certain?"

"Because I'm innocent. And I sure as hell don't want you marrying me just to provide me a family in my last hours."

Her chin rose with a show of her former spirit. "That isn't why, and you know it. I want you for my husband, Jake. If . . . *when* you get out of jail, I want us to be a family."

"You want me for Ryan's pa?" he asked skeptically.

Caitlin turned to pace the small cell in agitation, her blue gingham skirts swaying. Breakfast forgotten, Jake watched as she launched into the arguments she had prepared during the night.

"You were right, Jake, and so was my aunt. Ryan needs a father. He needs *you*. A boy needs a man to help him grow up, to protect him and teach him to survive."

"He won't survive long if he gets caught in the middle of a gunfight like the one yesterday," Jake observed grimly as he fought the hope in his heart. "There's still danger. What about that, Cat? That won't go away just because you want it to."

"I know, but we can deal with it. You were right. Ryan could be in danger anywhere. And there will be two of us to look after him. I think having two parents to love and care for him outweighs the risk he might face from your past."

"He won't have bounty hunters showing up on his doorstep if someone else is his pa."

Caitlin shook her head. "We'll deal with hunters if they come."

"Only a few weeks ago you said you didn't want a man with my past near your son—or anyone who'd been twisted by violence like your father."

"I was wrong. You aren't anything like my father. You don't live for revenge like he did." Her eyes misted. "If four years of being forced to live as an outlaw didn't darken your heart, then nothing will. I don't have to worry about you twisting our son the way my father did my brother. I've watched you with Ryan. You're good with him, good *for* him."

It was Jake's turn to shake his head. "I'm not so sure that really matters."

"It does so. That's *all* that matters. Ryan loves you. And you love him, you know you do."

"Yeah, I do. Too much to risk his life."

In growing frustration, Caitlin turned to stare at him. "Are you trying to get out of marrying me, Jake?" Her doubtful tone held an edge of hurt he couldn't mistake.

Jake forced himself to meet her gaze steadily.

"No, dammit. I'm giving you one last chance to back out."

She swallowed and held his gaze levelly. "I don't want to back out. I waited four years for you, and I think that's long enough. I want you for my husband, and the father of our child . . . our children. I want to face the future with you, whatever that is. If trouble comes, we'll get through it together . . . as a family."

Jake let himself exhale slowly, feeling as if a heavy weight had been lifted from his chest. He hadn't realized how badly he'd needed to hear her say the words. If Cat was willing to make a future with him, then he could face anything life threw at him. He would give his life to protect her and Ryan if need be, but he would do his damnedest to see it never came to that—

The door to the jail opened just then, and Marshal Netherson walked in, grinning. "Good news, Jake—" He stopped short when he saw Caitlin. "Ah . . . sorry, Miz Hughes, but I just got Judge Roper's wire. It confirms your acquittal, Jake, just like you said. You're free to go."

Caitlin looked at Jake questioningly. "What acquittal? Who is Judge Roper?"

"He's the judge who presided at my murder trial." Jake looked at her keenly. "I guess you could say he straightened me out. He's one of the few men I call friend these days. In fact, he's the one who suggested I study law—"

"What acquittal?" Caitlin repeated impatiently.

"I was tried and acquitted on the charge of murder of that bank clerk."

"You were tried? . . ." She gazed at him, dumbfounded.

"And found innocent. I never took part in that holdup, Cat. I'd left the Dolby gang by then. Dolby put out word that I'd shot that clerk, but I had witnesses to prove I wasn't even in the territory at the time. I'd done a lot of soul-searching by then, and since I didn't want to keep running for the rest of my life, I turned myself in. I spent two months in jail while I was waiting for the trial to start. Even after it was over, though, I was still wanted in Colorado for killing your brother. That's when I started studying law, to see if I could come up with a defense that would clear me."

"Then . . . that wanted poster Grimes had . . ."

"It was almost a year out of date."

"A *year*?" Her eyes widened as she stared at Jake. "You knew it was outdated?" A slow-burning fury spread through Caitlin's veins. "You *knew* all this time? You were acquitted of murder and you never told me? Damn you, Jake, how could you!"

"What are you so riled about?"

Her hands went to her hips. "You let me think you might be hanged! You never told me you were cleared by the law."

His gaze held her relentlessly. "I thought you should have known I wasn't a murderer, Cat, without me having to prove it to you."

"I never thought you were a murderer! I thought you had shot that clerk by accident! Why didn't you tell me you had nothing to do with that holdup?"

"You never asked."

"I did so!"

Jake had the grace to look contrite. Caitlin *had* asked him about the bank job, but his fool pride had kept him from letting her in on the facts. He'd wanted her to take him on faith, to believe in him enough to know he was innocent without his having to prove it to her.

Evidently she didn't see it the same way, though. She was still bristling with fury—nearly sputtering, in fact, as she railed at him. "You . . . you . . . arrogant fool! Of all the idiotic, *imbecilic* things to do! Grimes would never have come gunning for you if he'd known he couldn't collect the reward! And I never would have tried to bribe him to leave town!"

"Is it any worse than the secret you kept from me?"

When Caitlin winced, Jake suddenly remembered they had an audience. He gave the marshal an apologetic glance. "Luther, I hate to run you out of your office, but would you mind letting us have a few minutes alone?"

"Okay, a few minutes. But I'd be obliged if you got the heck out of my jail, Jake. Makes a man feel like a low-bellied snake, arresting his own deputy."

Netherson let himself out and shut the door behind him, leaving Jake alone with Caitlin.

"Now, calm down, Cat," Jake said soothingly—unnecessarily, he realized, for she seemed to have settled down already. No longer glaring at him, she had pressed a hand to her temple as if she was thinking furiously.

"No one knows you're innocent, Jake, that's the trouble. That's why Grimes came after you. But if we were to publicize the verdict of your trial . . ."

"Come here, Cat, will you?"

She went on as if she hadn't heard. "I know. . . . We'll send the news of your acquittal to every paper in Colorado. If it becomes common knowledge—"

"Cat, come here."

"Jake, don't you *see*, people need to know you're innocent. You wouldn't have to worry about bounty hunters on your trail, then—"

"Right now I don't give a fig about my innocence. We have a more important matter to discuss."

She stopped to stare at him. "What could be more important?"

"Our future, that's what. Are you going to marry me, woman, or do I have to resort to drastic measures, like arresting you for disobeying the law? I'm still a deputy, remember?"

The laughter lurking in his eyes reminded Caitlin of her aggravation. Her hands went to her hips, while her jaw set mutinously. "Give me one good reason why I should marry you."

"Because you love me like crazy."

Her lips trembled on a smile that she refused to allow. "You drive me crazy, all right. You should be *shot* for what you put me through."

"But you love me anyway."

She eyed Jake up and down, the way she might a prize ram she was considering buying. "Do I? You're a scoundrel, Jake McCord. No proper husband for a law-abiding widow."

"Maybe so, but you can fix that."

"Can I?"

Since she wouldn't come to him, Jake pushed himself to his feet and moved toward her determinedly. "If you won't reform me, who will, hellcat?"

Recognizing that glint in his green eyes, Caitlin took a defensive step backward, but the bars at her back left her nowhere to run. "How do I know you aren't going to surprise me with some other unlawful deed in your wicked past?"

"I haven't committed any other crimes, Cat. None that I know of." Tenderly he drew her into his arms, while his voice dropped to a husky murmur. "I wish I could wipe out those years of my past, but I can't.

I can't promise that some greedy bounty hunter won't come looking for me, either. . . . " His expression grew serious, while his voice held a quiet promise. "But I swear, Cat, I love you. I want to be a good husband to you, and a good father to Ryan. I want to make a life with you, if not here, then wherever you want to go. Hell, I'll even go back to St. Louis with you, if that's what you want."

"No. . . . There's nothing much in St. Louis for me. Maybe not even a job. This is my home, too, Jake."

He gazed down at her lovingly, with eyes that shone a brilliant emerald green. "I swear I'll be there for you for the rest of our lives, if you'll have me."

Caitlin felt herself melting inside. She trusted Jake. She believed in him and loved him with all her heart. But she didn't want to make it too easy for him, after all he'd put her through. "What if I say no?"

A slow grin moved his hard, beautiful mouth as he bent to brush her lips with a fleeting kiss. "I think I could enjoy getting you to change your mind."

Still piqued, she averted her face and pressed her palms against his hard-muscled chest. "Where would we live if we stayed here? Should I still sell the ranch?"

"That's up to you. If you want to hold on to it for Ryan, that's okay with me. But I mean to build us a place of our own, just like we planned years ago."

"A cattle ranch?"

Jake shook his head. "There's no future in cattle any longer. Too many head grazing too few acres. Prices are going down already, and some day the market's going bust. Keeping sheep as a hedge against losses would be the smartest thing we could do."

Caitlin couldn't help but laugh. "You mean you might really have a use for those 'smelly woollies' after all?"

Grinning, Jake gave her a little shake. "Don't push your luck, Juliet."

In response, she reached up to twine her arms around his neck, but Jake stopped her from pulling his head down for a kiss.

"Cat, there's something else I haven't told you. . . . What would you think about being the wife of a judge?"

"A judge?"

"I was thinking about running for the county judgeship. Walt Sanders means to retire in a few months and his position will be open."

Caitlin stared at him, speechless.

"What's wrong? You don't like the idea? I think I'd make a damn good judge, since I've seen both sides of the law."

"No . . . I'm just surprised. Really . . . I think it's a marvelous idea. I just never knew you were interested in a career like that."

"There's a lot you still don't know about me, wildcat." His gaze slid to her mouth and darkened. "You better get started finding out. We already have too many wasted years to make up for as it is."

Yes, Caitlin thought with a bittersweet ache inside. If she had trusted her heart in the first place, if she'd believed in Jake's innocence as she should have, she could have avoided a lot of heartache. Certainly he wouldn't have felt the need to test her faith in him by keeping the facts of his trial and acquittal secret, or letting her fear for his life.

He bent his head to kiss her—but this time it was she who held back as a thought suddenly occurred to her. "Jake . . . if you become a judge, no bounty hunter would dare try to take you in."

"Cat, dammit, hush, will you? I'm trying to kiss you."

This time Caitlin responded as he wanted, eagerly surrendering to his embrace. Helplessly she opened her mouth to his probing tongue, whimpering a little as the banked fires of desire ignited instantly between them. Yet there was far more than passion in their kiss. This was a kiss of promise and commitment, a pledge for the future.

"Oh, Cat," Jake whispered in her ear as he drew back, all the love he was feeling riding on the sound of her name. "This is a hell of a place for a proposal."

"I don't care," she murmured.

He bent his head to kiss her again when a throat being cleared behind them made them abruptly pull apart. Neither had heard Sloan enter, but he was lounging casually against the marshal's desk, eyeing them with amusement as they stood there, breathless and overheated. "Am I to take it congratulations are finally in order, little brother?"

"Yeah, finally," Jake said with a grin. "But don't you know when you're unwanted, big brother?"

Crossing his arms over his chest, Sloan hitched one hip on the desk, looking prepared to stay for some time. "I think maybe I should play chaperon till I can get you two to a preacher."

"There's no need. I'm not going to risk Cat getting away again. I mean to hunt down the preacher shortly myself—but there's something I need to do first."

"What's that?"

"Have a little talk with my son." When he

caught Caitlin's sharp look, Jake grinned reassuringly. "Sloan knows about Ryan. I couldn't keep something like that from him."

Sloan spoke up before she could reply. "I doubt you'll be able to keep it from anyone else, either," he observed, "given that the boy's eyes are the spitting image of Jake's. But I've been thinking about that," he added, seeing Caitlin's blush. "I figure your best bet is to tell everyone you're already married. Say you eloped in secret four years ago because you didn't want your fathers to know. Back then the feud was already raging."

"But everyone thinks I'm widowed," Caitlin protested. "If I eloped with Jake first, that would make me a bigamist."

"You changed your name to conceal your connection to Jake. And you went along with it, Jake, because you wanted to protect her. With a price on your head, you didn't want Caitlin to suffer as the wife of an outlaw. You give out that story, and I'll back you up."

"Do you think anyone would believe it?" she asked slowly.

"Does it really matter what anyone else believes?"

"No . . . I just want to shield Ryan from the gossips."

Jake looked at Caitlin quizzically. "It wouldn't be a lie. I married you in my heart years ago, even though we never said the words."

Her blue eyes softened with love, a look so tender it took his breath away. "I feel that way, too," she answered.

The emotion that shot through him was so strong his knees felt weak. Jake had to wrap his arms around her in order to keep standing. "I want to do it right this time, hellcat," he said huskily, rest-

ing his forehead on hers. "I intend to come court-
ing you and pay my addresses in the proper
fashion."

Drawing back, she held his gaze as she raised
her eyebrows skeptically. "You? Proper?"

"Yes, proper. But foiling the gossips has nothing
to do with it. I want to make completely sure our
son approves the notion of having me for his pa."

He rode up to the Kingsly ranch on a flashy roan
less than two hours later. He had spruced up for
the occasion, and wore a black suit and string tie.
He had obviously shaved, Caitlin noted when she
greeted Jake at the front door, and he smelled deliciously of bay rum.

She thought she had never seen a more devastating man, and she found herself battling a sudden
case of butterflies.

Disappointingly, Jake gave her the briefest of
kisses before asking impatiently, "Is Ryan here?"

"He's in the parlor—"

Before the words were even out of her mouth,
Ryan ran out into the hall to meet him. "Jake, I
missed you and missed you!"

"Hello, pardner!" He swung the child high into
the air, making him gurgle with laughter. "You
been galloping any horses while I was gone?"

Winifred joined them in the hallway just then.
"Goodness, I'm glad you're here. He nearly wore
me out, asking when you were going to come back
to visit."

Jake grinned and kissed Aunt Winnie on the
cheek. "To tell the truth, that's just what I wanted
to discuss. Mind if Ryan and I have a talk, man to
man?"

Caitlin and Winnie glanced at one another, and
then withdrew to the kitchen.

Jake hunkered down in front of his son, and lowered his voice, as if sharing a confidence. "I have something important to ask you, pardner, and I want your honest answer."

The child's green eyes grew wide. "What?"

"Well, you see, it's like this. . . . I love your mother very much, and I want to marry her. But I don't want to do it without your permission. If I did marry your ma, I'd come live with you."

"You would *live* with me?"

"And your ma, Ryan. I would be a pa to you. What do you say to that? Would that be okay with you?"

"I don't have a pa."

"You would if I married your mother. I would be your pa, Ryan."

"You *would*?"

In the kitchen, Caitlin held her breath as she strained to hear Ryan's response. A child so young wouldn't completely understand what was being asked of him, but he was obviously charmed and delighted by Jake, and she hoped that would be enough.

She didn't have long to wait. Ryan suddenly let out a whoop and galloped down the hall in search of her, exclaiming as he burst into the kitchen, "Mama, Mama! Jake's gonna live with us and be my pa!"

Laughing in relief, Caitlin bent and scooped her son up in her arms, giving him a fierce hug.

When Jake joined them in the kitchen, she smiled as she met his green gaze over their son's dark head. Her last fears were laid to rest. She needed and loved Jake. Her son needed and loved him. And nothing else mattered.

Chapter 21

~~~⟨⟨⟩⟩~~~

Rivulets of water cascaded down Jake's gleaming golden body as he emerged from the mountain pool. Watching him from the sun-baked rocks above, Caitlin caught her breath at the brazen, magnificent sight of her husband of three hours. Jake stood gloriously naked, gloriously masculine, crystalline drops of water glistening on his bronzed skin like diamonds in the bright mountain sunshine. Just looking at him made a familiar shivery heat settle between her thighs. Just looking at him made her heart full.

Her husband.

They had been married this morning, only a few short hours ago, in the presence of their families and friends. As soon as they could graciously manage to slip away, though, they'd ridden up into the hills to the old hideaway where they'd once met as young lovers, in order to consummate their marriage.

Caitlin had been reluctant to face this beautiful place again, to confront the haunting memory of her brother's death so soon after the ceremony, yet somehow this sojourn had reaffirmed a sense of homecoming, of rightness. She felt as if she'd closed the final chapter of a tragedy. As if she'd finally laid her brother to rest.

To her surprise and gratitude, she'd discovered Jake had placed a stone grave marker for Neal near the entrance to the glen, a touching gesture that brought tears to her eyes and eased a little of the bittersweet ache in her heart.

She wished devoutly that Neal were still alive, yet she'd come to terms with his death. Her brother had made a terrible mistake, not just in ruthlessly shooting Jake, but by blindly following in their father's vengeful footsteps. And he'd paid for it with his life.

But the past was over, Caitlin reminded herself. She would always live with regrets, but now wasn't the time for tears. More than ever, she had to look to the future. A future with an adorable son and adoring husband.

A future with Jake.

Her sad thoughts faded as her gaze riveted on the breathtaking sight of her husband. Here in this jeweled lovers' haven there was no past. Only the present mattered. Here, they were the only two people in the world.

Awareness shimmered through Caitlin as she thought of the union to come. In a few moments she would give herself to the man who had always possessed her heart. Jake would take her then, with all the hungry need in him. Their mating would be raw, tender, elemental, like always. The reflection sent shivers of delight rippling through her.

Jake must have sensed her anticipation for his white teeth flashed up at her in a knee-melting grin—purely sexual, entirely masculine. "You ke looking at me like that, hellcat, and I won't be responsible for my actions."

"I think I'll risk it," she retorted, unafraid.

"Getting pretty sassy, aren't you?" His hands hooked on his narrow hips, while his smile grew challenging, daring, flagrantly arrogant.

Yet he had every right to be arrogant about his virile beauty, Caitlin reflected. He was already boldly aroused, his rigid shaft straining nearly to his navel.

Spellbound, mesmerized, fascinated, Caitlin watched as Jake started up the rocky incline toward her, awed by the graceful power of his lean, muscular body. He moved with an earthy sensuality that was bewitching . . . and he was even more devastating up close.

In only moments he stood towering over the rock where Caitlin sat with her legs curled beneath her. She could feel the heat of the sun beating down on her bare body, but it was nothing compared to the scorching scrutiny Jake was giving her. His narrowed eyes gleamed with wicked knowledge, a flicker of something dangerously, sinfully warm.

Desire, hot and potent, curled inside her at his seductive gaze. A song of longing, of fierce, restless, feminine need whispered through her body.

His eyes swept over her face in a way that made her feel beautiful and desirable, a compelling scrutiny that made her pulse tremble. Already her muscles were tensing in anticipation of the pleasure of his strong hands upon her skin, of his tender mouth moving over her flesh. Her breath arrested when Jake lowered himself beside her.

He didn't touch her, though. Not yet. His heated gaze roamed her pale, bare body, lingering on her breasts . . . her slim legs and boyishly rounded hips . . . the dusky curls crowning her thighs.

Jake's own pulse raced at the sight of Cat's nudity, but when he reached for her, it was only to trace the lovely curve of her cheek and throat with tender fingers. He leaned closer, but only to slide his hands beneath the silken curtain of her hair, his callus-roughened palms framing her face.

"Wife," he murmured softly, as if testing the word. "I think I like the sound of that."

Caitlin's rapt, welcoming smile was so loving, he damned near stopped breathing. "So do I," she agreed.

His heart hammering in his chest at her low, husky reply, Jake forcibly restrained his urgency. His body was already hardened in tense, coiled readiness to claim her. Need trampled through him—a wild need to mark her as his—but he fought it back. He wanted to take until the hunger in his heart had been satisfied, but he wanted more to relish every nuance of this moment, to wring out every drop of pleasure and enchantment, the moment when Caitlin finally, fully became his wife.

Even though they'd made love innumerable times before, *this* time was different somehow. Nothing had prepared him for the well of love and need that sang savagely in his blood. Love was a relentless ache inside him. Love for his Cat.

He crushed down the urge to ravish her and commanded himself to go slow, even though desire raged through him like a fever. Even though she'd never looked more beautiful. Just now her blue eyes were wide dreamy pools, shining with joy and love, but before he was done, he would watch them darken with desire, turn hot and smoky with sensuality.

Her breasts were swollen, small and perfect . . . and responsive to the slightest touch, he discovered when he filled his palms with their weight.

His first caress sent a jolt through Caitlin's entire body. She had thought her breasts sensitive, but when his hands cupped and fondled the soft mounds, she suddenly went weak all over. Desire, primitive and raw, shot through her as Jake brushed his rough thumbs across the aureoles.

Her pulse thudded recklessly. Her skin felt over-sensitive, her nipples tight and feverish. She gave a helpless murmur of pleasure as he bent to find the beat of her pulse at her throat and licked it.

"I love the way your skin tastes," he muttered, letting his tongue savor her skin.

Urgently Caitlin reached for him, wanting, needing his kiss. His lips found hers then, yet Jake seemed determined to tease her, to make her arousal long and slow and deliberately drawn out. He kissed her lingeringly, lazily, taking his own sweet time. When she strained toward him eagerly, he drew away and gently pressed her down to lie on her back.

"How do you want it, hellcat?" Jake asked in a languid, amused voice. "Hard and fast? Wild and wicked?" His hands covered her breasts, lightly massaging, enjoying what his eyes were treasuring. "Or slow and easy?"

"Jake . . ." she whimpered, impatient with his torment.

"How do you want me to love you, Cat, hard or easy?"

She shook her head restlessly, unable to choose. It didn't matter how he loved her; she wanted it all. She wanted their mating to be fierce and wild, gentle and loving. She wanted tenderness and shar-ing, taking and giving, demanding and surrender-ing. And she knew Jake would give her what she wanted, satisfy her completely . . . eventually. "Both . . . either . . . I don't care. Just love me."

"All in good time," Jake answered. "I've waited too long for this moment, and I'm sure as hell not going to rush it."

"Jake, damn you . . . make love to me."

He chuckled in a very male way. "Is that any way to talk to your loving husband?"

"I swear . . . I'll poison you if you don't get on with it."

He bent and kissed a swollen nipple, letting his tongue flick the peaked flesh. "Like this?" he murmured wickedly. Closing his lips over the taut bud with a hard, sucking motion, he made her gasp and arch her back fitfully.

"Yes . . . Jake . . . please . . ."

"Settle down, hellcat," he drawled, impervious to her pleas. "I told you, I won't rush this. I'm going to enjoy every single precious minute."

"Jake, you're making me crazy. . . ."

"That's exactly what I intend to do, Cat."

His eyes fierce with tenderness and intent, he slid his palm down her naked belly to the juncture of her thighs, stroking beneath the soft curls there, seeking out her heat. Parting the folds he loved to touch, his fingers spread her open and began a slow and easy exploration . . . deliberately, boldly probing . . . fondling . . . brushing the tiny bud that was the seat of her ecstasy, finding the most exquisite pleasure points with an expertise that made her gasp and shudder.

When he slipped a finger into her cleft that was already slick with moisture, Caitlin arched her throat and made a soft, wild sound. His arousing fingers teased her, lingering inside her . . . withdrawing to stroke her weeping flesh again . . . sliding back inside even more deeply. . . . making desire coil ever tighter within her.

"Jake . . . please. . . ."

To her delight, he bent over her then, pressing her thighs wide apart as he let his mouth replace his stroking fingers. His lips and tongue savored her, gently, relentlessly, worshiping the very center of her femaleness. Caitlin thought she might die of bliss.

Jake murmured something wicked and soft and loving against her flesh, urging her on . . . but then to her incredulous dismay, he drew back. She was trembling now, but Jake left her there on the brink.

Savoring her shivers, he pressed his hot cheek against her bare stomach. "No sponges this time," he murmured huskily. "I want another son like Ryan. I want a daughter like her beautiful mother."

Their eyes locked, hers misty and soft, his like green fire. When Caitlin reached blindly for him, this time Jake allowed her to pull his head down to hers, his lips meeting her searching mouth. His fierce control slipped just a little as he buried his hands in her hair.

The kiss was deep this time, branding her as his woman. Caitlin tasted her own essence on his lips as she yielded willingly to the possessive crush of his hungry mouth. He kissed her until she forgot to inhale or exhale, until she quivered with need for him. Her flesh was hot enough to burn, hot and tender and exquisitely sensitive to his touch. . . .

But even then Jake withheld part of himself. With a sharp breath and a forced effort at mastery, he stretched out beside her. Holding her gaze, he pulled Caitlin into his arms so that all her slender softness was enfolded in his powerful embrace, imprisoning her against the naked, muscular length of him.

"Is this what you want, Cat?" he murmured tauntingly, holding her tight against his lightly furred chest still damp from his swim in the pool;

making her aware of the bold, corded length of his thighs, the searing heat of his loins. She felt the pulsating hardness against her stomach, the ripple of muscle as he moved, the heat of his skin. His hips rocked leisurely, rhythmically, pressing his sex against hers, showing her without words what he intended to do to her when he finally deigned to satisfy her.

"Yes," she rasped. "Yes, Jake . . . please." This was what she wanted. She wanted Jake, wanted him, wanted . . . Dizzy with desire, Caitlin buried her face in the hollow of his throat, twisting against him with sweet, strong urgency. She was so aroused she thought she might burst into flames the moment he entered her.

But he didn't enter her. He simply held her captive until she could stand it no longer. Want had become craving, a fierce longing for so much more than Jake was giving her.

His deliberate restraint igniting her recklessness, Caitlin suddenly went on the offensive. Pushing herself up on one elbow, she pressed Jake back to lie on the rocks and rolled partway over him, pinning him beneath her.

"Enough!" she whispered almost fiercely. "Now it's my turn to torment you."

His green eyes gleamed up at her brazenly. "Time for revenge?"

"Yes, revenge. . . . "

Determined to retaliate for his torment of her, she bent and kissed his shoulder, her lips nuzzling the brown satin of his skin, savoring how smooth and hard was his flesh, tenderly caressing the scar her brother's bullet had made. Lingeringly, her mouth moved on, pressing light, scattered kisses over her husband's strong throat, his collarbone, his chest . . . letting her tongue flick a flat male nipple in a deliberate attempt to arouse him as he had her.

Her touch was gossamer light, but Jake felt it in every nerve ending he possessed. Her mouth drew a pleasured sigh from him as he lay back contentedly, feeling the hot sun touching his bare body, the warm mountain air caressing his naked skin, the woman he loved worshiping his body. He felt the soft crush of her breasts, the feminine weight of her thighs, and thought there could be no greater pleasure on earth than having Cat make love to him. . . .

His serenity lasted only a moment longer, however, for Caitlin trailed her hand down his lean, furred chest to close deliberately around his thrusting shaft. Jake felt a shudder of stark heat sizzle through him, and he went rigid, tensing all his muscles at once.

She didn't release him, though, or stop her exquisite ministrations. Instead, her curling fingers caressed him, stroking . . . gently squeezing . . . slowly gliding up and down . . . making his aching, swollen erection that much stiffer.

"Witch," Jake muttered.

Caitlin only smiled. His heated shaft was burning hot to the touch, hard as a steel rod, yet covered with velvety skin. The feel of him pulsing and burning in her hand excited her unbearably, but it was the stark play of emotion on his face that exhilarated her. Desire made his beautiful features harder, the creases and planes sharper in intensity. Her magnificent, practiced lover wasn't nearly so indifferent as he pretended, Caitlin reflected with exultation. Not when she was driving him to distraction with her caresses. Not when she nuzzled her face into his firm belly just below his lowest ribs. Certainly not when she bent and closed her mouth over the engorged tip of his manhood.

Jake sucked in a sharp breath in an effort to keep from breaking, his chest muscles contracting harshly. He made no other sound, but Caitlin understood his total rigidness. Control. He was fighting like hell for it as he throbbed beneath her touch.

A sharp, answering throb quivered deep within her own body. Intoxicated by her feminine power, Caitlin gave a defiant smile of triumph and set about destroying Jake's will completely. She dredged a groan from him as she took him in her mouth again, and another, harsher groan as her fingers cupped the swollen sacs at the thick base of his shaft. She tasted him lingeringly, pressing her tongue along the huge, rigid length . . . stroking, licking, savoring . . . her hunger changing to greed as she lapped at him. . . .

She could only play with fire for so long, though, before it turned against her. When Jake surged upward into her mouth, Caitlin felt a tremulous wave of longing rack her body. More than willing to end her game, she made no protest when he abruptly grasped her shoulders and pulled her face up to his.

His eyes were hard and bright and hungry, his lean features taut with passion. "Enough!" His whisper was wild and low, his look of fire and emotion hot enough to burn. "Cat . . . if I don't get inside you, I'm going to die right now."

"Will you?" she taunted. "Seems like you have a big problem, doesn't it?"

"Cat, dammit. . . ."

"I think you should beg me, Jake."

With trembling fingers he captured her nape and drew her lips down to his, his fierce kiss scalding. "All right, I'll beg. Cat, please . . . let me in. . . . " he whispered, his voice hoarse, dark, just this side of pleading, his body alive with desire.

In tantalizing response, she raised herself up and slid one slender leg over him till she straddled his hips. Then positioning the swollen head of his shaft, she slowly, carefully impaled herself on that glistening rod and took him inside her, hard and deep. Her sheath tightened upon him with strong muscles, wantonly locking him inside her. She gloved him so tight, Jake thought he would explode at the slightest provocation. He gritted his teeth as she took over riding him slowly, fighting for tenuous control.

"Christ," he rasped hoarsely as her sleek heat scorched him. He loved lying on his back and letting her ride him, loved feeling the exquisite sensations shudder through him. His hands moved blindly in her hair while he let himself cherish the moment.

This was desire. This was need. Rich, potent, surging so strongly through him he thought his heart would burst. The need of his body to have her engulfed every part of his spirit. He was filled with a wild joy that threatened to shatter him.

And yet Caitlin was far too composed, far too tranquil. He wanted her hot and wanton, all hungry woman. He wanted her clawing with need for him. Taking a silken bottom cheek in each hand, he surged upward till he was anchored deep, deeper. . . .

The soft gasp she gave filled him with immense satisfaction. When her hips gave an instinctive jerk, his grip tightened, holding her still.

"Slow . . . down," Jake commanded in a roughened tone as he took over the pace and rhythm. His clasp startling in its strength and tenderness, he drove inside her with slow, strong thrusts, generating a hot, pulsing friction while he whispered to her, wild sinful things that urged her on. The fever that was eating him alive spread to her. The love that raged in him like a tempest burgeoned in her.

Love, she was filled with it. Desire, she was shaking with it, just as Jake was. She heard him make a low desperate sound even as a scream built in her own throat. When the passion suddenly ignited between them, it was like a brushfire. Caitlin surged against him, holding him tightly within her, moaning wildly as she yielded to abandon. Catching her writhing hips, he gripped her fiercely, possessing her with a savage tenderness that was like nothing she'd ever experienced before, the sweetest pleasure she had ever known. She could no longer tell where she ended and he began.

Jake felt her joy and responded with one final savage thrust. Crying out at the bright flare of sensation, he convulsed with hot, shuddering spasms, his body shivering and throbbing deep inside her, the hot flood of his release drenching her completely.

When the last, faint, delicious spasm was spent, she collapsed on his chest, exhausted, her skin and his flushed with erotic warmth. For long, panting moments neither of them moved. His hand tangled in her hair, Jake cradled her against him, simply holding Caitlin, cherishing her, while the erratic rhythm of his heart eased, the violent thud of his pulse slowed. Love filled him up, so deep, so rich, that he felt as if he were drowning in it.

"God, I love you, Mrs. McCord," he breathed on a husky sigh.

"Mmmmm." She stirred against him languorously, but that was her only response. In a love daze, Caitlin rested her head contentedly against the hard sinew of his shoulder. She felt a fullness and a wonder that this magnificent man was hers.

Their joining had been different this time: the same wondrous ecstasy as always, but with another precious dimension. This had the sweet, yearning taste of something lost, now found again. She felt complete, whole, fulfilled, in a way she had never imagined possible.

His fingers brushed the clinging tendrils of hair from her temples. "I love you, Cat," he whispered. "I always will. I'll be there for you, for the rest of our lives."

"Forever?"

"Forever and always."

"I love you, too, Jake . . ." she murmured dreamily.

"You mean that?" Finding the underside of Caitlin's chin with one finger, he tilted her face up to his. She gave him a smile so loving, it trapped his breath in his throat. Her blue eyes held a liquid radiance that he couldn't mistake.

This time his kiss was less fierce, a caress of ownership and promise. His hands held her nape, curtained in a mass of blue-black tresses, while his lips worshiped hers.

"Cat," he whispered when he finally allowed her up for air. "Why don't you show me how much you love me?"

She drew a breath of surprise as Jake gave a small, sensual movement of his hips. He was growing inside her, Caitlin realized with delight. Summoning a new surge of energy, she lifted her head, just a little, to look into his eyes.

A wicked slash of a dominantly male grin curved Jake's mouth—one of those devastating smiles that never failed to rock her to the core.

Desire stung with fresh insistence at his seductive look; her heart felt unbearably full as she gazed up at him. He could be brazenly arrogant, intimately mischievous, ruthlessly tender. And he was hers, her enchanting outlaw lover.

"Show me how much you love me," Jake challenged in that provocative, beguiling way of his. His bright gaze held hers intently, never wavering.

"Show me, hellcat . . ." he demanded huskily as he drew Caitlin's lips down to his again.

Author's Note

Dear Reader,

From the first moment Jake McCord rode into my imagination, the outrageous rogue of an outlaw captured my heart. Jake's story is actually Book One of my *Rocky Mountain Trilogy*. Eventually I plan to tell the tales of two more fascinating heroes—maverick Sloan McCord and renegade Wolf Logan—and the indomitable women they love.

But first I mean to detour through Georgian Scotland for my next historical romance. You see, there's this certain, sensual Highland lover who's taken possession of my fantasies. . . .

I love hearing from readers. For an autographed bookmark, please send a self-addressed, stamped envelope to:

> Nicole Jordan,
> c/o Avon Books
> 1350 Avenue of the Americas
> New York, New York 10019

> With warmest regards,
> Nicole Jordan

Avon Romantic Treasures

*Unforgettable, enthralling love stories,
sparkling with passion and adventure
from Romance's bestselling authors*

LADY OF SUMMER *by Emma Merritt*
77984-6/$5.50 US/$7.50 Can

TIMESWEPT BRIDE *by Eugenia Riley*
77157-8/$5.50 US/$7.50 Can

A KISS IN THE NIGHT *by Jennifer Horsman*
77597-2/$5.50 US/$7.50 Can

SHAWNEE MOON *by Judith E. French*
77705-3/$5.50 US/$7.50 Can

PROMISE ME *by Kathleen Harrington*
77833-5/ $5.50 US/ $7.50 Can

COMANCHE RAIN *by Genell Dellin*
77525-5/ $4.99 US/ $5.99 Can

MY LORD CONQUEROR *by Samantha James*
77548-4/ $4.99 US/ $5.99 Can

ONCE UPON A KISS *by Tanya Anne Crosby*
77680-4/$4.99 US/ $5.99 Can

America Loves Lindsey!

The Timeless Romances
of #1 Bestselling Author

Johanna Lindsey

KEEPER OF THE HEART	77493-3/$5.99 US/$6.99 Can
THE MAGIC OF YOU	75629-3/$5.99 US/$6.99 Can
ANGEL	75628-5/$5.99 US/$6.99 Can
PRISONER OF MY DESIRE	75627-7/$6.50 US/$8.50 Can
ONCE A PRINCESS	75625-0/$6.50 US/$8.50 Can
WARRIOR'S WOMAN	75301-4/$5.99 US/$6.99 Can
MAN OF MY DREAMS	75626-9/$5.99 US/$6.99 Can
SURRENDER MY LOVE	76256-0/$6.50 US/$7.50 Can
YOU BELONG TO ME	76258-7/$6.50 US/$7.50 Can
UNTIL FOREVER	76259-5/$6.50 US/$8.50 Can

And Now in Hardcover
LOVE ME FOREVER

America Loves Lindsey!

The Timeless Romances
of #1 Bestselling Author

GENTLE ROGUE	75302-2/$6.50 US/$8.50 Can
DEFY NOT THE HEART	75299-9/$5.99 US/$6.99 Can
SILVER ANGEL	75294-8/$6.50 US/$8.50 Can
TENDER REBEL	75086-4/$5.99 US/$7.99 Can
SECRET FIRE	75087-2/$6.50 US/$8.50 Can
HEARTS AFLAME	89982-5/$6.50 US/$8.50 Can
A HEART SO WILD	75084-8/$5.99 US/$6.99 Can
WHEN LOVE AWAITS	89739-3/$5.99 US/$6.99 Can
LOVE ONLY ONCE	89953-1/$5.99 US/$6.99 Can
BRAVE THE WILD WIND	89284-7/$6.50 US/$8.50 Can
A GENTLE FEUDING	87155-6/$5.99 US/$6.99 Can
HEART OF THUNDER	85118-0/$5.99 US/$7.99 Can
SO SPEAKS THE HEART	81471-4/$5.99 US/$6.99 Can
GLORIOUS ANGEL	84947-X/$5.99 US/$7.99 Can
PARADISE WILD	77651-0/$5.99 US/$6.99 Can
FIRES OF WINTER	75747-8/$6.50 US/$8.50 Can
A PIRATE'S LOVE	40048-0/$6.50 US/$8.50 Can
CAPTIVE BRIDE	01697-4/$5.99 US/$6.99 Can
TENDER IS THE STORM	89693-1/$6.50 US/$8.50 Can
SAVAGE THUNDER	75300-6/$5.99 US/$7.99 Can